Outstanding praise for

MW00985214

Such ⌣

"A deeply immersive and endlessly fascinating novel grounded in a true story I only thought I knew. Greco constantly surprised me with fresh perspectives and new insights as the story unfolded, seamlessly weaving together fact and fiction. An essential read for anyone fascinated by the fabulous life of famed writer Truman Capote and his complicated friendships with some of New York City's most celebrated socialites. I was dazzled by the life of Lee Radziwill, wife of a Polish prince, sister to an American First Lady, and mother-in-law to a Real Housewife. A deeply personal portrait of a friendship between two unique people whose lives encompassed world travel, high society, popular culture, and human frailty."
—Kim van Alkemade, *New York Times*
bestselling author of *Orphan #8*

"Explores with aplomb the luxurious jet-set life of its subjects, and their abiding friendship in the 1960s and 1970s. . . . With cameos from Leonard Bernstein, Rudolf Nureyev and Andy Warhol, it's a crash course in the pop culture of the time. A rollicking ride that's equal parts gossip, tenderness and emotional truth."
—*The Toronto Star*

"A fascinating and effervescent portrayal of 1960s Manhattan high society and the complex friendship at its heart between legendary writer Truman Capote and Lee Radziwill, sister-in-law to President John F. Kennedy and one of Capote's infamous 'swans.' Using a brilliant narrative overlay, author Stephen Greco brings the charismatic author of *Breakfast at Tiffany's* and *In Cold Blood* to life with the type of biting wit, trenchant social commentary, and keen grasp of human nature for which he was celebrated. Insightful, intriguing and endlessly entertaining, *Such Good Friends* captures a platonic yet deeply passionate friendship that had all the faultlines of a doomed romance, and the seismic influence of Capote and Radziwill on their respective worlds, and each other."
—Natalie Jenner, author of the international
bestseller *Every Time We Say Goodbye*

"A rollicking story."
—*The Buzz* magazine

Please turn the page for more outstanding praise!

Such Good Friends

"A thoughtful examination of the precarious bonds of friendship, fame and fortune. Greco's *Such Good Friends* stars two of the most notable personalities of their time, Truman Capote and Lee Radziwill, sister of Jackie Kennedy. Sweepingly detailed, with glamour and mystery woven throughout. Fans of Capote and the era of Camelot should be delighted."
—Shana Abé, bestselling author of *An American Beauty*

"A mesmerizing account of extravagance, glamour, privileged celebrity, and crushing betrayal. Greco's fabled protagonists capture the explosive alchemy between privacy and ambition, and the self-destructive caprices that upended an era."
—C. W. Gortner, author of *The American Adventuress*

"Stephen Greco's book is the highest form of confection I've read in years. Highly readable. . . . Truman Capote is the beating heart of this novel."
—*The Gay & Lesbian Review*

"*Such Good Friends* seamlessly blends high-society glamour with human frailties in this vivid re-creation of celebrated writer Truman Capote's and New York socialite Lee Radziwill's complicated friendship that spanned from the 1950s into the 1970s."
—Mary Ellen Taylor, author of *When the Rain Ends*

"Well worth reading."
—*Historical Novel Society*

Now and Yesterday

"Stephen Greco knows his New York from the seventies on, its gleam and tarnish. Through quickly and brightly delineated characters, he populates his present-day Manhattan, ground zero of the corporate 'mediasphere,' with a cast of bright young things who come to suffer at the city's altar to itself, get rich, and carry the message of branding and eternal happiness to the next generation. And yet the men and women of all ages that Greco depicts are sympathetic, warm and witty, each of them inspired with a generous capacity for love and friendship. *Now and Yesterday* is an often poignant, and sometimes chilling, romance of the creative class."
—Edmund White, author of *The Humble Lover*

The LAST AMERICAN HEIRESSES

Books by Stephen Greco

NOW AND YESTERDAY

SUCH GOOD FRIENDS

THE LAST AMERICAN HEIRESSES

Published by Kensington Publishing Corp.

The LAST AMERICAN HEIRESSES

STEPHEN GRECO

John Scognamiglio Books
Kensington Publishing Corp.
kensingtonbooks.com

JOHN SCOGNAMIGLIO BOOKS are published by

Kensington Publishing Corp.
900 Third Avenue
New York, NY 10022

All Kensington titles, imprints, and distributed lines are available at special quantity discounts for bulk purchases for sales promotion, premiums, fund-raising, and educational or institutional use.

Special book excerpts or customized printings can also be created to fit specific needs. For details, write or phone the office of the Kensington Sales Manager: Kensington Publishing Corp., 900 Third Avenue, New York, NY 10022. Attn. Sales Department. Phone: 1-800-221-2647.

The JS and John Scognamiglio Books logo is a trademark of Kensington Publishing Corp.

ISBN: 978-1-4967-4651-1

ISBN: 978-1-4967-4652-8 (ebook)

First Kensington Trade Paperback Edition: March 2025

10 9 8 7 6 5 4 3 2 1

Printed in the United States of America

To my sister, Mary Ellen

PROLOGUE

Ollie checked his iPhone and saw that he was right on time. It was 7:15 on a temperate evening in mid-May, and long, low rays of copper sunlight were streaming through the slots between midtown towers, illuminating the limestone façades of Rockefeller Center's central buildings and bathing the plaza below in an ethereal glow. Down in the rink, which was converted into an outdoor bar during months when it is too warm for ice, scores of pleasure-seekers were enjoying cocktails and nibbles at tables sheltered by gaily striped umbrellas. Emanating from the crowd was the happy roar of an outdoor party in springtime. Surrounding the bar were wooden planters bursting with lush greenery, and above it, on banks of poles lining all four sides of the rink, were artist-designed flags undulating gently in the breeze. And presiding over the entire scene was that mighty, golden figure of Prometheus thrusting forward, proffering the fire that he'd stolen from the gods for the benefit of humankind.

This is the kind of optimistic urban energy they had in mind when they built this place, thought Ollie, tucking away his phone as he headed past the rink and crossed 48th Street, toward the entrance of Christie's New York, the auction house where the film premiere was to take place.

Now in his mid-eighties, Ollie had made it a point to dress sharply for the occasion, in a tailored, dark blue suit and white shirt with no tie, but a pocket square in a foulard print of blue, green, and purple. Emma had reminded him that the premiere was not a black-tie thing; and indeed Ollie, a longtime writer on cultural matters and well-known man-about-town, had understood for years that festive occasions like this—unlike weddings and funerals, where a tie can help communicate respect—could be done without any tie at all, as long as the sartorial details said *something*.

A bit of Charvet in your pocket does send a nice signal to people who are paying attention.

Inside the storied auction house, several well-dressed individuals and groups were arriving for the event that Ollie was headed for, the VIP premiere of the documentary film he had helped produce during the past year, *Radiant: Great Women of the 20th Century and Their Historic Jewelry.* Dominating the auction house's triple-story lobby was a mural by the late contemporary artist Sol LeWitt, in broad, wavy patches of stark color, whose abutments with each other—red, yellow, orange, lavender, green, black—lent the space a kind of punchy vibrance. The mural's surface was as glossy as a sheet of glass, and Ollie knew that one of the duties of the black-suited men and women stationed discreetly around the lobby was to keep people from touching the walls.

A woman at the reception desk checked her list and welcomed Ollie. She directed him toward the grand staircase and elevators, which were located just past a wall inset with vitrines bearing items to be auctioned in an upcoming sale that the film premiere had been scheduled to coincide with. The sale was called "Magnificent Jewels of the World," and Ollie stopped on his way to the elevators to admire several items: a regal necklace in yellow and white diamonds by Van Cleef & Arpels; a Deco-style diamond-and-platinum bangle by Harry Winston; an enormous, fancy vivid blue diamond ring by Cartier; an Etruscanish ruby-sapphire-and-diamond bracelet by Bulgari—all of which and more were displayed behind bulletproof glass, under brilliant, blue-white light. This was merchandise that would soon change hands for millions of dollars. Most of the buyers and sellers would remain anonymous, though some would be publicly acknowledged. All would be interested in value, of course, but two or three might even be as deeply moved as Ollie was, he hoped, by the beauty and power of both the gemstones and their settings.

The premiere was taking place that night in one of Christie's main salerooms, which had been specially configured for the event. Walking toward the bar in the gallery attached to the saleroom, Ollie spotted socialites of several generations and countries of origin—people with money whom he either knew or knew of, the kind of people who would once have been called "boldface names" for their appearance in the gossip and society columns of newspapers and stylish print magazines. Most were people who had not managed, or wanted, to transform themselves into visible figures for a post-print era in which truly influential people seemed to matter less than so-called influencers. They were standing in small groups, chatting, laughing, sipping champagne, but it was a markedly subdued gathering—no one speaking in loud tones, no one rushing to or from the bar. *Maybe it's the décor,* thought Ollie. In contrast with the wild vibrancy of Christie's lobby, the rest of the building's interior was done in a markedly restrained manner, with white walls, featureless oak door surrounds, and white oak flooring—sedate modern luxe, just the thing to contain the combustion of multi-million-dollar commerce.

And there in the middle of it all was Emma, the film's young director, whom Ollie had advised on historical and cultural matters, as well as helped execute interviews with some of the *grandes dames* who agreed to be part of the film. He had also provided Emma with moral support through the difficulties involved in getting the film made—shortfalls of funding, crises of faith, and Emma's encounter with cancer. Tonight was a vindication of all the hard work, all the worry.

Dressed in an elegant gray pants suit, her dark hair characteristically short, Emma was standing with two women: Artemis, a seventy-something British socialite and philanthropist who'd participated in the film, and Kelly, a school chum of Emma's and also the film's co-producer. An auctioneer at Christie's, Kelly had arranged for the house to lend Emma a piece of jewelry from the upcoming sale to wear for the evening—a brooch of pavé-set rubies in the form of a camellia, by Joel Arthur Rosenthal, known professionally as JAR. The brooch, one of the priciest items in the sale, had been commissioned by the late socialite and philanthropist Maia Saracin, who collected quantities of the renowned jeweler's work. Brilliantly, alluringly, the camellia was glittering from the lapel of Emma's suit. Even from across the room, Ollie thought, the thing was a beacon of something more than wealth and social status—more, even, than earthly beauty.

Now, that's glamour, Ollie thought.

It was the glamour, in the sense of magic or enchantment, that Ollie remembered most from personally handling some of the legendary pieces they'd included in the film. These things radiated an aura that could be described as celestial, almost metaphysical. They possessed a quality whose true power Ollie was convinced was best understood only by individuals who were rich or famous enough to be completely undistracted by issues of cost and monetary value. And many of the women who were in a position to wear such things—movie stars like Elizabeth Taylor, aristocrats like the Duchess of Windsor, socialites like Doris Duke and Barbara Hutton—quite knowingly and sometimes even mindfully commanded this otherworldly power in the exercise of their most essential occupations, whether seduction, or celebration, or simply self-recognition—reminding themselves who the hell they were in addition to puppet playthings for a mass audience.

Artemis had flown in for the premiere from Monte Carlo, where she lived with her billionaire husband. She had been critically helpful to the project, allowing some of her historic jewelry to be included, rounding up some of her friends who also owned historic pieces, and even agreeing to speak on camera, which was something that most of the film's women had not been willing to do. Dressed simply in a blue shift, Artemis was wearing the Bulgari pearl-and-diamond earrings that Ollie knew her husband bought for her years before as a birthday gift, from the

Sotheby's sale of a collection of Gina Lollobrigida's treasures, the proceeds from which went toward stem-cell research.

One of the security people posted discreetly around the room, dressed in black, might well belong to Artemis, Ollie thought. *That's the way she rolls.*

Ollie accepted a glass of champagne from a waiter's tray and waved to Emma, who had spotted him. He was attending far fewer parties nowadays. People still invited the distinguished writer and all-around mandarin to important gatherings—openings of the ballet and opera, art preview dinners, better book launches, etc.—but the mandarin now had very particular ideas about which of the gatherings were worthy enough for him to put on a good pair of shoes. The footwear he wore most nowadays were easier on the feet and came from a little down-town shop called Stadium Goods, where the cool kids got their rare and limited-edition sneakers.

He joined Emma, Kelly, and Artemis with warm greetings for all and a round of catch-up small talk.

"You look great," he whispered to Emma.

"So do you," she said.

"You're sparkling."

Emma struck a pose that was meant to model the brooch.

"No Robert?" said Ollie.

"Nope."

"You didn't invite him?"

"I've made my decision."

Ollie nodded knowingly.

"So it's kaput, finally."

"I'm giving back the damned ring," she said.

"You're better off," he said.

"You saw what he was the moment you met him, didn't you?"

"I did. And I can say that now."

Emma smirked.

"And I've only been married to the guy for five years. . . ."

Ollie squeezed her arm affectionately.

"This is *your* night," he said. "Enjoy it."

Most of the sixty or so guests had already arrived.

"And to think it almost didn't happen," said Emma.

"You know very well that there was never a chance it wouldn't happen," said Ollie. "You faced a few blips—very normal—and you managed them beautifully."

"I suppose."

"Though I do take *some* credit, since perspective on blips is one thing that an old man can give his younger friends."

They shared a little laugh; then an assistant interrupted, with Kelly by his side.

"We're all set," said the assistant. "Shall we begin moving guests to their seats?"

"That would be great," said Emma.

"Will you want to say a few words first?"

"I'll introduce her," said Kelly. "Then yes, Emma will say a few words."

"What are you going to say?" asked Ollie, as they started walking toward the screening area.

"I dunno," said Emma. "Thank you all for coming?"

Ollie snorted in amusement.

"Em, you're wearing a pin estimated at four million dollars. Can't you come up with something better than that?"

PART 1

PARTIES

CHAPTER 1

October 1928

They were the picture of young American aristocrats in the affluent 1920s: two sixteen-year-old girls dressed for a morning's horseback ride in jodhpurs, hacking jackets, boots, and riding hats, looking sharp atop affable, retired thoroughbreds. One girl was notably taller and more athletic than the other, sitting assuredly on her horse and clearly at one with him. The other girl was a bit stiffer and more decorous in the saddle, though not exactly "ladylike," since these were both decidedly modern girls, whose young adulthood was happily syncing with all the enticing new social opportunities presented by the unprecedentedly fast-moving decade. Given recent weather, the girls knew they were lucky to be able to go riding as they'd planned to do since spending a week together that summer at one of the girls' country estates—called a farm—in New Jersey's Raritan Valley. October had already brought two nasty nor'easters, the most recent of which had rained out several activities at both their schools, as well as, indeed, much of the daily business of New York and the rest of the tri-state area. But for two days now, the skies had been clear, and the trail, they found, was not especially mucky, so the ride had been nice enough, through the pretty Connecticut countryside—picturesque fields and meadows and forest whose brilliant reds, yellows, and oranges were just past the peak of autumn glory.

The ride was ending, and the girls were emerging from the

woods and heading for the paddock and barn. There had been little conversation possible between them on the trail, as they galloped and cantered and trotted along, but now the horses were in a slow walk and knew where they were going.

"I have to go to the bathroom," said Barbara in a mock whisper, with a squirm in her saddle.

"Sorry—what?" said Doris.

"Bathroom, Dodo! As soon as possible! All that tea we had."

Doris adjusted the cuff of her glove, one corner of which had been pulled into an annoying fold by the leather rein.

"Tell me, Babbo," she said, "do you do number one in the shower?"

"What do you mean. . . ?" said Barbara, surprised.

"Do you or don't you?"

"In the shower? Of course I don't. Do you?"

"You should try it," said Doris, with teasing wickedness.

The field they were crossing, once farmland but now maintained as a wildflower meadow, was a swath of season-worn, wild rye grass sprinkled with violet aster and purple coneflower, edged by the narrow road to the school. A cool breeze was laced with the smell of a nearby farmer's field fire. Beyond that, enclosed by a weathered rail fence and gate, was the stable complex, featuring a long, neat wooden barn painted white, with a gable roof and topped by a ventilation cupola—all quiet on this late-October morning, except for two stable hands, who were bringing bales of hay into the barn, and three horses in the paddock that had been let out for the day.

"Isn't it . . . unsanitary?" said Barbara.

"Of course not."

Barbara smirked.

"Maybe it's a Southern thing," she said sharply.

It was a running joke between them that previous generations of their families had been on different sides of the Civil War—notwithstanding that both families were now based in New York, a few blocks from each other, in substantial limestone mansions just off Fifth Avenue.

"I don't know where I first heard about it," said Doris. "Certainly not from Mother. Certainly not from Mademoiselle Renaud."

"Perhaps from some mechanic or field hand?"

"I think it must have been one of the other Brearly girls. Anyway, it's quite natural and relaxing."

"Really, Dodo, I can't imagine it," said Barbara.

"Maybe I invented it," said Doris, with immodesty that she often felt about many of her accomplishments and rarely bothered to hide. "Anyway, isn't showering the only time when we're really, really, really alone? Think about it, Babbo."

"I guess so."

Both girls, who had already lost one parent each, and whose extremely wealthy families had always ensured that they be supervised by nannies and governesses, were now usually protected, except for private, rural get-togethers like this, by retired policemen dressed in business suits—bodyguards. Each girl was the target of death and kidnapping threats, and desperate appeals from strangers for money. The fact that they were unsupervised for this ride at Barbara's school, Miss Porter's, was a condition that the girls themselves had engineered. Doris's late father had left her not only money but significant control over major family assets and thus the terms of her life; she did as she pleased. Moreover, she was more enterprising than Barbara, and with the help of a new Duke employee, an assistant butler-cum-chauffeur named Henrik, she'd found it easy enough to devise a plan that assured their respective guardians that the other's guardians would be responsible for them. And this scheme had already worked several times for small outings like this one, in so-called "safe" settings—meaning expensive and socially exclusive parts of rural Connecticut, New Jersey, and Long Island. Whether or not the girls could arrange to pull off this scheme in the city—say, for a museum visit or a Broadway show—was another story.

"Father always said how healthy showering was. He had showers installed in all our houses," said Doris. "He encouraged me to shower when I wanted to—instead of that whole bathing ritual. When I am in the bathtub, Mademoiselle is usually right there beside me, being helpful. But who needs that kind of help? Anyway, even if she happens to be in the room when I'm showering, she hardly knows what's going on under the streaming water, does she?"

Barbara shook her head, with a frowny smile.

"You're terrible," she said.

"I suppose I am," said Doris.

Barbara was the more conventionally pretty of the two, with a face as sweet as a doll's, a pert, composed demeanor, and short dark hair that was carefully styled twice a week by one of her family's maids, who traveled to Farmington especially for the task, since the hairdresser from nearby Hartford who was brought in regularly by the school for the girls would not do for Miss Hutton. A creature of determined whimsy and originality, Barbara was not afraid to style her hair adventurously and frequently experimented with shades like gold and silver, in the manner of her favorite movie stars. Currently, her hair was a vibrant auburn, styled in a mophead-with-spit-curls look she had recently seen on Marion Davies in *The Patsy*. Doris's attractiveness was less in her exotically angular facial features than in her engagingly animated spirit, which seemed to fuel an instant and detailed focus on any matter at hand and boundless curiosity about everything else. She kept her straw-colored, shoulder-length hair in such a plain style that it hardly looked styled at all—something for which her mother disparaged her constantly but could do nothing about.

They halted at the edge of the road, for an auto that was approaching from the direction of school—a small disturbance of the pastoral peace. The horses, both well-trained, remained perfectly calm.

"It's Mr. and Mrs. Keep, the heads of school," said Barbara, waving weakly as the auto drove past—a snazzy, new 1928 Auburn roadster in racing green, whose tan convertible top was down. The Keeps waved back, with a warbly "Hello, girls!" from Mrs. Keep barely audible over the puttering motor, the lady twisting slightly in their direction, apparently to get a better look.

"I didn't tell them I had a guest," said Barbara.

"Good thinking," said Doris.

"If she knew it was you, she'd make a big fuss."

"I know."

The girls dismounted and led their horses past the paddock toward the barn. Miss Porter's allowed girls to keep their horses there during the school year. Barbara had brought her ten-year-old bay mare, Reckless, there from her family's Long Island estate, Winfield Hall, in Glen Cove; Doris had had Ten Grand, a seven-year-old chestnut gelding, one of her favorites, trailered over especially for the weekend from Duke Farms, in Hillsborough, New Jersey.

"You should be more comfortable with yourself, Babbo," said Doris. "Your riding—it's so proper. I'm surprised you're not riding sidesaddle."

"I did, once," said Barbara. "I love the way it looks."

"Have you ever ridden bareback?"

"Well, is that even safe?"

"So you haven't."

"Of course not. Have you?"

"All the time. My hack at the farm—Bluebell? Remember the very sweet one?—when I'm alone, we always ride that way. My father used to say how lucky we human beings were to have horses in our lives. He used to say how terrible it is that horses are passing out of everyday life. He made me promise to always have horses and keep them well."

"I know you miss him."

"I do," said Doris.

As they approached the barn, leading their horses, Doris glanced out over the tidy stable grounds. Her own stables at the farm would soon be even nicer than this, she thought, since the renovations she'd ordered and helped plan were now underway. Her father had adored her and taught her about life and people and money and purpose, and though he had been dead now for three years, she still missed him achingly—his advice, his support. Her mother, on the other hand, had always resented her. A vain and brittle woman who adored no one and whom no one adored, Nanaline Duke was doing her best to live up to the term *grande dame*, resentful of the will that had granted so much of the family fortune and property exclusively to her daughter.

At the door to the barn, Barbara wordlessly handed the reins of her horse to a groom.

"You're not going to wipe down the saddle or anything?" said Doris, loosening her saddle's girth a bit and ready to walk her horse to a tie ring.

"He'll do it," said Barbara casually. "Let him take yours, too."

Doris reluctantly complied, and the girls headed to the tack room, talking and occasionally laughing.

"Tiki would have a stroke if she ever saw me riding bareback . . ." said Barbara.

After handing their horses over to the groom, Doris and Barbara needed to stop in the tack room only for the toilet and to wash their hands. Henrik was waiting for them at the door of the stable with the car, to drive the girls first back to Barbara's rooms on campus and then back to New York.

"Ladies," said Henrik cheerfully with a bow. He was standing in uniform—double-breasted jacket with brass buttons emblazoned with the initial "D," breeches, boots, and cap—next to the Dukes' stately green-and-black Rolls-Royce Phantom Sedanca.

"He's so handsome," whispered Barbara, who had made the same comment the day before, when Doris arrived at Miss Porter's.

"Everyone likes him, except maybe Weston," said Doris, referring to the Duke household's majordomo.

"French?"

"Swedish. But that accent is partly British. His last position was in London."

"Dreamy."

"Weston doesn't trust him yet."

"But your mother adores him, right?"

"Well, yes. But you know Nanaline. A few days ago, she

made it a point to tell me that with my blond hair, I look more like Henrik than my father."

Barbara grimaced in dismay.

"Bunk."

"'So tall and Scandinavian!'" said Doris, mocking her mother.

"What could she possibly mean by that? That she and Henrik. . . ?"

"Or someone like him, years ago. She's obviously mad."

"And rather mean, if you ask me."

It was only a few weeks after he began working at the Duke Mansion on 78th Street that Henrik, who'd taken a liking to the smart and spirited little girl who was obviously the household's true mistress, first quietly intimated to Doris that under his supervision, for certain outings, he might be able to arrange for her and a friend to go out safely without the encumbrance of bodyguards. It was Doris who was clever enough to do the actual arranging, though, and Henrik who followed her orders and saw to the details. This overnight visit to Barbara at Miss Porter's was the first family-sanctioned outing under Henrik's supervision. Two previous ones that Doris made on her own— to the Cloisters in Washington Heights and Coney Island in Brooklyn—went unsuspected by both Weston and Nanaline Duke. Doris was now cooking up the most elaborate adventure yet, for her and Barbara, despite the vigilance of Doris's finishing governess, Mlle. Jenny Renaud, and Barbara's governess, Tiki: a secret visit to a Broadway show.

After a stop at Barbara's rooms to change clothing, they were on the road to New York. The drive was pleasant. In the privacy of the car's passenger cabin, the girls tucked into a luncheon hamper that Henrik had placed on one of the fold-down seats across from them. As the Connecticut scenery sailed by, they nibbled on cold chicken, scotch eggs, chunks of crusty bread, Stilton cheese, and apple slices. They chattered away about school, French lessons, the books Barbara was reading and the poetry she was writing, and the private tutoring Doris was receiving in classical piano, jazz piano, ballet, and voice.

An exchange of family gossip prompted Doris to mention a

trip she had taken recently to the Dukes' home territory in Durham, North Carolina.

"It's going to have six white columns in front—quite imposing. I've seen the drawings—I mean, I approved them last year," said Doris. She had laid the cornerstone of the new student union at Duke University, of which her father had been a founding patron.

"Was it messy?" asked Barbara. "With mortar and a trowel and all that?"

"More like cutting a wedding cake. You hold the trowel and just touch the mortar and stone, and then someone takes the trowel from you and finishes laying the stone. It's ceremonial. Then there's champagne."

"Ooh, I like that part."

With their lunch, the girls were enjoying a bottle of Veuve Clicquot that Henrik had procured at Doris's request.

"Technically, I'm the patron now that my father's gone," said Doris, "and I want to honor that commitment. But these people. . . ! Always asking for more money. Clearly, they think we're not giving them enough."

"Thank God I don't have any of that," said Barbara, with a laugh. "I don't think I'd know how to do it anyway. You're so clever with it all."

"Well, I am my father's daughter. He showed me everything he could about the business. 'Make the most of what you have,' he used to say."

"I don't know whose daughter I am," said Barbara wistfully, precipitating an awkward moment that she dissipated with a sour smile. "Oh, wait—that came out wrong. I only meant . . ."

"I know," said Doris. "It's alright. You noodle."

Barbara's mother, Edna, a daughter of F.W. Woolworth, founder of the great chain of five-and-dime stores, had committed suicide at the age of thirty-three, when Barbara was only four. Edna, distraught over the philandering of her husband, Franklyn Laws Hutton, had decamped from the family mansion to the Plaza Hotel with her only child; and it was in their suite there, tragically, that Barbara had discovered her mother's lifeless body. Franklyn took steps afterward to ensure Barbara's well-being by sending her to live temporarily with relatives in San Francisco and elsewhere, and by hiring a young French woman, Mlle. Germaine "Tiki" Tocquet, to serve as nurse, governess, and surrogate mother. And soon it seemed to the Woolworth family that Barbara had not been too badly scarred by the horrible incident, except that she remained moody and sensitive and dramatic, insisting on wearing makeup, even at such an early age, and writing pages and pages of pensive verse.

Doris's loss of her father, when she was thirteen, had a similarly bitter dimension. Doting always on his loving daughter, reinforcing her belief that no one would ever love her as much as he did, James Buchanan "Buck" Duke, founder of American Tobacco and Duke Energy, did his best to impart financial and other practical wisdom to her that had been part of his and his family's fortune-building heritage. And Doris, always a quick study, had taken it all in eagerly, including the solid Tar Heel values, like respect for others, that Buck always said shaped his personal ethos. When Buck became ill with pernicious anemia, Nanaline, his second wife, a fading Southern belle who favored the rather dull son she had by her first husband over the bright, young daughter she had by her second, did little to slow his demise. Doris may have complained about the Duke University trustees asking for more money, but willingly and quite capably she was now, even as a student, overseeing the operation of all the Duke businesses, properties, and philanthropic enterprises, with the help of a squad of loyal family employees.

Buck Duke also imparted to his daughter what he always said was the most important thing to remember about personal wealth: it was "only the tip of our iceberg." The other nine-tenths of us, he said, was the important part—the part that really influences life and other human beings, whether we ever see the results or not.

Doris had once mentioned this maxim to Barbara, who only sniggered.

"We're such visible creatures, you and me," mused Doris. "In the papers all the time. People say we're so influential. But I wonder if nine-tenths of our influence, anyone's influence, is invisible. I don't think we can comprehend it."

"Dream on," said Barbara, dismissively.

CHAPTER 2

A year and a half before the premiere at Christie's, Emma had been anything but certain that the film would ever be completed the way she was hoping. A filmmaker in her early thirties with several prize-winning shorts to her credit, she had made a good start on the project with her friend Kelly, who was proving an effective conduit to several people within the auction house who could help connect Emma with the owners or sellers of important pieces of jewelry who'd be willing to consider participating. But it was still unclear how the project would be funded. So far, Emma was out of pocket, and she'd been turned down for several of the grants she applied for.

The project was thus only just getting underway when Emma emerged from the subway at 86th and Broadway one afternoon and found two messages on her phone. Before going up to her apartment, she stopped to listen at one of the garden benches in the landscaped courtyard of her building, the venerable Belnord. The first message was from her husband, Robert, from whom she was separated.

"Ems, I'm so sorry, but I just found out that one of my Singapore people is coming in for a meeting on the day of your doctor thing, and I have to do it. But you know I would if I could. Gimme a call, okay?"

Emma had agreed to let Robert, an IP attorney, accompany her to an appointment she had with a rheumatologist later in the week, ostensibly for moral support. Living apart for the past year, Emma and Robert had little acrimony between them, or indeed much of anything else now, except a residual physical attraction that a couples therapist had helped them see was not enough to ensure compatibility, let alone a continuing happy marriage. They had recently run into each other at a restaurant party and shared a drunken, ill-advised kiss in the passageway to the restrooms, and since then, improbably, Robert had been calling for . . . what, a date? He said he wanted to have coffee or a drink or something, "to see what our options are," but Emma wasn't sure she wanted any options at all in this regard, so she was partly relieved to hear that Robert was bailing on the doctor appointment. Did she need the sex *enough*? Did she need it with *him*, who was undoubtedly still enough of the dickhead he was when they separated? Would he ever value her work as an artist or what she felt was her accruing existential *weight*, as much as she thought necessary? Was she keeping him on the hook as a kind of hedge—and, if so, a hedge against *what*? Was divorce really the next step—the only one?

I liked him once. Maybe . . . I will grow back into him?

She could easily do the doctor appointment alone. The rheumatologist was going to look at the x-rays and probably tell her she had arthritis or something, as her regular doctor indicated could be possible. The ailment didn't seem too dire—only a persistent ache in her elbow. Yet this was the first ache that she'd ever had that didn't simply disappear on its own after a few days. Her regular doctor thought it made sense to refer her to a specialist, but Emma had been a little surprised at the doctor's lack of alarm. Rather too philosophically, when Emma said she couldn't remember injuring the elbow, the doctor offered the explanation that "sometimes these things just happen as we get older," which Emma thought no explanation at all.

The other message was from an old friend of Emma's family, Oliver Wendell Shaw, a distinguished gentleman of a certain age and then some. A retired columnist often described as a connoisseur, he was one of a vanishing breed of New York cognoscenti who knew something about everything, from Renaissance art to epic poetry, from antique timepieces to vintage

automobiles, from the great doyennes of twentieth-century society to the promising young poets who were cut down in the
trenches of World War I. For years, Ollie, as he was known, had
written for the lavishly produced, now defunct monthly arts-
and-culture magazine *Nota Bene*, of which Emma's late father,
Martin, had been the editor.

"Emma, Ollie Shaw here," went the message. "It is so nice to
hear from you. It's been years, hasn't it? Thank you so much for
thinking of me. Of course, I'd be delighted to talk about helping
you with your project, in any way I can—*if* I can. Please feel
free to call me back, and we'll set up a time to meet. I'll be home
this evening, if you'd care to call then. Tomorrow morning also
works, any time before eleven-thirty. Then I'm off to the Mor-
gan Library to see some autograph scores by Ravel."

Emma smiled weakly and shook her head. The message
contained more information than necessary—a generational
thing, she thought—but also typical of Ollie's mode of self-
presentation: prolix, performative, mildly self-amused.

She had known him since childhood, as one of her father's
most eminent writers—someone who would often command the
dinner table when invited to one of the salon-like, at-home get-
togethers hosted by her parents: Martin, who years before had
been named editor of his legendary publication as a relatively
young man, and Janet, a painter now enjoying mid-career success with a prominent gallery. As a child and teenager, a bright
student at the progressive St. Ann's school in Brooklyn Heights,
Emma felt lucky to be included as a kind of equal among the
accomplished guests at these parties. Despite her young age, she
often occupied a place at the dinner table and engaged in conversation with everyone. She'd liked Ollie well enough then, especially when he brought her gifts, like an antique fountain pen
and an original Broadway playbill from *Oklahoma!*, but always
found him "too fancy" in an old-fashioned way. And there was
a darker side of her youthful antipathy. The man's self-assurance
as someone with an informative or at least charming word to say
about anything may well have been justified by his intellect or
his experience, but Emma saw this otherwise admirable quality

in context with the embarrassing if not contemptible "discreet-ness" Ollie maintained about his sexual identity. Even as a kid, she well knew that his coyly semi-closeted demeanor had grown less and less common among New York's intellectual class since the so-called Stonewall revolution of the late 1960s.

She simply assumed that Ollie was gay, and so what. Later Emma learned that there had once, during the '90s, been some kind of affair between this older gentleman and her father, then a newly married man in his thirties—an affair that had led no-where, and that she now understood, given the kind of men they were, may or may not have been very physical. That her father had a gay side was not particularly shocking. An other-wise devoted and loving family man, Martin was like several of the other St. Ann parents she knew: complicated individuals who made up their own pathways through life and created func-tional families in collaboration with partners who themselves were committed to highly individualized agendas. No, what Emma found embarrassing was the fact that her father, appar-ently always a bit naïve in the romance department, despite so-cial revolutions, might have found Ollie's old-fashioned brand of homosexuality appealing, or at least serviceable enough to emulate, and that this had led to a bad end. On a business trip to São Paulo a few years before, Martin had been murdered during the early morning hours while apparently cruising in a notori-ously dangerous city park. Aside from sad, Martin's secret life seemed unnecessarily sordid to Emma.

Upstairs, in her apartment, Emma made herself a cup of tea and settled at her desk in the book-lined library, which she was using as a base for her project: a documentary film about notable women of the twentieth century and the historic jew-elry they collected. It was her first full-length project, and she was enormously excited about it. The idea of developing her thoughts about women, power, and identity through the stories of legendary socialites and their wearable treasures excited her as a way to create something that was as beautiful to look at and fun to watch as it was intellectually revealing. Though she had self-funded her previous films, which were smaller in scope—

including *Broadway Tiresias*, an earnest encounter with a well-known, marginally housed Upper West Side nonconformist, and *Passion for Paint*, a sweet-and-sometimes-lovingly-sour portrait of her mother—she had been approaching all the usual foundations for support on this new one; and the months-long enterprise of application writing had been taking up at least as much time as research and planning for the film itself.

Emma remembered that Ollie had often spoken of his acquaintance with several of the women whom she was thinking about featuring in her film—including the Duchess of Windsor, whose jewelry collection was so extensive that it was sometimes referred to as "the alternative crown jewels"; heiress Marjorie Merriweather Post, who once lost a twenty-one-carat emerald, previously owned by an Aztec king, at a Buckingham Palace soirée; Elizabeth Taylor, whose Bulgari love baubles from Richard Burton often made their way to the screen in the star's movies on her neck, chest, or fingers; socialite Evalyn Walsh McLean, one-time owner of the supposedly cursed Hope Diamond, who said that "when I neglect to wear jewels, astute members of my family call in doctors because it is a sign I'm becoming ill." Emma wanted to dive deeper into the stories of these women and their acquisitions, looking for strains of feminism, creativity, self-confidence, and autonomy, and she hoped to interview, if not the original owners, then the present owners of legendary pieces.

She remembered that Ollie had once spoken of visiting Hawaii with his "great friend" Barbara Hutton, and she knew that Hutton, on the day of her first wedding—of seven!—was wearing a string of pearls said to have been owned by Marie Antoinette. This was the spot where Emma wanted to start the next phase of her new film project.

And if the grand Mr. Shaw liked the project and was interested in supporting it with some funding of his own, so much the better.

Emma lived alone in the generously proportioned, four-bedroom apartment that her parents had bought back in the 1980s, when they were newlyweds and the only thing that allowed them to afford such spaciousness was the run-down state of the grand, old building. Emma had grown up in the art-and-antique–filled apartment, which was now, after a first-class renovation of the entire building, comfortable to the point of luxuriousness; and both she and her mother saw no reason for them to sell the place after Martin's death. Janet was currently living in London with her new, much-younger boyfriend, but Emma, now separated from Robert, was happy to return to the Belnord. The main change was that Emma now lived there without the housekeeper, who had been with the family for years, and rescheduled the cleaning lady and her assistant to come twice a month rather than once a week.

Opening her laptop and checking her email, Emma found a message from her mother with some installation shots of an exhibition of her mother's work that would be opening in London later in the week.

"They're keeping one of the larger pieces for a private room, in back," Janet wrote. "Normal people can see it only if they start talking with one of the staff and are invited. Collectors, of course, get pulled back there right away!"

Emma was disappointed not to be going to London for the opening, but the timing wasn't right. There was all the grant application work that she wanted to stay on track with, and the doctor's appointment, which she didn't want to reschedule. She talked to her mother often, but not usually about things as trivial as aches and pains. They had never been that kind of family; Martin liked to preside over a loftier level of exchange. Yet Emma did wonder, girlishly, if a worrisome case of tennis elbow, or whatever it was, would be a good enough reason to call Mommy. Was it so terrible to need a little mothering? When was the last time that Emma had played tennis, anyway—two summers ago?

She picked up her phone and called Ollie. It wasn't technically evening yet, but who actually observes the precise onset of evening anymore?

The call began with Ollie clearing his throat.

"This is Oliver Shaw," he said.

"Mr. Shaw, this is Emma Radetzky," she said. "Thank you for returning my call. I'm so grateful."

"Of course. Not at all."

"I'm glad you're interested in my idea and wonder if it might be convenient for us to meet."

"Well, yes. I'm interested in helping both you and your idea."

Emma wasn't clear on the distinction between the two, but she continued.

"Then when might we meet?" she said. "May I take you to lunch sometime?"

"Lunch sounds lovely, but I wonder if I may invite you to my home instead and give you some lunch here? It would be so much quieter, and we could really talk."

"That would be very nice, thank you."

"Some lunches are for public consumption, at a restaurant, and some are better à la maison, no?"

"Yes. Hopefully we'll be talking about substantive issues, not society gossip."

"Oh, I'm afraid I don't see the difference there, but never mind."

"I remember your speaking about Barbara Hutton. I'd love to hear more. Maybe we can start there. Anything you can tell me would be valuable, anything at all."

"Dear Babbo!" said Ollie. "Well, I can't say that all shall be revealed, because I'm a gentleman, but I can certainly offer you a few tidbits."

"About her jewels? I've read about this magnificent suite of emeralds she owned that were once the property of the Romanov Duchess Vladimir Alexandrovich . . ."

"Ah, yes—the emeralds. She had them made into a tiara—an enormous thing. Wore it often when she was playing queen in her palace in Tangier. Huge house parties! People flying in and out! Certainly, I know something about the emeralds, but I can tell you a great deal more, if you like."

"That would be great."

"And since it's treasure you're interested in, you might also consider Doris Duke for your project. I trust you've heard of Doris Duke?"

"Oh, yes. Definitely she's on my list."

"I knew Barbara Hutton well—I knew her first—but Doris Duke became my great friend, my great friend for life, except for a little blip back in the sixties, shortly after we met."

"Oh?"

"Doris practically stole me away from Barbara and kept me in a little niche, as a prize in this game of one-upmanship they used to play."

"Game?"

Ollie laughed.

"It was always a game," he said. "They had a friendship as strong as you like, but they pretended to row. And though the press covered them madly, no one ever got it right. Because that was the game."

"I can't wait to hear more."

Emma was tempted to keep talking but was suddenly afraid of Ollie pouring out too much now, when there was no recorder in front of him. He went on.

"Doris not only had great jewels—some she inherited, some she commissioned—but she had *piles and piles* of gold and un-set gems sitting in a vault in Switzerland. Did you know that?"

"No, I didn't."

"Her father made that fortune bulletproof. Bomb-proof! It only got bigger through two world wars and the Depression. Whereas Babbo—*poverina . . .*"

"What do you mean?"

"She died penniless, as you may know."

Emma suddenly saw how much more she'd have to learn as she proceeded, not only about the specific pieces of jewelry her subjects owned—the story of their commissioning, the process of their design, the provenance of the stones, the subsequent histories of various pieces—but the nature of the fortunes that made the possession of such pieces possible.

"I can't tell you how delighted I am that you'll help me, Mr. Shaw," said Emma.

"'Mr. Shaw'!" said Ollie. "Emma, didn't you used to sit on my knee? Didn't I once take you to *The Nutcracker*? It's Ollie, please."

"Thank you, Ollie. So when can we meet?"

"Let me see," said Ollie, his words giving way to the sound of what Emma realized was the pages of an actual datebook being turned. "What about next Thursday—does that work for you?"

"Perfect."

"Good. Shall we say one o'clock? I'm on Seventy-Seventh, between Madison and Park. Let me give you the address. Do you have a pen handy?"

Ollie was glad to hear back from Emma, but did take note that she chose to call at five-thirty, rather than during the six-to-seven slot that some would imagine to be optimum for reaching a man-about-town who might then casually be dressing for an evening and have a moment for a word with an old friend. Was this old-mannish of him? At any rate, there was no point in letting the girl know she'd awakened him from his regular afternoon nap. Social norms might erode, he thought, but never kindness and consideration.

Moreover, he had come to understand that being called for almost any reason these days by someone younger than sixty was a blessing. This was a new phase of his life, not simply a continuation of the *last* new phase that had started in 1961, when after a spin through Princeton, he arrived in New York ready for anything, with two tuxedos—one black, one midnight blue. Naps were now a daily necessity, and he was no longer really a man-about-town. At eighty-four, he was spry enough for his age, more socially mobile than most, but no longer nearly as necessary to the city's social swim in which he'd been immersed for so long. For a while, even as his wonky feet slowed him up a bit, he continued going out to the openings and galas and private parties he was invited to, until it dawned on him one night, at a dinner party hosted by a ninety-year-old media mogul, that the invitations he was still receiving were from people of his generation, not from what he used to think of as just . . . people. Then he started hearing about events and parties that he would have expected to be invited to but wasn't—yet all that had begun to matter less and less in this new phase, partly because he'd also begun tackling all the big books he'd always meant to read, that he suddenly knew he'd have to read now or never: *The Count of Monte Cristo, War and Peace, In Search of Lost Time*. . . . When you're over eighty, he thought, turning the pages of Proust's *Sodom and Gomorrah* made for at least as compelling an evening as a place at the next flawlessly set dinner table, or repartee from the next impeccably dressed hostess, or financial advice from the next self-made billionaire.

The most recent pandemic had proved a landmark for Ollie. He'd gone into quarantine as a mature New Yorker and emerged as an elderly one. He hadn't fully realized until starting to go out again how much social stamina was required just to walk down a city street, let alone interact in a civil manner with restaurant hosts and theater ushers, let alone sparkle for party guests, let alone endure the jostling involved in any mode of transportation whatsoever, whether public or private. And this was just fine, he thought, especially if his expectation of social viability looked foolish to anyone outside of his generational bubble. Fine: he was no longer the guy who dropped in to see friends at the Chalet Eugenia every winter for some skiing, or looked into Charvet seasonally to poke through the new silks, or took a few days in one of his favorite suites at the Danieli any time he was traveling within a thousand kilometers of Venice. Fine: he was now someone who *once did* these things and might be lucky enough to do any of them again one or two more times—that is, if he hadn't already seen Venice for the last time, without framing his visit that way, in '22, when he stopped in to see an artist friend's installation at the Biennale.

Anyway, there was no choice but to be fine with it. For this reason, Ollie relished Emma's invitation to talk at length about some of the great gals he'd been lucky enough to know. His friendships with them had allowed him to see these women as they really were, beyond the mentions in society columns and appearances in paparazzi shots. They were real people who, even within their rarefied social stratum, had to handle family problems, juggle social conflicts, and even—though eviction and starvation were rarely issues for them—manage financial troubles. Ollie was disturbed when strangers spoke or wrote about such women without the empathy necessary to understand them as fellow human beings.

The depictions of Doris Duke and Barbara Hutton, in particular, were always off the mark by miles, he thought. From the get-go, their births in 1912 within days of each other, the fantastically rich baby heiresses were dubbed "the Gold Dust Twins" by the popular press, and a caricature of them was set, defined chiefly by wealth and, moreover, by the cartoonish notions that most people held then about wealth. Great American fortunes of the Gilded Age were more than cartoonish, of course, and the inequality between the tycoons and the workers on whose backs the fortunes were built was abhorrent. Most newspaper readers back then may have been appalled by stories of exploited laborers, but they were still hungry for details of excessively opulent lifestyles—an appetite that newspaper publishers knew well how to manipulate. Thus, reporting on the lives of the children of Gilded Age tycoons was useful in keeping up newspaper sales; and reporting on the two richest girls in the world was a nicely buffed-up way to keep talking about the increasingly vilified robber barons, even as government reforms were leading the country toward more progressive times.

Gawking through the eyes of sweet little girls at palatial townhomes and country estates, chauffeured limousines and private railroad cars, strict governesses and permissive nannies was a delirious dream that both publishers and readers could enjoy. Like anyone else in the world, Ollie thought, his friends Dodo and Babbo had started out with hopes and dreams and the simple instinct to be known and loved for who they were; and though shielded from the wrong kind of attention from birth, and relentlessly in search of the right kind of attention for the rest of their lives, both gals suffered unnecessarily from their gold dust, even as they also sought, throughout the years, to give so much of their gold away.

In fact, these gals, even when quite young, were perfectly savvy about their bittersweet lot in life and determined to make the best of it. Dodo, in particular, did so with the grit of an Air Force test pilot flying an experimental jet. At least, that's how Ollie saw it.

He'd had a life among society types that his mother, his sole parent for most of his childhood, never imagined for him. His family was from a Main Line Philadelphia town, middle-class until Ollie's father, an insurance executive, died of cirrhosis when Ollie was three; at which point Ollie's mother was forced to move with Ollie and his younger brother, Ambrose, from a comfortable house in which each boy had his own room to a respectable but decidedly unspecial two-bedroom apartment. It was the middle of World War II, and women were needed to build munitions and such, but rather than go into defense work, which would have been difficult with two small boys to care for, Ollie's mother took a job at a Bryn Mawr college cafeteria, first as a server, and then, after the War, as a cashier, and then as a purchase manager. Yet she needed her boys, now in high school, to have part-time jobs, in order to make ends meet, and the boys went off in very different directions.

Ambrose, the younger and always more outgoing one, never a particularly good student, took up with a decidedly unsavory crowd, via the jobs he found as a bowling alley pin boy and then a pool shark. Nominally, Ambrose continued to live at home with his mother and brother, but then he started not coming home, and when he did choose to make an appearance, he was dressed like a street tough, in a *Wild One*-style leather jacket and dungarees—looking not quite like a criminal, but certainly not like the good middle-class boy he was once cut out to be.

Ollie, on the other hand, was always a good student and interested in the aspects of art and architecture that were touched on in English or Social Studies. So he took a general helper job at Robertson's Flowers in Chestnut Hill, an old guard Philadelphia institution that served all the grand old families. As an eager assistant at Robertson's, under the tutelage of the head floral designer and through occasional encounters with clients of discerning taste, Ollie learned all about botany, composition, classical still-life painting, Main Line customs and manners, and the antique pottery of many nations in which Main Line types liked to display their flowers. Eventually, he applied to Princeton and aced an entry interview at the home of a Princeton alumnus, a tweedy gentleman who lived in the gatehouse of a formerly grand estate, in whose quiet study Ollie found himself discussing not only campus life but the peonies and hydrangeas of the room's splendid floral arrangement, as well as the Chinese emperor Kangxi, whose reign was associated with the antique vase the arrangement was sitting in. Judged by the alum to be "Princeton material," Ollie was not surprised when he was admitted to the school's undergraduate architecture program, with a full scholarship.

Arriving in New York with a bachelor's degree in the early '60s, Ollie had no trouble finding work in the field of interior design. He landed an assistant position on a Park Avenue drawing room project led by British designer David Hicks, then worked for years as an associate designer at Hicks's London office, on a series of splendid rooms for Lady This and the Marquis of That—while at the same time meeting clients, finding entrée into "a certain world," and taking on the social role of the penniless but nicely dressed American with decent manners and an easy way with conversation. At a boozy Cornwall house party, a viscount offered Ollie the opportunity to write a column called "Poking About" for a stylish British publication; and then a few years later, in the mid-'60s, after Ollie had returned to New York, a bright, new wunderkind editor of the venerable magazine *Nota Bene* brought Ollie in when looking for fresh talent. And soon, with a column entitled "Poking Around," Ollie took his place in the New York cultural firmament. In addition to writing, he advised friends on the purchase of art and antiques, and then on dresses and houses, while appearing as a connoisseur on TV shows like *Open End* and *Jack Paar*, and happily available as one of society's most useful participants, the extra man.

New York society was evolving fast. Café society was giving

way to the jet-set, and women were liberating themselves from their mothers' social norms. A whole class of old-school extra men—socially adroit and ready to fill in at a hostess's dinner table—was passing from the scene, many of whom were also known as walkers, their elbows available for a fun evening out with a socialite whose husband might not want to see the ballet or dance the night away at a nightclub. Most of these walkers were natural gentlemen, some of whom were of means or breeding, some endowed only with style and wit; usually they were unflappably agreeable, curious about everything, good at listening, and most important, talented at being best friends. Many, too, like Ollie, were "confirmed bachelors," as homosexuals were often referred to in polite society at the time, though even as ancient norms relaxed, a certain kind of finesse was called for when discussing matters of the heart with great gal pals, who expected honesty but only a certain level of clarity. Ollie was a generation younger than legendary walkers like Johnny Galliher and Jerry Zipkin, who were in high demand when he appeared in New York, but soon enough Ollie did find himself going out with fabulous ladies, often meeting them through friends—which was how he first encountered Barbara Hutton on one of his evenings out in town.

December 1962

The heiress was hosting one of her big parties—noisy, boozy, bouncy . . .

"Sorry we're late, Barbara," said Kin.

"People come, people go . . ." said Barbara languidly, taking a puff of her cigarette through a foot-long golden holder, exhaling, and giving Kin a light kiss.

They were in the middle of a crowded drawing room of her suite at the Pierre, her usual digs in New York in the early '60s, when she was jetting among Sidi Hosni, her luxurious "orientalist" residence in Tangier; Sumiya, the new Japanese-inspired home she was building near Cuernavaca; and her regular suite at Claridge's, in London.

"I think you know everyone," she said absently, with a little sweep of the hand.

The scene was something out of a Hollywood movie: a pianist was playing an upbeat version of "All the Things You Are" on a gleaming white grand, while smartly dressed party guests buzzed away with one another. The hostess seemed pleasantly tipsy but nonetheless regal, her gray-streaked hair stylishly upswept, her relatively slender body draped sari-like in loose layers of sheer, shimmering blue-green silk that exposed one shoulder and a large portion of décolletage.

"Cecil's over there, I think," said Barbara, pointing across the room with the cigarette holder. "Talking to some actress." Around Barbara's throat was a necklace of seven monstrous emeralds, six square ones and a hexagonal one as broad as a matchbook.

"Barbara, this is Oliver Wendell Shaw," said Kin.

Barbara took a moment to register Ollie's presence.

"And what are you?" she purred.

"A friend of Kin's, Miss Hutton," said Ollie. "From school."

"I mean, what is your purpose in life?"

"Oh. I'm a decorator. I work with David Hicks."

She proffered the back of her hand so bewitchingly that Ollie had no choice but to bow and kiss it lightly.

Was this coquettishness? Ollie wondered. He was twenty-two; the lady must be fifty. Also, he noticed that she was wearing nothing under those layers of sheer silk.

"Well, boys, have a drink and see what you can do to liven up this funeral. I was about to call the circus to see if they could send over some jugglers."

Ollie had been brought to the party by a former fencing teammate of his at Princeton, Kinmont Hoitsma, who had met famed photographer and stage designer Cecil Beaton recently in London and had already become a close friend of the much older man.

Ollie and Kin found their way over to Cecil, who looked slightly trapped as he stood there conversing with a short, dark-haired young woman in a fluffy yellow dress.

"Miss Paget, may I present my great friend Kin Hoitsma?" said Cecil. "Kin, I'm sure you know Debra Paget. *Broken Arrow? The Ten Commandments?* She's just finished shooting an epic in Italy."

"My old school chum, Ollie Shaw," said Kin.

"Delighted," said Cecil, extending a hand.

"Mr. Beaton," said Ollie.

"Hi, guys," said Debra, with a big smile. "I don't know if it's an epic, but it sure is an adventure. Set in the year 1585! Can you imagine? I play a Spanish princess."

"She's heaven in a period costume, you know," said Cecil dryly, adjusting the cuff of his impeccably tailored blue suit.

"May I steal Debra for a moment?" said a mannish woman in glasses and a black dress, grabbing the star by the elbow and practically dragging her away. Paget beamed sheepishly as she allowed herself to be led off.

"School chums, then?" said Cecil, putting a hand possessively on Kin's shoulder.

"Ollie and I were both All Ivy," said Kin.

"I was so proud when he went to the Olympics," said Ollie.

"How's the party?" said Kin.

"Winding down," said Cecil. "Just like the Empire."

"Seems fantastic," said Ollie, who was accustomed to more decorous behavior at London parties. The volume of everything here at the Pierre seemed louder—the chatter, the laughter—and the gilded highlights of the room's white plaster architectural moldings were notably glossier.

"The time to leave a party is when you look around and realize you're having the best time ever," observed Cecil.

"We went to a huge party last year at Barbara's place in Tangier," said Kin. "It's really a palace. She had everyone in, from movie stars and diplomats to the local baker. People flew in from all over."

"Another costume epic," said Cecil.

"And you did that wonderful portrait of her, didn't you," said Kin proudly. In a lushly landscaped courtyard of Barbara's elaborate Tangier townhouse, its walls adorned with Moroccan terra-cotta *zellige* tiles in typically intricate geometric patterns, Cecil had shot the lady draped in similar silky eastern garb and adorned with the same emeralds she was wearing at this party, only fashioned as a tiara.

"I'd shot her before, of course, several times," said Cecil, "but it's a whole new game now that she's been fixed."

"Fixed?" said Ollie.

"Plastic surgery," said Cecil. "Our hostess is one of the last great works of the late Sir Archibald Hector MacIndoe. Really, Kin, we must help your friend stay up to speed. The good doctor is the one who helped all those disfigured RAF fighter pilots— you must have read about it. Though quite wisely, he found time for movie stars and members of the royal family. For our hostess, he did a full-frontal facelift, a breast reduction, and something or other in the rear, or so I'm told."

"In Tangier, she was so proud of her lovely small breasts," said Kin, miming the opening of his shirt.

"Really?" said Ollie.

"They're brand new!" said Cecil. "And the face, too—brand-new architecture! I had to rethink her lighting completely."

Then Cecil spotted Barbara approaching them.

"We'd better get out of here while we can," he said. "Let's go somewhere, the three of us, for a proper drink."

Ollie nodded willingly. Cecil seemed to be good company, and there was something charming in the way this fifty-seven-year-old seemed to behave almost as one of the college boys.

"Though we're in for it now," whispered Cecil. "She probably wants to know more about you, Ollie. She likes sensitive boys with blue eyes and masses of dark hair."

Barbara insinuated herself between Ollie and Kin. On closer look, Ollie noticed how heavily made-up she was, especially the eyes, which bore heavy, black eyeliner and smoky aquamarine shadow.

"Cecily," said Barbara silkily, "you have two of these and I have none. Does that seem very fair?"

Cecil, always comfortable to let his great height—six-foot-two—fortify his self-assurance, drew himself up magisterially.

"Barts," he said, "you've just dumped husband number six, poor Herr Baron von Cramm, and we all know that that nervous little Eurasian creature over there by the bar, Monsieur Doan, will probably be number seven. So I don't know what you have to complain about."

"*You,*" said Barbara, turning to Ollie and rubbing her shoulder against the side of his arm. "It's Theodore, isn't it. . . ?"

"Oliver."

"Oliver, you must come to Sumiya for the weekend," she said. "*These two* are coming. We're having dancers and musicians and whatnot. I want you to be my guest. Don't say no."

"This weekend?"

"Mmm."

"Well, I . . ."

Barbara stopped him by wagging a manicured finger, still wielding the cigarette holder in the same hand.

"I told you, you *can't say* no," she said, shaking her head woozily, her eyes nearly closed. "Not remotely. Alright. We fly in the morning. My car will collect you. It's going to be fun. And then on Monday, you'll come with me to a party that my dear friend Elsa is giving in Hollywood. You've heard of Elsa Maxwell, of course. She practically invented parties."

"Back when man domesticated dogs," muttered Cecil.

"We're having fireworks, truckloads of them," said Barbara. "Moderation is a bore, I always say. So it's settled. Just tell . . ."—she scanned the room and pointed to the mannish woman in glasses—"*her* where you live."

"Alright," said Ollie. "Thank you."

"You *will* thank me," said Barbara, "if you like art. And all the young men these days seem to like art. Isn't that so, Cecil?"

"That's what I hear," said Cecil.

"We have a Kano screen from the Imperial Household, some very nice Chinese porcelains . . ."

"Oh!" said Ollie. "Now I happen to know a bit about Chinese . . ."

"And, of course," continued Barbara, "there is this . . ."

With that, she undid a bit of silk cord at her shoulder and

allowed the top part of her diaphanous habit to drop away, exposing her naked breasts. With theatrical flourish, she assumed the attitude of a classical statue: Diana the Huntress, her arm extended and elbow raised, poised to shoot, her bow symbolized by the cigarette holder. The gesture was a shock, but taking place as it did, in an expensive hotel suite, surrounded by world-weary guests of one of the world's richest people, it was not a very seismic shock. The other guests barely took note. To Ollie, Barbara seemed daring, sexy, vulgar, and magnificent all at the same time. He didn't know what to do, so he did nothing but continue to smile.

"That scarecrow Miss Duke has been showing her new face to everyone on four continents," said the lady sharply. "Well, that's just not good enough anymore. . . ."

Her breasts were small yet full, and so miraculously youthful-looking that they rivaled four hundred carats of emeralds for attention.

"The human body is indeed the ultimate masterpiece, is it not?" said Cecil, calmly taking a fall of the lady's blue-green silk and draping it back over her shoulder. "Now cover up, dear, or we'll all turn to stone."

"She'll probably do it again this weekend," said Kin twenty minutes later, as he, Cecil, and Ollie rode the elevator down from the party. "It's in Mexico, by the way."

"It's her new party trick for at-home," said Cecil. "She'll be able to get away with it once more maybe in London, and then Miss Hutton's going to need some new material."

"Why me, though?" said Ollie.

"Probably for Elsa's party. It's a big deal, a West Coast version of Elsa's 'April in a Coma' thing."

Ollie drew a blank.

"She doesn't even know me," he said.

"Don't be too flattered," said Cecil. "It was either a new boy or a new bracelet."

CHAPTER 3

October 1928

Even if the quality of American highways was fast improving—parts of the Boston Post Road were now four lanes wide!—the drive back to New York from Miss Porter's school was taking longer than two energetic teenagers found comfortable. Doris and Barbara had not been fatigued in the least by their ride on horseback through the Connecticut countryside. In fact, their energy led to constant chatting, rather than naps, and since the heating in the Sedanca's passenger compartment was more than adequate, they slipped off their coats and cracked a window.

Doris mentioned that she had taken up modern dance.

"What is modern dance?" asked Barbara. "The Charleston?"

"No, no," said Doris. "It's about free artistic expression—simple movement and natural rhythms. Much different from the Charleston, and from the waltz and fox trot—and from ballet, too, for that matter."

"So . . . wiggling around?"

"Yes, that's more like it. Interpretive. Like Isadora Duncan."

"Oh, I know who you mean—the dancer. I was in Nice last year when she died in a ghastly accident. Tiki and I were in Biarritz for a week, then Cannes, then Nice, while Father and Irene were in Paris. We had a ball. Mornings *à la plage*, afternoons on the terrace with Flaubert and Maupassant and Zola, and of course at night, we went out."

"Parties?"

Barbara made a gesture indicating festivity.

"The most fun!" she said. "Tiki may be very strict when she's here, but she's practically another person in France."

"How so?"

"She's a woman, after all! Anyway, people there are so much more sophisticated. I love titles, don't you? Europe is the height of civilization."

Doris made a glum face.

"I went with Nanaline once," she said. "She took all the fun out of it."

"In Cannes I also ran into that tennis pro again," continued Barbara gaily, "the one I was telling you about, Peter Storey—at the Carlton. It was perfectly dreamy."

"The one from Cambridge?"

Barbara nodded knowingly.

"I couldn't help myself," she burbled. "After a few glasses of champagne, I was *complètement perdue* . . ."

Her tone was especially suggestive.

"Wait," said Doris, "you don't mean that you and he. . . ?"

"*Mais bien sur.*"

"Babbo—*again?!*"

"Why not? It's 1928. Now, don't be shocked. You're practically the only one I can talk to about these things, besides Jeem."

"Sometimes I think you exaggerate."

"Jeem understands me."

Though two years younger than Barbara, her spoiled cousin, James Paul Donohue, Jr., was a bit of a bad influence on her. Known among intimates as Jeem, Donohue was already happily posturing as something of an international playboy, bouncing among the East Coast private schools that would have him, the best Palm Beach tennis clubs, and even, despite his tender age, cocktail lounges in New York, London, and Paris. The baby playboy was fast adopting the habit of living extravagantly and essentially independently, except for a family-appointed valet in tow. Donohue's attentions to young women were already being reported in gossip columns; and those to young men, while not quite printable, were also noted by many.

"Just last Christmas, we rode down to Mar-a-Lago together in Aunt Marjorie's rail car, and yakked and yakked the whole way," continued Barbara, who shared an aunt with Donohue in socialite Marjorie Merriweather Post. "He's really a sketch. One night at Aunt Marjorie's, a lady's necklace came apart at dinner, and pearls went all over, mostly into her soup. And then a butler who tried to help splashed soup into the lady's lap. It was slightly hilarious. Anyway, afterwards Jeem found one of the pearls on the floor and made me watch him swallow it. Do you think that's dangerous? He said it could be."

Doris shook her head.

"I suppose it depends on how big it was . . ." she said.

"I want to be more like him," said Barbara. "He called it 'taking his vitamins.' Isn't that clever? We know everything about each other. When I told him every last detail about, you know, Jonesy last year, he absolutely *consumed* it. . . ."

Barbara was referring to the loss of her virginity, which she accomplished the year before with the help of a family gardener, Jones. She extended her palms one above the other, about seven inches apart, as if to show Doris the height of something.

"What's that?" said Doris.

"Now who's a noodle? My friend Millicent told me always to hold your hands this way, when talking about a boy's . . . you know—instead of horizontally. So it looks like you're talking about a vase or something."

She rotated the gesture ninety degrees and was now obviously indicating the length of something.

"See?" she said.

Doris raised an eyebrow.

"Oh. Hmm. Really?" said Doris.

"I *told* you!" continued Barbara, with declarative satisfaction. "We did it in my bedroom at Winfield. No one was home. We made love for hours, and I was *utterly* destroyed."

Barbara took a slice of fruitcake from the hamper with a fresh napkin.

"Of course, Father found out and fired him," she added, before taking a bite. "Poor Jonesy."

They were speaking in low tones and had no need of speaking any louder, since the car they were sitting in, according to its manufacturer, was "so quiet, the loudest sound will be the ticking of the clock." In front of them, under the window into the chauffeur's compartment, which was shut, a clock and a speedometer were mounted in beautifully polished panels of book-matched Macassar ebony. And on each side of the back seat, secured with leather straps to the ebony trim of the padded roof pillars, were crystal bud vases, each containing a fresh yellow rose. Dove-gray wool upholstery and darker gray wool carpeting further helped the ride remain utterly squeak-and-rattle free, even though some patches of highway were bumpy. Also in front of them was the car's intercom, via which Henrik spoke to them only once during the three-hour drive, as they were approaching Bridgeport, to see if either of them needed a comfort stop. Neither did.

They had dressed that afternoon as properly for motoring—in suits and hats, with coats and bags and gloves at their side—as they had been earlier for riding. The shawl collar and deep cuffs of Barbara's coat, from the house of Chanel, were trimmed in sable, and her shoes and bag, also purchased in Paris, were of alligator. Doris's clothes, from the palatial new Bergdorf Goodman store at Fifth Avenue and 57th Street, were of plainer design but just as sumptuous. Changing clothes several times a day, to appear suitably garbed for whatever occasion, was simply a habit of the women of their class. Details of tailoring and etiquette and deportment and language had seeped into Doris and Barbara's brains during childhood, via the examples, let alone the actual instructions, of the adult women surrounding them. Money, of course, had made Doris and Barbara more sophisticated than almost any other human beings on Earth, including heads of state. They had been raised about as differently as possible from the era's dominating rubric of children being seen and not heard. But they were also teenagers, and it was probably this simple biological fact that balanced their polished self-confidence and sense of automatic entitlement with occasional moments of girlish nervousness and uncertainty. To hide or compensate for any whiff of immaturity, especially around boys and men, both girls worked hard on perfecting the womanly moves and throaty laughter they observed from the great divas and doyennes they encountered both on the stage and in real life.

Doris casually admired the smooth skin of the back of her hand, then raised it to her nose for a little sniff.

"The Chanel is lovely, isn't it?" said Doris.

"She was so smart to introduce skin care," said Barbara, who, when they were getting dressed, had suggested that Doris try some of the new *crème de beauté* she had picked up in the Chanel shop in Paris. "It's part of her vision for a woman. I knew you'd like it. I absolutely could not have endured the Riviera without her *huile tan*."

Around Stamford, conversation returned to a subject they had been touching on during dinner and again at bedtime the night before: their upcoming debut seasons, which were already being planned though they were more than a year away. Doris's debut was planned for August of 1930, at Rough Point, the family's place in Newport, on a cliff overlooking the Atlantic Ocean; Barbara's for the following December, at the Ritz-Carlton in New York.

"Nanaline's got five hundred on the list so far," said Doris.

"We're up to eight-fifty," said Barbara, a bit triumphantly.

"It's not a competition, you know."

"Isn't it, sister?"

"Well, maybe for Nanaline and Irene, it is."

"You know that all of the same names are on both lists, don't you? Astor, Rhinelander, Winthrop, Rockefeller, Pierrepont, Cushing . . . and the studs are being lined up. Irene has her eye on all the princes of Europe, most of whom haven't a *sou*, though some are quite handsome. There are a couple of Russian brothers she keeps pushing at me—doubtlessly looking for dollar princesses."

Doris sighed.

"They keep throwing Jimmy Cromwell at me," she said. "You know, his mother is married to Stotesbury, the banker. He's handsome enough, I suppose. . . ."

"Isn't he married to that Dodge person?"

"They just divorced."

"Well, we might as well have some fun with these circuses," said Barbara.

"Might as well."

"We've got Max Schling," added Barbara proudly, naming one of New York's most sought-after florists. "And Jeem says that the party favors should be little gold purses filled with un-set diamonds, emeralds, rubies, and sapphires. He read that some Byzantine emperor did that, so Irene is looking into it."

"At Duke Farms, we've got one of the greenhouses devoted just to smilax for the ball," said Doris. "It's already growing."

Barbara turned to face Doris directly.

"Irene's already arranging for me to be presented at the Court of St. James," she said.

"Next year?!"

"Thirty-one."

"Oh," said Doris, with a poker face. "I'm on the list for '30, three months before my party."

The girls were silent for a split second; then both burst out laughing.

"You rascal!" said Barbara. "Good day, Your Majesty!"

"Nice weather we're having, Your Royal Highness!"

Outside the car, rural countryside was giving way to a more settled landscape.

"Look, we're being manipulated," said Doris.

"Don't I know it."

"It's not fair. We've got to do something about it."

"But what can we do?"

"I may have an idea. The receptions and dinners and teas and luncheons are all very well, but the manipulation of this coming-out business is positively medieval. This is something Mae West would never put up with."

"No, that's right."

The Broadway outing they were planning was to see the star Mae West in the play she had written and was appearing in, *Diamond Lil*. The show was said to be as bawdy as her play

Sex, which had been produced on Broadway two years before and then shut down by the police, who carted West off to the Jefferson Market Courthouse and, after a conviction on morals charges, to Welfare Island, to serve a ten-day incarceration. West, choosing jail over the payment of a fine she could easily afford, served eight days and then was given two days off for good behavior. Moreover, she delighted in the publicity her little scandal garnered for her. Thus, West was naturally something of an idol to many, including young women of the forward-looking 1920s, who wanted to make more of their own choices about how to think and behave.

Diamond Lil had been running for months, and Doris insisted that she and Barbara needed to see it, though of course the responsible adults of both their households would never hear of such a thing. Aside from the usual threats of assault and kidnapping, there were morals to protect. Yet "corrupting the morals of youth," feared by so many adults born in the previous century, was exactly what smart and rich young American girls like Doris and Barbara were after.

Henrik was set to help the girls secretly get to and from the theater the following week, in an elaborately planned evening that depended on little white lies that both Doris and Barbara knew well how to pull off. It was going to be great fun, doubtlessly culturally enriching, and a little bit subversive, which Doris pointed out could be a good thing.

"Manipulated!" repeated Doris. "We're being sold to the world, and the world is buying. It may be time for us to do a little manipulation of our own. They say such ridiculous things about us in the papers. We bathe in bathtubs of pure gold! We eat caviar at every meal! We're rivals for all the nice, eligible young men. If they only knew that most of the nice, eligible young men won't go near either of us, for fear of being thought fortune hunters."

"Ha!"

"Newspapermen are such dolts—Father always said so. We might be able to use their doltishness to our benefit, or at least for our amusement."

"They're the ones who stir up all these madmen and kidnappers," said Barbara.

"I'm working on a plan for us," said Doris.

"Broadway?"

"Something bigger."

"That reminds me. I have something for you."

From her handbag, Barbara produced a little notebook she used for jotting down ideas for poems. From between the pages of the book, she took a folded sheet of notepaper and handed it to Doris. It was a few lines of poetry, which Doris read aloud with respectful feeling.

Appeal

Show your face to me
And guide the way across
The river great and wide,
Dear friend;
Your words are always
Clear and strong,
And tamp the doubt
That rattles in my soul.

Flows fast the river
And deep, which drowns weak souls.
My fear is great,
And skills alone,
I know, can fail me.

Won't you smile and speak
Then, from that far shore,
And show the way—
And more, the faith
That any way there exists. . . ?

"I wrote it yesterday, before you came. I hope you like it."

"Babbo, it's . . . quite beautiful! I am so touched."

Barbara looked down at her folded hands.

"Thank you," she said.

The car was crossing a bridge into Manhattan, and Henrik announced that they were minutes away from dropping Barbara off at her house.

"Promise me this, Dodo," said Barbara, as both girls reached for their gloves and began to prepare for disembarking. "We'll always be friends. No matter what the newspapers say."

"Always," said Doris. "In fact, we can use people's interest in us somehow to get to the other side of that river, right?"

"Right."

"You have millions. I have millions. We should be able to afford our own freedom and stay true to our souls."

"True to our own souls."

Doris refolded the poem and tucked it into her handbag.

"I'll treasure this always," she said.

Twenty minutes later, at the door of the Hutton home on East 80th Street, Henrik walked Barbara to her door and saw her safely into the hands of the Woolworth family butler. Doris, from the window of the car, shouted farewell.

"Remember the promise!"

"Yes, always!" shouted Barbara. "And remember, Westward ho!"

It took Doris only a second to understand that this was a reference to the star at the center of their upcoming Broadway adventure.

"Westward ho!" she shouted gleefully.

CHAPTER 4

After speaking with Emma, Ollie decided to go shop for some dinner, since there was nothing in the house and he had a hankering for the potato-crusted, herb-baked chicken paillard that was regularly offered at the prepared food counter of Babbidge's market a few blocks from his place, on Madison. Babbidge's was wildly expensive, but the gracious experience of shopping there made a visit well worth the price. The entrees, side dishes, and desserts were displayed as tastefully as in a buffet at someone's home. Interior design and lighting were exquisite. Customer selections were as beautifully packaged as fashion accessories in a luxury-brand boutique, in conspicuously high-quality cardboard boxes and cups whose lids featured little cellophane windows, then packed in heavy-duty shopping bags embossed with the market's signature initial "B," in the typeface Bookman Swash Italic. And especially popular with the neighborhood's finicky, well-to-do retirees was the apparent delight of the staff to package any portion of any selection that might be wanted, no matter how small, even a single stalk of Parmesan-roasted asparagus. Since the folding of *Nota Bene* and the shrinking of the market for most connoisseur-type writing, Ollie had to be careful with money. He was surviving by writing notes and essays for auction houses and realtors specializing in historic properties, as well as, in a recent foray into new media, scripts for specialized auction house videos that were circulated among potential blue-chip buyers. Most nights, Ollie was content to stay home and cook up something like a pot of soup with Bob's Red Mill Vegi Soup Mix and Better Than Bouillon Reduced Sodium Roasted Chicken Base. But he allowed himself a night or two per week of take-out extravagance, and tonight Babbidge's was offering, in addition to the chicken paillard he liked, a yummy-looking veal cordon bleu, gorgeous slices of baked salmon with a mustard-and-maple-syrup glaze, and an invitingly plump moussaka. Should he also go crazy and pick up a mini-quiche for breakfast?

"Mr. Shaw?"

Ollie turned and found his tailor, Sandro, standing there, a distinguished-looking man almost as old as Ollie, dressed nattily in a flawlessly wrinkle-free suit. Sandro's shop, an Upper East Side landmark for men accustomed to bespoke wear, was on the second floor of a small building that was once a private house, a few blocks down Madison, above a French leather goods boutique.

"Sandro, my goodness. It's wonderful to see you."

They shook hands warmly.

"Good to see you, too, Mr. Shaw. It's been a long time."

"Indeed it has!"

"You're looking very well."

Sandro's accent was of the cultivated, northern Italian sort; and Ollie detected a tone of relief in the tailor's voice. This aspect of advanced age, too, Ollie had come to peace with, when he encountered it.

"No, my friend," said Ollie. "I haven't died yet."

"No, no, no . . ." protested Sandro, with a forced but good-natured laugh.

"Getting some dinner?"

"Carlo and I—you remember my assistant, Carlo—we're working late tonight on a deadline for a customer. I am bringing back some sandwiches and wine. The gentleman is getting married in two days—I don't think you know him—and we have a fitting tomorrow morning."

"Last-minute! How dramatic! What kind of suit? Morning clothes?"

"Ah," said Sandro, rolling his eyes, as if to indicate regret over how rarely that kind of attire was required anymore for weddings or any other daytime event. "No. Double-breasted, six-by-two, peaked lapels."

"Aha. Fabric?"

"A nice glen plaid—Zignone."

"Oh, my! An informal wedding, I see. I can imagine that suit going quite nicely with a bright, new pair of Chuck Taylor high-tops."

The tailor looked mystified.

"Sneakers, Sandro. Just my little joke. Well, so be it. I can well imagine how beautiful a suit you are going to give him."

"We try. Now, will we . . . be seeing you again sometime?"

There was such intelligence in that face, Ollie thought, such skill in those hands. What he had learned from Sandro over the years was volumes about how the best tailored clothes are constructed and how magically they sit and move on the body, and conceal or emphasize a physiognomic feature—how powerfully they can boost the wearer's self-confidence and even his attitude toward life.

"I haven't changed tailors, my friend," said Ollie. "To be perfectly honest, my wardrobe budget is a fraction of what it used to be. And I have so many wonderful things that you've made for me. . . ."

Over the years, Ollie had commissioned numerous suits, sport jackets, and coats from Sandro, and had brought him things bought off the rack to be altered or copied. Ollie once even devoted a column to Sandro's work with a Katharine Hamnett sport jacket in heavy wool melton that Ollie had picked up in London in 1982, that Sandro relined once and copied twice, most recently in a dense camel hair fabric that Ollie complemented with handmade elk horn buttons that he'd found in an antique store in Prague.

"I like my work to give good value," said Sandro modestly.

"You make beautiful things that will last forever, and I will wear them forever, even if the kids tell me that my style dates me."

"You've been such a good customer, Mr. Shaw. Bring me

something, and I will update it for you pro bono, for old times' sake—even rebuild it, if that's what it takes. I miss working with you."

"Thank you, Sandro," said Ollie with a small bow. "I may take you up on that. That is, if the Met costume collection doesn't come calling first, asking for my old things."

Ollie lived in a pre-war apartment building on East 77th Street. With a façade of sandy-brown brick, accented by string-courses of Art Deco zigzagging in turquoise and black terra-cotta, the building was a co-op and considered "good" because it was well-maintained, boasted nicely designed apartment layouts, was home to a stable group of upper-middle-class residents, and had a super who lived on the premises. The place was just around the block from the Hotel Carlyle, where during his heyday, Ollie would often meet friends for dinner and a cabaret show at the Café Carlyle or hold court over cocktails at the hotel's storied Bemelmans Bar. For many years, too, whenever he hosted a cocktail party at his own place, he'd arrange for the hotel to send over one of their red-jacketed bartenders, though those days were long gone.

The lobby was small but conspicuously chic, with its original, sleekly modernist details intact.

"Emma Radetzky for Oliver Shaw, please," said Emma.

"Of course, miss—he's expecting you," said the doorman. "Sixteen-F."

Ollie's apartment was small but thoughtfully detailed, with a small foyer dominated by what appeared to be a minimalist sculpture in the form of a pile of packing crates, a dining alcove off the kitchen, a fairly spacious living room that doubled as a library and study, and a modest-sized bedroom and bath. As Ollie showed Emma into the living room, she recognized the décor of the place as in the same general style as other homes of New York intellectuals she'd seen over the years: a genial mix of contemporary furniture and European antiques, rugs from Central Asia and the American Southwest, a riot of framed drawings, prints, and paintings; personal photographs and other memorabilia; and books everywhere, stacked on tables and on the floor, lined up on the mantelpiece and packed inside the disused fireplace, as well as shelved in actual bookcases. Within this kind of décor was a wide range of possibilities for order and cleanliness, ranging from elegantly-composed-and-flawlessly-tidy to downright-dusty-messy-and-neglected; and Emma had learned through experience that neither of these poles necessarily connoted the frame of mind of the homes' occupants. Neat could easily mean sad and miserable, and sloppy might well express contentment or even Buddha-like bliss. The East Village home of one Pulitzer Prize-winning author whom Emma once visited, for instance, would probably have been described by an outsider as "squalid"—with empty, days-old take-out food containers on the kitchen table and a dead roach in the earthenware mug that the author started to pour tea into—yet on a kitchen shelf, the man had a tiny sculpture given him by his great friend, the artist Hans Arp, and in the bathroom, on a window ledge, he had an Emmy won for the television miniseries adaptation of his second novel. Ollie's apartment was right in the middle of this range of décor, neither too neat nor too messy, and Emma wondered, as she was shown to an amply proportioned, antique-looking chair upholstered in well-worn, pastel plaid silk, if she could draw any conclusion about the frame of Ollie's mind—or his financial health—from the fact that the upholstery of the chair's armrests was badly frayed and showing its padding.

"Shall we have an aperitif before lunch?" asked Ollie, at which point, a woman in an apron emerged from the kitchen, whom Emma had passed without noticing. "This is Mrs. Welland. She's getting lunch ready for us. May I offer you a Campari and soda?"

The woman, in her seventies or maybe even eighties, nodded hello, quietly beaming. With tightly arranged gray hair and small, gold button earrings, she did not look to Emma like a servant, despite the apron she was wearing over her impeccable, forest-green sweater set.

"Campari and soda would be lovely," said Emma.

"Right away," said the woman.

"No, I do not have a servant," said Ollie slyly, as the woman withdrew. "Mrs. Welland lives in the building. We're old friends—met at a benefit for the Central Park Conservancy. She's retired, as I am, and a widow. We help each other out as needed. Last week, I served dinner for her when she entertained her daughter and son-in-law."

"Very nice," said Emma, though she'd never heard of such an arrangement before.

"Makes life a bit easier."

Emma took in the room.

"What a nice apartment," she said. "How long have you been here?"

"Oh, let's see—almost thirty years now," said Ollie. "I moved in just after Doris died."

"So that would be . . . mid-nineties."

"That's right. And before that, I had a little place in Brooklyn Heights, where I lived, gosh, in the sixties, when I returned from London. I worked in London for a few years when I was just starting out."

"That must have been exciting—London then."

"Oh, marvelous! Pure madness."

"The Beatles?"

"Yes, the Beatles were already playing in London during those years. But I never saw them. I was doing interior design at the time and more tuned in to opera and ballet and all that—Joan Sutherland, Margot Fonteyn . . . Nureyev had just arrived on the scene."

Emma wasn't much of a day drinker, but did find herself thinking, as she sipped the Campari that Mrs. Welland served and Ollie went on about Sutherland's *Sonnambula*, that a little drink before lunch made a lot of sense, especially when comfortably surrounded by so many attention-worthy objects and artworks. Opposite her, framed in gilt, was a yard-wide "orientalist" watercolor that looked like some sort of temple interior scene—nineteenth-century, Emma guessed. Below that was a star-shaped, white-and-ochre-glazed ceramic tile, obviously antique, possibly Middle Eastern, set into a rustic wooden frame; and next to it, a silver-framed, full-scale drawing of a very similar tile.

"Moroccan?" asked Emma, referring to the actual tile, during a pause in the conversation.

"Good eye—close," said Ollie. "Persian, thirteenth- or fourteenth-century. A gift from Doris, actually. You may have read that she used to collect all sorts of fabulous antiquities and artworks on her travels through Asia and the Middle East, and have them shipped home. . . ."

"I've read about Shangri La."

"It's a museum now, but once, Emma, oh, it was the most fabulous spot on Earth—positively another dimension—and to actually live there. . . !"

For a moment, Ollie looked completely transported to the Eastern-inspired retreat that Duke built for herself in Hawaii—a world of shimmering ocean and caressing sunlight, tranquil loggias and fragrant floral breezes. Then he continued.

"Next to it, the drawing—that's by Doris."

"Really?"

"She did it as a child—well, as a teenager—on a visit to the Met Museum. Then, as an adult, she found dozens more tiles in Iran just like the museum's, and purchased them for Shangri La."

"Ha."

"She was always outbidding museums for antiquities, always hiring native artisans to create reproductions and even new works. She was fascinated by these things from a very young age."

"And above that?"

On closer view, Emma could see that the watercolor depicted a naked boy seen from the rear, with an immense serpent wrapped around his body, being watched by a group of reclining men in robes as if he were performing, in a beautifully tiled room. The performance was accompanied by a seated flute player. The boy was holding the serpent's head calmly above his own, in quiet mastery.

"That's Gérôme—Jean-Léon Gérôme, 1879. A study for a much larger oil he did, that's now in Chicago. *The Snake Charmer.* Isn't it delirious?"

"Lovely."

"The blue-and-white tile wall is from the Topkapi Palace in Istanbul. . . ."

"You mean copied?"

"Practically verbatim. And the floor is from the Amr Mosque in Cairo."

"Wow."

"A European fantasy about the Islamic world."

"Amazing."

"Also a gift from Doris. She was quite savvy, Doris was, about this thing we now call the Western gaze. She was quite a thoughtful scholar in her collecting, and consulted top experts, always. She was so much more than a rich lady who shopped the world."

When the aperitifs were finished, Mrs. Welland appeared without her apron to announce that lunch was ready. Ollie and Emma went to the dining alcove, and Emma examined the set of six botanical prints that hung there while Ollie said a quiet goodbye to his friend at the front door.

On the intimately sized table were two place settings of white china with silver, and serving dishes of poached salmon with tzatziki sauce, charred marinated string beans, and an orzo salad with feta, olives, and green peppers. On a counter between the dining table and the kitchen were two small linzer tortes on little plates, a dish of maple roasted nuts, and a small bowl of clementines.

"Please sit," said Ollie.

"Yummy," said Emma.

"And no, I don't cook. Neither does Mrs. Welland. This is all from our favorite market."

Ollie served the food and poured some white wine.

"Okay, women and jewels—I get it," he said, as they began eating. "Very nice idea. One of the first projects that Jackie O. proposed when she got to Viking was a history of gold. Never happened. But then she scored with a book she did with Diana Vreeland—*In the Russian Style*, about clothing and other artifacts from Czarist Russia. So Emma, why not a book?"

Emma nodded.

"Well, first of all, I'm a filmmaker, so film is how I work," she said. "It's a visual medium, and motion photography, more than still photography, I think, can show these jewels as they are in real life, with the sparkly vitality they have right before our eyes."

"Fair point."

"And I want to use the documentary angle as much as I can—talking to the women who now own some of the great jewels of the past few centuries, about what these fabulous things mean to them."

"So you want to shoot both some women and some historic jewels."

"That's what I'm proposing, yes. I know it will involve some preliminary back-and-forth."

"More than some, I should think," said Ollie.

"I have two, maybe three women already lined up. I have a friend at Christie's who's helping me."

"But it's not a Christie's project *per se*."

"No."

Ollie was silent for a moment.

"A small thought . . ." he said.

"Please, that's what I am here for—why I am so glad you've agreed to help me."

"You may find it difficult to learn who owns some of the most important of these pieces. I mean, all these historic auctions—the Elizabeth Taylor collection, the Claudia Cardinale collection, the Oppenheimer Blue diamond, the Hancock Red. . . . The people who purchase these things may not want to be known, much less interviewed. And many times, they are not even people but *entities*."

"So I understand. And yet some women . . ."

"Yes, some women will be very happy to be known and filmed, and I will be happy to help you identify one or two. Not sure, though, that we can be awfully strategic about who we get. It's going to be catch as catch can."

"I understand. We collaborate with fate."

"Exactly."

Emma explained also that she had applied to all of the likely philanthropic organizations that fund projects like hers, including the Doris Duke Charitable Foundation, and had so far been turned down by all of them in the nicest terms. One application, her last possibility, was still pending. Hesitantly, she offered that she was also open to private sponsorship, but knew that raising funds was its own arduous task, apart from the whole creative side.

"Well, I'm afraid I won't be of much help there," said Ollie. "I'm a terrible fundraiser. I learned that long ago after one too many gala committees."

Emma nodded.

"As you know, I'm no expert in jewelry," Ollie continued, "but I'm happy to tell you what I can about the women I've known. I've seen heaps of the world's most important pieces of jewelry up close, in their natural habitat—meaning great parties, historic balls—and I think I can give you some background about who these women were, especially Miss Duke and Miss Hutton, how they functioned, maybe some insight into the world they managed to navigate."

A devilish grin came over Ollie's face.

"And I may know a secret or two that could bring some extra sparkle to your project," he said with a wink.

"Okay, then," said Emma. "First things first. I have to ask: was Barbara Hutton really a man? I read a newspaper quote from the 1940s where Doris Duke hints at it. Do you have any knowledge about this?"

Ollie burst out laughing.

"Of course I do," he said. "Dodo tried that trick more than once. She outright called Elsa Maxwell a man, too, to some London reporter, probably around the same time."

"So it was true?"

"Of course it wasn't true. Dodo was a devil. So was Babbo.

It was their trick—their game together. Elsa was parading Barbara around as one of her prize herd of globe-hopping partygoers, and Doris didn't think that this was such a good influence for her friend, so *bang*, Elsa is a man. So silly—those days when such things were whispered about and thought shameful or dangerous or I don't know what."

"What do you mean, 'their game together'?"

"Barbara inherited twenty million dollars when she was sixteen. Doris inherited a hundred million when she was fourteen. Or something like that. And both would inherit millions more as the terms of various wills and trust funds kicked in. These girls couldn't eliminate the constant attention that was on them since birth, the constant stereotyping, not just from the press but often from people of their own class, who thought that ladies should be mentioned in the press only three times during their lives—at birth, marriage, and death. All the lies and exaggerations printed about these two as children, Emma, and as teenagers and as women—can you imagine? All that money and no way to eliminate the single most annoying condition of your life? Let alone the most dangerous one. Being seen constantly as an object and not as a human being. It can kill your soul—you know? And trying to ignore all that was a fool's errand back then, before we had filter bubbles and private realities. And besides, to ignore it would require more energy than these gals wanted to waste on it. So they decided to respond by using the attention to their advantage."

"How?"

"For their amusement. By pretending to be the rivals that the press cast them as, after that first splashy moment when they both came out."

"Nineteen-thirty?"

"That's right—their debuts. They had been planning these huge debut seasons, each with a round of lunches and receptions and balls, hugely extravagant, more lavish than any other society debuts had ever been—and then Black Tuesday happened. Wall Street crashed."

"Oh."

"The Dukes tried to scale back a bit, but the Huttons didn't. Barbara's ball at the Ritz-Carlton had four orchestras and endless dancing, two hundred waiters serving a seven-course meal to a thousand guests; Rudy Vallée was the entertainment, and because this was December, they hired Maurice Chevalier, who was a big star at the time, to dress as Santa Claus and greet guests at the door."

"Wow."

"The thing cost a hundred thousand dollars, which is probably almost two million in today's money. This at a time when the average family in Depression-era America was surviving on a thousand dollars a year, if that. People lost their jobs and their homes and their sense of dignity on an immense scale. Of course, the press liked nothing more than to report on the most conspicuous waste of money in history, while half the world was suddenly starving."

"So how did a pretended or exaggerated rivalry help anything?"

Ollie seemed more emotional than Emma would have expected when relating these facts.

"Well, it certainly wasn't going to help the Depression," he said. "Though, by the way, both of these women were always very generous human beings and gave lots of money and gifts away to both friends and strangers, even if as time went on, their generosity came to function in very different ways. But they also had to think about themselves, about their sanity. They had to survive in a world where even the bodyguards might not be as trustworthy as they should be."

"So it amused them to pretend to get the better of each other?"

"Privately, these gals knew who they were. Each had her circle, her habits, her projects. But this thing between them, this pretend rivalry, was a way to keep alive the oldest friendship either of them ever had. It wasn't ideal, it wasn't the stuff of grand opera. But it was all they could contrive, when no one else was going to contrive anything better for them."

"Huh."

"Sometimes one bought a mansion that the other one coveted. The next time, the other one placed the winning bid on an old master painting that both of them wanted."

"And with husbands . . ."

"Well, yes, yes. Both of them got Rubirosa—and both cast him aside, probably for the same reason—and they both pretended to want Cary Grant, though only Barbara got that particular prize."

"What reason to cast Rubirosa aside, may I ask? Though this has nothing to do with jewels."

"It has everything to do with jewels," said Ollie, with an amused sniff. "Crown jewels. I'm sure you've read about his enormous penis. Apparently, kids learn about it in elementary school nowadays. Well, both ladies wanted to try it, and both were rich enough to afford it—he was a notoriously expensive playboy, who expected gifts of polo ponies and private airplanes—and both of them wound up after marriage to him feeling something like, 'Nice. But what's next?'"

"It sounds like a chess game," said Emma, taking a sip of wine.

"Exactly," said Ollie. "It was a chess game, and they were the only two grand masters in the world. Some fish?"

Emma accepted another slice of salmon and another spoonful of orzo salad.

"This is exactly the kind of material I was hoping for," she said.

"Good," said Ollie, finishing his wine and pouring more for both Emma and himself. A shaft of genial midday light was poking in from the alcove's window, which looked onto the building's quiet inner courtyard.

"They were hungry for sex, hungry for men, hungry for experience," he said. "I mean, this was a time when hostesses of their mothers' generation kept lists of eligible men in categories like 'men who will dance,' 'men who can lunch,' and 'men who will go to the theater but not the opera.' Pshaw! And it was Doris who was the real instigator between them—the inventor of the game. She was a pioneer—a social pioneer, a real inventor, a big soul, an explorer, an astronaut—and I so much admired that. I know that you think I am not much of a social pioneer myself, Emma. . . ."

She started to make a gesture of protest, which Ollie resisted by raising a finger to quiet her as he continued.

"It's true, and I know very well I am the poorer for it," he said, "but it is simply the way I am, the way I was brought up to be, and I am too old to change now. I think your father saw this quickly enough and maybe even came to revile me for it a little, even if he still respected me as a writer. He was smart enough not to try to change me, and my ways might indeed have given me a lonely life, except for this redeeming friendship I had with Doris. It was really the most important relationship of my life—and actually more fulfilling than people can imagine, even without sex. . . ."

For the moment, Emma didn't feel comfortable being diverted into a conversation about her father, even if Ollie was holding onto some issues about that relationship and wanted to use this opportunity with Emma as a way of addressing or neutralizing them.

"So she wasn't a monster," said Emma quietly. "There are those movie versions played by Lauren Bacall and wasn't it Susan Sarandon. . . ?"

"Please, those were garbage," said Ollie, "if I may say that with respect for both Miss Bacall's and Miss Sarandon's work. No, she wasn't a monster. What she was, was Cixi, the dowager empress of China, and who can even grasp that?"

Emma chuckled.

"I was Doris's best friend for years, if I may claim that honor," continued Ollie, "and the empress was always present, the one who hobnobbed with First Ladies, even when we also got the girl who rode horses bareback, the young woman who swam in the ocean naked, the white lady who flirted with handsome Black guys while sitting in at the piano for a set with a jazz combo in a Harlem *boîte*."

By the middle of his second glass of wine, Ollie was waxing philosophical about Duke and Hutton's world. He explained that during a historical moment of unprecedented prosperity and permissiveness, the two came of age with more money and more permission than anyone else. Through much of the twentieth century, they were among the ten richest people in the world, including Henry Ford and Queen Elizabeth. When they came out, it was not just society with a capital S that was waiting for them, but a new elite called "café society," that mixed old and new money, and connected "people like us" with attractive types who were not quite like us but looked and sounded awfully attractive.

"They were basically teenagers when they started hanging out in speakeasies and private clubs that after Prohibition would become chic watering holes like El Morocco and the Stork Club," he said. "They were dropping into those legendary parties thrown by Condé Nast in his three-story penthouse at 1040 Fifth. This was the *ne plus ultra* invitation in New York for this new society, from the publisher who believed that people were no longer to be classified only by wealth, education, and refinement, but by their interests. Society types came to mix with *culturati* like George Gershwin and Josephine Baker, which is exactly the kind of thing that Doris and Barbara craved. Columnists like Maury Paul—who wrote as Cholly Knickerbocker— and Walter Winchell were turning newspaper journalism into entertainment with reports from this world, and photographers like Louise Dahl-Wolfe and George Hoyningen-Huene were capturing the very flattering side of it in pictures.

"And the rich, remember, were not in the least embarrassed about being rich during the twenties *or* during the Depression. You hear about financiers jumping out of windows, but 'I did nothing wrong!' was much more the state of mind of rich folks then. Anyway, by the time of Barbara's first marriage, to Alexis Mdivani, a polo-playing Russian playboy from a princely family of declining fortunes, and Doris's first, to James H.R. "Jimmy" Cromwell, a rising politician also from a family of declining fortunes, Prohibition was over, and nice young American women no longer needed the company of a husband to step out for an evening.

"These were some of the first girls who didn't wait around to be asked to dance, if you know what I mean."

When lunch was finished, Ollie suggested they move into the living room for coffee.

"Sure," said Emma. "Bathroom?"

"On the right," said Ollie, indicating the passage to the bedroom.

The fixtures in the bathroom looked old enough to be original, and though spotlessly clean, they were in poor condition. The foil backing the glass of the bathroom mirror was badly mottled around the edges, and the porcelain on the rim of the sink was chipped, exposing the cast iron underneath. Going for shabby chic was one thing, but Emma decided that it was more likely that Ollie could not afford the repairs or renovation that a fastidious gentleman like him might prefer—which, together with the frayed armchair upholstery, confirmed that Ollie would not be helping her project financially.

"This is fun," said Ollie, when they were reseated in the living room, in the same chairs they'd occupied earlier. "I don't know what kind of plan or schedule you may have for your film, but I suspect we should just go forward meeting and talking, and see what happens over the next few weeks."

"That sounds good to me," said Emma.

"I just remembered that my dear friend Artemis Qasim will be in town next week for the ABT gala. She's a Brit married to a Syrian billionaire, whose very thoughtful husband picked up several baubles for her from the Duchess of Windsor's collection, when they went on the block in Geneva back in the eighties. If you like, you could come with me to the ballet, and I could introduce you two. Though no promises. Artsy likes to dress up, but I have no idea if she'll be wearing any of the Windsor things."

"Oh, that would be tremendous. American Ballet Theatre?"

"Monday, a week."

Emma opened the calendar on her phone.

"Mrs. Welland was to have come with me," said Ollie, "but she just told me she can't make it."

"Perfect," said Emma. "Thank you."

"I have no idea what the program will be—probably a 'mixed grill,' as we used to say at the Royal Ballet. But afterwards will be fun."

Ollie had brought in the clementines and nuts, and poured coffee from a glass pot that was being kept warm in the kitchen.

"Thank goodness Mrs. Welland knows how to work my coffee maker," he said. "I can barely manage it."

"Say, Ollie, may I ask a question about that? Forgive me or just shut me up if I'm being impertinent, but . . . do you two really have an arrangement where you do domestic tasks for each other?"

Ollie chuckled.

"I've just never heard of anything like that," continued Emma. "It's not like going to the drugstore for a sick friend or accepting a neighbor's FedEx delivery."

"Well, it's interesting that you should ask," said Ollie. "First of all, as I've said, we're old friends. And the reality is that for various reasons, we are both coping with vastly reduced means, though in the past we've both had domestic help, especially when entertaining; and given that she and I now do only some very small-scale entertaining here in the building, under the same roof, it's fun for us, I guess you'd say, to play-act the old lifestyle."

"Interesting. Nice, actually."

"I suppose it's about the ritual of living in a certain way. Nothing fancy—just with a little grace."

"What a nice aspect of a friendship."

"I'm glad you see it that way. Living in a certain manner has always been important to me, though it's never just about money or manners or anything like that. And in a way—well, even more so—that's how it was with Doris and me. A certain understanding. I don't know—maybe that was *our* little game."

"You say you knew Barbara first," said Emma. "How did you meet Doris?"

"'Doris!'" said Ollie. "I suppose that's the way that we two may refer to her. You'll probably simply use 'Duke' in the film, no? In those biopics you mention, they made the butler, Lafferty, say 'Miss Duke' so many times, it made my skin crawl. Maybe the actors liked to say that phrase. Until she was an invalid and dependent on her staff, she was not really a 'Miss Duke.' She who was known by so many names! I called her 'Dodo,' which is kind of a British way of making a nickname; no reference to the extinct flightless bird of Mauritius. Joey Castro called her 'Dorshka'—that was her boyfriend for a long time, a jazz musician. Bobby Farrah—another beau who had a little Middle Eastern dance company she liked—he called her 'Dolly Ditz.' Duke Kahanamoku, her handsome prince of a Hawaiian surfer boyfriend, called her 'Lahi Lahi,' which I think means 'fragile' or 'gentle' or something like that—you know, because she had this surprisingly soft voice."

"Did she?"

"An empress doesn't need to raise her voice. Oh, and at the OSS, during World War Two, she was known by the code name 'Daisy.'"

"The OSS?"

"Office of Strategic Services, which after the war became the CIA. Intelligence gathering."

"Doris was a *spy*?"

"Well, she took her patriotic duty very seriously during the war, and as one of the most prominent Americans in the world, she was in a position to hear *certain things*. Remember, this was only twenty years after Mata Hari. The OSS thought that pillow talk was one way that comely young American women might discover secret things that could be useful to their country's armed forces. They recruited scores of 'em. Though Dodo's chief conquest during the war was no enemy—I refer, of course, to General George Smith Patton, Jr., who commanded the Seventh United States Army in the Mediterranean theater and led the Allied invasion of Normandy."

"Golly. An affair?"

"She always wanted to be part of the action. During the war, she was in Italy, Egypt, London. . . . Patton tried to get her to go to Austria, where she might be able to pick up something useful, but that got her into trouble with the State Department, which complicated her ability to get the visas and such she needed to move around as a war correspondent for the Associated Press."

"Really—a war correspondent?"

"Really."

Emma shook her head in amazement.

"Daisy," she said.

"For Daisy Mae Yokum, *née* Scragg, Li'l Abner's girlfriend."

"The cartoon!"

"Americans took their cartoons very seriously back then. Why do you think all these stories about 'the Gold Dust Twins' were so popular?"

"You make a lot of connections, Ollie."

"Emma, I like to keep my eyes open. And Dodo and I did a lot of talking, especially after Barbara died, when I was blessed with some of the benefits of oldest-and-dearest-best-friend status, and the game that those two had contrived for themselves became, in some small way, a game between Dodo and me."

"Fascinating. Competition but trust? Rivalry but respect?"

"Something like that. I was there, I knew the rules. I had graciously survived an assault, and I had a tuxedo."

"Assault?!"

Ollie snickered.

"I'll come to that some other time," he said. "First things first. I'd seen Dodo at parties, and she even said hello to Babbo once in passing when I was standing right there. But I was first introduced to her on a mountaintop. . . ."

CHAPTER 5

May 1964

The house was at the top of one of the Shawangunk Mountains, the so-called foothills of the Catskills, in Ulster County, about ninety miles north of New York City, not far from Cragsmoor, a tiny settlement that was founded in the 1800s as an artists' colony. A handsomely proportioned bluestone mansion dating from 1878, the house was designed by British-American architect and landscape designer Calvert Vaux in the Gothic Revival style. It was commissioned by Cornelius Dewitt Prescott for his young wife, Amelia, to replace an earlier, much smaller mansion of wood built by Cornelius's father, Dewitt Prescott, the transportation baron, whose canal and railroad lines both supported and helped drive the phenomenal growth of New York City throughout the second half of the nineteenth century. The family's fortune was hit hard by the Crash of '29, and Cornelius's Wall Street financier son, James, was forced in 1930 to retreat from his New York mansion back to the house, which was called Church Lake Road for the private road that led to it and to now-demolished stables—at which point the adequate maintenance of such a grand estate became impossible to continue.

When Ollie saw the place in 1964, in the company of Barbara, who was thinking of buying and restoring it, Church Lake Road was run-down. Its great lawn, the site of so many elegant summer parties attended by guests who came from as far away as New York and Washington, D.C., had reverted to meadow, and so many trees and shrubs had grown wild that the valley views from the house's terraces were now partially obscured. The property's most striking feature was a freestanding stone chapel down the road from the mansion, also designed by Vaux, in a picturesque, asymmetrical Gothic style meant to suit the building's rustic site. The chapel looked like a ruin, but begun only in 1927, it was actually never finished—another victim of the Prescott family's reversal of fortune.

It was late morning on an early fall day, and Barbara had asked the driver to take the most scenic route from the city, so he avoided the New York State Thruway, which had opened a few years before, and used local roads, the last of which, before they turned onto Church Lake Road itself, was New York State Route 52, affording panoramic lookout views east, toward the Hudson Valley, and then west, over the Shawangunk Valley.

"You're one of only very few parties I'm talking to about the house," said Dewitt August Prescott, James Prescott's son. "We love the place—it's not just our history, it's New York State history—but we can't keep it up, and it would be a crime to see it go completely to ruin."

"Mm-hmm," said Barbara, a little hazy from the pills she'd taken earlier in the morning and the champagne she'd drunk in the car.

She was nominally shopping for a country house. Barbara, Ollie, and Barbara's current secretary, Mrs. Fisk, were standing on a terrace off the parlor and dining room with Prescott and his lawyer. They had toured the house and seen the gracious public rooms, and grand staircase, and spacious bedrooms whose original water closets had been renovated in the 1920s into then-modern bathrooms—all now sadly battered, wallpaper faded, furniture that had been new and fashionable in the 1870s now shaky or shabby or both, empty spots on the walls where paintings had been taken down to be sold. Barbara was doing most of the talking, asking questions; Mrs. Fisk was taking notes and staying mostly silent; and Ollie would sometimes chime in with a question or remark that Barbara always seemed glad he was adding, as he had been included partly because of his knowledge of antiques and architecture, and partly because at that point, he was a steady companion of Barbara's, accompanying her often to social events and on shopping expeditions.

"We're so eager to see it go to the right owner," said Prescott, a distinguished-looking man in his mid-forties, who was known as Augie. "We hope to find someone who can understand the place and who would be in a position to give it the care it needs."

"Of course," said Barbara, gazing out over the wild meadow. She had put her sunglasses back on, now that they were out of the house again. "It's a splendid site, isn't it? This must have been a splendid lawn."

"The far edge, where those trees start," said Prescott, pointing, "that was always kept trim in my father's time, so that even in the summer, when everything was in full foliage, you could still see a big view across the valley, to the hills on the other side. All through the twenties, the lawn was always flawless, trees in white lattice planter boxes, ladies in white dresses. . . . We have pictures in the library from as far back as the 1890s. Great parties. Now, we can't afford to keep up any kind of proper lawn here—this is an acre-and-a-half alone—but we do try to keep it clear of big stuff, so helicopters can land."

It was meant as a joke, and Prescott winked, and Barbara and Mrs. Fisk shared a glance of amusement at such a preposterous idea.

"What's the elevation?" asked Ollie.

"Twenty-eight hundred feet," said Prescott.

"Isn't that nice?" said Barbara. "Good, fresh air."

"Though even now, as you can see, even with the leaves on the trees, there is still a bit of that view . . ." said Prescott, pointing.

"Yes, I see," said Barbara. "And the architecture is so charming. Ollie's told me so much about Calvin Fox."

"Yes—Calvert Vaux," said Prescott, gently correcting her. "I'm sure you know his work from Central Park. . . ."

"Oh, that's right. . . !"

"He did many houses here upstate and in Connecticut, and of course important public buildings in New York and Boston.

He used to summer in Kingston, I believe; came to a few parties right here, in fact. He was a friend of my grandfather, and was entertained by my grandmother very often at their townhouse in New York."

"The light is quite special, isn't it?" said Ollie.

"Vaux wrote about it somewhere," said Prescott. "And apparently, he chose the stone and the mortar, everything, with the specific light of the sites he built on in mind. For the chapel, my father had originally wanted marble, but Vaux convinced him that bluestone—a different variety from the house—was the better choice."

Trailing the party on the house tour, and now still close by on the terrace, were Prescott's two daughters, Elizabeth, called Liddy, who was ten years old, and Margaret, called Maggie, who was eight. Both girls, who seemed so curious about the proceedings, were sporting short brown hair and matching wool jumpers over white blouses. Each was wearing a modest little circle pin on the shoulder of her jumper.

"Are you going to live here?" asked Maggie, piping up.

Everyone laughed.

"I don't know, my dear," said Barbara, with a smile meant to be angelic. "It *is* a wonderful house, isn't it? Are you happy here?"

Maggie nodded shyly.

"We've talked about it as a family," said Prescott in a half-whisper, "but it's an awfully big change for the girls to contemplate. This is the only place they've ever lived."

"The president came here once," said Maggie.

"Did he, dear?" said Barbara, with routine solicitousness.

Prescott laughed, putting a hand on Maggie's head.

"Teddy Roosevelt," he said. "He was a guest here several times, in fact. The girls are very proud of their family's history."

"He came here in 1902, to open a train station," offered Liddy.

"That's right," said Prescott. "They're also wild about trains. My grandfather knew the president rather well."

"What a coincidence—so did mine," said Barbara blithely.

Ollie and Mrs. Fisk shared a discreet look, as they sometimes did when Barbara was being Miss Hutton, or even the Baroness, though she was long divorced from her most recent husband, tennis champion and German homosexual Baron Gottfried von Cramm.

"Well, you've given us a lot to think about," said Barbara.

Coming from above them, far away, was the buzz of what sounded like an airplane.

"As you well know, we've conferred with your people in New York," said the lawyer. "If there's anything else you need, please don't hesitate to ask. Mrs. Fisk has my private line."

"Or call me directly," said Prescott. "I love to talk about the house."

The buzz in the sky was becoming noticeably louder.

"Are you going straight back to New York?" asked Prescott.

"Well, we were to have," said Barbara, "and poor Ollie has tickets to a play tonight—don't you, Ollie?—but on the drive up, I got a call from my dear friend Millicent, over in Rhinebeck, and she practically begged me to come to a party she's throwing tonight, so we're having some things sent up there. . . . What *is* that sound?"

The buzz had become a roar, dominated by a *thwup-thwup-thwup*-ing sound, as from a helicopter.

"By the way, Mr. Prescott," said Mrs. Fisk in a loud voice, "you mentioned another party who was interested in the property?"

And then in the sky close by, above the trees at the far edge of the meadow, appeared a helicopter that had apparently been flying up the valley from the south and was positioning itself as if to touch down right there in the meadow in front of them. The sound was deafening.

"I gather this is her, Ed?" shouted Prescott, to his lawyer.

"Her pilot confirmed the route and landing site this morning," shouted the lawyer. "But as you know, she wasn't due until three."

It was then around noon. With everyone speechless in enthrallment, they watched as the helicopter landed and shut down its rotor. From its door emerged first a young man in a blue blazer and gray slacks, and then, with his help, a woman in a parrot-green pants suit and matching green hat with a large, floppy brim. Her oversize sunglasses covered half her face, but everyone knew it was Doris Duke.

She waved amiably to the party on the terrace as she approached, with a great big, beaming smile.

"Hello, hello, all! Augie, good to see you again!" said Doris, stepping up onto the terrace and shaking Prescott's hand. "Oh, my word, well, hello there, Babbo!"

"Well, of course it's Dodo," said Barbara, in an aside to Ollie. "Who else would it be?"

"Am I late?" said Doris.

"We expected you at three," said the lawyer, "but you're . . . right on time."

Doris embraced Barbara with a big hug.

"What a surprise, Babs," she said. "Are you looking for a house, too?"

Barbara smirked. She knew that Doris understood very well that she had been looking for a specific kind of property— something close to New York with the character of her ex-husband von Cramm's family castle, Schloss Brüggen, in Lower Saxony, Germany, where Barbara had once told a newspaper reporter that she felt "very comfortable with myself." Doris had noted her saying this, and was known to be looking herself for something historically interesting in the Catskills, as she had been a fan of Colonial Williamsburg since childhood and was thinking about involving herself in historic preservation.

Barbara introduced Ollie to Doris as her "architecture consultant," and Doris introduced the man in the blazer simply as Dennis. The small round of pleasantries that ensued had to do with the pros and cons of helicopter travel, while the pilot out in the meadow methodically inspected his craft.

"Give us a moment, will you, Augie?" said Doris, as she gently steered Barbara several steps down the terrace to a spot where they wouldn't be overheard.

"A helicopter, Dodo?" said Barbara.

"It was the fastest way," said Doris, still wearing her sunglasses.

"We usually plan these little encounters ahead, don't we?"

"I thought a surprise would be fun, and here's why: Dennis is from *Time* magazine."

"Oh."

"He's following me around all week, so I thought . . ."

"Yes, I see—a nice little run-in with your dear old friend."

"See how that works?"

"You might have called."

"Then it wouldn't have been a surprise."

"I suppose so. You've always known more about how to stage these things than I do."

Doris glanced over at the others, who were talking among themselves.

"Say, I thought your new beau was Eurasian," she said.

"No, no. Ollie's just a friend—a very convenient friend," said Barbara. "Besides, he's not that way."

"When has that ever stopped you?"

"He really knows his stuff around art and architecture."

"Really?"

"Princeton."

"*Really?*" said Doris, lowering her sunglasses slightly and looking at Ollie over the top of them. "Not bad looking."

"I suppose so. You look completely wonderful yourself in that suit, by the way."

"Thank you. It's Irene Galitzine," said Doris, striking a pose.

"You can wear those youngish things," grumbled Barbara. "They make me look ridiculous."

"When has that ever. . . ?"

There was a beat, and then both women laughed.

"New perfume?" said Doris.

"From Yves Saint Laurent—his first," said Barbara.

"It's lovely."

"'Like a walk in the woods,' he says."

"Oh, brother. Anyway, we'd better break this up, or it will seem too friendly," said Doris. "Listen, now that I think of it,

I have an even better idea than the two of us haggling over a house. Ready?"

"What do you have in mind?"

"The boy."

"Ollie?"

"Why don't I just fly away and take him with me? Just like that."

"Hmm . . ."

"We won't have to say a word about it. Let *Time* magazine make of it what it will."

"Clever girl."

"Are you going to take the house?"

Barbara made a face and shook her head.

"I should probably concentrate on the improvements I'm making to Sidi Hosni. You *must* come back soon. There are always fun people tramping through . . ."

"Your three-day-long costume parties?"

". . . Including Raymond. That's the man I've been seeing. He's Vietnamese."

"He's in antiquities, I hear?"

"He was trained as a chemist, was working for some French oil company. He does sell antiques, with his brother, but now he's doing the most marvelous oil paintings."

"Good for you."

"Quite handsome, in an exotic way—you'll see," drawled Barbara. "An adopted son of the former royal family of Champasak. That's a kingdom in Laos."

"I also heard you bought him a title."

"Is that what you heard?"

"Good for him," said Doris.

At the same time, they noticed that the little girls, Maggie and Liddy, were standing near them, obviously curious about the two great ladies conferring on their terrace, let alone the helicopter.

"And who have we here?" said Doris.

"It's Liddy, isn't it?" said Barbara, of the younger girl she'd been speaking to.

"Maggie," said the girl.

"Sorry—Maggie."

"Hello, Maggie," said Doris, bending a bit at the waist to shake the girl's hand. "I'm Doris."

"Hello," said Maggie. "I like your pin. It's pretty."

Doris, too, like Maggie, was wearing a circle pin, only Doris's was not made of stamped, ten-karat gold, as Liddy's was, but beautifully crafted of three intertwined strands of eighteen-karat gold, about an inch-and-a-quarter in diameter.

"Thank you, dear," said Doris. "I like yours, too."

"Thank you," said Maggie. "Liddy has the same one, but we told Mommy we wanted different ones."

"Did you? Well, rightly so," said Doris tenderly, crouching down to be at Maggie's level. "You know, sisters can be alike in so many ways, but they have to be unique, too. Right? Do you know what 'unique' means?"

Maggie shook her head but was obviously bright and inquisitive.

"It means very special," said Doris. "Each person is very special in his or her own way, even if they're also just like someone else."

Maggie was fascinated.

"Okay," she said.

"Do you know what might be fun?" said Doris. "We could trade pins, you and me. I'll give you mine, and you could give me yours. Do you like that idea?"

Maggie nodded enthusiastically.

"Then you'll have your own unique look," said Doris, removing her pin, then gently removing Maggie's and replacing it with her own. A moment later, Maggie's pin looked just as splendid on Doris's suit jacket as Doris's three-strand pin did on Maggie's jumper, and Maggie's face was aglow with a great big smile.

"Now I want you to remember one thing . . ." said Doris, crouching down so they could continue their conversation in whispers.

And they palavered intimately like this for a few minutes

while Barbara, standing by with mild impatience, used the moment to fix her makeup. She reapplied her lipstick, the medium-dark burgundy shade by Chanel called "Mysterieuse" being a bit too obviously mysterious for daytime wear. A thousand times, Doris had advised her friend to go lighter on makeup, since Barbara's preferred look did nothing so much as make her look old.

As Maggie listened intently to Doris's whispered words, her eyes widened and she nodded yes several times.

"You won't forget?" said Doris, returning to her normal voice.

Maggie shook her head.

"Good," said Doris, rising from her crouch. She smoothed the pants of her suit and turned to Barbara.

"So . . . the kidnapping—are you in?" said Doris.

"Fine," said Barbara. "We'll do it your way. We'll be doing Ollie a favor, anyway. He has tickets to a show tonight in town, and I've decided to stop for the night at Millicent's."

As Doris stepped back over to Prescott, Barbara, before rejoining them, and intent on not being outdone by Doris's gift to one of the sisters, quickly slipped off the gold bangle she was wearing, which featured black enamel stripes and two fierce-looking tiger heads.

"Here," she said to the other sister, tucking the bangle adroitly into the pocket of Liddy's jumper. "That's for you. Wear it when you're older, but right now you should probably keep it a secret. Alright, dear?"

Liddy, astonished at a fearsome kind of bracelet that she had never seen before, nodded yes.

"Augie, I'm afraid I must run," said Doris, imperiously. "I love the house, but it's not quite right for me."

Prescott and his lawyer tried to conceal their chagrin.

"We had hoped to show you around . . ." said the lawyer.

"I think fast," said Doris. "I know you'll understand. Maybe Miss Hutton will take it."

"Well . . . thank you for coming," said Prescott, slightly confused but doing his best to remain gracious.

Doris turned to Ollie.

"And *you*," she said loudly enough for Dennis, the magazine writer, to hear. "It's Ollie, isn't it? I understand you know something about architectural restoration?"

"Um, well, I do know something about it," said Ollie. "In Bryn Mawr, there's an historic house where I—"

"Restoration is a passion of mine," declared Doris. "I want you to tell me everything you know about it. Do you know Newport at all? I am giving you a ride back to New York—it's all been arranged. We're leaving right now. Dennis, this is Ollie, a gift to me from Miss Hutton. Ollie, say a quick goodbye to Miss Hutton."

CHAPTER 6

"Assault?" repeated Emma.

"Me and my big mouth," said Ollie, as they sat there after lunch at his place, having finished their coffee, Emma having declined the offer of a refill. "I'll tell you about it when I know you better. It was no big deal."

"I'm already looking forward to our next meeting," said Emma.

"We've made a good start," said Ollie, expansively. "An old man is grateful for a young ear. It all seems like another world, now."

"Well, this has been wonderful—really wonderful, Ollie," said Emma, taking his words about a good start as her cue to rise from her seat. She'd already stayed longer than she expected to. "Thank you so much for a delicious lunch."

Ollie made a courtly nod.

"A pleasure," he said automatically, rising too, though realizing that he was genuinely caught up in his own enjoyment in these reminiscences.

Emma found and gathered her things, and Ollie showed her to the door, where he remarked in passing that he'd always wished he'd been able to know Doris and Barbara as young women.

"What do you mean?" asked Emma.

"By the time I met them, both of them were playing very fast and loose with men and money," said Ollie. "Barbara was about to enter her last marriage, with Doan—and that would last only two years—and Doris had long ago said goodbye to her second and final marriage, with Rubi. At that point, for both of them, it was all about 'our bodies, ourselves,' obsessively: extramarital sex and the pursuit of youth; ailments and illnesses and any treatments that money could buy. And I suppose all that was magnificent, in a manic way. Barbara was taking peat baths at Swiss clinics, and Doris was trying to get a dying Nat King Cole to join her in using a contraption she financed that supposedly prevented cancer. Both women entertained a parade of charlatans and witch doctors who were as eager as the young suitors who had buzzed around them thirty years before."

"Oh, dear."

"Barbara was fading visibly," continued Ollie. "Liquor, drugs, alcohol—and this brought out a certain protective quality in Doris, who was always begging her to take better care of herself. I think there was always this push-and-pull between them. Barbara was maybe more daring, and Doris was more headstrong, if I can make that distinction. Barbara had the impulse to do wild things, whereas Doris wasn't particularly wild, but she had the gumption to do unconventional things. I think Doris thought Barbara a little aimless, with her society caravans around the Middle East and her endless parties with Elsa Maxwell on the Riviera. She once told me that she thought there wasn't a clear enough line in Barbara's life between generosity and profligacy, whereas I think Doris's generosity was more thoughtful, if you know what I mean."

"'Profligate' is a strong word."

Ollie sighed.

"They were both giving away lavish gifts and huge amounts of money at the time," he said. "Doris by then had bought organs for several small, Black churches throughout the South, whereas Barbara would breeze into a four-star hotel in Morocco with a party of twenty and hand out custom-made silk robes and gold jewelry for the staff to wear, so her guests would be served in style.

"And of course, Barbara died a pauper, while Doris had a billion dollars in the bank when she died."

"What happened?"

"To Barbara? Doris always said, 'Make the most of what you have.' Poor Barbara had a knack for making the least of it."

Emma shook her head.

"Maybe next time, we can talk specifically about some of the jewelry?" she said.

"Absolutely," said Ollie. "But may I make a suggestion?"

"Of course."

"That you should be thinking not simply about the possessions of these women but their personal histories and legacies, too."

"Sure."

"Both were extremely generous, but in different ways, undoubtedly based on their hopes and dreams as young women. And different kinds of traces remained after their deaths. Duke funded at least one charitable foundation that is still very active. Hutton, as I said, left no money at all—though the Woolworth family mausoleum, where she is interred up at Woodlawn in the Bronx, is undeniably handsome. . . ."

After saying goodbye to Ollie and confirming their date for the ballet gala, Emma walked the ten blocks north to the specialist's office where she had an appointment. The weather was pleasant, and since she was missing the gym that day, she thought a walk would be especially useful exercise. The only annoyance was a near-mishap with a food delivery guy barreling down the Park Avenue sidewalk on an e-bike. The incident gave her pause. She'd recently heard of an actor who funded a production of a play he'd written, by purposefully getting himself injured by one of those sidewalk warriors and accepting a cash settlement from the man's employer—a thought Emma instantly put out of her mind, since she was already feeling frail enough because of her elbow.

Bikes on a Park Avenue sidewalk! she thought. *What is this world coming to?* Then she chuckled to think of herself reacting like Ollie might. There was more to him than she had known, she realized. The way he spoke—with apparent relish for both his words and the reception he expected for them—struck her as overdramatic, self-important, and downright old-fashioned, yet this was a man with obvious intelligence and experience, and she supposed that this alone deserved respect in the form of tolerance. If the way he presented himself was to disguise some essential brokenness, as she assumed before they met, then there had been no evidence of it during their conversation. He's just the way he is, she thought—really engaged with a big idea about himself—and that *is* something that her father would have been interested in, aside from romance or whatever. Maybe she didn't even know her father as well as she thought she did. Maybe, though she was a reasonably smart, liberal upper-middle-class New York woman in her mid-thirties, she wasn't as savvy about men in general as she thought she was.

So much was changing in her world—notions of identity, gender, privilege, power—and so much had changed in her, since the death of her father and the departure of her mother for London. Chiefly, she had moved from arts administration to creating art herself, as a filmmaker. She had gone back to school for a while, which she thoroughly enjoyed, then jumped eagerly right into the field, wondering why she had taken so long to commit to this side of herself—though somehow, in the bargain, she may have lost her marriage.

Robert could never quite accept the new choices she was making about how to spend her time, as she evolved from serving a board of directors to serving her own creative agenda. Robert would tell her, in annoyed amusement he didn't bother to hide, that "as an artist or whatever" she no longer sounded like herself—a criticism that soon engendered in Emma an annoyed amusement of her own.

She had known Robert since their St. Ann's days. He was tall and slender, muscular in a graceful way, with beautifully creamy, practically hairless skin, and expressive eyes and mouth. He was outgoing, clearly addicted to being the center of attention, and from the start, Emma had accepted this for the typically male thing that it was, and even found herself wanting to know what was fueling all the show-off energy. He impressed her one day in their history class, Writing the Revolution: 20th Century Literature of Protest and Dissent, by arguing an absurd idea that nonetheless made for enjoyable watching.

"Great political writers own their great ideas," asserted Robert.

"'Own' an idea?" said the teacher. "How's that?"

"Yes, if they created it."

"Writers can earn a great reputation, yes," said the teacher. "But 'own,' as in 'having exclusive rights to' or 'profiting from'. . . ?"

"Absolutely."

"But how, Robert? Ideas are meant to spread freely, for one thing. No one owns them. The concept of ownership is irrelevant. For another thing, how can a writer profit when a political movement grows from his ideas?"

"He should get the credit."

"Credit, yes. That's reputation. And why 'he,' by the way? You're not forgetting Emma Goldman, are you?"

After class, Emma laughed when she told Robert she liked watching him make a clown of himself.

"I was serious," he protested.

"You were not. You were being a jerk. But it stimulated an interesting conversation."

"I'm glad you thought so."

Later, when sitting with Robert on the Brooklyn Heights promenade with paper cups of matcha in their hands, Emma lied and said that Emma Goldman was her namesake.

"That's amazing," said Robert.

She didn't know why she suddenly blurted out this lie, but knew at the moment Robert said "amazing"—the favorite dumb encomium of their generation—that they would be getting together as soon as it could be arranged. And sex led to dating, and that led to marriage.

They lived at the Belnord apartment for a while, until they found their own place in Prospect Heights. Then, after things started shifting between them, Emma moved back to the Belnord, alone.

And marriage led to this, thought Emma, as she stood on the sidewalk in Park Avenue's center median, waiting for the light to allow her to cross the downtown-bound lanes.

With the help of a couples therapist who functioned as something of a hospice caregiver for their marriage, they discovered that separation might well be the inevitable next step for them, because they were simply incompatible. That was the word the therapist used, "incompatible," and though Robert merely nodded when he heard the word, Emma greeted it as a kind of antidote to the co-dependency she feared was replacing her marriage. She took the word as a kind of gift to them, describing a welcome doorway out of the marriage that involved no guilt or blame or even much disappointment, since it would probably lead to better things for each of them.

Whether or not to stay married was the question. Neither party was seeing someone else, or even wanted to do so, apparently. Would divorce be the decisive move or just rocking the boat? Part of the question was their families, which had never been more than cordial to each other and didn't move in the same social circles. Emma's parents were upper-middle-class intellectuals. Their home functioned as a lively, bohemian salon. Her artist mother, Janet Fremont, was from a modest but old, Protestant California family; her editor father, Martin Radetzky, had been from a poor, Russian Jewish family that had migrated from Odessa to Brooklyn in 1905, after a pogrom. Robert's family were solidly upper-class and socially prominent—"Our Crowd" German Jews who'd come to New York as prosperous merchants in 1848. Their home was like a museum. Two of his ancestors had been founding members of the Harmonie Club, formed in 1852 when rich Jews were denied membership in the city's exclusive Union Club. The disparity between the families was not a particular problem operationally, but what continued to stick in Emma's mind was that once when she and Robert tenderly broached the subject of divorce, his first thoughts were about the engagement ring he'd given her. It was an old family piece, a sapphire-and-diamond ring that Robert's great-great-grandfather had had made in the 1890s at Garrard's, in London, for his aristocratic English bride.

"Mother was happy for you to have it while you and I . . . well, you understand," said Robert.

"Your mother. . . ? Is *that* what you're thinking about?" said Emma. She knew it wasn't a joke, but she found Robert's instinct laughable.

"We don't have to think about it now," he said dismissively.

"I don't see how we can think about anything else, frankly."

Emma was actually calmer than her words may have indicated. She wasn't particularly attached to the ring as a *thing*. It was just that she thought it meant something about a unique, rom-com-y kind of relationship that began over cups of green tea on the promenade . . .

But apparently, that's not us.

Maybe it's well enough, she thought, to pass out of what nineteenth-century novelists sometimes called a woman's first youth and on to the next one. To be more defined by individual achievement and personal satisfaction than by husband and children! This was something she thought she and her generation would already have well absorbed from their wise, feminist forbears, but so be it. Maybe Doris Duke and Barbara Hutton, whom Emma had thought she had little in common with when she started this project, could offer something of value after all: an example of the kind of autonomy that everyone deserves and no one ever has enough of. There is always more autonomy to manifest, thought Emma with a chuckle—though, really: peat baths and cancer-curing machines? If it were only that easy.

The specialist that Emma's regular doctor had referred her to was Dr. Harmon, a rheumatologist whose office, on the ground level of a 1970s-era apartment building, was small but nicely appointed with mid-century furniture and artworks. Emma was early for her appointment, and the doctor was able to see her right away.

"I've had a look at the x-rays," said Dr. Harmon, after chatting with Emma a bit about her diet and fitness practices, and examining her elbow and the rest of her body carefully. Several gray images were displayed on a large digital screen on one side of the exam table that Emma was sitting on. "Do you see this?" He was pointing to a whitish-gray shape between what were clearly her bones. "I want to know more about this."

Emma could feel some alarm building. If it were arthritis, wouldn't that be easy to identify?

"What is it?" said Emma.

"It appears to be soft tissue . . ." said Dr. Harmon.

"Something that shouldn't be there?"

"Well, no, it shouldn't be there. It's a nonspecific, round-to-oval juxta-articular soft-tissue mass, is how we describe it."

"Lord."

"And what I recommend is that we find out more about it."

"How do we do that?"

"I want you to see an oncologist."

"Cancer?!"

"Don't be alarmed. Cancer of the elbow is extremely rare. But I'd like to rule it out before we go further. If it does happen to be cancer, which as I say is rare, then you wouldn't want to waste any time about it."

The alarm was suddenly full-on. Emma's heart was racing. She felt a tightness in her chest. Something about her hearing felt off.

"So it's not arthritis? You can tell that?"

"It's not osteoarthritis or rheumatoid arthritis or fibromyalgia, as they would normally present themselves, no. And we have other tests that we can pursue, but first let's rule out—"

"Rule out what? Cancer of the elbow?"

"Synovial sarcoma would be something I would be concerned about. Same with something called myxofibrosarcoma. Sorry about these names. My best advice would be for you to let me make a referral, let Dr. Lee examine you—she's at Sloan Kettering, very experienced—and then we'll see where we stand."

Emma was feeling stunned.

"It's a lot to think about," she said.

"I know it is," said Dr. Harmon. "Most of the time these referrals turn up nothing, and then we go back to treating something that's very treatable."

From the sidewalk, outside Dr. Harmon's office, Emma reached Kelly, who had just come out of a meeting at Christie's and was eager to hear Emma's account of the oncologist visit.

Kelly could hear the fear in her friend's voice.

"He's just doing the prudent thing, Ems," she said.

"I know," said Emma.

"Rule it out, and keep going. I can't believe Robert let you go there alone. I will go with you next time, if you want."

"Okay—thanks."

"You should have company for a thing like that—if only just to help you process what the doctor says."

"You're right."

"Something's wrong with that guy, if I may say so," said Kelly.

"Robert? Maybe."

"He called you 'cuckoo' at my party, remember?"

"He was trying to be funny."

"Not cool."

"I know."

"You were talking about your work! I'll never forget it. A joke in the worst possible taste, at best."

They took a moment to update each other on the film.

"So I've been asking around about important pieces," said Kelly. "We will definitely be able to come up with more candidates, but so far this week is a bust. Two of Hutton's pieces—a ruby necklace and pair of Deco earrings, both Cartier—wound up with one of our clients, a woman from Mexico City; and one of the Taylor pieces, a diamond tiara, is owned by a woman we know in London. But neither one is going to be accessible."

"Okay."

It was hard for Emma to concentrate on work, though she knew that work was probably the best thing for her at the moment, and she knew that Kelly probably thought so, too.

"The other ones we already have—I feel good about them," said Kelly.

"My friend Oliver Shaw, the writer I was telling you about . . ." said Emma.

"Oh, sure."

"He's promised to introduce me next week to a woman who apparently has some of the Duchess of Windsor's things. Artemis Qasim?"

"Oh, Ems, that would be great."

"You know her? Of her?"

"Of her. She's been a client. She's fabulously rich, has a huge jewelry collection. Art, too, for that matter. She and her husband are great collectors."

"And patrons of the ballet, too, I gather. He's taking me to the ABT gala."

"Maybe she'll wear something."

"Maybe."

"Bring your phone."

"Ha! You think I should interview her right there at the Met, during intermission?"

"Just kidding."

"Her million-dollar earrings photobombing a selfie?"

"She's British. He's Syrian. The money is from construction. His business was in London until he got kicked out for something. Arms dealing, maybe? They live in Monaco now, I think. Big patrons of the arts and education. Medicine, too, I think."

"How convenient. Maybe she can recommend a good cancer treatment center."

CHAPTER 7

November 1928

On the night of Doris and Barbara's secret theater outing, Henrik was already waiting with the car in front of the Duke residence at Fifth Avenue and 78th Street when the Hutton chauffeur drove up and parked in back of him, to deliver Barbara and her governess, Tiki, to the door. Though the Hutton mansion was only two blocks away, at Fifth and 80th, driving to Doris's house was considered the only suitable way for a girl like Barbara to get to her friend's house.

The mansion that Buck Duke built for his family was designed in the Louis XV style by prominent Gilded Age architect Horace Trumbauer, who based his design, like that of so many other New York mansions of the era, on a French château. Constructed of limestone so fine that it looked like marble, the mansion boasted an imposing double-story entrance portico flanked by columns and topped with a pediment featuring carved reclining figures that Doris, as a child, dubbed Sadie and Lady.

Doris was already there at the door with her governess, Jenny.

"Off to our party!" exclaimed Doris, embracing Barbara.

"Off we go!" said Barbara.

Both girls were dressed in plain wool coats over plain wool dresses. Their cloche-style hats were similar—of the moment, but distinctly unostentatious.

"Do you need to come in?" said Doris. Behind her was the mansion's stately black-and-white-paved entry hall, with massive, unlit fireplaces on either side and a monumental stairway rising at the back. Positioned a yard or two in front of each fireplace was a Louis XV pier table topped with a pair of majestic, three-foot-tall Chinese vases; and set off to the left, atop a pedestal, was a full-size white marble statue of Mercury, the Roman god who ruled over commerce and good fortune.

"No, thank you," said Barbara.

"Are you sure?" said Jenny.

"Yes, thank you."

"They don't look dressed properly for a party, do they?" said Jenny, to Tiki.

"This is what she insisted on," said Tiki.

"I told you," said Doris. "It's not that kind of party."

"No, it's for her Latin teacher," said Barbara, in a manner that neither governess suspected was well-rehearsed.

"It's to honor Mr. Applegate—I told you," said Doris. "And he lives just a few blocks away, so we'll be very safe. And the school is providing a guard at the door."

"All right then, off you go," said Jenny, as the girls headed down the front steps and clambered into the Dukes' car. *"Amuse-toi bien, ma puce!"*

"Have a good time!" said Tiki, with a little kiss for Barbara at the door of the car.

With the girls in the back seat and the door secured, Henrik took his position behind the wheel, and they were off.

"It's the Royale Theatre," said Doris into the intercom.

"Yes, miss, I have it," said Henrik. "Forty-fifth Street."

"I'm so excited," said Barbara, with a little shiver.

"I am, too," said Doris. "Henrik, did you remember the refreshments?"

"Right there, miss—in front of you, under the blanket."

From a picnic hamper that Henrik had covered with a plaid blanket, Doris served Barbara and herself a glass of champagne.

"There," she said. "A night at the theater!"

"A night at the theater," said Barbara, clinking her glass with Doris's.

*   *   *

The streets around Times Square were bright with theater marquees and illuminated billboards for products like Maxwell House coffee, Squibb's dental cream, and Camel cigarettes, and for Cecil B. DeMille's epic silent film, *King of Kings*, which had been running for months. New Yorkers dressed for an evening were scurrying about here and there, excitedly on their way to a show or to dinner. Doris and Barbara got out of the car around the corner from the Royale Theatre and made their way to the lobby and then to their seats without being recognized by either ushers or other theatergoers. The house was packed and buzzing with anticipation. Dressed and made up plainly, as they were, Doris and Barbara might have been any other pair of young New York ladies at Broadway's naughtiest hit show. Their seats were in the front row of the mezzanine, on the aisle; and just before the curtain went up, Doris turned to see that Henrik had taken his place, too, in an aisle seat two rows directly in back of them. He had parked the car and changed from his double-breasted uniform jacket into a regular men's suit jacket.

After a sentimental overture stuffed with snatches of old-time tunes like "The Old Gray Mare," "A Bicycle Built for Two," and "Ach, Du Lieber Augustin," the curtain went up on a bustling saloon on the Bowery in the Gay '90s—lots of jawing among men in handlebar mustaches, about local politics and shady business and desperate times; lots of plaudits about the singer and femme fatale Lil, who's described as "a pretty slick article" and "no easy gal to handle"; and then the lady herself appears, warmly hailed by the saloon patrons and rapturously cheered by the theater audience. There's friction between Lil's boyfriend, Jordan, owner of the saloon, who wants to run as city sheriff, and Jordan's rival, Dan, who plans to become sheriff himself by exposing the counterfeit racket that Jordan is running. Meanwhile, Lil also has her eye on Captain Cummings, the righteous and handsome preacher from the mission next door.

"I've heard so much about you," says one of Lil's suitors, a handsome foreigner. "Yeah, but you can't prove it," replies Lil—to more roaring applause.

West was onstage for most of the play's three acts, and Doris and Barbara could not have been more thrilled to stare at her the whole time and listen intently. The character Lil and the playwright herself were both so smart and tough, and blessed with the proverbial heart of gold; and both were absolutely correct in their implicit ridicule of society's stuffier attitudes, especially toward women and sex.

"We're going backstage," said Doris resolutely, at the end of the play, as the house lights went up. She knew all about such theater practices from her nights with adults at concerts and the opera.

"How?" said Barbara.

"Follow me," said Doris.

Henrik, whom Doris had already informed of her intentions, knew just where to lead them, downstairs to the orchestra level and against the exiting crowd, to an unmarked door at the side of the stage.

"I have invited guests of Miss West," he said in his best Nordic-British accent, to the cigar-huffing gentleman in shirt and vest at the door. The gentleman summoned a stagehand to guide them.

"We are Miss West's nieces," said Doris, as demurely as possible. "From Brooklyn."

"We're from Flatbush," said Barbara, sounding very little like a Brooklyn native.

A party of ten or so was leaving West's dressing room, with boisterous farewells, when the stagehand knocked on the room's open door.

"Excuse me, Miss West?" he said. "I believe you're expecting your nieces?"

West, still splendidly dressed in her third act costume and wig, turned, and her eyes brightened as she took a moment to look over the visiting trio.

"My nieces, huh?" she said, without missing a beat. "Well, ladies, you'd better come in and make yourselves comfortable, and tell me what you thought of the show."

The room was entirely mauve, with mauve wallpaper in a floral pattern, an oriental rug in soft shades of rose and powder blue, and elaborate mauve drapery dressing, or perhaps over-dressing, two small windows. Doris and Barbara took seats on the silk-upholstered settee toward which West gestured, and Henrik settled in one of the two matching armchairs. West, who had asked the stagehand to close the door when he left, seated herself at the commodious dressing table, which was crowded with floral arrangements, telegrams, unwrapped gifts, and tins, bottles, tubes, and jars of beauty products. Turned to face her guests, the brilliantly lit back of the star's gown and of her elaborate hairdo were reflected theatrically in the dressing table's large round mirror, which was edged in blazing lights. Hanging in the air was a very feminine scent with notes of rose, jasmine, and sandalwood.

"I'm Dodo, Miss West, and this is Babbo," said Doris. "We absolutely loved the play, and you were divine in it."

"Why, thank you," said West.

"You're so clever," said Barbara. "The way you can make the whole theater laugh and cry and cheer. . . !"

"Not all at the same time, I hope," said West, with an easy laugh. "Well, wait a minute—maybe I *do* hope that!" The star was only thirty-five, and up close, despite the stage makeup, she looked voluptuously younger than that. Her manner was both grand and down-to-earth.

"We learn about Shakespeare in school, Miss West," said Doris, "and they tell us that when those plays were first produced, the audience wasn't dead silent. They cheered whenever they wanted and cried at the murders and talked back to the actors, too. Now I can really imagine what that was like."

"That's a beautiful compliment, Dodo—thank you very much. Tell me, girls, where do you go to school?"

"Brearly," said Doris.

"Miss Porter's," said Barbara.

"I see," said West. "A couple of society girls."

Then the star noticed Henrik's silence.

"Doesn't he say anything?" she asked.

"A very enjoyable play, miss—very enjoyable indeed," said Henrik.

"Why, thank you, too . . . uh . . ." said West, clearly wishing to use his name.

"Henrik, ma'am."

"Henrik, forgive me," said West, "but I can't help thinking that your top and bottom don't quite match."

The girls giggled, and the chauffeur reflexively gave the collar of his suit jacket a little neatening tug. He was still dressed in the bottom half of his uniform.

"I don't often have breeches and boots in my dressing room," continued West, "unless they're on a character from a play down the street."

She said this in a lightly amusing way, but Henrik flushed.

"Well, I, uh . . ." he said.

"That's all he had to put on," said Doris, decisively.

"It was, was it?" said West, who also took note of Doris's commanding attitude.

"Say," said West, looking more closely at Doris and Barbara, "you two look awfully familiar. If you're not my nieces, and I happen to know you're not, then who are you?"

"I'm Doris Duke, Miss West, and this is my friend Barbara Hutton. Please forgive our little deception. We're here incognito."

"I see."

"Even our families don't know we're here," said Doris.

"They would never have let us come," said Barbara.

"I'll bet they wouldn't," said West, with a chuckle. "And of course he's the bodyguard?"

"He's my driver," said Doris. "And our friend."

"Well, well—the Gold Dust Twins in the flesh," said West. "Isn't that what the papers call you girls?"

"We think it's stupid," said Barbara.

"Mm-hmm. The newspapers can definitely be stupid," said West. "But you can use 'em to your advantage."

"That's exactly what we want to do, Miss West," said Doris.

"Well, just think of the dumbest things that men will believe, and make something up along those lines. And then double it. That's all playwrightin' is, really."

Both girls nodded enthusiastically.

"Now I'm doubly honored!" said West. "To think that three of this country's most famous women are right here in the same room."

Everyone laughed, then clucked over West's announcement that *Diamond Lil* was going to be made into a Hollywood film. Then it was time to go.

"It's such a pleasure and an honor to meet you," said Doris, rising and indicating to Barbara that she should rise, too.

"The pleasure was all mine—really," said West. "I'd offer you my own car and driver, who's waiting right outside in the alley, but you gals seem to have everything under control."

Henrik bowed punctiliously.

"By the way, Miss West," said Barbara, "I approve of your choice of perfume."

"You do?"

"That's Joy, isn't it?" Barbara pronounced the name in French.

"Why, yes it is. What a nose, what a nose," said West, chuckling again. "Now how did you happen to know that? This perfume is supposed to be brand new."

"My aunt bought me some when we were in Paris, just a few months ago," said Barbara. "Monsieur Patou said that we were among the first people in the world to have it."

"Oh, yeah, sure—*him*," said West. "Johnny gave me the same line. He's a smooth one, that Frenchman."

CHAPTER 8

After his lunch with Emma, Ollie wondered if he should have told her more about the assault, or if he should have mentioned it at all. Was his subconscious telling him that it was finally time to talk about it with someone? And what would be the point of that? In many ways when Doris, after apologizing, suggested they never speak of it again, she was right, and she certainly made up for her indiscretion afterwards by giving Ollie gift after gift. As for feelings about what had happened, and questions about why it happened and what it all meant—there was a time when people could just put something like that away. Now, it seems, it was a national pastime to memorialize grievances and injuries in an ongoing theater of woundedness. Otherwise, he knew, he wouldn't even have used a word like "assault," which had become so popular with Emma's generation. Was this a sign that he wanted her to hear about it?

And why her, and not someone of his own generation? Did this have something to do with Martin? There were no assaults in *that* story, certainly. The story was simple: Ollie was the older, well-known writer, with global connections in what used to be called "a certain world"; Martin was the young *wunderkind* editor, looking for the entrée and erudition that would produce unique, entertaining features for his magazine. Ollie's first piece for *Nota Bene* had been on the portrait Beaton shot of Barbara Hutton at Sidi Hosni, with her emerald tiara and Pasha diamond ring—a quiet interlude, he wrote, in a raucous weekend house party in which rich Americans and penniless European aristocrats mixed with "Gypsies, tramps, and thieves." Though he hadn't attended the party himself. He and Martin started meeting each other for lunch, then accompanying each other to social events, casually, for about a year. Then the relationship faded into a purely business thing revolving around the column.

Early on, between them, there had been some inexplicit affectional bargaining, maybe; some private, individual cost-benefit analysis, maybe; some fumbling around in a train compartment, a limousine, a hotel room, but nothing involving real momentum, let alone thrust. For different reasons, neither of them could plug any juice into it. They weren't the same kind of man. They certainly didn't have the same kind of homosexual impulses, though to an outsider, even an outsider of their sophisticated, intellectual class, the descriptor "homosexual" alone could be enough to link them, to make them equivalent. No, Martin probably was bisexual—though they didn't use clinical terms like that between them—and his passions for men, when they occurred, were honestly felt; but he also was clearly in love with Janet, and the physical affection that Ollie saw between them at those wonderful dinner parties made Ollie happy for them and maybe even a little jealous—to have that kind of a connection with another human being, and to think that a new human life could result from that. Ollie, on the other hand, would have been "gay" if he had had that kind of physical need at all. But he just didn't, and he noticed this quality in himself long before, as a kid in elementary school, clueless about all the palaver he witnessed from other boys and from the girls who were his friends, about their crushes and their fantasies. *What is this?* he wondered. *Why don't I feel the same thing? Will I one day feel it?* He never did feel it, much—maybe a little with Dodo, before the incident—but he did learn quickly enough, especially after he got to Princeton, whose company he felt most comfortable in, and that was often discerning gay men and the discerning women who were friends with gay men; and in *that* company, it was much easier wordlessly to indicate how hesitant he might be with romance, how inclined he might be to curb amorous passions, how carefully he might intend to formulate the balance between the emotional and the physical.

Didn't passion too often end in assault, anyway? Wasn't it a pathway to infamy, as it was for Doris in the '60s, in the case of poor Eddie Tirella? "Doris Duke Kills Friend in Crash." "Death Called Accident for Heiress' Friend." Would Ollie wind up telling Emma what he knew about all that—how he suspected that his own position with Doris, several months before the crash, was similar to Eddie's position in the days leading up to it? Or would Emma, in the way of her generation, though they blabbed and blabbed about victimhood, enforce the strict lines *they* happened to draw around the things *they* didn't think merited talking about, like the younger days of old people?

Ollie was amused to think that not only was he no longer part of a certain world, he would soon be part of *another* world—the next one. As a cultivated gentleman with old friends, he still hobnobbed socially with aristocrats and billionaires, but as a writer-slash-public intellectual he had slipped from the A-list to the B-list, and then he'd fallen off lists entirely, especially with new publicity directors who didn't understand particularly well the history of their publications or the importance of continuity in the media. Maybe discontinuity was the point, but this was a point Ollie couldn't fathom. Wouldn't it be welcome, even valuable, for a publication to maintain continuity with people who had experienced, for example, being alone in the King's Chamber of the Great Pyramid of Giza, attending a private performance in the opulent Imperial Theater at the Hermitage, sitting in at a recording session of Glenn Gould, discussing electoral politics with James Baldwin over lunch, let alone attending the mock-wedding of Paul Reubens, aka Pee-wee Herman, to Doris Duke's adopted daughter Chandi at Shangri La, in the company of Imelda Marcos? Yet Ollie was philosophical. Less time to provide this continuity to baby publicists meant more time for him to read Proust, and to devote himself to the opportunity of doing small good works that, oddly enough, had resulted from the assault.

* * *

"Ollie, it's Liz."

"Liz, darling."

"I feel terrible about this ABT thing. . . ."

"No, no, don't worry about it. We'll go later in the season. I'm actually now going to be able to take my friend Emma, whom you met the other day. It might be good for the project she's working on."

Ollie was speaking on the phone with his friend and neighbor, Elizabeth Prescott Welland.

"We didn't exactly meet," said Mrs. Welland, "but she seemed charming."

"You were an angel to help out, as always."

"We are angels for each other. Isn't that the point? Now listen, since I won't see you at ABT, I'm wondering if I can invite you to my party at the Brooklyn Academy this Friday. I have a table for ten, and I know you'll have a good time. It's forty-five minutes of Mark Morris, then dinner."

"Oh, Liz, I wish I could—that sounds heavenly—but I'm off to Zürich on Thursday night."

"So soon again?"

"It's been six months."

"More castles and churches?"

"As always."

"I know you can't tell me more."

"It's better if you don't know. I am but a simple tourist."

"Twice a year for thirty years."

"Now, Liz . . ."

"That never sounded like tourism to me. And people know it's not for a facelift. You can't have had sixty of those."

"But we do know some people who have, don't we?"

"Ha!"

"Would you believe the waters, Liz? Taking the waters can be very beneficial."

"Well, I believe you are the kind of person who might go and take the water cure at some exclusive thermal spa. Except that nobody does that anymore."

"No?"

"Nobody rich and fabulous. That kind of thing was old-fashioned even for Truman Capote's swans."

"I don't know about that. Healing waters are healing waters. There might be some secret *grand hôtel du lac* up in a high Alpine valley, where Proust is still writing and Adelina Patti is still recovering from her Red Cross concert of 1914."

"On second thought," said Mrs. Welland, "you might fit in very well with that crowd—two-hundred-year-old celebrities."

"I might very well just."

CHAPTER 9

December 1930

"Society Debs Battle Over Crown," screamed the headline from the bottom-right of the newspaper's front page, the day after Barbara's debutante ball.

The headline didn't appear in a society column, because Maury Paul and Walter Winchell were both with the other invited guests, several rooms away from the private passageway where the incident took place. And anyway, as guests, the columnists would have to hold themselves to the norms governing their inclusion in such events, limiting them to writing only, if at all, about who was there, what they were wearing, what they ate, and what the orchestra played. No, the headline appeared in a news item, written by a reporter who was not invited, and would never have been invited, to such a party or normally allowed anywhere near it.

"The incident took place in a 'secret' passageway between the hotel's ballroom lobby and a private elevator to the guest rooms, where Hutton had taken a suite for her gala debut evening," ran the story. "Dressed ethereally in a long white gown, wearing that essential deb adornment, a single-strand pearl necklace, Hutton was alone when she came face-to-face with rival deb Doris Duke, a guest, also in white, and wearing a diamond tiara—a crown-like headpiece—of elaborate floral design. Alone with them in the passageway, concealed by a group of potted palms, this reporter chanced upon the encounter and heard Duke explain to Hutton that she was searching for the rest rooms. For those of you who know more about soup kitchens and breadlines than debutante balls, it is typical for a deb, wishing to strike the properly virginal tone, to wear nothing in her hair, or maybe some fresh flowers. Tiaras, especially spectacularly jeweled ones like Duke's, are just not worn by debs, and yet Duke—several inches taller than Hutton—looked like the queen of the evening. Sharp words were exchanged between the ladies, and Hutton insisted, in a voice more suitable to a racetrack than a ballroom, that it was *her* night and that Duke should remove the offending adornment. Duke reluctantly complied and gave the thing to her chauffeur, whom this reporter noticed was standing by to ensure Duke's safe arrival in the ballroom."

On the night of Barbara's debutante ball, December 22, 1930, the streets surrounding New York's Ritz-Carlton Hotel were barricaded and posted with police, to contain the crush of press and other onlookers, and to allow the steady flow of limousines to drop their formally dressed passengers off at the curb. The hotel's entrance, marquee, and surrounding stretches of street and sidewalk were ablaze in the light of scores of floodlamps and thousands of flashbulbs. The ball, for a thousand guests, was the culmination of a week of coming-out festivities—receptions, luncheons, and such. Earlier that same day, there had been a tea for five hundred at the Fifth Avenue triplex of Barbara's Uncle Edward and Aunt Marjorie, then dinner and dancing for five hundred at the fashionable Central Park Casino.

Inside the Ritz-Carlton, the festivities occupied an entire floor: reception room, two ballrooms, a restaurant, several lounges—all decorated in a winter holiday fantasy theme, with bowers of silvery white birch trees arching up out of beds of red poinsettias and dressed with tropical greenery shipped in from as far away as California. Columns and balustrades were wrapped in smilax, and mounds and drifts of sparkly artificial snow were everywhere, including a festive North Pole tableau set up at the door of the main ballroom.

Doris had planned her little scheme for the evening carefully and gone over it twice with Barbara. On an "official" errand,

Henrik had visited the hotel the day before the ball, as preparations were taking place, carefully noting the ballroom floor's architectural layout. He conferred casually with several members of the hotel's and florist's staff, about how the evening was planned to run. Then, later, in Doris's car, supposedly on a drive around the city to see holiday decorations, he showed Doris and Barbara the floor plan he drew up, with all the relevant entrances and exits clearly marked; he explained what he had learned about which passageways would be used for guests and which would be private, and which might be best for the needs of Doris's scheme on the night of the ball.

Instantly Doris was able to come up with a plan: how and where she and Barbara would encounter each other, what they would say, who the onlooker from the press would be, what time it would happen.

"Will it work?" said Barbara.

"Of course it will work," said Doris. "We'll make it work."

"Good! Some of these parties are *intolerable*," drawled Barbara. "At least the guest of honor should have a little fun. What do I have to look forward to except seeing a lot of very dull, old Palm Beach men that Father wants me to know?"

On one hand, coming out for Barbara was a pleasant ritual that rich girls were swept into—a round of lovely parties, a chance to show off some pretty new clothes. On the other hand, it was a Stone Age rite grounded in the sanctity of virginity and family property. In 1930, people were trying to be modern about it, but the old rules were clear: daughters are chattel.

"We were down at Mar-a-Lago for a party that Aunt Marjorie gave," she continued, "and suddenly all of Father's cronies noticed that I wasn't a little girl anymore. It gave me the heebie-jeebies. One old toad said I was now the ideal *Vogue* woman."

"He probably just meant to be nice," said Doris.

Barbara shivered.

"Heebie-jeebies! Thank God Jeem was there to brighten things up. He was positively drooling over one of the dancers. Aunt Marjorie hired some dancers to perform."

"Oh? Which dancers?"

"Dennis Something."

"Denishawn? How marvelous!"

"Yes, that's it. Jeem had to rip off his shirt to show everybody that he was as trim as a dancer."

"Art can do that to people."

"Anyway, that's why I am looking forward to our little scandal at the Penitentiary Ritz-Carlton. Now *your* party, Dodo, that was fun—so free and open, those great lawns, the ocean breezes . . ."

Doris's coming-out party, which had taken place the previous August, was mounted in the gardens of Rough Point. Where a guest list of a thousand or more would have been usual, Nanaline scaled back to six hundred, "out of good taste," she said— the former Southern belle being eager to stay on good terms with Newport society, but also happy to save money on a party for the daughter who was often so "difficult." The guests were the usual people, the luncheons and dinner-dances were the usual parties, but Doris's ball, under great tents with two orchestras, with the usual potted palms and baskets of gladioli, veered from the usual by including a small combo of Black jazz musicians that Doris had found on one of her and her beau Jimmy Cromwell's visits to the Cotton Club, up in Harlem.

On the night of Barbara's ball, around ten-thirty, as guests began to enter the madly thronged ballroom entrance of the Ritz-Carlton on 46th Street, a man in a brown overcoat and fedora waited patiently around the corner on Madison Avenue, near an unmarked service door of the same building. Then Henrik opened the door from the inside and admitted the man, whom Doris agreed was exactly the person for this mission: a newspaper reporter who frequented the same Third Avenue gin joint that Henrik did—a young man always full of bluster about the scoops he racked up and exclusive leads he sniffed out. Through a hallway, a janitor's room, and then another hallway, Henrik led the man to the appointed spot, a private elevator lobby, while the innocently sultry sounds of Rudy Vallée crooning "My Sweetest Souvenirs" in the main ballroom, with the Meyer Davis Orchestra, echoed in the background.

We danced away the night,
We kissed or thought we might,
They're now my sweetest souvenirs.

Henrik positioned the man behind a group of potted palms.
"Wait here," he said.

"Here?" said the reporter, incredulous.

"Do you want a scoop about Barbara Hutton or not?"

"Sure, but . . ."

"Then stay right here. She will come off that elevator there
and walk this way. I will greet her and ask if she has a moment
to speak with you."

"Okay."

"But as I told you, I can't promise anything."

"Okay, thanks."

"If we're lucky, you might have a word with her. Otherwise,
you can still write something about just being here and spotting
her. 'Behind the scenes at the party of the year'—something like
that." It was Doris who had suggested the headline.

The moonlight on your face,
The joy of our embrace,
They're now my sweetest souvenirs.

"Okay," said the reporter. "But now that I think of it, how
will I be able to prove to my editor I was really here and didn't
make it all up?"

"I've got that covered," said Henrik, taking a small item
out of his pocket and handing it to the reporter. It was a box
of matches, covered in gold foil and stamped with Barbara's
name and the date. "No one will have this who didn't attend
the party."

"Golly," said the reporter.

"Good luck."

Henrik went over to the elevator door and waited for a few
minutes. Then the elevator car arrived with a *ding* and Barbara

emerged, alone, holding herself in a conspicuously aristocratic manner. Henrik greeted her respectfully, but before anything else could happen, Doris appeared from another direction and the supposedly accidental encounter between the two women was played out exactly as planned. Except for the chauffeur and the reporter hidden by the palms, the debutantes were alone—the tall, athletic one in a glorious crown, with a face that had recently been described in the press as "sphynx-like," and the other, prettier in a doll-like way, with brown eyes that were as expressive as those of a star in a silent movie.

Within a few seconds, after the scripted sharp words, Doris stormed off in the direction she'd been going, having handed off the tiara huffily to Henrik, who tucked the thing into a leather satchel he was carrying, while Barbara uttered a curt "Excuse me!" to the chauffeur and hustled past him on her way to the ballroom.

"I heard it all, I heard it all," said the reporter, popping out from behind the palms, after Barbara was gone. "Jeepers."

"Good," said Henrik. "I'm sure your story about *that* will be better than any silly little quote that Miss Hutton may have given you."

The reporter, though clearly thrilled with his good luck, was also fixated on the treasure concealed in Henrik's satchel.

"Can I see it?" said the reporter.

From out of the satchel, Henrik carefully took the tiara—some of whose rose-shaped diamond clusters were set *en tremblant*, which meant that they seemed to flutter when worn or handled.

"Beautiful, isn't it?" said the reporter, obviously awed.

"That it is," said Henrik.

And with that, the reporter thanked Henrik and went off to exit the hotel the way he'd come in.

Our dance was long ago;
The heart has ceased its flow,
But I am still aglow
With all my sweetest memories.

Moments later, Doris reappeared.

"It went off like a charm, miss," said Henrik.

"Good," said Doris. "I knew it would. Now if you'd kindly walk me to the reception room, where Jimmy is waiting for me."

"Of course, miss."

"And keep that thing safe," said Doris, indicating the satchel. "I'll give it to Barbara tomorrow, and she'll get it back to her aunt. Dear Aunt Marjorie! Apparently, she was so excited when Babbo told her she was thinking of breaking holy tradition by wearing it herself."

The girls were delighted the next day when they saw the newspaper story that resulted, which proved that they could indeed manipulate the media and frame their friendship/rivalry exactly as they wanted.

"It was more fun than I imagined it would be," said Barbara.

"Told you."

"You're a real danger to yourself and others."

"I'm sure you mean that in the nicest way."

Over the next few months, Doris and Barbara pulled off many similar capers with Henrik's help, including attendance at a Carnegie Hall performance of the progressive German choreographer Mary Wigman, whose lyricism seduced them; a Salmagundi Club poetry reading by Elinor Wylie, whose sensuous sonnet series, "One Man," inspired by the poet's affair with a married man, enflamed them; and a midnight visit to a jazz-filled speakeasy on Harlem's "Swing Street," which happened to be the place where, two years later, a seventeen-year-old Billie Holiday would be discovered. All those adventurous outings would certainly have been frowned upon by the girls' families, which made the outings even more exciting.

But these flings soon became more difficult to arrange. Doris arrived home from shopping one afternoon to discover that Henrik had been fired. Weston, the majordomo, had found a pint of bourbon in the chauffeur's room. When Doris tried to countermand the order, she was informed that Henrik was already on his way to the docks, to catch a ship back to England.

PART 2

MARRIAGES

CHAPTER 10

March 1931

But even within a year of their debuts, Doris and Barbara knew their paths were beginning to diverge. Though they knew many of the same people and were accepting several of the same social commitments, they were also consolidating different social circles, based on their different interests and inclinations. Barbara liked nothing better than to party with party people; Doris was growing more serious about the arts, especially the performing arts, where her passion was both in the watching of musical and dance performances and doing the performing herself. Every now and then, because of this growing divergence, there were strong differences of opinion and an occasional barbed comment between the two women over a certain person or thing—a comment that when they were girls would have been framed more gently.

"He's a poseur, that one."

"*Au contraire*. He's a very important man who holds himself accordingly."

"You're crazy to like him."

"You're crazy not to."

"You're misguided."

"No, *you're* deluded."

And what with differing social schedules, there were fewer times for Doris and Barbara to do simple things together, like ride horses through the countryside, since less and less were they actually in the same city—which meant that capers required more and more planning.

"It's so complicated to arrange these things—you'd think we were embarking on some kind of world voyage," said Barbara one day on a call from Biarritz, to Doris, who was in New York. Transatlantic telephone service was still thrillingly new, though ridiculously expensive. They were planning to stage a mutual public snub three months hence in New York, at a big movie premiere for which both of them would show up in the same dress. They would "happen" to be photographed together for a newspaper, looking terribly upset. Doris had lined up a dressmaker who would create the same slinky Vionnet counterfeit for them in floor-length, gold silk crepe georgette.

"It'll be fun," said Doris. "Can you be in New York around the fifteenth for a fitting?"

"Oh, Dodo, I don't know . . ."

"I even know a drama coach who can help us stage it."

"I'm really not planning that far ahead, these days."

"Of course you are, Babs. What about the Everglades Ball, the Belmont Stakes, Bitsy's wedding, for goodness' sake . . ."

"But something like this? Is it really worth all the fuss? All these details that Henrik used to take care of . . ."

"Henrik would not have been able to organize the dresses."

"It's just that . . ." Barbara trailed off.

"Look," said Doris resolutely. "You said it yourself: these little escapades are the antidote to dull. I don't know about you, but for me, that's why they're more than just games. They're a kind of, oh, performance that only we can mount. Isn't it kind of wonderful that, with all the dull motions we're compelled to go through, these are roles that *we* make up and only *we* can play?"

"I don't know."

"The world is our theater, Babs. We have to take the stage! I know you think I'm a drip for my dancing, and you know what I think of your excessive partying. The point is, we're two of a kind, and we need each other, even if we don't necessarily like each other every second of every day."

Barbara thought for a moment, in a pause peppered with the sound of crackly transatlantic static.

"I suppose you're right," she finally said.

"Good," said Doris. "Now, I can send the dressmaker to you in France this week, if that would make it easier for you."

"Okay. Thanks. Let's do that."

"Just remember: the men can't know. They'd give it away for sure."

Plans were that Barbara would be escorted to the premiere by newly divorced millionaire playboy Phil Plant, while Doris would attend with Dr. Lenox Baker, from Duke University's medical school.

"No, that's at least one thing we can still agree on," said Barbara. "Keeping secrets from men."

The American Ballet Theatre gala took place on a warm, fall evening, and the façades of all the Lincoln Center theaters were lit up dramatically. Emma and Ollie were standing with Ollie's friend Artemis Qasim on the outdoor portico terrace of the Koch Theater's grand promenade, at the cocktail reception before the performance.

"Gone," said Artemis sadly. "I'm afraid we lost some very nice things, and so did a lot of other people."

They were speaking about a 2004 fire in an art warehouse in London in which Artemis and her husband lost several important pieces, including a Modigliani reclining nude that Ollie had once written about.

"By 'other people,'" said Ollie, "Artsy means multibillionaires who don't want themselves or their art collections to be especially visible."

Emma nodded knowingly. Below them, in Lincoln Center plaza, the fountain was cycling through one of its less flamboyant sequences, while inside, under the promenade's vast gold-leafed ceiling, hung for the evening with inflatable silver clouds and specially lit in shades of blue and purple, the tables set up for the post-performance dinner were being given final touches.

"And it's ironic," continued Artemis, "because we'd just

agreed to lend two pieces to a show being organized for next year called 'Unstored,' which will feature masterworks that are usually in storage."

"Fantastic idea for a show," said Ollie.

"I've always thought it sad to store artworks," said Artemis. "Tragic, in fact. Saalih says it's a reality we have to accept as collectors, but I don't know about that. These things draw life from being seen, don't they?"

In 1971, Artemis Payne, as she was then called, was a tall, lively arts-and-humanities girl at Cambridge, with fetching green eyes and cascades of flaxen hair, who met a dashing Syrian businessman named Saalih Qasim one night at a fireside lounge in Gstaad. They found they had hiking, cross-country skiing, and British sporting art in common, so the next day, they sneaked away from their respective ski parties and went for a quiet, snowy hike together around the Lauenensee. They chatted merrily about Landseer's dogs and Stubbs's horses, and six months later, they were married. Qasim soon made his fortune in the Saudi construction industry, and by the 1980s, the couple were well-known as discerning art collectors and generous philanthropists, based in London and in an historic manor house in Oxfordshire. But they seemed determinedly reclusive, maintaining a low social profile. Headlines resulting from an arms deal that Qasim helped negotiate during the Thatcher years, and more recently from charges of international money laundering, induced the couple ultimately to take up residence in Monaco, though Artemis was still active on four continents as a patron of the arts.

She was in her early seventies, Emma guessed, expensively dressed and flawlessly groomed, as the women of her class must be at an event like this. Her hair was up and big, expensively colored, and distinctly lustrous; her face and body were obviously well-cared-for, in that way that's meant to restore the look of youth but also, in itself, connotes a certain age. Yet still, Emma thought, the bright young Brit who was a star among the international set in the go-go '70s was visible now and then in quick flashes of smile and smart cracks of wit. Emma even thought, as they chatted, that she might be able to see in Artemis some ongoing tension—deftly managed, as simply one more requirement of an exalted social position—between the billionaire lifestyle and ordinary human existence.

Artemis was attending the gala unescorted, but had invited several guests to join her for the post-performance dinner, including Ollie and Emma. As the three of them stood there on the terrace, champagne flutes in hand, Emma could see that Ollie was paying Artemis the deference due an evening's host, as well as due an old friend and ranking doyenne, though he was balancing this gallantry with his responsibility, assured of the lady's automatic understanding of it, to Emma as his date.

Emma knew that all of this conduct—and her previous experience at galas, balls, and such—would in some way be coloring the film she was making. It was all context. Artemis was in a long, blue gown; and in fact, almost all the women that evening were in gowns, and standing and moving in that way that Emma had always thought of as "that gown way," which in Artemis's case seemed powered by some extra energy beyond that of fashion or modeling or good deportment. As an Upper West Sider whose family lived in a fancy apartment and sent her to private school, Emma had nonetheless always identified more with her middle-class friends than her super-rich ones. There were obviously both kinds at St. Ann's and at Yale, and in her wide social experience, there was always that polite adherence to an agreement to "be cool" about people's relative wealth. And the wealthier, the cooler. Yet at an event like this, among a more homogeneous mix of more super-rich people than at most events, there was a special atmosphere of general ease about "being among ourselves," though no one talked about this or was probably even conscious of it. It was an ease that emerges when doubt is neutralized about a possible encounter with someone who might revile your expensive dress or your expensive jewels or your expensive face. This condition of ease was certainly not evil, yet Emma had seen it characterized that way in so many political discussions. Whatever the case, she had chosen never to aspire to that kind of ease, fearing it to be numbing, anesthetizing. Instead of a gown, she had selected a black suit to wear to the gala—elegant, appropriate, and with the added benefit that it covered up the bandage on her elbow from the biopsy that Dr. Lee, the oncologist, had ordered for the day before.

Then there was the brooch Artemis was wearing on the shoulder of her gown, in the form of a four-inch-high flamingo balancing on a single slender leg, the other leg tucked up elegantly, its body and neck feathered in white diamonds, its magnificent tail fanning out in a dazzling spray of emeralds, rubies, and sapphires. This was a legendary piece, Emma knew: a birthday present for the Duchess of Windsor that the Duke had commissioned from Cartier in Paris. A favorite bird of the Duchess, the flamingo was the national animal of the Bahamas, and the pin was meant to be a reminder of the pleasant times the royal couple had spent in those islands. It was a piece that the Duchess normally wore for day, with a suit or dress, but Artemis made it clear that the flamingo could dazzle for an evening, too. After the Duchess's death in 1986, the brooch was sold at auction—purchased by Qasim with other Windsor pieces as a surprise for Artemis, who had developed a taste for what the French call *haute joaillerie.*

"He had to outbid Cartier for it," said Artemis, responding graciously to Emma's compliment on the brooch. "Isn't that ridiculous?"

"Ridiculous," said Emma.

"Thank God there are some assets invulnerable to fire," said Artemis.

"Are they?" said Ollie, who had never really thought about such a thing.

"Though I hear that diamonds can go cloudy in a conflagration," said Artemis. "But that could be kind of fabulous, too, couldn't it?"

"Like a sailor getting a tattoo after crossing the Equator," said Ollie.

They all laughed, though the observation didn't quite track.

"Odd, the way I see the phrase *haute joaillerie* translated into English as 'high jewelry,'" said Artemis. "Even the luxury brands do it, even Cartier, in their ads. I find it so clumsy."

"Why?" said Ollie. "We say *haute couture* for high fashion."

"Maybe it's the British in me," said Artemis. "When I see 'high jewelry,' I think 'high tea,' and that feels so working-class. I mean, even 'high fashion' begins to feel a little bit Barbie doll, no. . . ?"

Above the chatter of the dozen conversations surrounding them, the sound of the waters jetting and falling into the fountain's pool, and the mild beat of a DJ set streaming from inside, Emma was captivated by the brooch—the inexplicable allure of a woman like Artemis adorned with a flamingo like this. *This* was what she wanted to capture for her film, this *effect* and its function.

On an intellectual level, Emma understood the basics of jewelry design and construction; the physics of precious metals; the geology, chemistry, and crystallography of gemstones; the optics governing light and color, refraction and dispersion, clarity and fire. She understood something of the history of this particular brooch, which had been commissioned by a former King of England of a Parisian *maison* founded in 1847. In the presence of such a bauble, historical facts can command your attention, take it over, hijack it, if the bauble is not worn by an individual of suitable . . . what? Presence? Power? When worn by such an individual, the total effect is greater than the sum of the individual's presence and the bauble's beauty and value; and we find ourselves in a realm of effulgence that cannot be described, only felt and then fondly remembered—*if* something so improbably indescribable can register deeply enough on most people's quotidian brain to be fully remembered at all. To Emma, whose parents had trained her to aim beyond the quotidian in life, this effect felt as close to a blessing as anything she had ever experienced. Was it okay, Emma wondered, that this was a blessing that relatively few human beings would ever feel? If reserved for the rich, how should such a blessing be talked about, if talked about at all?

A gong was struck to summon the guests into the theater.

"Living is just easier for us in Monaco, than in London, that's all," Artemis was saying to Ollie. "Saalih is just not a political animal."

"Though they persist in treating him like one, don't they?" said Ollie.

"Remember, I have you at my table," said Artemis, beginning to lead the way inside. "See you after the performance."

CHAPTER 11

August 1939

And nine years after their debut season, the little game that Doris and Barbara invented for themselves was still going strong. They had both married, which chiefly meant being set free from their families; and they had taken their place in society, whatever that meant at a time when the Depression was eroding some of the prettier habits and myths of American life. Their uniquely unorthodox friendship was still flourishing, privately. In fact, they now agreed it was one of the few truly private things either of them had: and quite intentionally, they fueled the public image of rivalry, because it cast the truth of their relationship deeper into shadow, where it was better protected. During the '30s, they came to see their game as something of a lifeline—a vital running joke that was there when they cared to play; perhaps set aside for long stretches of time, then suddenly useful for a laugh or some strategic bit of publicity; sometimes bitter in flavor, sometimes sweet; a kind of refuge for them in a world where everyone wanted something from them and no one else could supply that reliable fellowship needed by all orphans of the storm. Certainly the game was more of a refuge than their husbands were. By then, Barbara had married and divorced Mdivani and Reventlow, the latter whom had given her a son, Lance, who was now three years old and largely in the charge of a nanny; Doris and Cromwell were leading essentially separate lives, except for the ceremonial occasions required for Cromwell's advancement as a politician. Doris was still technically married to him, but had been thinking about divorce almost since their wedding night, aboard the liner *Conte di Savoia*, on the first leg of their months-long honeymoon voyage around the world, when the groom unembarrassedly asked what his income from their union was going to be.

A prank the women pulled one night in the spring of '39, in a chic New York club called Fefe's, delighted them to no end. Fefe's Monte Carlo was a tiny *boîte* on East 54th Street, created and run by Monsieur Felix Ferry, a nightclub impresario and producer of revues and musical comedies. Like many of the smaller New York nightclubs of the era, Fefe's occupied a townhouse space that had previously housed several other clubs and would afterwards house several more. But for a few years before the war, Fefe brought magic to the spot. "A gigolo's conception of paradise," was how the *Times* described Dorothy Draper's indefatigably whimsical neoclassical design for the place, which featured dramatic alcove banquettes, painted balustrades on the walls, buckets of artificial greenery, and lush green-and-scarlet drapery. For two or three seasons, Fefe's was one of *the* places for debutantes, dowagers, and playboys, and even smartly dressed delivery boys with the right kind of good looks, to mix and drink and take in the miniature floor shows staged by the proprietor. One night when the club was packed, Doris arrived with a handsome young escort and was led to the table being held for her. Twenty minutes later, Barbara arrived with *her* handsome young escort and was led to *her* table—the two couples separated by a table occupied by a corpulent older gentleman in a tuxedo and a young blond woman in a satin gown. While pointedly ignoring each other, Doris and Barbara drank their champagne, watched the show, then swept out of the club with their escorts within half an hour of each other. And of course, there was an item on this apparent snub the next day in Maury Paul's Cholly Knickerbocker column.

"A slight out on the town" was how the incident was described.

They had planned the prank over the winter holidays, a few

months before, when Barbara stayed with Doris in Hawaii, during Shangri La's first days after completion. And they had staged essentially a dry run for the same thing earlier that spring in London, at the Silver Slipper Club on Regent Street, one of nightclub queen Ma Meyrick's establishments—only the snubbing incident didn't make it into the London papers, because the tabloids there had a juicier item to focus on, involving a naughty cabinet minister and a fashion model.

Doris and Barbara were still chuckling over their antics at Fefe's, one August day when they were both in Newport and chatting by phone about plans for a new outing together.

"I still think he might have mentioned my heavenly new Schiap," said Barbara, about the mention in Cholly Knickerbocker. By then, Barbara had become a regular customer of several Parisian couturiers, including Elsa Schiaparelli.

"It was probably Fefe who gave him the item," said Doris, "and he may not know his fashion."

"How could he not know fashion?" said Barbara. "He runs a club. Anyway, Maury did note my sidelong glance, remember?"

"I do. Did you rehearse that?"

"Of course I did."

And the day after the snubbing prank at Fefe's Monte Carlo, thirteen-year-old Nancy Creamer was reading about the incident in Cholly Knickerbocker's column, too, in Brooklyn, on her walk back home from a full day of Home Arts summer session classes at the Dyker Heights Intermediate School. She had picked up a paper at a newsstand and turned immediately to Cholly's column, before walking one step farther. The social doings she read about there were *so* much more interesting than the cooking and housecleaning tips she was learning in that ghastly red-brick temple of knowledge, not to mention the dreary goings-on in her family's modest house in Bay Ridge. All that was just short of an hour by subway away from where the real action was—Manhattan. Even as a young teenager, Nancy liked to dress her distinctly womanly body stylishly, as far as her budget would allow—sometimes to the derision of her classmates, who thought she was putting on airs. If only the Home Arts program offered sewing and pattern-making and the history of fashion! Not that Nancy wanted to be a couturier. Fashion executive was more her dream. Other program girls might dress for school in duddy dresses or modest skirts and sweaters, but Nancy felt it important to dress for the life of action she dreamed of, to be one step closer to being worthy of mention in columns like Cholly Knickerbocker's. Standing there at the newsstand in a fitted, almond-colored linen suit and three-inch Cuban heels, she might have been mistaken for a young Manhattan career woman instead of a neighborhood seventh-grader.

Even the column's headline was more clever by far than anything Nancy had heard in school: "A slight out on the town." This was wit, this was sophistication. A war might be coming, but America was separated from Europe by an ocean, and American women would remain free to lead the modern world with their style-setting ways!

But what were Doris Duke and Barbara Hutton wearing that night at Fefe's? How was their hair done? What accessories were they carrying? After devouring the column item, Nancy decided it was awfully thin on details. She didn't care at all about the identity of the corpulent gentleman whose table separated the two heiresses—Cholly Knickerbocker identified him by name as a prominent Wall Street banker, out with a woman who was not his wife. Who cared? What Nancy cared about were the couturier names and exact styles associated with the heiresses, so she could model her own wardrobe, hair, makeup, and general urbanity on theirs. Nor did the column give as much information as Nancy wanted about what actually happened during the incident, minute by minute. Who noticed whom first? Did either of the women suppress an initial reaction of distaste? Did both of them rely on automatic sangfroid? Did they steal glances at each other? Who rose to leave first, and how long after that did the other one leave? Did their escorts play any active role at all?

This was the world that Nancy intended to live in someday. Women like Duke and Hutton were her models—stylish, independent, involved only in the activities they wanted to be involved in, excluded from nothing. Working two days a week at Mme. Del Sarto's dress shop on Bay Ridge's Fifth Avenue, as nice as that was, would never be enough for Nancy. She was aiming at the real Fifth Avenue, perhaps one of the top department stores that sold high-fashion styles, like Lord & Taylor, Saks Fifth Avenue, or Best & Company. The least someone like Nancy could do, even at the age of thirteen, if she were heading toward a world like that, was always to look like a million dollars.

Now that it was the height of summer and both happened to be in Newport, Doris was at Rough Point, while Barbara was close by, staying with her friend Millicent, who liked to rent a Bellevue Avenue cottage for the season. The outing they were planning involved sailing. After flying by clipper from London to Boston, where she dropped off her three-year-old son, Lance, and the nanny, Barbara had motored to Newport and arranged to borrow Millicent's yacht, which was docked at the Newport Yacht Club, so she and Doris could sail across Long Island Sound for a short visit that Barbara wanted to make at Winfield Hall, the former Woolworth mansion in Glen Cove. The mansion, one of Barbara's favorite spots when growing up, had been sold not long before to Richard S. Reynolds, of the R.S. Reynolds Metal Company, and Barbara said she was eager to see "what they've done with the place."

Doris and Barbara were speaking by phone.

"What *have* they done, Babbo? New wallpaper?"

"Well, if you must know, they've set up some kind of laboratory on the grounds. I want to see that."

"A laboratory!"

"A metals laboratory. Apparently they are developing some kind of aluminum foil there that could be helpful if there's a war."

"Really, Babbo, you surprise me. War? Aluminum foil? When did you become interested in such things?"

"Madame Schiaparelli says there's going to be a war, sooner than we think."

"But, darling, you're not even interested in your own business. I happen to know that you've never attended even one board meeting of the Woolworth company."

"Oh, Dodo, *really* . . ."

"And *war*. . . ?"

"Alright. Cary says a war is coming, too. And he says we're going to be pulled into it, and it's going to be the most important thing in our lives. He says I should care about it."

"There had to be a man behind this."

"It's true, I *have* been seeing something of Cary," said Barbara provocatively, of the movie star she'd known for several years, Cary Grant.

"I know you have," said Doris. "Lining up Number Three?"

"I don't know. Maybe. Or maybe I won't do it again, ever."

"Good. Then I can take a run at him. I see Cary all the time in Hollywood."

"No, no," said Barbara with sudden sharpness. "Leave him alone until I decide what I'm doing with him." Then Barbara paused and harrumphed. "On second thought, do what you want. I think he's a little crazy."

Doris agreed, and had an idea that she wanted to work into their outing. She said that since Barbara was so interested in current affairs, she wanted to introduce her to someone who might be at least as knowledgeable about a coming war as Elsa Schiaparelli and Cary Grant.

"Who?" said Barbara.

"You'll see," said Doris. "It's a surprise—a friend of mine."

"Another opportunity to upstage me?"

"Just tell Millicent's captain that we'll be sailing to Greenport, not Glen Cove. I'll arrange a car for us. We'll have tea with my friend, and we'll be at Winfield by dinnertime."

Doris and Barbara arrived in the marina at ten o'clock in the morning and were met at Millicent's yacht, *Bonita*, by the captain and chief steward.

"We have smooth sailing the whole way," said the captain, as they boarded. "The sky is forecast to remain clear, and reports are that the sound is calm."

He confirmed Greenport as the destination, and they were underway almost immediately.

"How smart!" said Doris, of the ensemble Barbara had chosen for the day: a plaid silk summer dress and matching jacket, which she wore with a raffia hat designed with an integrated matching scarf that tied under the chin.

"Thank you," said Barbara. "Also Schiap."

Doris was dressed a bit more casually, in a white blouse and roomy, sailor-inspired trousers, with a white sweater draped over her shoulders.

"Best and Company," she said, modeling her own look with a quick, comical pose.

"You and department stores. We really must do something about that."

"They really have some very nice things."

Barbara sniffed.

"I prefer to have artists like Schiaparelli or Balenciaga touching my body."

Both women had brought several pieces of luggage with them, containing changes of daywear, and dresses and jewelry for evening, though their visit to Winfield Hall was planned to be informal and last only two days. This was less luggage than they might have brought along on a similar outing only ten years before, when packing even for a short jaunt had to accommodate clothing and accessories for a decidedly more formal social schedule—the world's current hard times for these two, born in the shadow of the Gilded Age, being one more welcome cue to modernize their social lives. Doris's net worth at that point was probably around a hundred million; Barbara's, seventy million—in a year when a Ford cost eight hundred dollars and few families could afford that. How were they able to weather the Great Depression so comfortably, when so many American fortunes established during the nineteenth century, already compromised by the introduction of corporate and personal income tax, were wiped out by the Crash? The answer was simple. The Depression was a fine inducement for people to smoke more of Doris's family's products and shop more at Barbara's family's five-and-dime stores.

The trip across the sound to Greenport would take a leisurely five hours. A steward had coffee, tea, and breakfast snacks ready for them in the galley, and Millicent's chef had sent down a cold lunch to be served later. They installed themselves on the pillowed banquette of the yacht's comfortably appointed foredeck and had coffee and croissants brought to them.

Bonita was a classic, eighty-foot craft built by the venerable John H. Mathis company and designed by renowned naval architect John Trumpy, who created many of the great yachts of the period, including the United States Presidential yacht, *Sequoia*. With a slender beam perfect for buzzing around intercoastal waterways, *Bonita* was used by its owners chiefly to go seasonally between their homes in Palm Beach and Newport, with occasional jaunts up the Hudson River to Millicent's family estate near Rhinebeck. With a hull of pine and oak, and deckhouse of teak, the yacht featured a commodious main saloon, card room, and two staterooms, all fitted with rubbed mahogany paneling and matching custom-made Venetian blinds.

"Father gave me a yacht when I turned eighteen," said Barbara, as *Bonita* made its stately way beyond ranks of moored boats, toward the marina's entrance.

"I remember," said Doris. "You never used it." On the harbor-front street lining the docks were brick and wooden façades of small businesses dating from the eighteenth century, in various states of repair.

"Sold it after a year."

"Not a sailor?"

"Not like you."

In Hawaii, Doris kept two boats—*Kimo*, a twenty-six-foot mahogany runabout that she sometimes used for jaunting into Honolulu, and *Kailani Lahilahi*, a fifty-eight-foot ocean-going yacht that she and husband Jimmy used for cruising the nearby islands and occasionally meeting guests arriving on incoming steamships. When building Shangri La, Doris also created—via the use of dynamite!—her own small harbor and private boat slip, with jetty, after lengthy negotiations with, and the ultimate expensive cooperation of, the Honolulu Harbor Board. For Doris, leaving a marina was always one of the most exciting parts of a shipboard outing—sailing past all the moored craft and those afloat in the basin, past where the land ends and out into the open water, where your sense of speed and forward thrust become balanced with the majestic impression of timelessness and suspension, for a pleasantly altered state that would last for hours or days, until land becomes visible again and the far shore beckons. Out there on the water, unobstructed by land or buildings, the elements themselves seem to have more to tell: the lyrical silence of boisterous breezes, the divine luminosity from above and all around and even from below, reflecting off the water's surface.

Heading past the Castle Hill Lighthouse, toward the mouth of Narragansett Bay, they talked about traveling with luggage and methods of packing clothing.

". . . And tissue paper, of course," said Doris, describing the way her maid usually packed for her.

"Plain tissue paper?" said Barbara.

"As plain as it gets. White-white. Sheets of it for every fold. Isn't that what you use?"

Barbara shook her head slowly.

"Silk paper, they call it. Aunt Marjorie swears by it. It's got some kind of matte surface on it. And we found some in Paris with lovely assorted floral patterns."

"Silk paper."

"We bought masses of it."

Barbara's face, framed by her hat, whose brim and scarf ends were snapping in the breeze, looked especially sweet in the morning light. Her expression seemed imperturbable, as if she were poised for anything, even a shipwreck. Yet the smile appeared to betray some fatigue, and there was a loginess about her speech.

"Are you alright, Babbo?" asked Doris.

"I'm fine," said Barbara. "Just a little dry mouth." She took a sip of her coffee.

"You could have a little nap before lunch."

"No, no. I'm fine."

"A touch of seasick?"

"Not a chance," said Barbara. "I'm so loaded with Scophedal."

"Scophedal?"

"It's German. For my tummy and my head, when I travel."

"What's in it?"

"Lord knows."

"But it works?"

Barbara grinned.

"Beautifully," she said. "Though I'm not supposed to drink with it, and I think it conflicts sometimes with my nerve medicine and diet pills."

Doris looked surprised.

"What nerve medicine?" she said.

"Don't worry, Dodo," said Barbara. "I'm perfectly fine."

"Are you sure? Since when do you need nerve medicine? And what is that, anyway?"

"It's nothing, really. I have the best doctors, as you know."

"Just because they're giving you what you want doesn't mean they're the best."

"I know they're the best, because they're the most expensive."

"I rest my case."

"I'll be fine."

Doris was growing concerned.

"Look, darling," she said, "forgive me for saying so, but you mean a lot to me, and I just want you to take care of yourself—the best care possible."

"You're sweet," said Barbara, patting her friend's hand.

Presently they asked for lunch to be served there on the foredeck—seafood salad, sliced steak, potato salad, rolls, cheese, and assorted fruit. They were finishing a bottle of Ayala *blanc de blancs* when off *Bonita*'s port side they spotted another yacht, at least as large as theirs, probably half a mile away and heading in the opposite direction. And even though the two craft were so far apart, Doris and Barbara could hear, echoing across the waves, the sound of a live jazz band playing the song "Ragtime Cowboy Joe."

"Now that's what we should have brought along—a band!" said Barbara.

"Noon is never too early for a band," said Doris. "Or for dancing."

First Doris got up, then Barbara, to improvise a giddy little swing dance together, for the few minutes that the music was audible. The foredeck wasn't huge, but it did accommodate their kicks, hops, and jitters.

". . . Hi-falutin', rootin' tootin', son-of-a-gun from Arizona," sang Doris gaily.

". . . Ragtime cowboy Joe!" they sang in unison, occasionally putting hands to each other's shoulders or waists.

Watching respectfully from just inside the saloon door was the steward, in case anything was needed. Then, as the distance between the boats grew, the music became too faint and the women sat down again, Barbara a little shakily. The steward cleared away the lunch things.

"Do you want to go in?" said Doris.

"No, no, I love the breeze—don't you?" said Barbara, adjusting the seat cushion behind her. She seemed a little winded. "Now, who's your friend?"

"Haha—in Greenport? You'll see," said Doris. "I'll give you only one clue. He or she knows a lot about current events, but that isn't his or her chief claim to fame."

"So there's a claim to fame here! Are you trying to best me again?"

"We'll see!"

"You're so cutthroat," exclaimed Barbara, retying the tails of her scarf, which had become loose with the dancing. Then she exhaled. "Tell me, why do we do it?"

"Our little jests?" said Doris. "You know why. Because we can, and it's fun—so much more fun than husbands. Didn't we both just learn that, in recent years?"

"We did indeed."

"Much more fun than Paris, Biarritz, Palm Beach—you know, the merry-go-round."

"The merry-go-round," repeated Barbara, in assent that sounded woeful. "Though homes do matter, don't they?"

Doris nodded.

"Do you miss Glen Cove very much?" she said. "You must. It's such a pretty spot."

"A little," said Barbara. "But now I have London, and I've been working on that. Though since the divorce, I've been finding it easier just to stay at Claridge's."

Shortly after marrying Count Kurt Haugwitz-Hardenberg-Reventlow in 1935, Barbara commissioned a very large neo-Georgian-style house in London's Regent's Park that she christened Winfield House, after the family name that was also used for the Long Island estate. She spared no expense in building and decorating the place, which saw the arrival, during her marriage, of all manner of antique furniture and fittings, including eighteenth-century Chinese wallpaper, a collection of Chinese porcelain, a collection of precious jade ornaments, a Savonnerie carpet that was said to have belonged to Marie Antoinette, gold taps for the bathrooms, and, for the garden, a life-sized sculpture of Barbara in a set of barely there, nominally Chinese-style pajamas, by a young Italian named Antonio Berti. Now that Barbara was divorced from Reventlow, the house was no longer useful for the social purposes she had envisioned for it, and she was considering selling it or donating it to the British government as an official residence for the American ambassador—a plan much to the liking of the Honorable Joseph P. Kennedy, who not only was appointed to that office in 1938 but also counted Barbara among the women he wanted to woo.

"You are so lucky to have Shangri La," mused Barbara. "I think I want a palace, too. Something . . . exotic. A place where I can be someone else, someone I really want to be. Isn't that fun?"

"Like play-acting?"

"Not onstage, with cardboard scenery. A real palace, with

marble walls and a full staff. Just different from all the faux-French and faux-Tudor and faux-Gothic applesauce we all grew up with."

"Well, you can come back to Shangri La any time you want, for as long as you want. Even if Jimmy's there. You see how he ignores us."

CHAPTER 12

December 1938

Six months before Doris and Barbara set out on the yacht *Bonita* to cross the Long Island Sound for Greenport, Barbara had spent Christmas with Doris and her husband in Hawaii.

"Welcome to paradise!" bubbled Doris, who was at the wheel of a red Alfa Romeo Villa d'Este convertible, its top down, having just picked up Barbara at the Honolulu airport.

"Oh, Dodo, it's marvelous. I've never been here in December!"

"Told you."

They were soaring through dazzling sunlight and fragrant breeze, speaking in loud tones, to be heard over the road noise.

"I'm breathless," warbled Barbara, craning around with almost uncharacteristic enthusiasm, to take in all the lush landscaping.

"We're very happy out here," said Doris.

Merrily, the two shouted bits of personal news back and forth to each other as Doris drove, and soon they were sailing up Shangri La's driveway of crushed white coral, past emerald lawns, rows of stately palm trees and bougainvillea, beds of brilliantly colored hibiscus, poinsettia, and anthurium, and an entire coconut grove that Doris had bought and installed on the grounds, fully grown. The temperature was in the low eighties, and fragrant trade winds were sweeping in off the ocean and mixing with the fruity-creamy scent of plumeria. The Bentley that was following them, with Barbara's luggage, peeled off toward the service courtyard.

The deceptively modest stucco façade of the house gleamed white in the morning sun. Guarding the entrance courtyard, flanking an antique, studded-wood Berber door, was a pair of immense, eighteenth-century Chinese stone camels.

"Jimmy and I only just moved in, before Thanksgiving," said Doris, as her secretary, Pansy, greeted them at the door and showed them inside. "And now the Roosevelt boys are here for a few days. . . ."

"The Roosevelt boys?" said Barbara.

"The president's sons, the younger ones—Franklin Junior and Johnny. They're lots of fun."

"Oh."

"I think they're all sailing right now. Jimmy was going to take them out. We'll see them at dinner."

"Lovely."

"Loretta Young was to have been here for Christmas, but you know Hollywood. Now it's going to be New Year's Eve, hopefully. You know Loretta, don't you. . . ?"

The sound of their voices and footsteps echoed pleasantly among the stucco and tile walls, as Doris and Pansy escorted Barbara through the place, on their way toward the guesthouse.

The pleasure palace called Shangri La that Doris built on Oahu, on the other side of Diamond Head from Honolulu, was inspired by the art and architecture of the Near East and Far East. But rather than strictly historical, its design reflected a mix of styles including Moghul, Seljuk, and Ottoman, as well as faux versions of those styles. The project began in 1935, when Doris and Cromwell were on their honeymoon trip around the world, which had been planned to take four weeks and wound up lasting nine months, culminating with a long stay in the United States territory of Hawaii. Lush and fragrant, populated with warm and friendly people, Hawaii seemed to offer more privacy and relaxation than Doris had previously been aware of needing. Instantly she felt at home there. From their suite at the Royal Hawaiian, she and Cromwell spent weeks roaming the island, looking for a suitable place to build, until at last they found a spot that sang to them, a promontory overlooking the Pacific in Honolulu's exclusive Black Point residential neighborhood. Doris hired architect Marion Sims Wyeth, the same architect who had designed Mar-a-Lago, to work with her on the house's design. She also bought a large, dockside warehouse on Honolulu Harbor, which would function as a depository for all the larger, museum-level Islamic artifacts and architectural elements she was buying or commissioning from artists, artisans, workshops, and dealers in India, Iran, Morocco, Spain, and the like.

When finished, Shangri La was basically a modernist house onto which all these elements had been applied. The interior was a fantasy-like succession of dazzling salons, terraces, courtyards, and pavilions, whose tranquil atmosphere was enhanced by delicately carved marble wall screens, inlaid with semiprecious stones in floral patterns; lattice-work windows admitting jewel-like beams of light through panes that shimmered in pink and green and lavender; florid mosaic panels depicting mythical gardens; soaring antique columns; massively scaled carved wood doors; elaborately coffered and painted ceilings; an oak floor imported from a sixteenth-century French château; an eleventh-century Moorish mantelpiece purchased from William Randolph Hearst. . . . It may have been located in a territory that was known as a playground for the rich, but for Doris, this was no vacation house. Shangri La was a refuge, a retreat far from New York nightclubs and newspapers, which is why she named it after the legendary domain of beauty and harmony where people did not grow old, as described in the popular 1937 movie of the same name and the 1933 novel by James Hilton that the movie was based on.

"This is the heart of the house," said Doris, on a small detour through her own bedroom suite. The sitting room featured a small fountain with a delicate *acequia*—or Moorish-style water channel set into the floor—streaming out to a pool in Doris's private lanai, which gave onto a larger terraced garden that was built around a lily pond. Her octagonal bathroom of white marble accented with jade featured a fancifully vaulted ceiling, studded with tiny mirrors, worthy of a palace or temple.

"Don't worry—your bathroom is nice, too," said Doris, noticing Barbara looking up in wonder. "This one is Moghul. The one in the guesthouse where I'm putting you is Moorish—from a twelfth-century palace in Córdoba."

"Fit for an empress," said Barbara.

"That was the idea," said Doris. "Right now, we've put the emperor in the theater—or what will soon be a theater, on the other side of the pool, as soon as the ceiling panels arrive for the portico. That's the next phase. I want to bring dancers and musicians out here. We've based the thing on this gorgeous little pavilion in Isfahan called the Chehel Sotoun, that Shah Abbas II built for receptions and such."

"You've put Jimmy in a theater?" said Barbara.

Doris shot her friend a look of patient determination.

"We've made it quite comfortable," she said.

"I'm sure."

"He and I are sorting things out."

By then, Barbara was living much of her life abroad, staying in London and Paris, where she could be closer to young Lance, who, after a bitter custody battle, lived mostly with his father, Reventlow, in Europe. She was also closer there to the social life she'd settled into with Elsa Maxwell's crowd, partying often on the Riviera while being pitied in the press for a variety of reported ailments and sometimes mocked for questionable medical treatments, or being positively vilified at a time when Woolworth workers were on strike and the chain's customers themselves were suffering unemployment or worse. And Barbara made further headlines for her spendthrift habits—for paying one-point-two million dollars for a group of opera singer Ganna Walska's emeralds, once given by Napoleon III to the Countess de Castiglione; for completely refurnishing a rented palazzo for just a weeklong residency; for dining at King Tutankhamun's tomb, inside the actual tomb itself, on top of the king's sarcophagus, using solid gold vessels and utensils, at a luncheon party hosted by the Sixth Earl of Carnarvon, whose father had funded the tomb's excavation. "The Most Hated Girl in America," one newspaper dubbed Barbara.

Doris was frequently in Europe, too, as well as in the Near and Far East, and she certainly didn't hate a party, but she was international in a different way from Barbara—more interested in the intricacies of culture and politics than in the excesses of society and high living. As a by-product of the financial savvy cultivated in her by her father, and as an active board member of several Duke enterprises, Doris expected to maintain a close view of what was happening politically around the world, especially in Europe, with an eye toward how current events could affect the United States. Though by then she was often living and traveling apart from Cromwell—and sometimes jaunting about with a series of other companions and beaux—including Captain Alec Cunningham-Reid, a handsome British MP and former World War I flying ace, who was known as something of an adventurer, in both the political and romantic senses.

Doris liked the access she had, through her politically ambitious husband, to intelligence sources in Washington. Cromwell had made a name for himself in the '30s with two books, *The Voice of Young America* ("alarming facts about our country and what we can do to save ourselves from ruin") and *In Defense of Capitalism* ("an explanation of the functioning of our capitalistic system of today and of specific measures which would correct its defects"). Even from as far away as Hawaii, Cromwell was speaking almost daily to movers and shakers in Washington, even sometimes to his good buddy Franklin Delano Roosevelt, as he angled for a political appointment—specifically, at that point, U.S. Ambassador to Canada. It had probably been, in fact, Cromwell's New Deal-ish leanings that caused his rich Republican stepfather, upon his death not long before, to leave Cromwell an inheritance of only four million dollars and not the hundred million he was expecting, thus rendering him so financially dependent on his wife.

In this way, Doris was more fervently patriotic than Barbara, and at a time when rumors of war were circulating, Doris was actively exploring possibilities for serving her country—something that both Cromwell and Cunningham-Reid admired. Whether or not she would actually be able to secure some kind of overseas assignment in or with the OSS—the intelligence-gathering U.S. Office of Strategic Services—remained to be seen. Of course, as a private citizen of nearly infinite means, Doris considered herself perfectly able to bash off on whatever international mission she might set for herself, with or without the official papers people might need to travel during increasingly restricted conditions. She was determined to be useful.

Later on the day of her arrival at Shangri La, Barbara emerged from the guesthouse at cocktail hour as instructed, wearing a black Chanel evening dress in ruffled chiffon and black heels, and the strand of pearls once owned by Marie Antoinette that her father had given her for her twenty-first birthday. The house was quiet, with no other guests and very few staff about, except for a cocktail steward at the bar on the pool terrace, whom Barbara was chatting with over a martini when Doris appeared in an informal summer dress and flat-heeled sandals, holding a kerchief for her hair.

"Oh no, no, that's all wrong," said Doris, seeing Barbara's attire. "It's not formal at all."

"I gather dinner isn't here," said Barbara.

"No, it's not here, and it's not formal—sorry, I should have made that clearer."

"But Chanel can go anywhere."

"Go change quickly and meet me at the door."

"Change into what?"

"Anything informal. Now, hurry. They're bringing my car around."

"You're driving again?"

"We're not going far."

"Where are we going?"

"To the beach!"

"A beach club?"

"The beach."

The drive took only ten minutes. Barbara, now in an informal dress, was still in heels.

"One of the great benefits about Hawaii is the boatloads of tanned, young Hawaiian men all over the place," said Doris, as she parked near several other cars in a small clearing on the side of a sandy, unpaved road that ran alongside the beach. "Muscular, and in the briefest of bathing suits, to be found everywhere—on the beach, on the streets, in the bars . . ."

The sound of ocean waves gently crashing on the shore was stronger and even more seductive than on Doris's promontory. A little path through some beach cabbage bushes led to a broad stretch of white sand on a secluded cove, where a gathering of thirty or so genial partygoers, casually dressed or barely dressed at all, were standing around or seated in the sand in small groups, talking and laughing and drinking. It was a mix of dark-skinned Hawaiians and those of lighter skin, including residents and visitors; children were running about, hooting and hollering, and a group of quite old-looking people sat chatting and laughing in a circle of folding wooden chairs. A trio of musicians on ukulele, steel guitar, and bass was playing a jazzy version of "Deck the Halls," while off to the side, a spirited beach game of tag football was taking place, with Jimmy Cromwell and the Roosevelt boys, all in khaki shorts and polo shirts, and several of the Hawaiian men and boys, most of them shirtless and in bathing suits. Almost everyone was barefoot and in a buoyant mood.

"The first few weeks here, I couldn't stop looking," said Doris, "and I couldn't stop smiling."

Doris pointed out the underground oven, a *kalua*, dug into the sand and lined with hot rocks and banana leaves, where a pig had been roasting for eight hours, for the traditional *luau* feast being prepared. Nearby, a table was being set up to serve what Doris said were other *luau* staples: bowls of various kinds of raw fish and noodles, a salad of salmon and tomato, a mashed taro root dish called *poi*, a platter of roasted purple sweet potato slices, bowls of fruit and bread, and a coconut pudding.

Two of the shirtless Hawaiian men and a Hawaiian woman in a blue-and-mauve, floral-patterned shift were approaching them.

"And the best part was that they thought *I* was beautiful," whispered Doris.

"*Mele Kalikimaka!*" said one of the men, whose smooth muscular body, black hair, and handsome face made him look like a cartoon superhero. He automatically wrapped Doris in a hug.

"*Mele Kalikimaka,*" said Doris, obviously relishing the warm greeting. "Barbara, this is Sarge Kahanamoku and his wife, Anna, and this is Sarge's brother Duke. . . ."

"Hey—*Mele Kalikimaka!*" said Duke Kahanamoku, squeezing Doris into an even more ardent hug than Sarge's, and then greeting Barbara with a bit more restraint, as Sarge and Anna had done.

"*Mele Kalikimaka* is our way of saying Merry Christmas," explained Duke, flashing a dazzling smile.

"Beautiful evening for it," said Doris.

"You celebrate Christmas . . ." said Barbara, as if she were trying to parse the idea.

"Well, remember," said Duke, "the missionaries did have their way with us. Now, if you're interested in what Hawaiian religion was like before that, we can ask one of these very intelligent college kids about that. They give courses today in the old ways."

"The Kahanamoku family is my *ohana*—which means extended family," said Doris. "Two of the brothers are . . ."—she turned toward the football game, scanned, then pointed—"there—Sam and Lewis, playing opposite my husband, of course. Sam was so helpful when Jimmy and I were looking for the perfect spot for Shangri La, during our first days here."

Doris squeezed Duke's wrist and told him that she was taking Barbara to meet everyone.

"Each one is handsomer than the last," whispered Barbara, taking in the attractiveness of the party guests.

"And the sweetest souls," said Doris.

"Damn. Now I want one, too."

"They are not objects, Babbo."

"Aren't they? Barons and counts and princes are, so why can't beach boys be?"

They were given mugs of beer by a boy tending a wooden keg girdled with iron bands; then Doris brought Barbara around to other partygoers, making introductions. With a round of hollering, the football game broke up, and several of the players ran straight to the surf and jumped in, while Cromwell walked over to Doris and Barbara with the Roosevelt boys, who were in their early twenties, to exchange automatic pleasantries.

"Good game?" said Doris.

"Great," said Cromwell.

"Looked like fun."

"Sam's a champion."

"I'm showing Babbo around."

"Have a good time."

Excusing themselves, the boys ran off, and Cromwell said he needed a beer.

A bonfire was started and torches were lit, as the sun sank lower and the sky turned hazy yellow, the underbelly of a bank of puffy white clouds stained with oranges and grays. Doris and Barbara found a spot to be by themselves for a moment, before the feast was ready.

At first, Barbara seemed a little reluctant to plunk herself down in the sand.

"We can find you a chair if you'd like, Grandma," said Doris.

"Oh no, I'm fine," said Barbara, managing to get down and make herself comfortable in the sand.

"Feel free to kick off your shoes. Walking on the sand in heels is murder."

"But my nylons!"

"Take 'em off."

"And the pedicure, Dodo . . ."

"We can have a girl come to the house tomorrow."

"On Christmas Day?"

Doris shot Barbara a look that said, "Of course on Christmas Day, if that's what we want."

"Well, alright . . ." said Barbara, removing her things as gracefully as possible, with some discreet rocking and leaning.

"Do you see why I wanted to get you out of your Chanel?" said Doris.

"Everyone's so friendly."

"One reason why I love Hawaii," said Doris.

"I've been here before, but I never really saw this side of it. The men. . . !"

According to Doris, "the great thing" was not so much that there was all this exposed male flesh around, but that the men were so comfortable being that way. This was an easy, natural thing for them, and their comfort with their own bodies was itself a kind of missionary message. It expressed a joy of living that wasn't precisely sexual but could indeed fuel sexual feelings.

"I suppose so," said Barbara, working her feet a bit into the sand.

"The women, too," said Doris. "They're so comfortable with themselves. That's what finally reaches you, beyond the breezes, and the ocean, and the beauty . . ."

"Am I wrong, or did the tall one greet you with a little extra fervor?" said Barbara.

"Duke?"

"Is that his name, too?"

Doris laughed.

"Yes, Duke and Duke," she said. "He and I swim together all the time. He's teaching me how to surf and sail, so we've been spending mornings in the ocean, alone, not far from here."

"I see. Naked on the beach."

"Well—practically. You may recall that he's an Olympic champion."

"Is he?"

"I told you. He won medals in 1912, 1920, 1924."

"Lord, he was competing in the year we were born? He can't be that old. He looks much younger."

"I *know*," said Doris, with emphasis that was meant to betray her strong interest in Duke, which she'd hinted at earlier, when responding to a comment Barbara made at the airport that she looked "completely invigorated."

"Great smile," said Barbara.

"Oh, yes. That, too."

"Does Jimmy know?"

Doris hesitated a moment, then spoke as frankly as she could.

"He must," she said.

"Is it serious?"

"It may be getting that way."

"Well, good for you. I can't imagine how good-looking your children would be."

As the sun was setting and the trio was playing "Silent Night," the beer began to have its effect, and the two women found themselves as comfortable in the sand as they might have been at a country club lounge.

"It might be . . . difficult for any child of ours," said Doris contemplatively.

Barbara nodded.

"In the US of A, anyway," she said.

"Yet I think everybody dreams about this kind of living without even being aware of it," continued Doris. "Rather, they think of it as a dream and take their own lives to be reality, in the stone canyons and noisy nightclubs. But *that's* the dream, Babbo—actually a nightmare, the damned city madness! And *this* is reality."

"Mmm, maybe."

"And we are lucky enough to see that, to discover that—to be able to *afford* to discover that. Do you know what I mean? The basic pleasure of everyday life is practically a sacrament."

"Steady, girl."

"No, really. It should not be misunderstood, or worse, wasted. It should be taken . . . oh, how does the Anglican wedding language go? Reverently, discreetly, advisedly, soberly, and in the fear of God."

Barbara pondered this for a moment.

"Well, maybe not soberly," she said.

The sun was almost gone when the trio suddenly halted their Christmas music. After a moment of silence, during which a set of lighted torches was planted in the sand at the edge of the water, almost like a gateway, the musicians and several other men began chanting and accompanying themselves on drums, Hawaiian-style, in a pulse-quickening, rapid-fire rhythm. The guests gathered at the edge of the ocean and waited expectantly. Then, cutting through the waves from down the beach and around a bend, came a sleek outrigger canoe, paddled vigorously by four shirtless men, the first three of whom were sporting fuzzy reindeer-horn headgear, and the fourth of whom, Duke, was wearing a Santa Claus hat. To waves of wild applause and cheering, the boat slipped up to the torch gate. The men hopped out and deftly turned the boat around and set it on the sand facing the ocean, and then turned to greet the crowd.

The drumming shifted from one rousing pattern to the next, and Barbara watched with envy as everyone joined in the chant as best they could, and Doris stepped forward to be the first to hail the arrival of the Hawaiian Santa. Tall and half-naked, so darkly tanned and gracefully robust, Duke Kahanamoku made a truly Hollywood-level tropical Saint Nick. Doris seemed aglow with high spirits and also, Barbara saw in the body language, a little possessive of Duke. That kind of desire looked so different from the passable compliance that the girls had learned to summon up for the dependably well-mannered milksops they'd been paired with for ten years. This Hawaiian scene between Duke and Duke looked much more deeply felt—though, Lord knows, even true love itself could well be a plaything for certain rich girls whose entire world is comprised of playthings, for whom even the highest stakes—maybe even continued existence—could sometimes feel a bore.

Prudently, Jimmy Cromwell was off near the beer keg, talking about European politics with the Roosevelt boys and some of the other young people.

Doris was on a slightly different path now, thought Barbara—not exactly parallel to her own, as Barbara might have imagined it would be, all those years ago when they went horseback riding and followed the same path through the Connecticut country-side. Who would have thought that there could be two such different paths for women like themselves, dubbed "twins" by the entire world? Barbara was happy for her friend but also slightly puzzled. How was Doris so confident in following, even forging, such a particular path? She was only twenty-six, and this half-naked, dark-skinned man she was embracing by torchlight must be close to fifty. Where could that lead? What was Doris thinking? Barbara knew that her friend was becoming intimate with homosexual decorators and Black jazz musicians, too—people with distinctive, even flamboyant style and talent. Fair enough. They didn't fawn over her and were not demanding in the same way that impoverished European nobles were. Here at the ocean, Doris, in the same way, was able to drop her heiress mask and be at peace with the simple pleasures of island life, singing and dancing and swimming with beach boys, like one of the beach girls. Yet wasn't Doris always the odd one, the gawky one? Wasn't Barbara always the pretty one, like a movie star?

Doesn't Alexandre of Paris do my hair? thought Barbara. *Didn't Horst photograph me for* Vogue?

"I didn't realize you went for the strong, silent type," said Barbara, when Doris was leading her, arm in arm, to the *luau* table.

"Duke isn't silent—not at all," said Doris. "He might be a little shy around my dearest, oldest friend, whom he's meeting for the first time. He's actually quite vocal and intelligent."

"And intelligence is high on your list of qualities for men, is it?"

"Of course it is. You know I like to speak with leaders in politics, science, religion. You know that Jimmy and I met with Gandhi when we were on our honeymoon."

"Yes, yes, and it was 'absolutely enlightening!'"

"It was, darling. I like people smarter than myself. That's how we learn. That's one reason why I like you."

"Hmmh," sniffed Barbara.

"You fit right in with those people," said Doris. "In fact, I know a card-carrying genius whom I think you'd rather like. Let me introduce you."

"Marriage material?"

"Mmm, no."

"Then I doubt I would relate to him."

"But dear, he does know a lot about relativity . . ."

CHAPTER 13

After the ballet performance, dinner was on the Koch Theater's grand promenade. Under the glistening silver clouds, a glamorous assembly of VIP guests was joined at each table by members of the ballet company. Artemis had seated herself between Ollie and Emma, and found herself conversing mostly with them over the usual chicken breast with potato gratin and bouquetière of seasonal vegetables. Meanwhile, Artemis's other friends and one of the evening's star dancers discussed things like gender roles in ballet and the relative ranking of gala chicken with wedding chicken, conference chicken, and airline chicken.

"Ollie tells me you're working on a movie about jewels," said Artemis.

"Yes," said Emma. "Well, it's actually about women and their jewels—or, I should say, the jewels of great women."

"I notice that you've been looking at my pin."

"It's beautiful."

"Thank you. It's one of the pieces I can travel with."

"How do you mean?"

"Insurance. It all depends on value and local security. It's complicated."

"I understand you have an extensive collection."

"I do have some nice things. Saalih is very generous. And I'm mad about the way these objects come into being. You must be, too."

"Did you know the Duchess?"

"I did, a bit, in the early seventies, in Paris. Saalih had business there, just after we were married. The Duke had just died, and Wallis was on the American Hospital's board of governors—she and the Duke had received so much good treatment there. My aunt was also on the board and knew Wallis—which is why I feel I can call her Wallis. We had lunch two or three times with her at the Bois—she lived in a beautiful house in the Bois de Boulogne."

"What was she like?"

"The Duke's death had obviously devastated her, but she was trying her best to go on. You could still see the wit. I think she feared becoming the isolated widow, which of course is exactly what happened. She stopped seeing visitors and eventually lost her ability to speak and eat, toward the end. . . . She was wearing this pin, actually, one day at lunch."

"Really—at home? That's interesting," said Emma, her eyes widening.

"It's fun, isn't it?" said Artemis. "Honestly, it's the taste expressed in such things, that the Duke commissioned from Cartier and other houses, that I find so interesting. Some people commission things that are too garish, or too whimsical, or not whimsical enough, or too austere and classical—you know. It's very personal, when you go to Cartier with a million dollars and tell them what you want. They try to guide you, but not everyone has particularly good taste. There was something about what the Duke, or Wallis and the Duke, asked Cartier to cook up for them that I really like—just the right balance between design and sentiment. The fact that there's history involved, and value—well, that's nice, too."

Emma hesitated for a moment, then spoke up.

"Do you think," she said, "that you would ever be interested in saying something like that to me on camera, for my film?"

Artemis cocked her head coquettishly.

"That would depend on who else you've got," she said.

Emma named two of the international socialites she'd already lined up for interviews through Kelly and the Christie's connection, and two more who'd indicated interest.

"I'd only need an hour or so," said Emma. "And if you were also willing to let me shoot a few pieces. . . ."

"Hmm," said Artemis. "I'd have to confer with Saalih. Maybe, if you'd like, I could invite you to Monte Carlo, where we could have lunch, and then, if it seems possible, you might bring in a small film crew."

August 1939

The yacht *Bonita* arrived in Greenport Harbor at 2:15, and one of the Duke cars was waiting at the dock for Doris and Barbara. Gulls were squawking and pennants snapping in the breeze, as the girls stepped carefully down the gangway, above the water lapping against the yacht's hull and dock pilings. They were met by a perfectly adequate chauffeur whom Nanaline liked but Doris found sadly less conspiratorial than dear Henrik had been.

A short drive to Nassau Point, near the village of Cutchogue, led them to a modest, two-story beachfront cottage on Great Peconic Bay, broad and peaceful on that August afternoon. The chauffeur stood by dutifully in the glaring sun as Doris stepped onto the shady porch, knocked on the screen door, and was greeted by a friendly and efficient-seeming woman with short dark hair.

"Oh, Miss Duke, hello," said the woman, in a light German accent. From behind her, a dog was barking in a friendly manner.

"Hello, Helen," said Doris. "So nice to see you again."

A wire fox terrier was with Helen at the door, being curious and very vocal.

"Right on time! Right on time! Quiet, Chico," she said, bending slightly to restrain the creature. "But unfortunately, the professor is not on time. He should be home by now."

"Perhaps he's lost track?"

Helen laughed, as if this were a common occurrence.

"Perhaps," she said. "But please come in. He takes his boat out on the cove in the morning, you know. It helps him think. He should be back quite soon."

"Well, why don't we go find him?" suggested Doris.

Helen seemed to think this was a good idea.

"Horseshoe Cove," she said. "It's only back down the road—Haywaters Road to Fisherman Beach. There's a little dock."

"We'll bring him back," said Doris.

"Who, Dodo?" said Barbara when they were back in the car.

"You'll see," said Doris. "He knows all about aluminum—and, I daresay, all the rest of the elements."

The few fishermen at the cove were unperturbed by the arrival of a great limousine and discharge of two splendidly dressed young women. As the women approached the tiny dock, they were spotted by a shortish, white-haired man who, standing in the shallow water, was handing off his small sailboat to a teenage boy, who was functioning as something of a dockhand. The man waved.

"Thank you, Tommy," said the man, speaking, too, in a German accent. "But what have we here? Two ladies?" Smiling broadly, he strode barefoot from the water and up onto the beach, and extended his hand.

"My good Doris," he said warmly.

"Herr Professor, *guten tag*," said Doris, taking his hand in both of hers.

A kindly looking gentleman of around fifty, with a corona of untamed white frizz on top of his head, he was dressed in baggy bathing trunks and a rumpled white shirt. He was clutching a newspaper under his arm and holding a pair of what looked like women's sandals in white, which he proceeded to put on with the steadying help of Doris's arm.

"I am late?" he said.

"No, we're early," said Doris.

"You are not a very good liar," said the man. "I sailed around the point to Southold for the paper, but the wind was not with me."

"Professor, let me introduce my friend Barbara. Barbara, this is Albert Einstein."

"I . . . I'm delighted, Mr. Einstein," said Barbara, slightly gobsmacked.

"We can take you home, Professor," said Doris, emphasizing the title for Barbara's sake and indicating the car.

"I usually walk," said Einstein. "I am very sweaty."

"Please," said Doris. The chauffeur was already holding the door open.

Einstein entered and took one of the fold-down jump seats, while the girls installed themselves as usual on the rear bench.

"The professor and I have known each other for many years," explained Doris. "Jimmy is helping him with American citizenship. We met . . . when, Professor?"

"Princeton, 1933, if I am not mistaken."

"Yes, that must be right. We were introduced at a reception, and of course I knew who he was, and he was terribly easy to talk to."

"We talked about photons!"

"Yes, photons! And we've stayed in touch."

In a whispered aside to Barbara, Doris explained that from one of her private funds, she was "helping" some of the scholars at Princeton's Institute for Advanced Study, where Einstein was teaching.

"And then," Doris continued, "a year later, he was in the United States again and decided to stay and become a citizen, because of this whole Hitler matter."

"And then in Washington, we met with the Senators . . ." said Einstein.

"So now you are an American citizen?" said Barbara.

"Very soon, I hope," said Einstein.

"It's all but done, as I understand it," said Doris. "Apparently, the FBI was a roadblock. . . ."

"Mr. J. Edgar Hoover does not particularly like German Jews," said Einstein, with a sad chuckle. "Nor does he like militant pacifists."

"But the president knows we need the professor's genius, especially now. . . ."

Back at the cottage, Einstein's sister Maja and his adult children, stepdaughter, Margot, and son, Hans, had returned from the market with a watermelon and fresh pastries for their tea.

In the cottage's cozy living room, over the light buffet that Maja and Helen, Einstein's secretary, laid out, with Chico relaxed after receiving some love from the visitors, the six of them enjoyed some genial conversation. Einstein said he was spending the summer sailing and, with Helen's help, working on a paper about the expansion of the universe. Maja, a scholar of Romance languages, was studying a fourteenth-century Catalan royal chronicle. Margot and Hans were going back and forth to New York, for museums and performances. Einstein seemed delighted to hear Doris and Barbara's report on social doings in Newport.

"It still goes on?" he said with a laugh.

"It still goes on," said Doris.

"And you sailed here on a yacht? My goodness! From Newport? How long does that take?"

"About five hours," said Barbara.

"And did you sit on the deck and stare at the horizon and contemplate the meaning of life?" asked Einstein.

"Well . . ." began Barbara.

"I'm afraid we gabbed and gabbed," said Doris.

Everyone laughed.

"And what did you gab about?" said Einstein.

"Husbands and boyfriends," said Doris.

"Very good," said Einstein, obviously amused. "Even if there is a war coming, we must remember love, no?"

"Who said anything about love?"

Laughter.

"And emeralds," said Barbara. "We talked about emeralds."

After the reference to war and love, Barbara's contribution struck an off note, though Einstein didn't seem to mind.

"Emeralds?" he said. "Did you just buy some lovely emeralds?"

"I bought them a few years ago. Doris is helping me figure out what to do with them."

"Such things!" said Einstein.

"Are you very nautical, Professor?" asked Barbara.

Einstein chuckled.

"Well, I use my *Tinef* to go for the newspaper and for oranges—my sailboat . . ." he said.

"*Tinef* in Yiddish means 'junk,'" added Maja.

". . . But I can't even swim."

"No?" said Barbara.

"A big wave and I am . . ." said Einstein, miming sinking under the water while holding his nose.

More laughter.

Doris hastened to add that her friend Barbara was a poetess and had recently published a slim volume entitled *The Enchanted*.

"Charming," said Maja.

"Professor Einstein is leading an effort to prevent a war," said Doris, for Barbara's benefit. "Or if there is one, he's thinking about how to prevent it from getting out of hand."

"I see," said Barbara, not quite seeing.

Einstein explained that he was helping scientists at nearby Stony Brook University set up a national lab for high-energy physics, as was also being envisioned for a place called Los Alamos, in New Mexico.

"Why is that?" said Barbara.

"To produce some kind of superbomb—isn't that right, Professor?" said Doris.

"Among other things," said Einstein.

"My goodness," said Barbara.

"Unfortunately," continued Einstein, "the Germans are already building such a device. I am trying now to see if Mr. Roosevelt can be persuaded to build one, too. The time grows short."

An hour later, as Maja and Helen began clearing away the tea things, Hans and Margot said goodbye and took Chico out for a walk.

"Such a sweetheart," said Doris, whom the dog had determined, during tea-time conversation, could be his next very best friend.

"He is very smart," said Einstein. "He feels sorry for me because I receive so much mail. That's why he tries to bite the mailman."

"He must be a great comfort," said Barbara.

"He helps me think," said Einstein. "When I am stuck on a problem, I just think of what his namesake might do."

"His namesake?"

"Chico Marx."

The women giggled.

"And in return, I do nice things for him—like feed him and pet him. And in our house in Princeton, I made it possible for him to go in and out on his own, through a little hatch I designed for him in the bottom of our kitchen door."

Einstein made a hinging-back-and-forth gesture with his hand.

"How clever," said Doris. "I must remember that and have some made for the farm."

"Will there really be a war, Professor?" asked Barbara.

"Yes," said Einstein. "I think so."

"Must we do something?"

He took on a serious look.

"The world will not be destroyed by those who do evil, but by those who watch without doing anything."

That statement provoked a short silence that not even Barbara felt inclined to break. Then Einstein continued.

"Germany will invade Poland within a month—I am sure of it. Then Great Britain and France will almost certainly respond by declaring war on Germany. I don't see how the United States can resist being drawn in—so many of our interests are at stake."

"Good Lord," said Barbara.

"This could be the biggest war ever, with the highest stakes ever, and we must be decisive in combatting Hitler."

"Hence the superbomb," mused Doris.

"You can't imagine the power," said Einstein. "But we all must imagine the responsibility for so much death and destruction, even when it does put a halt to evil."

"Yes," said Barbara.

"Though how much of an evil is the bomb, in itself?" said Doris.

"Ah—very good question, my good Doris," said Einstein. "My dearest hope is that we don't come to regret it, we physicists. All physicists will feel responsible, you know, even if we are not personally giving the orders."

The living room's furnishings included a Hamilton upright piano, on top of which were piled albums of sheet music. Next to it, leaning against a bookcase, was a black leather-covered violin case.

"Do you play, Professor?" asked Barbara, who seemed keen to change the subject.

"Do I play?" said Einstein gleefully. "I play this!"

He opened the case and took out his fiddle.

"Doris, shall we?" he said, while giving the instrument a quick tuning. "Do you have the time?"

"Oh, yes!" said Doris, eagerly seating herself on the piano bench, shuffling through a few albums, and selecting one. "How about some Mozart?"

"Perfect," said Einstein.

"The B-flat major?"

"Ah—nice!"

"We played this together once at a party in Princeton, Babbo," said Doris.

"It was a triumph," said Einstein, brightly. "Though sometimes, here, when I practice, the neighbor complains."

Doris and Einstein launched into the Mozart violin sonata— an introductory largo, then a spirited allegro. Maja and Helen emerged from the kitchen and took seats. And from the open windows of the little beach cottage on Great Peconic Bay came sublimely effervescent melodies, runs, arpeggios, and cadences from the mind of one of the eighteenth-century's most prodigious composers, as interpreted by one of the richest individuals of the twentieth century and one of the smartest.

At the end of the movement, everyone burst into applause.

"How about something a little more contemporary?" suggested Doris breezily, as she started improvising a version of a popular song that had debuted the year before, sung by Dick Powell in the movie *Hard to Get*, "You Must Have Been a Beautiful Baby." With gusto, Einstein jumped into doubling the melody that Doris was playing, then launched into a series of flamboyant violin embellishments. His playing was not bad, and what he lacked in technical expertise, he made up for with spirit.

For the refrain, Barbara started singing, though it was clear she didn't quite know the words.

You must have da da da-da-da da-da,
You must have da da da-da-da da . .

"Everybody!" said Doris, as she and Einstein were finishing the song, though Barbara was the only one singing.

'Cause baby, da da da da!

Then they moved on to a brand-new song that Doris said was yet to be published, that the composer Harold Arlen had taught her at a party one night at his apartment in the Upper West Side's posh San Remo building. It was something called "Blues in the Night" that he was working on for a movie, with lyricist Johnny Mercer. With smoothness reflecting the many years Doris had spent learning and playing jazz piano, she launched into the song, and with great ease, Einstein picked up the melody and got its bluesy mood, and began improvising and embellishing.

Again, Barbara tried to sing along, with the song's first line, which Doris prompted her with.

He knows things are wrong, and da da,
Da da-da da da da, da da-da da da da . .

Farewells after the tea were fond, and a promise was made for another get-together again soon. Doris said she'd call the professor in Princeton the next time she visited the Duke farm, to see if he were available. She reminded him that the farm was only twelve miles away from the university.

"Why didn't you say 'Hutton' when you introduced me?" said Barbara in the car, as she and Doris were on their way to Glen Cove. "You said, 'This is my friend Barbara'—that's all."

"He knew who you were the moment he saw you," said Doris.

"How do you know?"

"Babs, he's the smartest man in the world, and you're the second most famous woman. How could he not?"

"Well, you won that round."

"Doesn't that rather depend on what we learn about aluminum?"

Barbara gave Doris's shoulder an affectionate yet slightly aggressive little shove.

"*Second* most famous?" groused Barbara.

"Actually, third. After Eleanor Roosevelt and me."

CHAPTER 14

Ollie might be living in reduced circumstances, but he held that things should be done properly if they were done at all, so he had engaged a car and driver for his gala evening with Emma. He picked her up at the Belnord before the event and was dropping her there afterwards. Around midnight, they were heading north on Broadway, sitting in the back of a Lincoln town car.

"Doris knew Einstein?"

"They were friends until his death. She funded a quiet little program he put in place to get promising Blacks and women into his graduate physics institute."

"Students from Princeton?"

"From anywhere. Some were admitted even without a bachelor's degree."

"Wow."

"Some went on to NASA, some to the private sector or to teaching. They were very successful. You see, she liked to work behind the scenes."

"So I gather."

Ollie chuckled.

"And she could also have swum from Newport to Greenport," he said.

"What's that?"

"Never mind. So you and Artemis got along. Will you go to Monte Carlo?"

"I suppose so. If she invites me. I guess I will just have to pay for it myself."

"Good decision."

"And trust that it will pay off."

"It's called faith. And after a certain point, that's the thing you need if you want to make something big happen in this world—on top of all the clever stuff, like ideas and information. Full faith."

"It's a big risk for me."

"Of course it is. And the stakes are high. That's the price of admission for the game you want to play."

At home, after the gala, Emma changed into her sweats, made a cup of Sweet Dreams herbal tea, and sat down in front of her laptop. Usually, she wasn't aware of being alone in a sprawling four-bedroom apartment, but tonight she felt the place's echoes, its shadows. Wouldn't a smaller home suit her better, after all? She wanted to capture any thoughts or impressions about the evening, but first, before writing anything, she checked her calendar for the weeks that Artemis had said might work for a visit to Monaco. She checked her two flyer miles accounts for the current balance and determined that the trip would be possible without outlaying too much cash. Cursorily, she made a few notes on her impressions of Artemis, on the Windsor pin, on the beautiful *pas de deux* that had been on the ballet program, taken from a full-length, nineteenth-century ballet that she'd never heard of, whose convoluted story, summarized in the program, seemed awfully implausible—which prompted the question, What the hell did the Russian upper classes want to think about when they went out to the theater in 1870? What did they talk about when they came home afterward, to a light supper served by liveried servants in a fire-warmed salon? What do sapphires look like by candlelight?

Ollie's point about needing full faith for a project stuck with her. This was different, he said, from the conviction that a project should be successful, based on the confidence gained when project variables and assumptions were thoroughly excelled out in a spreadsheet over eighteen or twenty-four months. After all rational and strategic thoughts were worked out, there was still a more important factor that the greatest projects were never without, he explained: this faith by some "mover or shaker" that the thing was indispensable, fundamental. But Emma wondered, Why was this kind of faith so crucial? Because it inspired faith in others? Where did faith come from? Can you look for it, or must you just make yourself open to it and hope it finds you?

Something else Ollie said stuck with her. He said it in passing, the kind of thing that might come up in those long moments after a leisurely dinner, when you're in a reflective, philosophical mood—only Ollie jammed it into a brief aside as they were riding in the limo, where it sounded gratuitous and almost inappropriate, but as if he had been determined to get it in somewhere that evening and the opportunity was almost past. He said that her father had found his full faith in himself at last, and that Emma shouldn't judge him too harshly. Emma didn't respond to this remark, because the hour was late and they were almost at her door, but also because she found the remark presumptuous. She had never been explicit with Ollie about her distaste for his closeted ways and her assumption that her father had emulated some of them, and had been led to his death because of that. Yet Ollie seemed to have intuited both her distaste and its cause.

"He came to the magazine as a young star with faith in its mission, and for years, he did a damned good job of it," said Ollie. "But print was over, and maybe connoisseurship was, too. And your father got caught in a business-end play that just never could have worked."

"I don't know what that means."

"*Nota Bene* was already finished. His transfer to São Paulo and the publisher's idea of expanding the business globally online was only ever a pipe dream."

"Oh."

"Yet Martin knew it could be an opportunity for him personally, to follow a faith he'd always meant to do."

"With men."

"With men."

"I . . . don't know."

"With respect to you and your mom, I admired his move more than I can say," said Ollie. "It's something I could never do and will never do. I don't seem to have that faith. Which means I am condemned to be suspended between what I might have had—what maybe any human being has the right to have—and this other, perfectly good thing that I did have."

"What thing?"

"My friendship with Doris—which was actually a great thing."

This comment of Ollie's was what prompted Emma to make a few notes about her project. Who were women like Doris and what did they want? Maybe the Radetzky family business so far had been commenting on rich people's lives, and on the loveliest, most delightful moments in life that great art and precious possessions can bestow; and maybe that commentary had always, ridiculously, implied that the relationship between the possessions and the delightful moments was an entitlement of the rich and only of the rich. It was kind of a political impulse, after all, that impelled Emma to come up with the concept for this film in the first place; and maybe the whole effort was a little knee-jerk, the inevitable flowering of seeds planted during a liberal education and life on New York's affluent Upper West Side. But was there something more about people like Doris Duke and herself—something that they all had in common—that she needed to find and express with this film?

"There's a lot to tell you about the soul of these great women," Ollie told her. "It has nothing to do with jewels, but everything to do with intention, purpose, agency—things like that."

For one thing, Emma thought with a chuckle, those women wouldn't be dithering around with a husband who should have been an ex by now.

Clearly, that focus on his mother's ring was an important sign . . .

Emma took a sip of her tea.

And clearly Ollie has his suspicions . . .

Ollie didn't know Robert well, but now that Emma thought

about it, she remembered a reaction that Ollie had during their lunch, when she was explaining the nature of her and Robert's separation. Ollie winced ever so slightly when Emma said that this new arrangement was working fine, which she didn't think much of at the time. She believed on some level that the separation *was* working, which is why she said so. But Ollie's instinct, or at least his sharply honed curiosity, must have been working on a deeper level; he'd probably been too polite or respectful to express disapproval, and would not do so unless he were asked specifically for an opinion. Emma had not asked for one, and now she wished she had.

Then another thought struck her.

Lord, Kelly must think I'm a fool, too, and feel disloyal for wanting to tell me to dump my fool of a husband . . .

PART 3

DUTIES

"You're young, you're strong," said Dr. Lee. "The tumor is relatively small. You're a good candidate for surgery."

Emma and Kelly were at Memorial Sloan Kettering, New York's premier cancer center, in the office of Dr. Catherine Lee, the oncologist whom Dr. Harmon, the rheumatologist, had referred her to. Dr. Lee had sympathetically delivered the news that there was indeed a soft tissue cancer in Emma's elbow. Its proper name was synovial sarcoma, and Dr. Lee explained that its origin was likely genetic—a faulty gene, damaged DNA—but that no one could say for sure. It was unlikely to have been caused by playing tennis. The tumor was in an early stage and "very treatable."

To one side of the doctor's desk was a digital screen displaying images of Emma's elbow.

"'Synovial' just means joint," said Dr. Lee.

"Curable?" said Emma.

"Success rates are getting better all the time. Up to eighty-five percent of patients are clear after five years, with this sort of thing; seventy-five percent after ten years."

"So that's relatively good," said Kelly.

"Quite good," said Dr. Lee. "Now, surgery is usually the main treatment for soft tissue sarcomas like this—small, local. The tumor is removed, along with a small bit of the normal tissue surrounding it. The limb is saved . . ."

Emma was chilled to contemplate the idea of the limb not being saved.

"Ucch," she uttered.

"But as I say, I'm concerned about this," said the doctor, indicating a tiny spot on the MRI image. "The tumor is small, but it's very close to the ulnar nerve, see? That's one of the most important nerves in your arm, so we want to protect it, at all costs."

"Okay . . ." said Emma.

"So what I am recommending, after consulting with my surgical team, is a course of radiation first, to shrink the tumor, which should give us more room to operate in such a small space, and reduce the risk of nerve damage."

Under the doctor's immaculate white lab coat, she was wearing a sleek, green wool dress with long sleeves. Emma found herself both amused and ashamed to be thinking, at such a moment, about what the doctor was wearing: clothing nice enough to show good taste and judgment, but not so nice as to raise suspicions of vanity or extravagance. Emma forced herself not to think about how expensively manicured the doctor's colorless fingernails looked.

"Okay," said Emma, trying her best to hear and remember everything that Dr. Lee was saying. She was glad that Kelly was there to help with this task, as well as to provide emotional support. "So the radiation. . . ?"

"Right," said Dr. Lee. "It's called neoadjutant therapy. All that means is treatment delivered before the surgery. We treat just the area with an external beam—we can do it here in the hospital."

"How does that go? How often? How long?"

"I want to call in a radiation oncologist, but it's probably once a day, except for weekends, for several weeks."

"Oh Lord. Several weeks?"

"In a case like this, yes—maybe four to six. Each treatment is relatively short and efficient. Are you in the neighborhood?"

"Across the park."

"Well, that's not too bad. We could also look for a treatment center nearer where you live or work."

Emma shook her head.

"I have to remember that we're lucky to be living in a place and time where such treatments are available, right. . . ?" she said, trying to calm herself.

Dr. Lee nodded.

"I wish all my patients had such a good attitude."

"Side effects?"

"Fewer than with chemo. Maybe some nausea, fatigue, skin irritation at the site, but everyone is different. You are otherwise strong and healthy, so that's in our favor. And we will probably give you a drug to protect the normal tissue from damage."

"Hair loss?"

"Probably little or none, in your case."

Emma took in a deep breath and let it out slowly.

"Starting when?" she said.

"As soon as possible," said Dr. Lee.

"And you're sure it's this sarcoma?"

The doctor nodded soberly.

"I'm afraid so."

"And then the surgery?"

"Let's see where we are after radiation."

After the appointment, Emma and Kelly ducked into a nearby Greek restaurant, for some lunch.

"I've always taken care of myself, I've always eaten well, avoided added salt and sugar . . ." said Emma, over her plate of *tonosalata*.

"I know," said Kelly.

"I meditate when I can, I don't smoke . . ."

"I know."

"Is it environmental? Are we all doomed?"

"Dr. Lee said it was genetic."

"I suppose I should talk to my mother and my father's brother, Murray . . ."

"About family history?"

"Yeah."

"That might be a good idea—I mean, just to see what you can learn."

"It's not going to cure me, though, is it? Knowing any-thing . . ."

Kelly reached across the table and took Emma's hand.
"The bright side is that Dr. Lee said you're a good candidate. It's in an early stage, and you'll probably be able to work normally, even around those radiation appointments."

"Work!"

"It can be a great focus, Ems . . ." said Kelly.

"I know," said Emma. "If anything, this makes me more determined."

"Good for you."

Kelly sat back and grinned.

"Did you know that during the Middle Ages, they treated people medically with powdered gemstones?"

"Of course they did. Powdered frogs, too, I'll bet."

"No, really. A client told me all about it. They're either ground in a mortar with rose water or burned to ash and made into a paste."

"Yikes."

"Emerald for the liver, ruby for the heart . . ."

"Makes sense."

"And powdered pearl for just about everything."

"Like a daily multivitamin."

"Yes!"

"Sounds expensive, grinding up pearls."

"Well, you know—the rich."

"And for cancer?"

Kelly brightened, glad to remember so many details from the conversation with her client.

"Ashes of diamond!" she said cheerfully.

"Can there be such a thing? Can diamonds burn?"

"According to ayurvedic medicine, you shouldn't eat them raw. And we have several nice ones for under a million coming up at the 'Magnificent Jewels' sale."

"Now, I wonder if my medical insurance would cover something like that."

They were headed in different directions after lunch. As they were saying goodbye on the sidewalk in front of the restaurant, Emma suddenly took hold of Kelly's forearm.

"Kel, I should divorce Robert, shouldn't I?" she said. Somehow, it was easier to get the question out outside, with traffic rushing past, instead of at the table. "Really, we should divorce, he and I, shouldn't we?"

Kelly produced a sad smile and nodded yes. She looked relieved that this issue was out in the open.

"I don't know him as well as you do, of course, but . . ." began Kelly.

"He's a dope and I should divorce him."

The issue felt much less explosive now that they were talking about it.

"I want you to be open to something better, if it isn't working," said Kelly in a measured way. "Admittedly, it's a big step, and your feelings are complicated. . . ."

"No, this is helpful, Kel, it is. Let's stay focused on the film, but this is really helpful."

CHAPTER 16

Kelly had arranged for Christie's to make available a small studio for shooting the interviews and B-roll of jewelry pieces that Emma needed for her film. This was done at no cost, as Christie's agreed to become a sponsor of the project, with the understanding that the house could arrange for "two or three" of its clients, if they agreed, to be featured in the film with their property. There was still the cost of the crew to cover—people and equipment for sound, light, and camera—but Emma had decided to follow Ollie's advice and "go for it" on faith. She would be paying out of pocket until either a sponsor stepped forward or the last of the many grants she had applied for—still pending—was approved.

Christie's New York occupied a 300,000-square-foot facility at Rockefeller Center, featuring a main saleroom with double-height ceiling and two smaller salerooms, expansive exhibition spaces and galleries, and private viewing rooms and offices, in addition to its spectacular Sol LeWitt lobby. The studio assigned to Emma was on an upper floor and featured a small pantry and seating area at one end and a large, empty stage space at the other. Kelly had seen to the provisioning for the day—bottled water, fruit juice, fruit, and muffins, in addition to coffee and tea—and the setup in the stage area of two chairs and a table, brilliantly lit by lighting equipment that was both mounted on stands and suspended from a ceiling grid.

The day was planned for two sessions, the first of which was accomplished quickly and efficiently: a few minutes of footage from various angles of one of the star offerings of Christie's upcoming "Magnificent Jewels" sale: the emerald-and-diamond necklace with pendant by Bulgari that Richard Burton bought for Elizabeth Taylor while shooting *Cleopatra* in Rome, just after the two stars had fallen rapturously—and scandalously, since they were both married—in love. Right on time, the necklace was brought in by a member of the Fine Jewelry department, accompanied by a dark-suited security man; the necklace was admired by all, set up on a revolving, black-velvet–lined display bust, and shot by Tom, the camera guy, with only a few, minor adjustments in lighting by Scott, the lighting guy; then the necklace was taken away. Then Emma and Kelly set up, on the table, some of the historic original sketches of the necklace that had been loaned to Christies by Bulgari for the sale, and those were shot; after which Emma and Kelly pored over them breathlessly.

"The necklace was bought at auction here, in the 2011 sale of Taylor's estate," explained Kelly. "Thirteen million, including the pendant. And now it's going on the block again."

"No chance we could get the seller. . . ?" said Emma.

Kelly grimaced.

"I asked," she said. "No dice."

The necklace, made in 1962, was formed with a graduated series of sixteen rectangular-cut and square-cut stones, each framed by a diamond surround, spaced by graduated circular-cut, marquise-cut, and pear-shaped diamond quatrefoils. The rectangular-cut pendant emerald attached to the necklace, also framed in diamonds, dated from 1958 and could also be worn on its own as a brooch. The sixty-year-old sketches of the piece were exquisitely done in ink and gouache on heavy gray paper, mounted on board, and protected by a hinged sheet of tracing paper. Emma was mesmerized by the artistic expertise employed to depict the gemstones and platinum—tiny strokes of ink and daubs of paint to deftly emulate crystalline sparkle and metallic glow.

"We had originally thought that these might be Barbara Hutton's Romanoff emeralds repurposed, remember?" said Kelly.

"They're not?"

"Apparently not, according to my colleague's contact at Bulgari. They said that Hutton sold her tiara to Van Cleef and Arpels to fund her last divorce, and the set was broken up and sold separately. That was in '65—well after the Burton purchase, obviously."

"What a shame," said Emma. "That tiara was divine."

"At least it wasn't lost."

"Lost?"

"More Hutton lore here, from the Bulgari woman. Hutton was living in Rome in the seventies, falling apart physically. She fell in her hotel suite and broke her leg or hip or something, which wouldn't heal. So she skipped out of Italy for Cedars-Sinai in L.A., leaving a whole bunch of her jewelry for safekeeping with some Italian count who was connected, unbeknownst to her, to the neo-Fascist movement. When she came back to Rome a year later, the count claimed to know nothing about the jewelry—though rumor had it that he sold everything for the MSI, the Movimento Sociale Italiano, the neo-Fascist party."

"No!"

"Interesting, huh? The Marie Antoinette pearls, a ruby tiara of the Empress Eugénie . . . gone."

"Wow. And the Pasha—King Farouk's diamond?"

"Not that. She must have worn that to the hospital."

"Of course she did."

"And, get this: she simply wrote off the loss. Apparently, she didn't want to sue the count, because it would expose her to a trial and cross-examination."

"That Barbara!"

"Chubb wouldn't pay the insurance, either, since technically it wasn't a theft."

Emma returned to studying the Bulgari sketch, marveling at how well the artist's technique could render an emerald and imitate some of the stone's magic—by hand, in the days before computer rendering.

"That pendant, Kel—did you look closely at it?"

"Of course I did."

"Such a pure, deep green," mused Emma. "So free of the cloudiness and inclusions you see in lesser stones. You know, green glass can pack quite a punch. Lalique makes some lovely colored crystal rings. But the optics of a proper gemstone. . . ! I think you really have to be present for a cut gem, really look at it, see how the cutter optimized the material's optical qualities, in this deceptively tiny theater of light. . . ."

"Do you even like jewels?" interjected the cameraman, Tom, an old friend of Emma's from their St. Ann's days. "I never heard you talk like that before."

"Of course I like them," said Emma. "Doesn't everybody?"

"Not necessarily."

"Some people find them terribly dynamic, Tom—embodying the geological forces of their creation. Think of it! Over a hundred thousand years in the ground, of the earth but somehow extraterrestrial, emanating this great power from inside their crystalline architecture. . . ."

"Yeah, and some people think that thirteen million dollars could buy a lot of school lunches."

"C'mon, Tom, that's not fair. . . ."

"Hello, hello!" said Ollie brightly, entering the room with a flourish, accompanied by his friend, Mrs. Welland.

A round of greetings and the dropping of personal belongings was followed by a brief conference on how Ollie's session would run. Emma would interview him on set—at the table and chairs set up in the light; there were two stationary cameras and a hand-held one; they would go for three twenty-minute chunks, if that was alright with him.

"Of course," said Ollie, looking sharp in a well-tailored suit. "I hope you don't mind that I brought Liz along. I know you're on a budget, and there's no one for makeup, so Liz can touch me up if I need it. We just had the nicest lunch."

It turned out that Ollie had had some media training and was fairly smooth on camera. Emma explained that her film would include expert commentary about several of the great women she would be featuring, and Ollie would be used for context and commentary about the women he had known, including his friends Doris Duke and Barbara Hutton. Fed questions and comments by Emma, Ollie listened carefully and responded directly, speaking for the most part with a charming, upbeat mien, though every so often his corroborative and illustrative asides were ramble-y and not quite to the point.

"I've been thinking a lot about Duke and Hutton," he said, "and I think it's important to start with what we've been told about them and why we were told it, by the first entities to talk about them, the newspapers of the teens and 1920s. Remember, the scale of newspaper audiences and influence had been growing at a phenomenal rate since the turn of the century, and the appetites for muckraking and yellow journalism were really opening up a new mass market. So there was an automatic context for approaching any story about the richest baby girls in the world. They never had a chance."

Emma interrupted, as the camera kept rolling.

"Ollie, let me ask you to say that last bit again, but as a full sentence."

"What bit?"

"'They never had a chance.'"

"What about it?"

"They never had a chance at what?"

"Oh—okay, sure." Ollie composed himself and restated the line. "They never had a chance to be seen as normal human beings, which is something that surely everybody needs."

Emma made a chef's kiss gesture, and Ollie continued. Sure, they were rich, he said, but the most important thing he wanted people to know about them is that they were generous—generous in their own ways, in sometimes very different kinds of situations, which affected how they lived their lives, defined their marriages and other personal relationships, and governed the legacies that they left, financial and otherwise.

"I don't know if other people of the era defined themselves quite so very much in terms of the money they did or didn't have," said Ollie, "but that kind of self-definition was forced on these girls, and they made the best of it. For most people, you'd call this kind of self-definition superficial, but for these girls, it wasn't. Their wealth was an essential part of them—the newspapers weren't wrong about that part; and it was up to the girls to try—to *try!*—to turn this condition into something positive."

"And did they?" asked Emma. "Full sentence."

Ollie nodded.

"Duke and Hutton did so much good in their lifetimes, in terms of philanthropy, both organized and impromptu. And of course, Duke left a very vigorous charitable foundation, which is active to this day."

Emma winked at Ollie as a sign to keep going.

"I mean, how do you amplify this impulse to be generous, to share?" continued Ollie. "Both women started giving money away on their own, as teenagers. Why not? On some basic level, it feels good to help someone, to make someone else feel good—before the strings that can be attached to such acts present themselves. To some degree, both Doris and Barbara used their generosity as an expression of their humanity. That is, since it was so hard for them to be simple human beings and to do what other simple human beings did, coexist with each other, they both wanted to extend their good will with gifts. Both of them, by current standards, were completely haphazard in their philanthropy at this point, as girls. Doris was a little more organized, since there was the university that depended on her patronage, but she was still a bit scattershot about how she gave her personal money away. Same with Barbara—scattershot. She once gave one of her school classmates a horse, though this turned out to be a great burden for the other girl, and Barbara was miffed when the horse was returned."

Ollie sniffed, enjoying an amusing thought.

"And generosity even became part of a little game that the girls invented with each other," he said, "pretending to be rivals for the sake of the newspapers, which was kind of a naughty lark for them. Can I give an example? I'm not supposed to be going chronologically, am I?"

"Everything will be edited," said Emma. "Please feel free to speak as you would at a party."

"At a party?!" said Ollie. "Well, then . . . I can do *that*. Once,

when I was at Shangri La at the same time Barbara was there—
that's the palace Doris built in Hawaii—Barbara gave the majordomo a gold Rolex as a thank-you for some service he'd performed,
and it was reported in the papers that Doris was furious about
this, because the majordomo was one of Doris's beaux. But of
course, that was just the game. They staged the whole thing.
Well, not the gift itself and not the friendship between Doris
and the young man. In my experience, people of great means
are always giving away gold watches and diamond rings, because they enjoy shopping so much that they always have extra things on hand that are easier to give away than to return.
Who has time to return things? In Paris, once, Barbara casually
offered an acquaintance a diamond bracelet, and the acquaintance hesitated, feeling that she didn't deserve it; and Barbara
just snatched the thing away and immediately gave it to someone else, as if the original recipient were spoiling all the fun.
That story, by the way, was also amplified in the press by Doris
as part of their game."

Ollie took a sip from the glass of water that had been provided for him.

"This almost profligate generosity was the flip side of the no-
tion of pleasure as a sacrament that Doris, in particular, held
dear—about wanting to share pleasure and plenty with others,
in a naïve, almost innocent way. But sharing like this can often
prove as hard for rich people to achieve as it was for, oh, the
early Christians to share the faith through the rituals of holy
mass. Over time, some people will get it, but many won't."

"That's quite a thought," said Emma. "I take it that the possession and display of precious jewelry fits into your analysis
somehow?"

"You bet," said Ollie. "Let me give you a story. I remember
once arriving early for a party at Doris's penthouse on Park
Avenue—this was New York, mid-fifties. It was an unusually
warm Indian summer evening. She was alone in her bedroom
suite in a slip, having had a nap and a bath, and poised to select
just the right jewelry to resonate with the infinite possibilities of

the particular evening she'd planned. Shortly she would be stepping out to greet guests in her living room, itself a sort of stage set she had created for the pursuit of interesting pleasure—not idle pleasure, mind you. The evening was going to feature important discussion! I found her considering the choice between a strand of pearls, paired with a long blue dress, and a string of jade beads, paired with a long green dress, all laid out before her there on the bed. She knew she wanted luster, not sparkle, but for her there was so much more to go into the decision. So she stepped out onto the terrace and took a deep breath of fresh air, her choice of attire being, she explained, dependent on what the city was saying about itself that evening. I was amused, and did have a thought about the millions of other, less fortunate New Yorkers who at that very moment might be worrying about having something to eat or a place to sleep that night, or about taxes, or school work; and here was a Park Avenue priestess in her slip, trying to *be there* for the divinely sensual potentialities of the moment, as some guru had once suggested she should do. And you might think it a little nuts, but this was simply her way of really being present, to use the term for it that we use now. Doris was convinced that embodying and preaching this evangel was the moral and ethical thing to do, if one had the means. Her jewels were part of it. This was something she said she took from Gandhi and Einstein and the rest. . . ."

Tom, the cameraman, cleared his throat, unnoticed by Ollie.

"She went with the jade," said Ollie. "Now, Barbara, on the other hand—I don't think Barbara was as tuned in as Doris was to the sacramental aspect of jewelry. So when Barbara bought the Pasha diamond, for instance, all that was on her mind, I'd wager, was an expensive piece of merchandise, forty-odd carats, rather than some gemological apex of chthonic metaphysics. . . ."

Ollie halted.

"I may be going a little far astray here, aren't I?" he said.

"You're fine," said Emma patiently. "We're just getting started. This is good for context. We'll get there."

"We'll get where? Where are we going?"

Emma wanted to stay focused on what she was getting from Ollie's comments.

"You make Doris sound quite big spiritually," she said.

Ollie considered this for a moment.

"She *was* big," he said. "Big enough not to be overawed by million-dollar baubles. That is certainly a bigness, isn't it? On the level of James Bond, if not Gandhi or Einstein. And the funny thing is that I saw their jewels the way they did, not the way the press or the public or their boyfriends did. I was never in the suitor class, you see. Though that role of the walker was well in decline even as I began to be groomed for it. I went out with them simply as a friend. And the jewels were only part of their way of life; wearing them was some kind of duty—necessary glamour in the primal sense, meaning magical . . ."

"Oh, my God," said Kelly, who was watching the shoot attentively. "We were just talking about this, before you arrived—that aspect of glamour."

Ollie raised an eyebrow.

"Ah, well, all that has shifted now, hasn't it? And maybe that's fine . . . Liz, how's my forehead?"

A little later, during the break in the shooting, Kelly took Emma aside, while Mrs. Welland was lightly applying a bit of powder to Ollie's forehead and nose.

"He's rambling, right?" said Kelly.

"Big time," said Emma, with a patient smile.

"'Chthonic metaphysics'?"

"I know."

They giggled.

"But we let him go on for now, right?" said Kelly.

"I think so," said Emma. "Even if we use a snip of it, it's good to have. Besides, if this warms him up for juicier stuff later or in the next shoot, it will have been worth it."

"You're so good, Ems."

"It's called directing, yo."

Then the shoot continued.

"Let me give you the big picture first," said Ollie. "Hitler invades Poland in September of '39, and Poland's allies Britain and France immediately declare war on Germany. Hitler takes Paris the following June, and declares war on the United States four days after Japan attacks Pearl Harbor, in December of '41. I was only a kid, but I well remember my parents having to put plans for a new car on hold, since the future was suddenly contingent on an uncertain outcome. Yet the great masses of the world, except in war-torn territories, went about their business almost as usual, coping as best they could with shortages and restrictions. And for people like Doris and Barbara, for whom under most circumstances even an act of God meant just a higher price or minor rescheduling, the war worked devilishly on their sense of privilege, as seasonal patterns of social migration were interrupted, family fortunes were threatened, assets and properties were sometimes requisitioned. Fathers and sons of these families didn't necessarily put their bodies on the line, as other Americans did, but they certainly were susceptible to a new kind of shame or pride around how they responded to the war effort . . .

"I bring this up because Doris and Barbara really came into their own during the war. It's one of the good things that the experience of war can do for a person. Superficially, there were the obvious things for people like them to do. Shangri La was only fifteen miles away from Pearl Harbor, and after the attack, Doris offered the place to the Army as a kind of officers' club, which they refused as too impractical, though Army brass did avail themselves of the pool and tennis courts. Barbara's London place, Winfield House, was more or less commandeered for use by the RAF. The officers played football there in the gardens, and one of the teams was called 'Barbara's Own'—isn't that funny? Cary Grant, by the way, whom Barbara married in '42 and divorced in '45, felt that his dear wife never got the credit she deserved for her wartime generosity. Rather nobly, I think, he complained about a radio report by Edward R. Murrow that Barbara had abandoned her home and fled London. Cary called Murrow and invited him to the house and see it in use, after which Murrow apologized on the air. Barbara did, as the newspapers reported, continue to party, satisfied that her six-year-old son was in someone's very capable, well-paid hands, but she was sending money to the French Resistance. And she took refuge where she could, in Paris and London and in people's villas on the Riviera, as a card-carrying member of Elsa Maxwell's caravan of lotus eaters. They were like characters in a Graham Greene novel, floating giddily from masquerade balls to week-long house parties, sipping cocktails on a terrace in Juan-les-Pins while the smoke was clearing after a day's battle on the other side of the Mediterranean, which might determine who would still have a fortune the next morning and who would not.

"Anyway, Doris was hellbent on doing something, joining something. I think the war finally freed her of the last link to that old-fashioned society thing. Actually, she was dropped from the Social Register around that time—they both were—probably because of too much fucking around. Can I say 'fucking'? It was an open secret that Doris had been pregnant with Duke Kahanamoku's child, and then, after a miscarriage or possibly an abortion, she referred for decades to the girl, whom she posthumously named Arden, like some kind of guardian angel. And then she started going with her Shangri La majordomo, Johnny Gomez, well before she divorced Jimmy Cromwell, in '43.

"After the divorce, she was free to be herself, which during the war meant doing her duty."

For Doris, Ollie explained, duty meant using her high-level connections and deep pockets to secure work volunteering at the American Seaman's Club in Alexandria, Egypt, and joining the OSS as a "minor undercover operative" overseas. Even as the War Department kept trying to get her back to the U.S. for "proper training," and as air, maritime, and rail travel across borders was restricted to officially sanctioned business, Doris kept flying about Europe freely in special planes, on special passes, connecting with special people and learning what she could about relevant military and political matters. Everyone loved hobnobbing with the famous adventuress. Then, with no journalistic training or background, she got herself a position as a war correspondent for the International News Service in Rome, for which she wrote articles like "Doris Duke Finds Widow of Il Duce Happy in Exile" and "Doris Duke Finds Squalor in Rome." She may have entered wartime service partly in continuing pursuit of her rakish MP Alec Cunningham-Reid, Ollie said, but soon enough, she found other soldiers to suit her interest, including one young Brit who had no idea that his jaunty new squeeze was an internationally known heiress. By the end of the war, she was working in an Air Force hospital, helping wounded soldiers make tape recordings to send back to their hometown radio stations. She was always enormously popular with the men.

"Now, this was almost twenty years before I met Doris," said Ollie, "but we had so much time together, when she would tell me stories of the old days. I think she was a little proud that at the end of the war, she was more desirable to men than ever, even in her mid-thirties, even in that gawky way of hers; while Barbara, the conventionally pretty one, was getting obsessed about gaining weight and losing her hair, always on crash diets and bingeing on caviar and blinis, and sinking deeper into alcohol and drugs.

"Doris met Rubi at that time, in Rome—the notorious playboy Porfirio Rubirosa—her second husband, who wound up being Barbara's fifth. But that's another story."

CHAPTER 17

May 1947

When Barbara told Doris that they were going to be looking at Barbara's new horses, Doris naturally thought they would be visiting a stable. A week before, Barbara had visited Duke Farms and *ooh*ed and *ahh*ed over two new Arabian thoroughbreds that Doris had bought, Pharaoh and Moonshine. Since these were some of the most expensive animals on the planet, Doris didn't see how Barbara could better her with any new horses of her own. Yet Barbara challenged Doris to come with her to see these superb new creatures because, she said, they were "worth their weight in gold." So gamely Doris went along with her friend, one spring afternoon.

It was a bracingly aggressive challenge, which Doris liked. In the two years since the end of the war, their little private game was beginning to take on a more sharply competitive edge, especially from Barbara's side, since her enjoyment of her triumphs seemed to be growing in direct proportion to her fears about the loss of youth and beauty. They were both thirty-five, but in very different physical shape for their age. Doris was regularly playing tennis and golf, and swimming, surfing, and scuba diving in the ocean, while Barbara, who had ditched third husband Cary Grant, rarely did anything physically demanding and, indeed, had spent much of her honeymoon with her fourth husband, Prince Igor Troubetzkoy, being treated for a kidney ailment in a Swiss clinic, and then undergoing the removal of an ovarian tumor and both her ovaries.

After Barbara picked up Doris at home, the car headed not north toward Connecticut horse country, nor west toward rural New Jersey, but across the Queensboro Bridge into Long Island City, then down across Newtown Creek into Greenpoint, Brooklyn. Doris was mystified, but asked no questions; and conversation between the women in the car was only small talk, as the rules of the game had evolved to require a certain decorum between the players when directly involved in a contest.

"I saw Cary last week," said Barbara.

"Did you find yourself craving more 'grievous mental stress'?" asked Doris mockingly. The phrase, taken from Barbara's divorce papers, had been tossed around gleefully in the press.

"He and Lance are still very close. And I'm still in this tug-of-war with Kurt"—second husband Reventlow, the boy's father—"who wants Lance in Europe."

"How old is Lance now?"

"Eleven."

"It's a shame. I thought Cary made a good stepfather. I was hoping that you and he would last."

"So was I! But Dodo, after a few weeks, we both knew that it wouldn't last. Cary's a nice guy, sure, but kind of a homebody. We never went out. I hardly saw anyone else. And I thought I would be getting Hollywood! He loathed my friends. I can't live that way."

"Your new prince isn't quite as handsome, is he?"

"No, nobody is. I'll give Cary that. But he's soft, in a way."

"Cary Grant is soft?"

"His personality. Sometimes practically feminine. I prefer a man with a bit more . . ."

Barbara made a ladylike punching gesture and Doris nodded.

"So do I, sister," said Doris. "And you gave him that pretty little Utrillo."

Barbara smiled mirthlessly.

"It wasn't so little. Anyway, he didn't ask me for any alimony—like the first two. So that's something."

The building where they arrived was obviously no horse stable. Located in an almost treeless industrial neighborhood of one- and two-story structures, with loading docks and feature-less parking lots, this was a part of New York that Doris had never seen before. Painted in white block letters on the red brick façade of the modest factory-type building was BEDI-RASSY FOUNDRY, above the main entrance and front windows.

Doris looked quizzical.

"No, we won't be looking at horseshoes," said Barbara.

Inside, in a cramped hallway furnished only with three wooden side chairs with cracked leather upholstery, they were met by a man wearing coveralls and an apron over a white shirt and tie.

"Hello, Miss Hutton. Mr. Haseltine hasn't arrived yet."

"Thank you, Harvey," said Barbara. "May I see them right away?"

"Of course," said Harvey. "They're in the studio."

Doris and Barbara were shown into a locked room whose central worktable was cluttered with drawings, sketches, blueprints, and examples, presumably, of metal items that had been cast at the foundry: a decorative architectural panel in a geometric Art Deco relief design; a gracefully posed human hand reaching upward; a stylized portrait bust of a stern-looking woman with hair arranged in a bun. An interior window looked out onto the foundry's work floor, which featured a furnace, several cranes and worktables, hanging hooks and chains, racks of metal tools, stacks and shelves of various kinds of molds and forms, and what appeared to be a bin of sand. A team of men in heavy aprons, gloves, goggles, and safety helmets was at work lifting a crucible of bright-hot liquid from the furnace, setting it down, and ladling liquid from it into some kind of form.

"It's a fine art foundry," said Doris.

"Very good," said Barbara.

"We've just been commissioned by the Marines to do a monument for Washington, D.C.," said Harvey. "Do you know that photo that was in all the papers, raising the flag at Iwo Jima? A sculptor is rendering that in 3-D, life-size, and we've got the commission to manufacture it."

"Fascinating," said Doris.

"Is this them?" said Barbara, referring to a square yard of canvas that was draped over what seemed to be two foot-high objects.

"Yes, ma'am. We haven't buffed them yet," said Harvey, gently pulling off the canvas. "Mr. Haseltine said to wait until he could inspect them."

Revealed were two golden sculptures of horses' heads. They were fairly realistic but in an unfinished state, with small cavities for the eyes and ears and at the top of the head, and with raised strips lined with series of small holes, depicting bridles and defining the bottom edge of the horses' necks.

"The eyes and bridles will be jeweled," said Barbara, softly feeling the surface of one of the heads. On her finger, her Pasha diamond, the size of a silver dollar, flashed enticingly. "And each head will have a feather or turban jewel on top. And Lakshmi's mane will also be jeweled—that's the mare. Indra is the stallion."

"My goodness," said Doris. "Do you mean those are gold?"

Barbara didn't bother to contain her satisfaction.

"Cast twenty-four-karat gold," she cooed.

Even in the office's fluorescent light, the two sculptures glowed warmly with a sumptuous, beguiling yellow. Several times, Doris had seen gold bullion—bars that Buck Duke stored in a private vault in Zürich, along with several drawers of unset gemstones. But these horse heads comprised the largest amount of gold she had ever seen, wrought into objects, outside of a vault or museum.

"How do you cast gold?" said Doris.

"Same as bronze," said Harvey. "You model whatever you want in clay. Mr. Haseltine modeled these, of course. Then you make a plaster cast with the lost-wax method, just like the Greeks did, and pour the liquid gold into that and let it cool. We did these the day before yesterday."

For a moment, Doris was speechless. Was it the stylized nobility of the sculptural heads that was so affecting? The palpable, individual personality of each of the horses? The fact that, unfinished as they were, the objects were as haunting as the relics of an ancient civilization? The fact that they were made of, oh, pounds and pounds of gold; or that sometime in the previous week, an armored car had pulled up at this obscure factory in Brooklyn, to deliver a load of gold bars?

Doris thought better of asking how much the heads weighed. But to a question she asked about security, Harvey explained that the project was "as secret as the atomic bomb."

"Game, set, and match, Babs," Doris said, extending her hand. "Really. I'm flabbergasted."

"I thought you might be," said Barbara, shaking her friend's hand. "Cary done and dusted, a year ago; now this. I'm doing rather well, aren't I?"

An assistant popped into the office, a man also dressed in coveralls.

"Excuse me, Harv—Haseltine is here."

Doris and Barbara looked up to see an elegantly dressed man of around seventy enter the foundry's office. Barbara rose to greet him warmly.

"*Cher maître*," she said, "so good to see you again. May I present my friend, Doris Jones? Doris, this is the sculptor Herbert Haseltine."

Haseltine greeted the women courteously but was clearly fixated on the golden heads. He stepped over to them impatiently.

"Harvey, they look pretty good, pretty good indeed," he said.

"We're quite happy with the way they turned out," said Harvey.

"They're brilliant," said Barbara. "They are going to be masterpieces."

The sculptor picked up one of the heads and turned it over. It was hollow, though the gold was quite thick, making the thing almost too heavy for an old man to handle easily. He gave the horse's neck a sharp tap with a knuckle, producing a dull *thung* sound, like an untuned bell.

Haseltine was American, Barbara explained, as the sculptor and the foundryman discussed details of the buffing process. Born in Rome, his father a well-known painter, he now lived and worked in Paris and would be bringing the heads there for finishing.

"We could only get the gold on this side of the Atlantic," said Barbara, while the men conferred. "It's been quite an odyssey with these horse heads. Herbert does the best horses, of course—he's known for that. I ran into him before the war at a Paris salon, where he was showing a new bronze head, a little larger than these. I found him charming—I love the passion he has to capture the animals' personality! He told me about having been commissioned by a maharaja to do these wonderful golden portraits. . . ."

"Portraits. . . ?" said Doris.

"Yes, they're real horses—the maharaja's favorites! But then the maharaja lost all his money or something, so Herbert had only the clay models. The detailing, those lovely braids, the jeweled bridles, see?—he took those right out of those Moghul miniatures. I was so touched when he said he was looking for a new patron to execute his vision. You know what a soft touch I am."

"You're a softy, alright," said Doris.

"He has the best patrons—Edward VII and Queen Alexandra, Prince Schönburg-Hartenstein of Vienna . . . I had to step up."

"Well, dear, they're magnificent."

"To be mounted on globes of rock crystal, I think. Either that or lapis, or maybe malachite."

"Malachite might be nice."

"The maharaja had assembled most of the stones. I simply bought them from him. We're working with a jeweler who knows how to mount these things—diamonds, pearls, rubies, sapphires, emeralds, garnets, and jade. Oh, and rock crystal for a feather that will be on top of Lakshmi's head. Isn't that cute? There are sketches around here somewhere."

"Quite a nice change from ordering couture, no? Buttons and pockets and linings. . . ?"

"That's just the thing, Dodo—I've missed clothes so much! You can't imagine. And I am finally going back to Balenciaga.

You have no idea how inconvenient it was, during those war years. I know you love your department stores—and we will cure you of that—but can I tell you. . . ?"

September 1943

Four years earlier, on the brink of the occupation of Paris during World War II, many of the non-French designers, including the American Mainbocher, the British Molyneux, and the Italian Schiaparelli, either closed their houses or fled the country for places like London and New York. Chanel closed her *maison* but kept her perfume and cosmetics boutique open, and lived, during the occupation, at the Nazi-occupied Ritz Hotel with her high-ranking Nazi lover, Baron Hans Gunther von Dincklage. But scores of the *haute couture* houses did remain open, after negotiations with the Nazis that were led by designer Lucien Lelong, who was tried after the war for collaboration. A supply of enough of the luxury fabrics needed by these houses to keep their business going was sometimes unofficially secured, and the customers included the wives of Nazi officials who needed to acquire special permission cards to buy fashion there—despite Nazi ideology's disapproval of Paris fashion and the slender, non-Aryan, "decadent and corruptive" feminine body that Paris idealized. Customers also included a sprinkling of British and American women who were brave enough to travel during wartime and rich enough to get their hands on the travel papers necessary to admit them to occupied France. Balenciaga, who had left Spain in 1937 because of the Spanish Civil War and reopened his business in Paris, was beginning to be highly celebrated just before the Nazis' arrival, and he was one of the designers who decided to keep their *maisons* open during the Occupation.

An ardent fan of this prodigious "master of masters," Barbara was one of the women who managed to make it to Balenciaga's salon during this dark period. One always needed some nice new clothes, of course, but even with the help of nannies, motherhood of a seven-year-old handful like Lance—obstreperous, demanding, trying hard to be one of the adults—was taking Barbara off her social course. His birth had nearly killed her, after all. She was feeling that, despite a war, she needed to re-assert the sense of herself that she was most comfortable with. The answer was new couture fashion.

For the city of Paris, both occupied by and resisting an enemy, it was a decidedly surreal period, made especially chilling by the lively conversation and loud laughter among natives and occupiers that continued to radiate from the city's sidewalk cafés, which the Nazis kept open. Situated in a stately six-story townhouse at 10 Avenue George V, built in 1887, the house of Balenciaga tried its best to welcome its guests as warmly as possible, despite the new wartime regulations.

"Welcome, Miss Hutton," said Nicholas, Balenciaga's chief business aide, in the house's dignified, white marble entry hall. "I hope you are comfortably installed."

"I am down the street at the George, as usual—thank you, Nicholas," said Barbara. "But the selection of mineral water has become so limited."

Nicholas was not sure whether or not his customer was making a joke.

"Well, the war . . ." he said.

"They've got a cellar full of wine, don't they?" snapped Barbara. "Why wouldn't they store some Vittel down there, too?"

Nicholas, a punctilious young man in a snappy blue suit, had no answer for this question, so he merely maintained his placid demeanor. Surely Miss Hutton had heard that several hotels in the spa town of Vittel were being used by the Nazis as an internment center.

"And Mr. Grant?"

"I am alone, Nicholas. Mr. Grant is in Hollywood, making a picture. Like the fashion industry, Hollywood soldiers on."

"Very good, Miss Hutton. Now, if we may only see . . ."

"See what?"

Then a buoyant salutation came from the grand staircase.

"Barbara, *charmante*! How are you?"

Descending the stairs in a rapid, graceful patter was Vladzio, the Franco-Polish millionaire who was both Balenciaga's backer and his romantic partner.

"Vlad—lovely to see you!" said Barbara. "I am fine, dear."

They exchanged kisses.

"Cristóbal is waiting for you, come," said Vladzio. "We have only to see the, you know . . ." He bowed slightly, as if the gesture could release him from saying the word.

"See what?" Barbara repeated.

"It is only the card, Miss Hutton . . ." said Nicholas, miming the half-page-size permit that was now required by a customer to do any business at a French couture house.

"The permit," said Vladzio.

"Oh, that!" said Barbara, annoyed. "Yes, someone did put that in my hand, but it's at my hotel."

"It is our protection," said Vladzio. "They make us note your number. So sorry."

"Alright, alright," said Barbara. "My driver will go fetch it, and we can go on with the fitting as usual. Is that alright?"

"Yes, of course," said Vlad. "This way."

The sanctum sanctorum of the *maison* was the design atelier, a daylight-filled laboratory on an upper floor, all in white, where the maestro, a slender, extremely handsome, dark-haired middle-aged man with soulful brown eyes, was waiting. Over navy blue trousers and a white shirt with a royal blue-and-white jacquard tie, he was wearing a freshly pressed, white cotton work coat. Attending him were three women staff members, also in white work coats.

Balenciaga bowed.

"Hello, maestro," said Barbara, extending her hand. "Wonderful to see you again."

Balenciaga kissed Barbara's hand, then gathered her into a warm but decorous embrace.

"You are an inspiration, *mi tesoro*," he said. "To come all this way. . . !"

"There may be a war on, but people just can't keep on wearing the same old clothes, can they?"

"We are honored."

"And the heathens cannot be permitted to stop an artist like Balenciaga in his tracks."

"Just so, Madame," said one of the women in white, holding a notebook and pencil.

"I mean, if the German wives are getting new dresses," said Barbara, "why can't we?"

After a fitting for a suit, Barbara and the designer went to work on a ball dress that was conceived in the spirit of what Balenciaga called "today's Infanta." It was to be of a new fabric that the designer was developing in collaboration with a Swiss manufacturer, a stiff and bulky silk gazar that Balenciaga said "masses beautifully."

Barbara lovingly handled the swatch Balenciaga showed her.

"We have it exclusively," said the designer. "This shipment was brought in over the Alps in a farmer's truck. Not even the Germans know it is here."

The color, as they agreed, was a rich, vibrant claret. The feel of the dress was to be what Balenciaga called "semi-fitted." That was where things were heading after the war, he said, though he knew that his respected colleague Dior had a different idea about the future of fit.

"I would like to blur the waistline and focus on the back, Barbara," he said, softly placing his hand on the small of her back. "We will create great drama with a simplified cut."

"Very good," said Barbara. "Show me."

And the master went to work.

Balenciaga's designs originated not in sketching but in draping, which for him was a gestural, emotional, and excitingly unpredictable process. It was a matter of discovering the behavior of fabric while taking into account the unique volumes of a client's body parts, her posture and the patterns of her movement, the asymmetries of her musculoskeletal system, etc. Feeling safe and comfortable in Balenciaga's atelier, Barbara was perfectly willing to be nude for the draping process, but Balenciaga's custom was to dress his client for draping in a loose, white silk chemise, with no undergarments. So while the assistants stood dutifully by—handing Balenciaga the tools and materials he needed, recording notes, making sure Barbara remained at ease—the master went about his explorations and discoveries and shapings, deftly manipulating scissors and fabric and pins, while conversing occasionally with his client in a tone just audible between the two of them, not so much in whispers but in soft sighs.

"Just like this," he murmured, perfecting the fold of a swag. It sounded like a lover's utterance. He went on sculpturing features of the dress, as Barbara stood there assuredly, accustomed to being the center of attention.

"See, here?" said Balenciaga with a little tug. "How does this feel?" His voice was deep and gentle, with something of a lilt—neither fully masculine nor quite feminine.

"It feels good," said Barbara.

Balenciaga nodded delicately.

"Almost airborne," he said. "Do you see how this can move?"

For a moment, from the windows, came a great commotion from the street—the sound of noisy motor vehicles rolling past, people both cheering and booing. One of Balenciaga's assistants went to the window, watched for a second while the others waited, then returned to her position.

"*Défilé militaire*," she said, with a mixture of boredom and contempt. It was a small procession of military vehicles—a frequent occurrence in Paris at this time, meant to reinforce the supremacy of the Germans.

Balenciaga shook his head, with a look of resignation.

"Shall we continue with our work?" he said. "Or maybe a little break to recover ourselves?"

"No, I'm fine," said Barbara. "Let's continue."

"Are you in Paris long, Madame?" asked the assistant with the notebook. It was clear she was in charge of scheduling the next fitting.

"I am on my way to Cairo tomorrow," said Barbara. "Then back to Paris in five days. If we can get across the Mediterranean."

"Not shopping in Egypt. . . !" said Balenciaga, meaning to be droll.

"Actually, yes, shopping," said Barbara. "In a manner of speaking. King Farouk needs money and is awfully eager to sell a certain diamond he owns, and my friends at Bulgari seem to think that I am the one to have it."

"Mmm, *encantado!*" purred Balenciaga.

"So we will see. Cary says no, that I like publicity too much and shouldn't go about in a war being so extravagant. But I ask you, Cristóbal, is it extravagant to keep pursuing beauty, even in the midst of a great storm?"

CHAPTER 18

May 1947

Doris made no mention of Rubi as she said goodbye to Barbara at the Brooklyn foundry, where Doris's colleague and confidante Pansy, whose given name was Marian Paschal, was waiting to collect her, in a Duke car. The world would find out soon enough that Doris was marrying handsome polo player and race car driver Porfirio Rubirosa, whose official role was diplomat of his native Dominican Republic. Doris was not yet quite sure when and how to go public with the upcoming marriage, given the few issues with her divorce from Jimmy Cromwell that were still lingering, and the fact that the State Department was concerned that the marriage could give Rubi, the agent of a foreign government, Rafael Trujillo's dictatorship, control over Doris's company Duke Energy, which generated electricity for homes and factories across the American South. Yet Doris was delighted with her catch, and was planning to subdue Rubi's objections to the State Department-required prenup with gifts of a sapphire-studded gold cigarette case, a stable of polo ponies, and a B-25 bomber fitted out as a private plane.

Neither had Barbara mentioned her new husband, Troubetzkoy, with whom she'd had a spat the night before, after an elaborate dinner party she threw at the Ritz for some very fancy friends. Though the dishes served were exquisite, Barbara barely touched a bite, and the prince was annoyed by this. Moreover, he was alarmed by his new wife's growing reliance on appetite suppressants, which gave her insomnia, and on sleeping pills, which contributed to violent mood swings. Whatever Troubetzkoy thought he was getting in his marriage was not, in fact, what he was getting.

Doris and Pansy drove back into Manhattan and over to Best & Co. at Fifth Avenue and 51st Street, where Doris had an appointment with a young woman named Nancy Creamer, a Bay Ridge, Brooklyn, girl who had assisted Doris as a personal shopper several times during the past year and was now the department store's head fashion buyer. Pansy, who also served as secretary of Independent Aid, Inc., the first charitable organization that Doris set up on her own, was coming along to weigh in as needed, with trusted advice about color, fit, etc. Though Doris had started buying cocktail and party clothing from the Paris haute couture houses, especially now that postwar fashion was more fun and feminine than it had been for a while, she was still buying suits made-to-order and even off-the-rack at stores like Best and Bergdorf's, because she liked being able to rely on the store's selection of appropriately sober attire for what she called her "work clothes." She had been sharply criticized several years before for wearing a full-length Russian mink coat and chic hat when joining First Lady Eleanor Roosevelt, at Jimmy Cromwell's behest, on a tour of Depression-stricken mining towns in West Virginia, so for more serious occasions nowadays, she was attempting to be more in tune with public opinion.

Nancy was waiting for Doris at the private elevator entrance of Best & Co.'s private shopping suite, adjacent to the store's eighth-floor "Better Suits and Dresses" department. She was clearly in her early twenties, but as composed as any older male executive, dressed in a chic, figure-hugging gray flannel suit and alligator high heels.

"Miss Duke, good to see you again," said Nancy, whose assistant, standing by, was at least a decade older than she was.

"Nancy, how are you?" said Doris. "You remember Miss Paschal."

Nancy showed the women into a living-room-like salon,

where coffee was waiting for them in a cozy seating area whose armchairs and sofa were of a sleek Art Moderne design. Around the room were three other groupings of armchairs with occasional tables, accented with several pots of schefflera and vitrines displaying accessories.

Nancy had hit it off with Doris the first time Doris came into the store seeking a cloth coat that would be appropriate for a charity function she was attending at one of the small churches she helped support in Harlem. Nancy listened carefully to her customer and didn't select items to show her that were outside of the carefully stated requirements, nor did Nancy use overly hyperbolic language in describing the items. Nancy and Doris both liked the clarity between them, and Nancy was flattered that a great lady like Doris would speak to her so directly and respectfully, almost as if they were colleagues.

"It's suits today, I believe?" said Nancy.

"Yes," said Doris. "But nothing too girly, as I said. That 'New Look' from Dior isn't right for me, especially at my office."

The fashion magazines had been full of pictures of the designer's new "Bar Suit," a luxuriantly full, black taffeta skirt topped by a fitted white jacket of silk shantung, well-padded and stiffened, with small, rounded shoulders and a sharply defined waist.

"Of course," said Nancy. "I've selected several options to show you, along the lines you expressed. 'Sober,' I think you said."

After the assistant served the coffee, Nancy made a signal, and from a backstage area came a model gliding as casually as fashionable ladies do along the Champs Élysées, looking chic, blithe, unpretentious. For one of the fashion shows that the store mounted regularly for favored clients, the model would do a full circuit of the salon, stopping at all the seating groups, which would be populated with well-dressed women. But for this private showing, she stayed close to Doris and Pansy, insouciantly cycling through a range of stylish postures, turning occasionally to allow for all views.

"Mitzi is wearing a double-breasted suit in dove gray silk

shantung, fully lined, by the American designer Maurice Rentner," said Nancy, standing to one side, holding a leather-bound notebook and silver pen. "You'll note the uncomplicated silhouette, the light padding in a relatively soft shoulder. And you see Rentner's prevailing theme of modern femininity expressed here in a suit of strict but nonetheless womanly lines."

"Lovely," said Doris, feeling the hem of the skirt.

"Very nice little kick pleat in back," noted Pansy.

"Also available in *café au lait*," said Nancy.

The women looked on admiringly as Mitzi opened the jacket to reveal a silk lining in a matching shade of gray. Unhurriedly, the model did several full turns, then stood aside graciously as the next model entered and began her routine, at which point Mitzi strolled away and disappeared backstage.

"Rita comes to us in a suit of dark burgundy cashmere tweed by Claire McCardell, for Townley," said Nancy. "Again, the suit is fully lined. The shoulders here are unpadded, to bring out what McCardell is calling 'the American look'—a more relaxed silhouette, in contrast with the more French-inspired 'New Look.'"

"I like that," said Doris.

"Me, too," said Pansy.

"You may recall that we carry a line of McCardell's suits and dresses exclusively," said Nancy. "We think she really understands what American women are thinking about now, as we approach the 1950s."

"Very nice," said Doris.

"She met with our fashion staff only last month and told us that she didn't want the French influences to confuse the American consumer."

"Is that the word she used—'confuse'?" said Pansy.

"What did she mean by that?" said Doris.

Nancy nodded, ready with a response.

"I think she was suggesting that the supremacy of the French *couturiers* is now to be rivalled by some of the best, rising American designers. . . ."

"I like that idea," said Doris. "Especially since America is such a melting pot of influences and different ways of thinking."

"Yes, exactly," said Nancy, pausing a second to see if more conversation was wanted, then continuing with the show. "And now I have for you an unusual three-piece suit by Irene, in slate wool gabardine, worn by Muriel. The suit is comprised of a slightly A-line skirt and a long sleeveless vest, and a short, long-sleeve jacket to complete the ensemble."

"Oooh, interesting," said Doris, leaning forward.

The model approached and opened the suit's jacket, so the women could see how it fit over the vest.

"Dramatic, yet not flamboyant," said Nancy.

"Indeed," said Pansy.

"As I'm sure you know," said Nancy, "Irene is a well-known name in Hollywood costume design. She has her own salon at Bullocks Wilshire in Los Angeles—the only designer other than Coco Chanel to have that honor."

"These are great choices, Nancy—I'm really impressed with your work," said Doris, standing, after six more suits had been shown and Doris, conferring briefly with Pansy, ordered three. After a seamstress took a series of measurements to update those that the store already had on file, Nancy walked Doris and Pansy slowly back toward the private elevator lobby, while exchanging a bit of small talk about the direction women's fashion might take in coming years. As they chatted, Doris's eye was caught by a selection of jewelry on display in one of the two obelisk-shaped vitrines flanking the portal to the lobby.

"Those are interesting," said Doris, of a velvet-lined tray of pins.

"Yes, we like to select accessories that make sense with our suit and dress lines," said Nancy.

"You select these especially for your offerings?" said Doris.

"Yes, indeed. Some clients like our advice when putting together a complete look. We like to be able to offer a complete design, our vision—for a woman who might want that."

"You do such a good job with the store's fashion direction,

and you certainly know how to divine what works best for a customer."

"Thank you, Miss Duke," said Nancy. "I appreciate that. It means a lot to me, coming from you."

"May we take a look at these?" said Doris, indicating the tray of pins.

"Of course," said Nancy, opening the vitrine's glass door. She removed the tray and set it down on a nearby table.

Without hesitation, Doris took up the item she had her eye on, a circle pin about an inch-and-a-quarter in diameter, in the form of three intertwined strands of gold.

"This is lovely," said Doris.

"Yes," said Nancy. "Solid eighteen-karat gold, Trabert and Hoeffer, the Chicago firm—we're their exclusive New York outlet."

"Nice, isn't it, Pansy?" said Doris, putting the pin up to the lapel of the suit she was wearing and regarding herself in a mirror.

"It is . . ." said Pansy hesitantly.

"But what?" said Doris.

"Well, only that we'll be in Paris next week, and we might have a look in Cartier and Van Cleef, if it's a circle pin you want. . . ."

Doris continued to look at her reflection.

"Mmm . . . no," she uttered, "I like this. I like it a lot. And I think it will really be right for the suits we just ordered—right, Nancy?"

"A good choice," said Nancy. "I'm really pleased that you see how they will work together."

"They will," said Doris.

"If I may say so, I do see lots of beautiful brooches applied to suits where they just don't work," added Nancy. "Too . . . *much.*"

"I agree," said Doris. "I've got plenty of too-much brooches for when I need 'em. This is how I want to look for charity work—simple, elegant. I'll take it."

*   *   *

The bill for that day's suit shopping at Best & Co., including the gold circle pin, was presented to Doris discreetly in a small leather portfolio. Doris barely glanced at the bill and signed it, then handed the portfolio back to Nancy.

"Thank you, Nancy. Well done," said Doris.

"You're welcome, Miss Duke," said Nancy, handing Pansy a receipt. "Always a pleasure."

Nancy's assistant stepped away to begin working on the order, and Nancy accompanied Doris and Pansy to the elevator lobby. From the gossip columns, Nancy knew very well that Doris had been divorced from Jimmy Cromwell for a few years now, and after her wartime exploits in Italy and Egypt, was back on the merry-go-round of parties, dinners, and balls. The socialite was even rumored to be seeing someone new romantically—playboy Porfirio Rubirosa.

If only we were close enough for me to ask her about Rubi! thought Nancy. That was the nickname the columnists used for the playboy—Rubi. It sounded so rakish and sophisticated! *Is he really like they say, all about sports cars and polo ponies? Is he solid enough for her. . . ?*

"Nancy, let me ask you something," said Doris. "Miss Paschal and I were speaking and . . . we were wondering if you were happy with your position here at Best."

The question surprised Nancy, but she was confident that the comment was not a rebuke of her work.

"Very happy, Miss Duke," she said. "Is there . . . anything else I can do for you?"

"Well, here's the thing. My charity, Independent Aid, is growing, and Miss Paschal, who is the director, is always on the lookout for bright, young people. . . ."

"Yes," agreed Pansy.

"Responsible people, personable—such as yourself."

"I see," said Nancy.

"We wondered whether you might want to talk about the possibility of joining us."

". . . As some sort of manager or director," said Pansy.

"A charity . . ." said Nancy.

"It would be more about managing relationships with clients and partners, than anything administrative or financial," said Doris.

"Trying to make the world a slightly better place," said Pansy. "Helping people is what we do."

"Well, I'm flattered, of course . . ." said Nancy.

"I know it's not fashion . . ." said Doris.

"No," said Nancy, "and I'm grateful for your thinking of me this way. . . ."

"But?"

"But the thing is that I will probably have to leave New York soon."

"Ah."

"My father has found a business opportunity upstate, and he's talking about moving the family up there."

"I see. And you would have to go, too?"

Nancy made a half-sour expression.

"I . . . don't see how I could avoid it," she said.

"But you're not looking forward to it," said Doris.

"I've been doing very well here, if I may say so. Youngest buyer in the store's history."

"That's quite an achievement."

"And I do love fashion."

"Of course. You want to build something. I understand."

"I want to." Nancy paused. "I wanted to—but I have a duty to follow my father."

The elevator arrived with the ding of a bell, and the door opened and closed, ignored, while the women continued speaking. Doris drew closer to Nancy.

"Believe me, I know about honoring your father," said Doris. "I admire that. But remember that, nowadays, we women have a duty to ourselves, too. Right?"

"Right."

"You know where to find me, if you change your mind."

Pansy produced a card and handed it to Nancy. And Nancy stared at it for a while, standing there at the elevator, after Doris and Pansy had left, considering the card's elegantly engraved letters and thinking about the gaping future—and more than anything else about her age. The youngest buyer in the history of Best & Co. was not twenty-three, as the company thought. Nancy had lied about her age two years before, when applying for a job and claiming to be twenty-one. She was actually seventeen then, and only nineteen now.

After a full day at the store, on her feet, dealing with exacting customers, supervising her staff, let alone enduring almost an hour's commute from Brooklyn to midtown on the crowded Fourth Avenue Local train and the hour-long commute back home from midtown, Nancy was still happy to help her mother clean up in the kitchen, after dinner.

"Plenty of pot roast left, darling," said her mother, at the sink. "Why don't you make a nice sandwich for yourself, for tomorrow's lunch?"

"The girls and I go to Toffenetti's on Wednesdays," said Nancy, drying silverware.

"Suit yourself."

Then Nancy dried the serving utensils, and replaced them in a drawer, and slammed the drawer shut with more force and clatter than usual.

"If I could suit myself, Mother, I wouldn't be going upstate," she said.

Her mother turned to her.

"You heard your father. He thinks it's best for all of us that . . ."

"And *you*," said Nancy, "you're just going along with it."

But Nancy wasn't all that surprised. Her mother was a typically dutiful middle-class wife, who'd been married at sixteen and had certainly said the word *obey* in her wedding vows.

"It'll work out—you'll see," said the mother. "I know it's not Fifth Avenue, but you'd just meet a boy anyway and get married. I'm sure you'll find a job in Prescottville and meet just as nice a boy in the country as you would here in the city. Nicer, even.

You've said so yourself, what some of those jokers in town are like . . ."

Nancy folded the towel and dropped it on the counter.

"I'm going upstairs."

She walked through the living room without a word to her father, who was reading the newspaper and waiting for nine o'clock, when his favorite radio program, *The Mysterious Traveler,* would come on the air. In her room, Nancy switched on her own radio, a black Bakelite Emerson portable, of a trim, modern design. On the music station was a new song from Ted Weems, "Broken," an updated, rumba-foxtrot version of the song, with oddly cheerful whistling instead of the wistful vocals of the much more sedate version of the song from her parents' generation. A shellac record of that old one, by Sid Phillips and his Melodians, happened to be sitting downstairs in a paper sleeve in a pile with other records in paper sleeves near the Victrola, in a corner of the living room.

The bedroom's beige-and-blue wallpaper was also very modern, in a geometric pattern that Nancy picked out because it reminded her of the grille of a European sports car. They had just repapered the room the year before.

A country boy! Nancy could just picture him: baggy overalls and a hay straw in his mouth. At least the jokers in town wore Botany 500 suits and Florsheim shoes. Besides, life wasn't all about men, was it? Obeisance to husbands? What an antediluvian concept!

Broken,
Broken,
Your sudden flight has left me broken . .

As if I were a child! I'm nineteen—and the store thinks I'm four years older than that!

What kind of jobs could there be in the mountains to compare with running your own floor of a big Fifth Avenue department store and helping customers like Miss Doris Duke? And

Nancy had impressed her—a woman who had inherited a fortune, traveled internationally, started a charity, and could easily hire Ted Weems and his orchestra to play at her next party.
In fact, at that very moment, while Nancy was sulking in her
bedroom in Bay Ridge, Miss Duke might well be hosting a big
party tonight at . . . now, where would Doris Duke's New York
pied-à-terre be? Park Avenue, of course. And what would the
place be like? Well, undoubtedly it would be a penthouse. Now,
in little ol' Prescottville, New York, were there any apartment
buildings even tall enough to have a penthouse?

CHAPTER 19

September 1947

A few months after their visit to the foundry to look at golden horse heads, Doris and Rubi were married at the Dominican Embassy in Paris. There was some last-minute dickering between their respective legal teams about whether France's Napoleonic code meant that Rubi, as husband, would now control all the family's wealth, including all the assets possessed by his wife before the marriage, but the outcome of the dickering was no, there would be no such control, the code be damned. Then, accompanied by Pansy, Doris and Rubi went on to Cannes, where they had rented a palatial nineteenth-century villa for their honeymoon.

Somerset Maugham had described the Riviera as "a sunny place for shady people" just a few years before, in his 1941 collection of essays, *Strictly Personal*. He had been spending time there since the '20s—in Saint-Jean-Cap-Ferrat, when it was an enclave for British and American writers, including F. Scott Fitzgerald, who set much of *Tender Is the Night* nearby. The French coast had been the site of human occupation for half a million years. The Greeks founded Nice as a colony, and the Romans made it a bustling trading port. The English elite flocked to the coast in the eighteenth century, as did the Russian elite in the nineteenth; and in the first decades of the twentieth century, more and more painters and poets kept coming to live simply and cheaply in little fishing towns along the sea. Then, in the early '20s, as princes and publicists were promoting the coast as a playground for the rich, and Coco Chanel decided that suntans were fashionable, the luxurious Train Blue started running overnight from Paris to Menton. Now, after a devastating war, the Riviera was a convenient canteen for a world of displaced types, to rest and regroup. In addition to the usual pleasures of the rich and idle, there was the afterglow of the utter upset of European society, which afforded a sad-but-thrilling new perspective on the primal satisfaction of showing skin and living easily on fish and sunshine and red Ferrari convertibles. Especially for those whose home ground had been wrecked by depression and ruined by war, the Riviera meant release from wounded, grieving societies and the massive responsibilities of reconstruction.

The honeymoon was bumpy at first. Rubi, in a snit about the prenup, refused to have sex with Doris, which meant that during the first few days, Doris and Pansy went out happily on their own, swimming and playing tennis and shopping, while Rubi motored up and down the coast visiting friends at various house parties. Then, after Doris promised to buy Rubi the seventeenth-century mansion in Paris that he'd been asking for, the newlyweds made up and all was well again. Together Doris and Rubi started attending the luncheons, cocktail parties, and dinners they were invited to, usually winding up at the end of an evening at the casino in Monte Carlo, where Rubi could gamble and Doris could be on the lookout for stories that might be right for the magazine she was now contributing to, for a nominal fifty dollars a week, *Harper's Bazaar*. The magazine's editor, the legendary eagle-eyed Carmel Snow, was eager to capitalize on Doris's connections to fashionable and creative types. Snow charged her new correspondent only to be on the lookout for "good taste with a dash of daring." On the Riviera, this posed a dilemma for Doris, since on those late nights under the casino's ornate Beaux Arts arches and vaulted ceilings, Doris saw again and again, in the gambling and often in the fashion and entertainment on hand, much that she considered reckless, but little that was interestingly daring.

The press noted that Doris and Rubi made an interesting-looking couple, the lady being almost six feet tall and the gentleman, barely five foot nine. At the beach, Doris looked as fit as an Olympian in one of her favorite Jantzen swimsuits, while Rubi, in his swim trunks, was happy to make a splash with the other women with his trim, athletic physique and, from under the trunks, hints of the masculine endowment that everyone whispered about. Doris, the girl who'd always had everything, was quite matter-of-fact about this endowment. It was part of what she'd quite knowingly purchased via the marriage. And guiltlessly she enjoyed the thing because, as she confided to Pansy, "it's so large that it seems to be in a state of eternal erection, and he's able to do whatever I want for hours."

Their presence in Cannes made a perfect excuse for celebrity hostess Elsa Maxwell to throw them a party, which Maxwell did not at her home, in the restored farmhouse she shared with longtime partner Dorothy "Dickie" Fellowes-Gordon, a Scottish heiress; and not at Le Sporting, the open-air dining and dancing pavilion attached to the Monte Carlo casino, where she hosted Friday-night galas for the rich and famous; but at the snazzy white Château de l'Horizon, a modernist villa she'd been "loaned" for the season by her friend, actress Maxine Elliott. It was at a party there at the villa, the year before, that Maxwell had introduced her dear friend Rita Hayworth to her dear friend Prince Aly Khan, and it was there, above ancient, jagged rocks and landscaped terraces, on a sleek arcaded loggia facing the sea, where Maxwell hosted a dinner for forty for her dear newlywed friends, Doris and Rubi.

It was a warm and fragrant evening. From one end of the loggia, a small band played a mix of pop standards, show tunes, and Latin numbers. The guests of honor looked regal—Doris in a white Grecian-inspired gown by Madame Grès, and Rubi in a perfectly fit tuxedo by his new, "secret" tailor in Rome, Guglielmo Battistoni, who was just then becoming popular among gentlemen of means—and happily, they mixed among the friends and celebrities Maxwell had gathered, which included the Duke and Duchess of Windsor; Lady Diana and Duff Cooper; Bolivian tin king Antenor Patiño and his wife, María Cristina; Aristotle Onassis and his new wife, Tina; Salvador and Gala Dalí; Tyrone Power and his wife-to-be, actress Linda Christian; Cyd Charisse and her husband-to-be, actor-and-singer Tony Martin; Khan and Hayworth, who were talking of marriage and already arranging to buy that very villa from Maxine Elliott; the dress designer Jean Dessès, who was coming into his own with a clientele of royalty and movie stars; and a grand-looking woman introduced by Maxwell as the Duchesse de Gramont, who was now, after the death of her first husband, divorce from her second, and the loss of her fortune, working at one of New York's better hair salons.

It was Pansy, also a dinner guest and dressed in a plain blue gown, who shared the latter detail with Doris as the two stood at a balustrade, after a dinner of sea scallops and lamb from the Pyrénées. On the other side of the terrace, Rubi was entertaining a contingent of tan, young women by showing them bachata and merengue dance movements.

"Apparently her salon was one of the liveliest in Paris, with all the best artists and writers and actors," said Pansy, of the Duchesse. "A great beauty, at one time; a princess from an old Roman family. Monsieur le Duc had previously married a Rothschild, so that's where all the money came from. But she squandered it."

"On what?" said Doris.

"Restoring a palace. Buying art. Giving parties."

"Why can't people be more careful with their money?"

"Apparently she's hung on to some of the art."

"I marvel that you know these things."

"People tell me these things. I only pay attention."

"A hair salon? I wonder which one. I am imagining her coming home to a fourth-floor, cold-water walk-up in Spanish Harlem, and on the wall there's a portrait of her as a teenager, by Boldini."

"Elsa insists on treating her as a duchess and a princess."

"Very decent of her."

"She does seem rather a decent sort."

"Who's indecent?" roared Maxwell, joining them.

"Such a nice party, Elsa, thank you," said Doris.

"I have a surprise for you and your new man, Doris," said Maxwell. She was decked out in an improbably fancy, floor-length meringue of green lace.

"Please tell me you've persuaded Wallis and David to revive their 'Sweet Georgia Brown' number," said Doris dryly.

Maxwell chuckled. A stout, "excitable tugboat of a woman" in her mid-sixties, to use a phrase that Cecil Beaton once applied to her, Maxwell was born in Keokuk, Iowa, and raised in San Francisco with a passion for music and theater. In the 1920s, she found her way to Venice and began dazzling the smart set there with lively parties that boasted more exciting guests and more interesting settings and themes than anyone else's. Since then, Maxwell had been setting up at will in world capitals like Paris, London, Rome, Vienna, New York, Washington, and Hollywood, in addition to the Riviera, to host splendid parties, scavenger hunts, murder-mystery evenings, "Come as You Are" parties, and all manner of fancy dress balls, at the latter of which the hostess might appear as anyone from Catherine de Medici to Herbert Hoover. Smart and well-versed in the accomplishments of "dear friends" like Albert Einstein and Fritz Kreisler, Maxwell was able to balance her strong sense of fun with a commitment to decorum that kept her quiet about the secrets that people inevitably shared with her. Since she entertained so lavishly and lived so well on no apparent income, some people speculated about possibly illegitimate means of support. But the truth was that Maxwell simply enjoyed the largesse of rich friends in the form of "birthday gifts" that were given her all year around, and had special arrangements with the fancy hotels where she stayed, because she was expected to attract the rich and famous there, which she did.

"Are you ready?" said Maxwell. Without waiting for a response, the hostess gave a cue, and the band launched into some bright intro music. Two servants appeared with tripod-mounted, electric theatrical lamps to illuminate a spot in the middle of the floor, and the crowd watched, hushed, as Cyd Charisse stepped barefoot into the light and launched into a brilliant, ten-minute dance number with the band, which progressed from a sexy rumba to a cool samba to a spirited mambo. Under contract as a dancer at MGM and a member of the Ballets Russes when she was thirteen, Charisse looked in complete command of her number, joyous, exultant, flinging arms and legs about energetically, as best she could on the hard terrazzo floor. The crowd roared its approval at the end, when Charisse took her bow and signaled her acknowledgment of the bride and groom and their generous hostess.

Doris stepped over to Charisse and was thanking her when she noticed that a new guest had arrived and was making it a point to stand facing them, clapping slowly, theatrically, while everyone else had gone back to their own conversations. It was Barbara Hutton, in a black satin gown and an elaborate, bib-like diamond-and-ruby necklace, with a lit cigarette dangling from her lips.

"Barbara, at last," said Maxwell, rushing over to her and the timid young man in black tie accompanying her. "I'm afraid you've missed dinner, dear."

"Thank you, but I never touch the stuff," said Barbara slowly and with some difficulty, her speech instantly giving her away as drunk or under the influence of drugs or possibly both.

Doris, who had not known that Barbara was on the Riviera and invited to the party, stepped over to her friend and spoke as quietly as she could over the music and conversation.

"Nice to see you, Babbo. Are you feeling alright?"

Barbara pulled away sullenly, an ash dropping from her cigarette.

"Never better," she snapped.

Instantly Doris saw that this was not a prank. Barbara was in worse shape than Doris had ever seen her—perhaps the way she was often nowadays when she wasn't in public.

"Barbara, let me get you a chair," said Maxwell, signaling a servant.

"No, no, we're going for a swim," said Barbara. "We were talking about going for a swim."

"Uh, I don't think you should go for a swim just now, Barbara dear," said Maxwell. "It's dark, and the steps down to the beach are awfully dangerous. Maybe we can find someone to go with you in a little while. But here, we're just about to have some coffee. Won't you and your friend join us for that?"

Barbara grunted something that didn't sound like either *yes* or *no*.

"Now . . . that adorable little boy of yours, Lance—how's he?" said Maxwell.

"He's not little," rasped Barbara. "He's eleven."

Maxwell was doing her best to contain a drunk's manic energy, but the renowned hostess also sensed that something wickedly memorable might also take place at her party, so she didn't feel inclined to spirit Barbara away to a bedroom. Her judgment proved correct, as Barbara, after extracting a fresh cigarette and a light from her companion, launched into a rambling speech about how sad it was to return to London and find Winfield House with buckled floorboards, peeling wallpaper, broken windows, and dangling wires—a visit that Doris knew had taken place two years prior, before repairs were made and the house was donated to the British government. Pansy tried to nudge Doris away from this disaster scene, but Doris stayed and so did Maxwell, so they both heard the terrible accusations that Barbara began to spew, as did some of the other guests, who'd started watching.

"She thinks she's a spy or something," slurred Barbara, jerking her head toward Doris. "Ha. The OSS. Most spies try to sleep with the enemy. Mata Hari here sleeps with the supreme commander of the allied forces—after the goddamn war is over."

"Don't be vulgar, Babbo," said Doris quietly, annoyed that Barbara was not in control of herself but satisfied that the memory of her behavior would eventually be Barbara's punishment, if she was even capable of feeling shame anymore.

Maxwell and Pansy both knew well the incident that Barbara was describing—one that had not been openly discussed in deference to the marriage partners of those involved. A few weeks after VE Day, Doris had been waiting at an airstrip in Linz, Austria, for a private plane back to Rome, when a plane landed with Douglas MacArthur and Soviet Field Marshall General Fyodor Tolbukhin, who were on their way to a little getaway at a château formerly belonging to the Emperor Franz Joseph. They persuaded Doris to come along with them for a few days, which led to a small vodka-filled house party and a brief affair between Doris and MacArthur.

"Just like a spy, but sleeping with the wrong side," said Barbara, almost to herself. "Instead of a German or an Italian, she sleeps with one of our own."

"What can I tell you?" said Doris. "I went with the supreme commander because I didn't have Hollywood's favorite leading man at home, like you did."

Barbara spurted out a laugh.

"Typical," she said. And just when it seemed she might have ended the rant, she started up again. "You might be smarter than me and richer than me, and you might be able to swim from here to Tripoli, but Cary married me because I'm prettier than you, and he told me so."

Doris smirked, rolled her eyes, and turned away.

"I was just doing my duty," she told Maxwell with a smile, and then asked Pansy to find Rubi and tell him it was time to go.

Elsa said goodnight to Doris, but of course offered no apology, since they both knew Barbara was an adult and in no immediate danger of harming herself, and was otherwise providing a kind of entertainment that was not unwelcome at a party like that, where bad behavior might always be diverting. From the edges of the crowd, people like the Duke and Duchess, and the tin king and his wife, were conversing amiably and drinking Maxwell's champagne, while also paying perfectly good attention to the party's main attraction.

In the car, on their way back to their villa, Rubi's question about what had happened provoked a conversation between Doris and Pansy that largely excluded him.

"She wasn't wrong," said Doris.

"What do you mean?" said Pansy.

"She was the pretty one."

"Doris . . ."

"She still is. Though it's all going to hell, as far as I can see."

"I'm so sorry."

"She stays in bed all day with the drapes pulled and drinks coffee, cup after cup. Amphetamines all day, and then it's the phenobarbital, Nembutal, chloral hydrate, what have you. It kills the appetite, it kills the sex drive. She receives people in bed now—did you know that? Except when they manage to get her up and dressed."

"It can't be as bad as all that."

"Can't it?"

"She's only thirty-five."

"She's a hundred, if she's a day."

Rubi chimed in with another question—"You are both the same age, aren't you?"—but it went unanswered.

"You didn't know she was here?" said Pansy.

"No," said Doris, "and I find that odd, too. We were just in L.A., and I tried to get her to see my psychic, but she wouldn't have it."

"There's only so much you can do for people."

"I can't . . . I hate watching this."

Around lunchtime the next day, Doris and Pansy returned from a morning of tennis to find the villa's broad, sun-filled entry hall filled with masses of flowers—baskets and baskets of yellow roses, bright orange Gerbera daisies, yellow billy balls, peach alstroemeria, and purple Veronica.

"These arrived an hour ago, Miss Duke," said Higgins, the houseman.

"Was there a card or something?" said Doris.

"No, but there was a gentleman in a green sports car, who drove up in back of the delivery truck—a young gentleman who did not remove his sunglasses."

"I see."

"He asked if you were at home."

"And when you said I wasn't?"

"He asked if I would deliver a message. 'Miss Hutton says she is very sorry.'"

"That's it?"

"That's all he said, ma'am. And then he left."

"A peace offering?" said Pansy.

"Something like it, I guess," said Doris, "the flowers, not the boy."

"Not the boy?"

Doris shook her head.

"Who knows," she said. "Higgins, is Mr. Rubirosa at home?"

"No, ma'am. I believe he's gone to look at some horses."

"Thank you, Higgins. We'll have lunch on the terrace in twenty minutes. Make up a little arrangement for the table with some of these flowers, would you?"

Doris and Pansy were having lunch under the terrace's green-and-white–striped awning when the houseman announced a telephone call from Miss Hutton. Doris flashed Pansy an expression of surprise as the houseman placed the phone on the table and plugged its cord into a nearby jack.

"I am a beast," said Barbara. Her voice was lower than usual and sounded gravelly.

"You certainly are," said Doris, forbearingly.

"Can you forgive me?"

"I might be able to forgive you, by the end of this phone call."

The edge of the awning was flapping in the fresh breeze. The sky was cloudless; the sea, shimmering beryl blue.

"It was a very cruel thing to do," said Barbara.

"It was a very *stupid* thing to do," said Doris.

"Yes. I'm sorry."

"And not least because it would have been a perfect opportunity for one of our little scenes."

"I know."

"I was hurt, Babbo—well, not very hurt, but I might have been. And it could have been so much better theater if someone had thrown a drink in someone's face, or something like that. Elsa would have been so pleased."

Barbara sighed. Doris knew she was calling from her bed.

"It's not even true what I said," mewled Barbara. "Cary never said that about you."

"It didn't sound much like Cary."

"If anything, I admire your body. Lord knows, mine is falling apart as we speak." Barbara paused to light a cigarette and take a first drag on it. "I don't know how we score this one, Dodo."

"Let's call it a draw."

"Fine. Listen—come with me to Paris?"

"When?"

"Soon. Now."

"Why?"

"Lance is there with his father, for those asthma treatments. . . ."

"Poor boy. . . !"

". . . And I have an appointment with Monsieur Lachassagne at Cartier. He's going to help me figure out what to do with those Russian emeralds. So I need your help, Dodo. You're so clever about these things."

"Is that what's on your mind right now—emeralds? Shouldn't you be thinking about your son's health? Or your own?"

"I'm thinking about a tiara—something Indian, some kind of sunburst or starburst. What do you think about that?"

"My advice is for you to come see Takata-sensei with me."

"What is that? More color therapy?"

"I told you about her—a very powerful healer I have been seeing. She uses reiki."

"What's that?"

"The hands deliver energy to the body."

"Not one of those healers who beat you up?"

"No, no. It's very gentle, sometimes not even physically touching. . . ."

"I don't need to be beaten up."

"Of course not, Babbo."

"Where is she?"

"Los Angeles, but I can fly her to New York, or Paris, or even here."

"Come to Paris, and we'll discuss it." She took another drag on the cigarette. "A tiara in the Indian style, I think—something I can wear around the house in Tangier. Did I tell you I bought a house in Tangier?"

"You did mention it."

"Several houses, actually. I'm combining them. It's going to be gorgeous—a palace. And not on *le Boulevard*, but right there in the Kasbah. I am going to base myself there. Enough with Paris and London and Hollywood."

"Why Tangier?"

"Because I am comfortable there. I can be myself."

"Alright, then."

"Does it work?"

"Does what work?"

"Reiki."

"It works for me."

"If you do it the wrong way, can it harm you?"

"What a funny question."

"Can it?"

"I would say probably not."

"Then how can it be powerful enough to help you?"

Doris laughed. At least part of her friend's mind was still sharp.

"Will you try it?" she said.

"For you, Dodo, yes."

Chapter 20

As the shoot at Christie's was winding down and Kelly ran off to meet her mother, Ollie proposed going out for a drink somewhere. Mrs. Welland declined to join them, so it was just Emma and Ollie who wound up not far away at the rooftop lounge of the Peninsula Hotel, where they were able to snag a terrace table for two that commanded spectacular views of midtown skyscrapers to the east and north. The strips of lighted windows on graph paper façades shone brighter and brighter as the sky's luminosity faded. It was classic martinis for both of them.

"We're off to a great start," said Ollie, raising his glass in a toast.

"A great start!" said Emma, gingerly raising her glass so as not to spill anything and clinking it with Ollie's. "Is this a favorite spot of yours?"

Ollie glanced around.

"Nope," he said. "But every rooftop bar in midtown serving a thirty-dollar martini is the same, isn't it?"

"It seems like your kind of place."

"All of my kind of places are long gone," said Ollie, with playful weariness. "These new places are meant to look like they've been here since the Jazz Age, but of course they are only hospitality-brand experiences cooked up yesterday by luxury hotel corporations."

Emma smirked. In the interpretation of Ollie's nostalgic observations, she was learning to weigh neither the bitterness nor the brightness too heavily. Neither seemed a baseline for the other. As she took a sip of her martini, she decided not to worry, for the moment, how this insight might guide her editing of Ollie's interview material.

"Yet you've always kept up, haven't you?" she said. "As someone in the whirl of New York media, always connected to the hot, new thing?"

"Until recently I was, sure," said Ollie. "Then I decided, what's the point? I'm certainly still curious about everything, but no one needs the smart, old white guy to be the arbiter of anything anymore."

"Mmm."

"My days of whirling and weighing in have come to a close. My chief responsibility now is simply to keep my body clean and stay out of bright lighting. Though, of course, I have my memories of the Peninsula and pretty much every other building that we see before us here in midtown." With a small sweep of one hand, Ollie indicated the sparkling urban panorama in front of them. "Right downstairs, in fact, in one of the suites, is where your father and I met with Oprah for breakfast one morning in the early- or maybe mid-2000s. . . ."

"Oprah Winfrey?"

"Is there another? We were proposing to do a shoot of her art collection and the house she'd just bought in Montecito. Do you know Montecito? Just outside Santa Barbara. Gorgeous little town. She had, probably still has, a Thomas Hart Benton painting of two slaves coming home to a cabin after their day in the fields."

"Did you get the shoot?"

"Oh, yes, we did. She very kindly invited us out there and could not have been nicer."

"You did the interview."

"I did."

"And what did you think?"

"Of the lady? Genius. Big soul. Force of nature."

"So you . . . traveled with my father?"

Ollie adjusted himself in his seat.

"We were colleagues, Emma. By that time, that's all we were. But we were a great team. And the older I get, the more I think I prefer teammates to any other kind of relationship."

"Why is that?"

"It's cleaner."

"Were you and Doris a team?"

"That's exactly what we were. That's exactly what she wanted. Husbands didn't work for her. Boyfriends never did either, really. At the end, she had Bernard, her butler, who was stranger than Jesus in a sun dress, but she was quite weak by then, and we should all be forgiven our weaknesses, no?"

"So my father was more of a protégé?"

"*I* was the protégé, darling, even if I was much the older party. He had the big magazine behind him. He was the wunderkind. I felt lucky to have the gig. Remember, even in the good old days, there were never too many slots for opinionated queens who knew a little about too much."

Now that Emma was getting to know a bit more about who Ollie was, she was better able to put into perspective some of the impressions she had gained about him over the years.

"It took me a while to know what was going on," she said. "I knew plenty of gay people when I was a kid, of course, and in school, but I never understood about my father until one time when I saw you put your hand on his shoulder, and you two shared a laugh over some private joke or something—this was at my own dinner table. . . !"

"And you suddenly got a vision of your father in a bouffant wig and a marabou boa."

"Well, not that, but . . ."

"Close."

"And you know, Ollie, I had friends whose fathers were gay, but they were gay-gay, if you know what I mean—*Will and Grace* gay, gays who vote and pay taxes and drive their kids to soccer practice in hybrid SUVs."

"Lord help us."

"And my father was not like that. He was another kind of creature entirely."

Ollie took a sip of his martini.

"Whatever he was, Emma, he loved you," he said. "Of course you know that. And he loved your mother. People are complicated."

Emma shook her head, suddenly feeling very emotional.

"I wanted to talk to him about it," she said plaintively, "but I didn't know if I was allowed to ask anything, if I was supposed to know anything—at least then, when I was younger. I was probably eleven or twelve when you were doing that Oprah article. By the time he actually had a boyfriend, years later, or something like a boyfriend, just before he died—this man Charles, Charles McKenna, much younger than Dad—by that time, the unspoken had morphed into the unexamined."

"Yup."

"Which I accepted but could never quite swallow."

They were silent for a moment. Muffled traffic sounds from the street below, almost as pleasant as white noise, echoed up between mute stone cliffs to mix genially with the plaintive melody of a classical Chinese flute, which was floating from a speaker concealed on the terrace in a nearby planter. Then Emma went on.

"What I'm realizing is that you may know more about certain parts of my father's life than I do, and I still feel like I don't know what I'm allowed to ask."

"What do you want to ask?"

"I don't know that, either."

Ollie took a deep breath and exhaled.

"Look, there are probably no big secrets here," he said. "But keep in mind that most kids don't know everything about their parents, and it's just as well."

"Right."

"Ask me anything, anytime. And then let me ask you what's going on under that bandage on your elbow."

"Ha! I hate to be a complainer, but for you, I'll tell all," said Emma, as her mood lightened under the influence of the cocktail. "I dunno. I begin to realize that the flip side of my curiosity, the thing that drives my filmmaking, is this . . . passivity.

I should have broached the subject with my father. Simple as that."

"I'm sure he would have valued the opportunity to talk to you about it."

"It was *easy*, it was *convenient*, not to go to that explicit place with him, you know? But that's not good. How did I ever pick up such a bad habit?"

"Civilization sits on normal people like—"

Emma made a gesture to pause Ollie's comment, and continued.

"And right now, it's the same thing with Robert. What do I feel about the guy, and what should I do about it? Why is it so *easy* to do nothing, and what's the cost of doing nothing?"

Ollie was listening and processing Emma's words.

"Okay, sorry, please continue," said Emma. "Civilization sits on normal people . . ."

"I only want to suggest," said Ollie quietly, "that things take the time they take, and that each thing is unique. Whether or not you stay married to Robert, you're on the only path you've got to get there. If that makes any sense."

"It will make a great deal of sense in a minute, I assure you," said Emma, blinking her eyes waggishly and reaching for her martini.

PART 4

TREASURES

CHAPTER 21

Though Dr. Lee maintained that beginning the radiation sooner was better, she did sign off on Emma's wish to delay the start of treatment until after the visit to Artemis in Monaco.

"Synovial sarcoma is slow-growing, and your symptoms seem manageable," said the doctor, "so as long as we get you started within a week or two, I think we're fine. More than that, I am not comfortable with. What we don't want is for any of the cells to break away and get started somewhere else."

Artemis had agreed to speak on camera about her Duchess of Windsor brooch, and arranged for two of her Monaco-based friends to be part of the project, too: a Russian woman who owned a diamond-and-seed-pearl tiara once belonging to Lady Marguerite Allan, a Canadian banker's wife who took the tiara with her on the ill-fated 1915 voyage of the *Lusitania*, and who was rescued from the wreck along with her diamonds and her maid; and an Emirati woman who owned the flawless, twenty-six-carat, pigeon-blood-red ruby nicknamed "Light of the Shan," said to have been owned by Supayalat, the last empress of Burma—a bauble that the woman purchased at Sotheby's in 2015 for thirty million dollars. The two women were participating anonymously, to be represented in the film only by their words in voice-over narration, paired with both moving and still shots of their glamorous property. Each woman's English bore a charming accent, which Emma thought would be good for the film. Moreover, Emma generally liked the fact that the texture of the film was evolving according to both the participants' respective baubles and personalities, since this was likely to present editing challenges that would stimulate Emma's creativity and might yield something more exciting than a typical documentary.

"That hint of mystery will be great fun," said Artemis. "People will think, who is the lady who secretly owns the Burmese ruby? And it will say something about the nature of ownership of such things in modern times, don't you agree?"

Emma did agree. The territory between transparency and concealment might be new to her, but she decided to embrace the secrecy as gamely as she was going forward with her medical procedures. There was no choice *but* to go forward. In the case of the film, going forward was thankfully made easier by a fifty-thousand-dollar "grant" from Emma's mother, Janet Fremont, who had just had a sold-out show in London and felt sorry that Emma had been turned down by the last of the institutions she'd applied to for support. The project's budget was about three times that amount, but Emma was still hoping that some possibility for private support might present itself—somehow—once the project was further underway.

Adding to her angst was the fact that she had turned down an offer of the same amount that Robert had made recently via text message, to help fund the film. He proposed coming on board as a "partner" in the project. Emma noted that he used the word "invest" and referred to the film as a "property."

"What made you think we need money?" asked Emma, when she responded to his text with a phone call.

"Tom mentioned it to me—your cameraman," said Robert. "He and I still have a beer now and then."

"Okay, so . . . I'm assuming you believe in my vision for the film as much as Tom does?"

"What do you mean?"

"I mean, do you believe in my vision for the film? Simple question."

"Well . . . sure I do."

"Tell me what it is."

"I don't understand."

"My vision for the film. If you believe in it, you should be able to express what it means to you."

"That, uh . . . that women have been great collectors of important jewelry."

"So that . . ."

"So that . . . when they wear it, people know that . . ."

Robert trailed off. He knew he was headed in the wrong direction.

"What do people know, my darling?" said Emma, as patiently as possible.

"Well, I'd love to learn *more* about the film and your vision for it, Ems. I really do think I could help."

"Fine," said Emma. "Will you let me keep that in mind?"

After she hung up, she realized that she was far less annoyed with Robert than she would have expected herself to be.

He doesn't get me as an artist, and maybe he never really got me as a person. And maybe—well, obviously—I never really got him, either . . .

CHAPTER 22

June 1957

Calling Doris and Barbara "best friends" was probably too schoolgirlish a way to describe two women who, by the 1950s, were much divorced—with seven former marriages between them, including one each to the same man, Rubirosa—and among the ten richest individuals in the world. They both enjoyed a privileged existence that was loosely organized around an international social circuit encompassing the world's most glamorous parties, where they more or less knew, if they cared to think about it, they might run into each other—as in a family, where members assume that on big holidays, they will see all of the usual faces. Which worked well enough for Doris and Barbara, for whom actual family now, aside from ex-husbands, meant Doris's mother, Nanaline, recently relocated with her butler, maid, and nurse from the Duke mansion to the Stanhope Hotel, and Barbara's son, Lance, who was growing interested in Grand Prix motor racing and the kind of women who went for race car drivers. At the age of nineteen, Lance now was living in Los Angeles under the watchful eye of ex-husband Cary Grant's ex-valet, who had agreed to keep on looking after the young man, as he had done when Barbara and Grant were married.

It was after running into each other in Venice, in early June 1957, at a costume party given by Elsa Maxwell on the rooftop of the Danieli Hotel, that Doris and Barbara decided on the spur of the moment to voyage together later that month to New

York, where they were both expected: Doris by a current beau, Joey Castro, a handsome young jazz pianist who was then based mostly in Los Angeles and had gotten a brief gig in a New York club; and Barbara by her sixth husband, Gottfried von Cramm, with whom she'd be going on to Mexico, to the Japanese-style house that she was building in Cuernavaca. In order to spend a few days catching up more or less privately, the women decided to sail, and Doris insisted on their going on the SS *United States*, the most modern ocean liner of the time, "the incarnation of our global superiority since the war."

Stealthily and separately, Doris and Barbara made their way to Le Havre and boarded the ship unobtrusively, unnoticed by the press. For herself, Doris had procured the ship's most luxurious accommodations, the Duck Suite, which comprised two bedrooms and a spacious parlor, decorated in an uncluttered, fashionably contemporary style, with gold-leafed aluminum wall panels featuring delicately painted vignettes with ducks. She was traveling with her companion May McFarland, who several years before had taken over Doris's Independent Aid charity, after dear Pansy died. Barbara had taken one of the ship's fourteen other first-class suites for herself and her new favorite beau, Jimmy Douglas—a handsome young American, eighteen years her junior, whom she'd met at Maxwell's party. Both women were so well-known that it was possible they'd be recognized by at least some on board, but in an effort to minimize unwanted fuss, May had seen to it that the ship's passenger list would identify these first-class travelers as "Miss May McFarland and maid" and "Mr. and Mrs. James Henderson Douglas." It was "Mrs. Douglas" who deposited with the purser a jewel case containing necklaces, bracelets, and earrings, but not the enormous thirty-eight-carat diamond ring that she wore practically every day; and it was "Miss McFarland's maid" who was delighted to learn that she could stash her mistress's jewels in the Duck Suite's own safe.

Dinner on the first night was informal, as on most ocean liners, and the women were still in their day clothes when they met for a pre-dinner cocktail in Doris's suite—Doris in a parakeet-green silk dress with sashed waist by Claire McCardell, Barbara in a black-and-white cotton gingham dress with fan-back peplum by Jacques Fath.

"Teetotaling?" remarked Doris, when she heard Barbara ask the cabin steward for a club soda and bitters on the rocks with a twist of lime.

"For the voyage, Dodo, yes," said Barbara. "Jimmy is helping me stay away from alcohol while we're shipboard."

"Good for you," said Doris.

"Yes. And he got me my Valium, which is apparently much better for me than the alcohol."

"So he's useful."

"That's exactly what he is."

"A friend of Elsa's?"

Barbara made an expression of indifference, while reassuring herself with a glance at her Pasha diamond.

"Lives in Paris," she said. "Originally from Chicago. Was staying in Venice with the Brandolinis—so there's that. It was his friend, Philip, whom Elsa invited to the party, and Philip brought Jimmy along. Did you meet Philip van Rensselaer? Quite good-looking. Good family, as far as that goes, but apparently he passes bad checks and sells fake paintings—Philip, that is."

"Oh, *that*."

"Exactly—*that*."

"It's not enough for men to be lazy anymore, is it? They've got to be reprobate now."

They both laughed.

"It's all the rage," said Barbara.

Jimmy, as per his instructions, was currently waiting in the first-class smoking room, where Barbara said she would find him. May, wanting to give Doris some privacy, was off poking around the ship's library.

"Anyway, it was tin whistles and kazoos at first sight," continued Barbara. "His father's Secretary of the Air Force, or something like that."

"I see," said Doris. "But what does the boy do? Anything?"

"Oh, you know. He seems to know a lot about furniture and paintings. He's terribly interested in restoring Venice, or at least one of the palazzos."

Doris shook her head with a smirk.

"Did Elsa tap you for the charity?" she said.

"Of course she did," said Barbara. "I gave them fifty. You too?"

"Yep—fifty. I mean, that's what we were there for, wasn't it? Elsa in her doge's cap—ha! She practically demanded her tribute."

"What I chiefly remember about Elsa that night was how intently she was pushing Ari Onassis on Maria Callas."

"Oh, I know! What was that all about?"

"Good question. They're both married; they both attended the party alone. And did you see the way they were snogging?"

"I did. Everyone did."

"I'm sure Ari asked Elsa to invite Maria. And since Elsa is completely enamored of Maria, I'm sure she was only too happy to do so."

"This is why I'm glad we have a few days on a boat," said Doris. "Peace and quiet, away from all that."

"I'll drink to that," said Barbara, raising her glass. "Well, you know what I mean." She took a sip of her club soda, then set it aside. "Shall we go find Jimmy?"

The sea was calm, and walking through the ship was as steady as in any hotel. They were aboard the largest ocean liner built in the United States and, at 53,300 tons and 240,000 horsepower, lighter but more powerful than its chief rival, the *Queen Mary*—which helped make it the fastest ocean liner ever to cross the Atlantic. Originally conceived in partnership with the U.S. Navy, for the possibility of converting to transport troops quickly anywhere in the world, the *United States* was basically an ocean-racing machine whose service speed—thirty-two knots, in comparison with the *Queen Mary*'s stately twenty-six—meant that its normal Atlantic crossing took four days instead of the usual five. In fact, the ship's top speed—forty-two knots, in comparison with the *Queen Mary*'s thirty-two—

resulted in so much wind that the deck promenades had to be built enclosed. The ship's portholes couldn't even be opened at such a speed. Though filled with aluminum structural elements and even part-aluminum furniture, because it was meant to be as fireproof as possible, the ship entered commercial service in 1952 as America's luxurious ship-of-state: thoroughly modern and sleekly contemporary, its first class an unstuffy alternative to the wood-paneled coziness of the British liners from Cunard and White Star. The interiors were designed by the all-female design firm of Smyth, Urquhart & Marckwald, which had done the interiors of 1930s widely hailed SS *America*. The goal for the *United States*, said interior designer Dorothy Marckwald, was to fit the vessel's interior for both luxury and function, to create "a look that emphasized simplicity over palatial, restrained elegance over glitz and glitter."

In the first-class dining room, the elegance was expressed by the bold red of upholstered armchairs of sleek modern design, punctuating a field of white-clothed tables. Commanding the airy, double-story space from a central wall was a golden relief sculpture entitled "Expressions of Freedom," depicting American life in the form of four scantily clad women bathing in the light of a star that one of them was holding aloft. A small band led by a pianist was providing a calmly buoyant atmosphere as Doris and Barbara, accompanied by May and Jimmy, were shown to the table that May had arranged for the voyage, off to one side of the room, partly obscured by one of the celery-white columns—"a little out of the way," as Doris had asked for. Still, an aging but decidedly grand countess from Elsa Maxwell's floating carnival of very important people, Lady Arabella DeCourcy Gresham, managed to spot Barbara as the lady and her second husband, the Earl of Sidwich, aged and doddering, were being shown to their table.

"*Polpettina*, I didn't know you were on board," said Lady Arabella. "I didn't see your name on the passenger list, or the baron's."

Jimmy began to rise from his seat, but Barbara, with one hand to his thigh, pressed him back down.

"We're traveling incognito," said Barbara, indicating the others at the table with a sweep of the hand but offering no introductions. To judge from the look of quiet amusement that crossed Lady Arabella's face, she knew exactly who or what everyone at the table was, and was delighted to play their game.

"Of course you are," said Lady Arabella, in a sly, low tone that seemed to be for Barbara alone. "And we wouldn't expect stewards on an American ship to recognize someone who's anyone, would we?"

Her manner of speaking identified her as a British aristocrat *at very least.*

"Well, if the ship is so *declassé,* one might ask what *you* are doing on it," said Barbara. Doris and May were trying to ignore the exchange, appearing to weigh dinner options behind a menu that May was holding open.

"My daughter is threatening to elope," said Lady Arabella. "So we have to get to New York as soon as possible. That's where she's based. Horace hates flying, and to be honest, so do I."

Barbara acknowledged the explanation with a nod.

"I hope you enjoy your dinner," she said.

"Since we're both here, we might as well see something of each other," said Lady Arabella, going off with her husband.

"Nice to meet you," muttered Doris, sarcastically.

"She's a bit of a snob, but I like her," said Barbara. "She always has good gossip."

"Is that so?" said Doris. "Then maybe we should give her something to gossip about."

"You're incorrigible."

"I admit it."

The signature motif of the United States Lines was the American eagle, as depicted on the country's Great Seal, with wings spread, grasping an olive branch in its right talon and a bundle of arrows in its left. This fearsome motif, and thus subliminally the theme of war and peace, was everywhere on board the ship—woven into carpets and peering down from plaques, crowning the top of swizzle sticks and etched onto the stemware. On the cover of the first-class dinner menu, featuring three horizontal stripes—red, white, and blue—were two of these eagles, one shadowed in the red stripe, one shadowed in the blue, with MENU in script and DINNER in block letters printed in the white stripe, in typefaces undoubtedly selected by Dorothy Marckwald for their elegant modernity—"Pax Americana Light" and "Martial Extended," respectively. It was stars only, though—blue-gray ones on a field of white—that were emblazoned on the ship's china; and the tabletop was further graced with a sleek trumpet vase of red and white carnations, and, instead of candles, since fire on the ship was kept to a minimum, a small, aluminum electric lamp whose space-age shade in four graduated, circular bands was exactly what the world's most modern ship required.

Dinner was leisurely, and conversation ranged from the 89th Belmont Stakes, to the Asian flu, to the benefits of fresh ocean air. Barbara announced that she had found the ship's swimming pool and gymnasium, and had already booked a massage for the following morning. Jimmy, who despite his laddish enthusiasm always seemed to rely on Barbara's cue as to whether to speak or not, surprised everyone when he reported having heard rumors the day before in Paris that Egypt was going to nationalize the Suez Canal.

"What's the big deal about that?" said Barbara. "Isn't the canal *in* Egypt?"

Jimmy looked concerned with the naïveté of Barbara's question but seemed patient.

"Well, the canal is owned by the French and the British, first of all," he said. "So taking it would be stealing. But the thing is a tremendous commercial and military asset. People are afraid of what would happen if the Egyptians controlled it—and by people, I mean the Americans and the Soviets."

"Lord," said Barbara.

"Lord," said May.

"This one's alright, Babbo," said Doris, impressed with Jimmy's knowledge of current affairs. The fact that he seemed to be so well-informed, as well as the fact that he was encouraging her friend not to drink so heavily, led Doris to approve of the man.

"If only she'd keep this one," whispered May to Doris, as Jimmy lit Barbara's cigarette.

"I know," said Doris sadly. "But at some point, she sends them all packing."

Spirits were high in the Navajo Lounge after dinner. If any of the ship's passengers were tired after a day of travel, boarding, and settling in, they didn't show it. The lounge's atmosphere was lively with everyone's excitement over being underway. With low lighting and walls and ceilings burnished in a lustrous shade of midnight blue, the lounge's décor was accented by elegant, sand-finished panels emblazoned with a series of Navajo *yei* figures—geometric stylized divine spirits—in enameled copper. The sound of dozens of conversations buzzed away over a string of Broadway hit songs spouting from the room's tiny bandstand. As waiters scurried about taking and delivering orders, Doris, Barbara, and party were shown to one of the small, fixed pedestal tables near an oversize porthole affording a view onto the enclosed promenade outside. Already installed at a table nearby was Lady Arabella and the earl, sitting with another grand-looking British couple. Waves were exchanged as Barbara took her seat.

"Perfect opportunity," said Doris.

"But we would need to rehearse . . ." said Barbara.

"*Carpe diem*, Babbo."

"Let's get a round of drinks in us first, though."

Jimmy placed his hand over Barbara's.

"Join me in a club soda and bitters, darling, won't you?" he said.

The ship's first-class passenger list included a senator, a congressman, a colonel, two judges, and numerous doctors of various sorts, among the "Mr. and Mrs.'s," presumably American, in addition to several "M. et Mme's" and "Sig. e Sig.ra's." Indeed, a glance over the Navajo Lounge that evening suggested that many of the ladies and gentlemen enjoying this trip's first night at sea were well-padded American businessmen and their well-padded wives, dressed in standard dark suits and conservatively fashionable dresses.

Yet there were several, small variations in informal, first-night style that spoke as much about America's regional differences as the ship's artworks did. Despite the fact that it was summer, one elderly couple were dressed in tweed, as if for a testimonial dinner at a northeastern university—he in a sober gray suit, she in a sober brown dress—while another couple were turned out with more southwestern flair, as if for a poolside barbecue in Santa Barbara—he in a robin's-egg blue suit, she in a full-skirted shirtwaist in a vibrant pink, green, and white plaid. Even the couple, misguided or not, who'd gone ahead and dressed formally fit perfectly well into the mosaic. As the lyrical strains of "On the Street Where You Live" poured forth, Tuxedo and Gown listened as respectfully as in a concert hall, though sipping champagne. Elsewhere in the room, a Japanese couple in black nursed cognacs; a trio of Africans in native garb conversed quietly over coffee; and a party of three German couples laughed uproariously and repeatedly over beers and more beers.

"There's that man again," said Doris to May, and then she drew Barbara's attention to the man. "Barbara, who *is* that?"

"Who is who?" said Barbara.

"Over there. He was staring at us just a second ago."

"People stare."

"I saw him watching us in the dining room, too."

"I wouldn't worry about it."

"He was at a table all by himself," said May.

"Why, May, are you interested?" said Barbara slyly.

Sitting alone at the bar, across the room, the man was middle-aged, slender, and mild-looking, and dressed in a stylish navy-blue suit and silver-toned tie, his dark hair rigorously combed and pomaded into a slick-back. He looked like he might be a banker or a government official. He seemed to be quietly savoring his view of the crowd, and was possibly glancing now and then in the direction of Doris and Barbara's table.

"*No*," said May, with an amused mock-sneer.

"I just think it's odd," said Doris.

Presently, May spotted Lady Arabella and her party rising from their table and nudged Doris discreetly with her elbow. Doris saw them and said, "Babbo, here we go."

"What—sorry?" said Barbara, initially confused. Then Doris launched right into it.

"I saw Rubi first, you know," announced Doris in a conspicuously dramatic tone, sounding sharp, if not angry.

"Oh—yes," said Barbara, catching on. "Well . . . *no*," she declared with theatrical flair. "*I* saw him first—in London, during the war, at a party. You bitch."

Doris raised her head triumphantly.

"Ahh, but I married him first, didn't I?" she said.

Barbara sneered almost as broadly as an actress might in a silent film.

"What I meant, Doris *dear*, is that I *had* him first," she said. "So technically, the round goes to me. . . ."

When approaching their table, Lady Arabella seemed ready to stop for a few words, but appeared to think better of it when she heard the women spatting. As she passed, she simply nodded, with a pleasant smile plastered on her face. Then, as she and her party swept out of the lounge, she seemed to be leaning into her female counterpart as if to share a private word.

"Do you think she heard?" said Barbara.

"Definitely," said Doris.

"Do you think she fell for it?"

"Hook, line, and sinker."

"I feel so wicked," said Barbara, with a giggle.

"I know the type," said Doris. "She'll be interested."

"Does she really strike you as too awful? She's very well-connected."

"A snob, as you say," said Doris.

"She seems a little biting to me," said May.

"Biting! How so?" said Barbara.

"'*Polpettina*'?"

"What about it? She always calls me that. You know the British and their Italianisms. It's an endearment. Isn't it?"

"Maybe between you two it is," said Doris.

"It means 'little meatball,'" said May, who knew Italian and had translated for Doris at the dinner table, behind their menu.

"Meatball?" said Barbara.

"It's something you might say to a chubby child," said May.

Barbara looked crestfallen.

"But it sounds so nice," she said.

Jimmy piped up.

"Listen, we can have a nice swim in the morning and get in some exercise," he said, trying to be helpful. He well knew Barbara's fears about getting old and plump. He knew, in fact, that for the moment, he was her chief form of remedy for that condition.

"No, no," Barbara told Jimmy. "I'll swim alone tomorrow morning, then my massage. You run along. Go play shuffleboard or something."

CHAPTER 23

September 1951

Doris had, in fact, encountered Lady Arabella once before, at Count Beistegui's legendary 1951 ball in Venice, at his sumptuous eighteenth-century Palazzo Labia. It began simply as a meeting in passing, not even an introduction.

Thousands of spectators lined the Grand Canal that night, jammed together in boats, and crowded on *vaporetto* landings and on private piers and balconies, watching the flotilla of guests proceed toward the blue-and-white-spiral–striped poles of the palazzo's pier. Doris's gondola was arriving at around ten p.m., the same time as dozens of other boats, including Lady Arabella's private *motoscafo*. Under the Hollywood-level floodlighting that had been set up for the occasion to illuminate the palazzo's façade and double-story *portone*, the great door onto the canal—and which also lit up a significant stretch of the Grand Canal itself—liveried servants were darting about frantically with lanterns, shouting, gesturing, trying to direct arriving water traffic as best they could, arranging the disembarkments from gondolas and *motoscafi* onto the stone steps in as orderly a fashion as possible, so that each party—indeed, each costume—could have its moment to be seen and admired by onlookers, which included the general press. It was a runway moment that would be repeated inside the palazzo at the entrance to the great ballroom, for invited guests and the Count's selected photographers.

Amidst the commotion, Lady Arabella's *motoscafo*, bearing her and three friends, all dressed alike as charmingly menacing "Phantoms of Venice," in voluminous black satin capes with black tricorn hats, masks, and gloves, chanced to nudge itself in front of Doris's boat, which had been approaching the pier first. As the *motoscafo*'s pilot was urgently commanded to go ahead and discharge his passengers immediately, Lady Arabella momentarily lowered her mask to flash a wordless frown of apology to her disguised fellow-guest in the other boat. Then, under a shower of photo flashes and with the help of a liveried arm, the lady resumed her grand progress toward the stone steps. After which Doris, costumed as an eighteenth-century gentleman, in a vivid blue justacorps, long vest, and breeches with matching mask and white wig, and her beau Joey Castro, as Papageno, the cheerful, flute-playing bird catcher from Mozart's opera *The Magic Flute*, themselves disembarked and headed into the palazzo under their own shower of flashbulbs.

The glitch in precedence wasn't necessarily a slight, Doris knew, and under the circumstances, it was perfectly understandable. And it was probable that in coming hours, such a lavishly mounted event would afford many more memorable moments than this near-slight. But Doris did take note of the moment, her American sense of fair play being put somewhat out of joint, before the usual *oh-so-what* feeling arose and she remembered Mlle. Renaud's cheerful advice about always bringing your smile to the party. She knew that inside the palazzo, during the course of the evening, she would be seeing several friends, including Barbara, who was attending the ball with the Italian author, opera expert, and publicist, Count Lanfranco Rasponi.

The ball was actually more Barbara's territory than her own, Doris knew. Since the war, their styles and paths had been diverging even more sharply than before. Especially now that Doris was divorcing Rubi—"No more husbands for me," she'd confided to Elsa Maxwell, at the Danieli; "marriage is for our mothers; for me, it's lovers from now on!"—she counted herself among those identifying as the era's spiritual "seekers," and was responding to middle age by going more deeply into her modern dance practice, jazz piano playing, and the pursuit of new-fashioned practices for body and mind, like aura therapy and ayurvedic naturopathy. Barbara, for her part, had positioned herself squarely among those who had already found something and weren't budging from it. Showing far more signs of illness and physical weakness than Doris was, Barbara was content to fall into many of the old-fashioned habits that people did in response to falling apart—costly purchases, elaborate parties, and visits to stodgy thermal spas where, for a week or a month, thalassotherapy and mashed carrots were substituted for champagne and caviar.

Having emerged from the war years questioning what her life was for, Doris had been thinking seriously about the meaning of husbands and duties and personal happiness and service to others. The exact balance among these elements had always been totally up to her, of course, but now the actual balancing maneuvers felt like a huger task than ever before—exciting, because everyone was talking about the bright, postwar future, but also a little frightening, since the future is always unknown. Was this feeling a result of aging? Of worldwide paroxysm? Did all women feel like this in 1951—facing a new decade of fresh social possibilities? Did all rich people feel like this now—shaken loose from the well-settled ways of their parents and grandparents?

In a way, these questions made Doris feel more reliant than ever on her unique friendship with Barbara, because the two women were of the same species. On the other hand, Barbara didn't seem interested in such questions and was perfectly happy with the well-settled ways, as in being recognized as one of the fifteen hundred people necessary for what the press on two continents were calling "the ball of the century"—the first truly spectacular social event of its scale since the war. Count Beistegui had created his ball specifically to reconvene the world's *crème de la crème: ancien régime* nobility and new Hollywood royalty, millionaire industrialists and superstar artists, fashion designers and prominent socialites. Some outsiders griped about the "moral indecency" of such theatrical opulence when so much of Europe still lay in ruins. Indeed, some expected the Mayor of Venice, who was a Communist, to disapprove of the ball, since so many of his people were still impoverished. Yet reports were that both the Mayor and his people were delighted with the spectacle, so with that in mind, Doris felt free to enter the Palazzo Labia delighted, too.

Don Carlos de Beistegui y de Yturbe was a Parisian-born, Eton-educated art collector and aesthete whose Mexican-Spanish family had made a fortune in mining. Known as Charlie to his friends, he was a flamboyant bachelor rumored to be heterosexual, with a taste for all things rare and beautiful. In the early 1930s, he commissioned Le Corbusier to add a modernist rooftop terrace-cum-open air salon to his penthouse near the Place de l'Étoile, with an electronically operated wall of hedge that could slide away to reveal a view of the Arc de Triomphe. In 1939, he bought the eighteenth-century Château de Groussay, outside of Paris, and made it a showplace. Then in 1948, he bought the Palazzo Labia, at the corner of the Grand and Cannaregio canals, and restored *that*.

Invitations to the ball had gone out nine months in advance, so guests would have adequate time to prepare. And because so many others *thought* they should be guests, the Count sequestered himself in a suite at the Grand Hotel on the day of the ball, away from a telephone, until he made a grand entrance in his palace's *salone della feste* at eleven, dressed as an historic Procurator of the Venetian Republic, in scarlet damask robes and a magnificent, white, sausage-curl wig, his normal height of five-foot-six boosted several inches by platform shoes.

The palazzo's grand, double-height ballroom was a stage piece of illusory Baroque architecture in multicolored marble. Designed and decorated theatrically to suggest both interior and exterior spaces, the room was graced with frescos by Tiepolo from the life of Cleopatra—"The Meeting of Anthony and Cleopatra" and "The Banquet of Cleopatra"—so the Count had set "Anthony and Cleopatra" as the ball's theme, and asked two friends to preside: actress, socialite, and wife of the former British ambassador to France, Lady Diana Cooper, costumed as the Egyptian queen, and *bon vivant* Baron Frédéric de Cabrol, as the Roman general.

Besides Doris and Barbara, Count Beistegui's guests that night included Salvador and Gala Dalí; the Aga Khan III and the Begum Aga Khan; actor/director Orson Welles and Brazilian socialite Aimée de Heeren; couturier Jacques Fath and his wife, Genevieve; Surrealist painter Leonor Fini and sculptor Count Sforzino Sforza; scores of princes and princesses; several collectors, connoisseurs, and prominent figures from the decorative arts; and about a thousand others. Many were costumed lavishly as historical or mythological personages, like the Empress of China, Le Roi Soleil, and the Queen of Africa; and many were disguised as phantoms, spectres, demons, angels, slaves, potentates, or simply *grand siècle* gentlepeople, in costumes featuring elaborate wigs, fanciful masks, exotic feathers, glittering sequins, and extravagant ruffles. Many of the palazzo's public rooms were open. Entertainment throughout the evening, besides the music of several orchestras, featured jugglers and puppets, as well as ballerinas from the famed company of the Marquis de Cuevas and acrobatics by a troupe of shirtless Venetian firemen. Outside, in the palazzo's courtyard, uninvited onlookers were dazzled by fireworks and treated to a Punch-and-Judy show for which some of the Count's staff unauthorizedly sold tickets. Residents of neighboring palazzos also sold tickets for the view of the spectacle from their windows.

"You look marvelous; it fits beautifully," said Cecil Beaton, finding Doris surveying the ball from a broad balcony overlooking the ballroom floor, at around midnight. It was Cecil who had suggested and designed Doris's costume, which was inspired by the composer Antonio Salieri, the great friend and/or rival of Mozart.

"Thank you," said Doris, happy to see her friend, whom she knew had been engaged by the Count to photograph selected guests of the ball. "Shouldn't you be snapping?"

"Oh, yes," said Cecil, pointing to the entrance to a salon nearby, where he and his assistants had set up a temporary studio. "I've gotten most of the ones the Count wanted already. They made their entrance and were shown directly to me for their portraits, and only then joined the party."

"Because the pictures will live on."

"That's the idea, anyway. My boys are doing some of the lesser people now. There's a bar in there, so it's quite jolly."

"He's paying you?"

"Of course he's paying me—a good price, too. Beistegui is utterly ruthless, so one has to be ruthless back. And then it's all hunky-dory."

"I've barely met the man."

"Keep it that way, sister. He has become the most self-engrossed, pleasure-seeking creature in Europe—a man of what the French call spleen. *'Chaque jour vers l'Enfer nous descendons d'un pas . . . à travers des ténèbres qui puent.'*"

Doris looked as though she were drawing a blank.

"Baudelaire," continued Cecil. "'Every day we descend one step toward Hell, through stinking darkness.' That's Charlie." He paused. "Which is one reason, I suppose, why he gives such splendid parties."

Below, the orchestra was playing a set of Latin dance music, and while some guests were swanning or lolling about, many were dancing as best they could, encumbered by costumes and/or headdresses with a life of their own.

Cecil was dressed in an austere black cassock with white linen preaching bands at the neck, and a short, silver-white wig.

"Now, are you a clergyman?" said Doris.

"Miss Duke, I am Mr. Collins, the vicar from *Pride and Prejudice*," said Cecil, with great dignity. "And pray where is your bird catcher?"

Doris pointed toward the orchestra.

"He knew the bandleader and asked if he could sit in for a while."

"Leaving you stranded."

"Who could be stranded at a party like this?" said Doris. Cecil chuckled.

"Probably any of us," he said.

"I think he was uncomfortable," said Doris, gazing down at the revelries. "He doesn't know too many people here. We'll have a bite together in a little while."

The sounds of a spirited mambo, punctuated by bongos and Joey's pulsing piano, were vibrating among the room's marble walls. Hundreds of what Count Beistegui considered the world's most important people were trying their best to rock their hips with the sensuality demanded by the music. Among them, partnered with Rasponi, was Barbara, dressed with grandeur as Mozart, in a black, lace-trimmed costume from Dior that had cost fifteen thousand dollars.

"Did you photograph *them?*" asked Doris.

"Of course I did," said Cecil. "Then one of my boys got Barts and me doing a little rumba."

"Lovely."

"Lovely is going to be the one I take of you and her—Salieri and Mozart together."

"You're a wicked one, Vicar Beaton—planning my costume after she told me about hers."

Cecil giggled.

"You didn't tell her?" he said.

"I'll tell her after we get the picture," said Doris. "She'll be fine. Though she may be a little fuzzy on who Salieri was."

"Mmm. And I'm sure her Mozart is the stronger for it, too. I'll have someone come and find you two."

Doris looked pensive, though echoes of "Mambo Jambo" were bouncing frenetically off the marbled walls of the cavernous ballroom.

"Do you think in a hundred years, anyone will understand?" she said.

"Understand what? This ball? My photographs?" said Cecil.

"*That* photograph, of Mozart and Salieri. That she and I are friends and not friends. Rivals but not rivals."

"Oh—honestly, no," said Cecil, glibly. "No one will understand something like that from a staged photograph at a costume ball. I mean, maybe eleven people will—but then they will die, and the photographs will be destroyed in some future war, and that will be that. Even frescos fall apart. So if there's anything you want said about your friendship with Miss Hutton, you'd better say it yourself today, sister, in plain English, and make sure it's repeated."

Doris smiled.

"Maybe Barbara will write something. She writes poetry, you know."

"I know. I have the slender volume to prove it."

"In fact, she once wrote something about me. . . ."

Doris quoted some lines from the poem that Barbara had given her long ago as a girl, in the back seat of a limousine:

Show your face to me
And guide the way across
The river great and wide,
Dear friend;
Your words are always
Clear and strong,
And tamp the doubt
That rattles in my soul . . .

"Barbara wrote that?" said Cecil.

"Yes, she did," said Doris.

"She should keep at it."

"Shouldn't she, though?"

Cecil glanced toward the door of his salon-studio.

"Well, I'd better get back," he said, leaning in to give Doris a little kiss. "Let's have a dance later, shall we? And speaking of history, do make it a point to inspect Diana Cooper's costume."

"Cleopatra?"

"Oliver Messel and I did it."

"I saw it—it's beautiful, though awfully Baroque. Not at all Egyptian or Middle Eastern. . . ."

"No, no, that's right. Look at the frescos, darling," said Cecil, as he went off. "It's all Tiepolo! We took it right off the walls!

Except the collar. Lady Miss Diana didn't want the damned collar. . . ."

On the dance floor, Barbara was now doing the cha-cha with Lady Arabella, whom she'd just been introduced to—both of them delighting in occasional gestures of exaggerated politesse that would be due a great Venetian lady and a famous Viennese composer. Their laughter, of course, was inaudible over the music and general hubbub. Would all this expensive, frivolous fun truly be forgotten one day, its evidence destroyed or uninterpretable, as Cecil suggested? Did this ball signal the last of something, or perhaps the first of something? Some of the guests, despite their costumes or maybe because of a sudden, exhilarating struggle against the costumes, were being led by the music a little more deeply into their cha-cha movements, the thrusts of their pelvises and pushes of their shoulders just a bit more dynamic than they might have expected of themselves earlier, when making their courtly disembarkments at the *portone*.

Are we approaching the wild and febrile, Doris wondered, *tonight, or sometime soon in this brave new decade? Or maybe it will come in the 1960s. . . ? Is there a good kind of hedonism as well as the bad?*

She turned away from the ballroom view, accepted a glass of champagne from a passing waiter, and found herself staring at a fresco whose exalted ancient personages, draped glamorously in silks and jewels, were depicted at the height of some gracefully exaggerated gesture. Was this a known historical moment, or simply an exchange of remarks between Cleopatra's courtiers, captured for all time? And why was there a half-naked teenage girl, painted *trompe l'oeil* style, emerging from the scene at one edge of the picture, trying to push beyond the fresco's painted frame, as if to escape out into reality and onto the balcony where Doris was standing?

1951. The second half of this damned century begins.

Doris took a sip of champagne and thought how little time had passed since she was helping wounded soldiers in a hospital make tape-recordings to send home to their local radio stations . . .

"Dodo, what on earth are you doing up here?"

It was Barbara in Mozart-form, champagne glass in hand, slightly out of breath.

"Oh, my," said Doris. "I was just watching you. . . ."

"I saw you from the dance floor."

"I was chatting with Cecil."

"Yes, I saw."

They were standing at the balustrade, looking out over the party.

"He wants to photograph us together."

"Marvelous. Let's do it now."

Doris set down her glass and put her arm around Barbara's waist.

"Babbo—all *this*," said Doris, gesturing toward the entire ballroom. "You're the poet. Is it a return to something or some kind of . . . departure?"

Barbara tilted her head and regarded her friend with a gently mocking expression.

"Blimey, Mr. Pantalone, listen to you. We clearly need something stronger than champagne. Let's go see Cecil. He's got bourbon in there."

CHAPTER 24

When he got off the crosstown bus, Ollie was relieved to discover a large Korean market with a good selection of fresh flowers out front. He got the attendant to combine two bunches of orange tea roses into one big bunch, paid for them, and headed around the corner to Emma's building. He'd been to the apartment several times before, long ago, as a guest of Emma's father and mother; and it was a slight surprise to be returning there two decades later, under circumstances he would scarcely have been able to imagine only a few weeks before.

"Oh, they're beautiful," said Emma, taking the flowers from him as she showed him into the apartment. "You can put your jacket there on the bench, if you like."

"Thanks, I think I'll keep it on for the moment," said Ollie. "Sometimes an old man feels chilly in the spring."

His eye was caught by the artworks and objects displayed in the commodious foyer, familiar and still, by and large, in the same positions they occupied two decades before.

"We'll eat in twenty, if that's okay with you. I have some pasta for us. Just throwing together a salad. Please go on in and make yourself comfortable."

"Alright."

"I put some Campari out for us," added Emma, as she headed back to the kitchen. "Or I could offer you some water, some wine. . . ."

Bottles of Campari and soda, and a small dish of orange

slices, were sitting on a tray near the sofa. There in the living room and the dining room, much as they were previously, were the walls of books, the assortment of pleasingly mismatched furniture, both contemporary and old or antique, the paintings by Janet Fremont and other artists, even the ficus bush in a pot on the floor, near a window—could it possibly be the same plant, or a descendant of it. . . ?

"We'll be in the kitchen tonight," said Emma, reappearing with a plate of artichoke bruschetta. "Much cozier for two people. The dining room, as you may remember, works better with a cast of thousands."

"I remember those," said Ollie, pointing across the room toward two paintings by Emma's mother, hung close together: a beach scene with a little girl in a floppy hat, and a verdant landscape with a stream or canal in the foreground.

"Did you realize that was me?" said Emma, referring to the little girl.

"I believe your father once did tell me that, yes."

"*On the Lido.* Isn't it sweet? May I?"

Emma served the Campari, and they settled into their seats. Ollie took a sip.

"You haven't changed the place much," he said.

"I haven't changed anything," said Emma. "It's my mother's apartment. She moved out not long after Daddy died. Robert and I tried living here, but it never felt right, even though we loved saving the money. Then we got a place in Prospect Heights, and things kind of went downhill from there—like I told you. So I came back."

"It's larger than I remember."

"Too large. I think of myself as the caretaker."

Ollie laughed.

"Nice of you to remember the aperitif," he said.

"Oh . . . yes," she said. "Learned that one from you."

"The last time I was here, I remember thinking I was the old man," he said. "Your parents and so many of those bright, young people at their table—most of them were a generation younger than me, or more. Now that I'm back, I'm thinking, Oh, to be sixty-five again!"

"You haven't changed a bit," said Emma, as sincerely as she could.

"Thank you for noticing," said Ollie, with an impish smile. "But *you* have."

"Good, because I'd never want to be ten again."

"Rightly so."

"Or twenty-eight."

Ollie raised an eyebrow.

"The year you were married," he guessed.

Emma sighed.

"He just called," she said. "So I can't . . ."

Emma waved a hand, as if to dismiss an annoying thought.

"It's okay," said Ollie.

"We dated for years. Actually, it wasn't dating, exactly. It was hanging out. And that's exactly the way the marriage went."

"And you wanted more."

"I wanted fair. That's all I ever wanted. Mutual . . . whatever, respect. That was part of the cool, millennial kind of relationship I thought we had. But Robert . . . it's like he reverted to some kind of boomer personality. No offense."

"None taken. Or . . . should I be flattered? I'm several centuries older than the Baby Boomers."

"Now he's making noises about getting back together, and I just don't know what to do."

"May I give you a thought?"

"Sure."

"It's like ballet. When in doubt, *jeté* out."

Emma looked confused.

"What I mean," continued Ollie, "is that if you are onstage and don't know what to do, head for the wings."

"Did I mention that we're still married?"

"Then you know what you ought to be thinking about."

Ollie heard himself speaking intimately, the way he allowed himself to do with close friends like Mrs. Welland. Since agreeing to help Emma with her film project, he had been feeling closer to her. He was also developing something like pride in seeing how successfully the precocious ten-year-old he encountered at her parents' dinner parties had matured into an autonomous adult—an equal. One is always grateful, he thought, to see the children of friends grow up well and become the kind of fellow citizens that we want to believe the world is full of. And he was proud to be working with Emma as a creative collaborator. Yet more was going on here. Ollie realized he was also proud of Martin for having transmitted to Emma so much of the very thing that had most attracted Ollie to Martin—intellectual curiosity. And in a way, Ollie's working with Emma now as an equal was a way of earning his right to this pride in Martin, and of nullifying some of the shame he'd always felt about not being capable of responding properly to Martin's curiosity in *him*.

An old man's thoughts!

Despite the intimacy, Ollie thought it might be a good idea to lighten the conversation.

"It's lovely how an aperitif can adjust the mood, isn't it?" he said, contemplating his glass and taking a sip. "Like dimming the lights."

"Nicely put," said Emma.

"It's more than a drink, isn't it? It's a moment, a way of experiencing a time of day when perhaps work is giving way to dinner, or to love and to rest—or something like that."

"Golly."

Ollie winked.

"Perhaps it's a subject that your father would've asked me to explore in twelve hundred words, with a three-hundred-word sidebar on the history of Suze."

"Suze?"

"An aperitif made from gentian root. You might try it next time."

"And that would be an article?"

Ollie feigned alarm.

"Did you never read *Nota Bene*?" he said. "There were articles like that all over the place, along with the huge spreads

on things like medieval Bavarian altar vessels and Marie Antoinette's favorite spring water. Your dad once asked me to write one of my 'Poking Around' columns on the meaning and function of the tricorn hat. I know: 'Does anyone still wear a hat?' So there was the original hat, which Spanish soldiers wore, and then all the iconography about Venice and the American Minuteman, and then suddenly it's goodbye to all that, and all Europe is wearing a bicorn and then the so-called top hat."

Emma was smiling.

"Daddy had a tricorn," she said. "He wore it for Halloween. He bought it in Venice."

"Of course he did."

"Dear Daddy," said Emma, closing her eyes for a moment, then opening them. "Ollie, once we were watching *Casablanca*—just him and me; I was probably eight or nine at the time—and right at the end, when Humphrey Bogart is explaining to Ingrid Bergman why she *must* get on that plane and the problems of three little people don't amount to a hill of beans, my father shouts, 'Look at that! Look at that!' and freezes the frame so we can take note of the behavior of their hats in that scene. That's what he called it, the 'behavior' of their hats. And I wouldn't have really registered it—you know, the brims and the angles and the lighting—without his explaining it to me. And I loved so much that he was eager for me to see this."

"That was Martin."

"I was eight, mind you, but after that, I started thinking about everything I was looking at every day but not really seeing."

"And you know, Emma, he was only talking to you about hats because he found them exciting and wanted you to find them exciting, too. That was his mind. You have a similar quality, if I may say so—enthusiasm that gets people thinking."

"I hope that's true, Ollie."

"It is. And an old pro like me is grateful for it."

Ollie was finding it stimulating to be working with Emma. He enjoyed the challenge of trying to say things on camera that were smart enough not to be cut. The challenge was even yield-

ing some new perspective on his dear departed gal pals. He had come to see, for instance, that where Barbara was the one who wanted to *be* something—a great lady, a titled eminence—Doris was the one who wanted to *do* something—improve herself, improve the world. Or did this kind of perspective simply come with advanced age? Sometimes, the shocking apprehension of the sheer number of years that he could remember—almost a century of observations and discoveries and learnings and epiphanies—required a pause, to take in the panorama. Was this Eliot's "still point of the turning world"? Was it a blessing? Was it a burden? Why did he not feel this so acutely when he was sixty-five?

"Anyway, I am glad you're coming to Monte Carlo," said Emma. "We'll need your sharp eye."

What you'll need, thought Ollie, is someone who knows how to talk to fancy rich ladies. Ollie's friend Artemis had decided to fly both him and Emma over as her guests, partly because she wanted Ollie to look at a drawing of a horse by Stubbs that she'd acquired, and partly because she thought he would have some nice chemistry with her Russian friend, Lyudmila, in conversation about the *Lusitania* tiara. It also was an opportunity, said Artemis, to help a promising filmmaker "tell a story about a certain type of woman who is always misunderstood."

Over dinner, Ollie and Emma got around to talking about two prime examples of this certain type of woman.

"I met Barbara at a party in New York, through a Princeton classmate," said Ollie, "and began helping her with Sumiya, her place in Mexico, inspired by an imperial courtesan's house in Kyoto. She hired me to do some furniture design—Meiji meets Biedermeier, as I recall—and to help her buy some things at auction."

"Was decorating always a special interest of yours?"

"At school, I studied architecture and decorative arts, and then I went to work at Christie's, in New York and then in London, where I met the designer David Hicks and started working for him—rooms in country houses and the townhomes of

the people who owned them. I always liked helping my mother select new wallpaper and furniture, and then we lost my father and couldn't afford to live that way anymore. Which was slightly inconvenient for my mother, except that the reduced circumstances made it less likely, or so she thought, that her son would grow up to be the fancy-pants he was tending toward."

"You wanted to be a decorator, and she wouldn't hear of it."

"It was the 1950s. Communists and homosexuals were not the most popular people in suburban Pennsylvania. In high school, I volunteered at the Harriton House, a historic residence in Bryn Mawr, where I met two wonderful gals from the college who knew a lot about antiques and kind of tacitly accepted me for the creature I was—whatever that was. I was only twenty-two when I met Barbara, and then, when I was twenty-five, I met Doris, on a mountaintop, in 1964."

"A mountaintop?"

Ollie recounted the tale of Barbara and Doris being interested in the same Hudson Valley mansion called Church Lake Road; Doris arriving by helicopter and taking a cursory glance at the house; Doris conferring with Barbara privately about something; and then Doris commanding Ollie to join her in the helicopter and, apparently with the approval of Barbara, accompany her back to New York.

"It was like an abduction," said Ollie. "Just what a fancy, transatlantic Princeton boy thought was a thrilling, James Bond-like caper. Yet there it was, in real life. And life with Doris was much more exciting than it was with Barbara."

"How so?"

"Well, from the very first. . . . We got into the helicopter, and Doris told the pilot, 'Straight down the Hudson, please. We want the scenic route.' The pilot said, 'I'm sorry, Miss Duke, but we haven't been cleared for that route'; and she looked at him incredulously and said, 'We'll go that way anyway.' And she said it in such a way that we all knew that, if necessary, she would get the governor on the phone in about a minute and have the route cleared. The helicopter had a phone, of course."

"So you went down the Hudson."

"We did, and it was like Marie de' Medici making her way to Marseilles—do you know the Rubens cycle at the Louvre? Inconceivably, breathtakingly grand. We gabbed the whole way, except when she was pointing out the window toward the estates of her friends, below, along the river. We instantly knew how to talk to each other. She was interested in my work at the Harriton House, and she told me all about Newport, where she was just beginning to put together her restoration project."

"Which she roped Jackie Kennedy into, didn't she?"

"Absolutely. Jackie-before-she-was-O. Doris lived larger, had a bigger idea about herself and others and the world, than anyone else I've ever known. And she was kind."

"What do you mean, 'kind'?"

"To be honest, Barbara could be a little cold. What she wanted mostly was obeisance. Doris was warmer. What she wanted was love. Didn't matter that she was what, fifty-something? She had a fire inside, not a forty-carat diamond. Doris was seductive."

"Seductive."

"A natural kind of seductiveness that begins in innocence and love, but can sometimes morph, as seductiveness can, into something weird."

"Sixty-four. So that was around the time of that incident in Newport when she killed or may have killed that boyfriend. . . ."

"Eddie Tirella. That was '66. It was an accident, a terrible accident."

"Are you sure about that?"

"That's what the police concluded."

"But wasn't there some funny business about the original investigation? *Vanity Fair* had a piece about some new evidence that was just uncovered."

"Well, I believed Doris, and she said it was an accident. By then, she and I were quite close. . . ."

"I see."

"And maybe I was being sized up, I don't know, as a fling, before the accident—despite her relationship with Eddie, and de-

spite my being, you know, whatever. At a certain point, Emma, two people are just two souls. . . ."

September 1966

It was a moment of tenderness in one of the gardens at Rough Point—a kiss that Doris stole from Ollie as sweetly as young lovers do in eighteenth-century operas; something that arose quite naturally between them, that Ollie had maybe seen coming, and anticipated in contentment mixed with panic; something that a month later, in October, he realized could have been the type of thing to precipitate the squabble between Doris and Eddie that some witnesses reported hearing on the day of Eddie's death.

Twelve years younger than Doris and openly gay, Eddie was a handsome New Jersey boy who did design and decoration work on Hollywood movie sets, and also sometimes appeared on screen as a bit player. Doris and Eddie had been close for about ten years. She relied on him for advice on refurbishing her residences, and had provided quarters for him in or near several of them. Sometimes they went out together. On the day he died, Doris and Eddie had been arguing over plans he announced to leave her and pursue his career in California. On their way out of Rough Point for an evening, Eddie stopped the car in the driveway and got out to open the gate. Moments later, he was dead—the car, having struck both him and the gate, now across the street, crashed into a tree, with Doris in it. According to a newspaper report, Doris told the police that "suddenly the car leaped forward, and I was on top of him." A subsequent investigation cleared Doris, but left lingering doubts. Had she, in anger, slipped over on the seat and stepped on the gas?

On the day of Ollie's stolen kiss, a month before the accident, Eddie was out on the West Coast, on a movie assignment that Elizabeth Taylor had arranged for him, since she'd admired his extra work on *The Sandpiper*. Ollie was spending a week at Rough Point to help Doris look over and refine some initial plans and maps for the Newport project. That day, after discussing dinner with the cook, Doris and Ollie visited the kitchen garden to pick some carrots. Then, instead of going right in, Doris suggested they stroll across the lawn and visit Rough Point's formal hedge garden. It was early on a mid-September evening, just before sunset, the weather still warm enough not to require a sweater, even with the fragrant ocean breezes sweeping across the cliff. Doris explained to Ollie what she knew about Frederick Law Olmsted's original 1887 design for the grounds, created when the house was built, which specified gently rolling lawns and not flat, level ones, for a more natural look.

"It always made entertaining out here a bit of a challenge," Doris said, rearranging a few strands of her hair that the wind kept blowing out of place.

The rhododendrons in the hedge garden were at the beginning of their fall blooming, radiantly purple, even in the failing light; and soon Doris and Ollie found themselves in front of the white marble statue of Cyparissus, the boy grieving over the accidental death of his beloved stag, which Nanaline Duke had had installed in a niche formed in a wall of boxwood hedge. It was moments before dusk, and the sky was still aglow, though in the gloom between the grassy ground and the lowest branches of the garden's great pines, all shades of green had begun to hide themselves in plain sight, and the crash of ocean breakers was hushed in the herbage.

"He was a favorite of Apollo," said Doris very quietly, as they gazed at the statue and her hand reached for his. She was wearing a long white cotton dress decorated with eyelets, in the style then known as "Rich Hippie," and she drew close and kissed Ollie's neck. And she persisted as he stiffened and then relaxed, both of them perhaps lulled by the citrus-fruitiness of Doris's Carnet de Bal, which enveloped them, and perhaps remembering that they were friends and had been laughing all morning and afternoon, and were holding a basket of carrots that was due in the kitchen. In one sense, the moment seemed so natural and unguarded, and neither would have been able to say precisely how much intention was in back of it and what they were supposed to derive from it. And Ollie, so typically of him, was thinking about this moment more from her point of view than from his, because he felt he owed her that. Instead of expressing some agenda of hers, the moment might simply be an infantile expression of her comfort and trustfulness with him, no matter how weird or scary it might be for him. In this regard, it was certainly less scary than the previous occasion on which someone had made an affectionate advance with him—a man, one of the fellow decorators at David Hicks, a few years before, in England, at a country house party, when a sort of mutual recoil and instant retreat to decorum saved both Ollie and the young man from stickiness.

Nothing really came of Doris's kiss. She sensed that Ollie was uncomfortable, and he understood that Doris was simply used to getting what she wanted from men like Kahanamoku, Rubirosa, Castro, and the like. She may have felt entitled, but she was not a predator. After their moment in the garden, Doris and Ollie were a little more formal with each other for a week or so. Their work together continued, and as a makeup offering, she gave him the Gérôme *Snake Charmer*, which was one of many Orientalist artworks she happened to have on hand in the library at Rough Point. Ollie was back in New York when he heard about the accident with Eddie. He thought twice about phoning Doris to see if he could be of any support, but he did call, and by the spring of the following year, he and Doris were back to something like normal. If there was anything in the kissing incident for Ollie to learn about desire, or sexuality, or the substitution of a great friendship for a great love, he didn't learn it. And the pang of regret about never trying to learn more about such things didn't appear in his thoughts until many decades later.

CHAPTER 25

June 1957

On their second day aboard the *United States*, Doris and May breakfasted in the Duck Suite and remained there for most of the morning, catching up on Doris's charity work correspondence. Then at eleven-thirty, Doris went out onto the first-class promenade to meet Barbara, who had spoken of spending her morning swimming, exercising, and getting massaged.

As Doris and Barbara sat chatting intermittently in the deck chairs that May had reserved for them, they returned the occasional greetings of fellow passengers who strolled by, a few of whom knew who one or both of the women were, most of whom didn't know either of them. A steward with a pushcart offered them a cup of bouillon, but they declined. At one point, Lady Arabella shuffled past with the doddering earl, assisted by a nurse they'd engaged to attend them. Cordial greetings were exchanged with nods and generic smiles.

"We're a thousand miles from anywhere, on top of two miles of water," observed Doris, after the trio passed. "Thousands have died at sea over thousands of years, while the seafaring skills that keep us afloat right now have been steadily improved, yet it's these little rituals of 'Hello, good morning,' isn't it, that keep us feeling safe."

"Mmm," said Barbara, her eyes half closed. "But the little things count, don't they? I saw her after breakfast. . . ."

"The lady?"

Barbara nodded.

"She was complaining about the way the toast soldiers were served with her three-minute egg. 'Not at all like on a Cunard queen,' she said, 'or even the pokey little P and O ships that piddle around the Orient.' The point being that only the British lines know how to do first class, and I must say I agree with her. Aluminum furniture, indeed."

In front of them, beyond the promenade's glass-paned wall, was a limitless horizon of gray ocean under a steel-blue cover of cloud, pierced in the distance with slanting blades of yellow-white sunlight.

"I called down to the pool earlier," said Doris. "They said you weren't there."

"Did they? I must have gone to the gift shop," said Barbara. "I wanted to get something for Jimmy."

"In the gift shop? When you just left Paris and will be in New York in two days?"

"It was a whim, Dodo. I felt like shopping."

"I see—shopping."

"What did you want?"

"To see if we could have lunch a little earlier."

"Well, let's go in now, if you're so ravenous."

In fact, Barbara had not visited the gift shop earlier that morning, nor the ship's indoor swimming pool, nor the masseur's studio. She had knocked on the door of first-class stateroom U-21 at 9:30 a.m. and been admitted by the slender, stylish, middle-aged man that Doris had spotted observing them in the ship's dining room and Navajo Lounge.

"Good morning, Miss Hutton," said the man, admitting her into the stateroom. He was dressed in a blue blazer with gold buttons and gray slacks. His accent was cultivated Italian.

"Signore Ottoboni," said Barbara, removing her sunglasses.

Waiting for them at the low table opposite the stateroom's green-and-gold upholstered sofa were a tray with coffee service and a cubic wooden case measuring about six inches square.

As they settled onto the sofa and Barbara reached for the cup of coffee that Ottoboni poured, her thirty-eight-carat diamond ring caught his eye.

"Ah—*che bello*," he said, almost involuntarily.

Barbara simpered and brought the cup to her lips perhaps a bit more slowly than she normally would have done.

"Thank you," she said. "Now please show me the other one."

Ottoboni unlatched the wooden case in front of them and swung back the hinged lid. On the pinkie finger of his left hand, he was wearing a baroque-style gold ring set with a large burnt-orange citrine intaglio carved with the profile of Apollo. With the grace of a surgeon, he removed from the case a smaller leather box whose lid was embossed in scrolls of gold, opened it, and took from it a small, black velvet bag. Loosening the bag's silk cord and gesturing toward Barbara's hand, he said, "May I?" Barbara opened and outstretched both hands to receive the bag's contents, an enormous unset diamond.

The diamond was of spectacular color, clarity, and brilliance. Barbara inspected it closely, as Ottoboni looked on, satisfied, while taking a sip of his coffee. Instinctively she brought the jewel next to the diamond of her ring, to compare the two.

"The other eye of Astarte," marveled Ottoboni, in a dramatically hushed pronouncement.

"It *is* nice," said Barbara.

The two diamonds might have been mates, the unset one octagonal in shape and just slightly larger than Barbara's, which was round. Both were of the same blue-white brilliance, magnificent, almost hypnotic in their seemingly infinite depth.

"You see they are sisters," said Ottoboni. "We believe they are of Indian origin, the Golconda mines, and, as I say, probably cut from the same ancient stone."

"Yes, I see," said Barbara, mesmerized by the sight of both diamonds.

When Barbara bought her diamond, from King Farouk of Egypt via the Roman jeweler Giorgio Bulgari, it was described as a Golconda stone, from the legendary diamond mines of southeastern India that were known for their beautiful stones—

mines that were pretty well exhausted of diamonds by the middle of the nineteenth century. The legendary clarity of Golconda diamonds is due to their chemistry, Barbara was told: formed of pure carbon and devoid of nitrogen.

"Only one percent of the world's diamonds are like this," said Ottoboni. "Classified as 1-1A."

Barbara's diamond was known as the Pasha diamond, for a nineteenth-century Viceroy of Egypt under Ottoman rule, Ismail Pasha, who purchased it for the Egyptian treasury. But the pasha ran up so much debt that he was eventually deposed by the Ottoman sultan and went into exile. He took the diamond with him, along with other Egyptian treasures, and sold it to an Englishman, who later sold it to a London firm, who sold it to Cartier, at which point the "Pasha of Egypt" was returned to that country in the possession of King Farouk. After World War II, the high-living king needed money and arranged with Bulgari to sell the diamond on, and of course, Miss Barbara Hutton was one of probably only ten people in the world who could consider making such a purchase. But the octagonal shape of the forty-carat diamond was not to Miss Hutton's liking, so she had Cartier recut it to a thirty-eight-point-one-nine-carat round and set into a ring. What Signore Ottoboni had told Miss Hutton in Paris, several days before she set sail at Le Havre, when he was introduced as "an independent dealer, very reputable," was that a companion stone to the Pasha had been discovered in the long-private collection of a noble Bavarian family, and was available for an historic reunion with its "sister," if Miss Hutton would care to purchase it. In accordance with her wish for discretion, Ottoboni could show her the stone on her Atlantic voyage.

"And why do you say 'historic'?" Barbara had asked.

The two stones originated with a rock mined in the first century BC, recounted Ottoboni, a century before Pliny the Elder, in his *Encyclopedia*, described the taste of discriminating, rich Roman ladies for the diamonds of South India. In fact, what is now known as the Pasha and its companion stone, both cut into an octagonal shape at the time, were set into a twice-life-size statue of Astarte, the Hellenistic goddess of love, war, and the hunt, as the goddess's eyes!

"The statue was at the altar in one of Alexandria's most important temples," said Ottoboni. "Cleopatra herself paid respects there. The Egyptians worshipped Astarte as the daughter of the sun god Ra. She did many good things. You may know the *ankh*—the symbol of eternal life. This is a representation of the eye of Astarte."

"Mm-hmm," said Barbara, regarding the unset diamond intently, as she tilted the stone at various angles, to see its flashing sparkle. "Then you might think one would be enough."

Ottoboni looked as though he couldn't tell whether or not Barbara was making a joke, but he continued.

"And of course, your lawyers have seen our appraisals and the bill of sale from the Bavarian family. . . ."

"Very fair, I'm sure," said Barbara.

"So the price that has been discussed . . ."

"No, no, Signore Ottoboni, I'm not here to discuss the price. Only to be ravished or not."

"Yes, of course."

Barbara continued to regard the diamond thoughtfully.

"And I am ravished, I must say," she said. "It *is* ravishing."

"I am delighted to hear you say it."

"And you say that I am the first and only one to be offered this piece?"

"Yes, of course—the first."

"The first and *only*?"

"Yes, the first and only."

"Then I will think about it and let you know after we arrive in New York," said Barbara, rising. "And for the meantime, Signore, I must ask you to be more discreet on board. Last night you were positively lurking around like a spy in a Hollywood B-movie."

Ottoboni was nowhere in evidence that night at dinner, which was formal. Doris wore orange silk brocade, with a pair of diamond-and-pearl ear pendants by David Webb; Barbara wore black-and-white chiffon, with her necklace of luscious, antique jadeite beads, which her father had given her on the occasion of marriage to Mdivani. The atmosphere in the Navajo Lounge was much livelier than it had been the night before, with hotter music from the small orchestra led by pianist Al Menconi.

"Miss Duke, Miss Hutton," said Menconi, oozing Latin charm and dressed in a white dinner jacket, when he came over to their table during a short break.

"Good to see you again, Al," said Doris. "How's your season?"

"Fair winds and following seas, as they say," said Menconi, whose orchestra sometimes played at parties that Doris hosted in New York and Newport. "We'd be honored if you'd care to join us for a song, Miss Duke. The men always like that."

"Not tonight, thank you, Al," said Doris.

"Any requests, then?"

"Hmm. Any requests, Babbo?"

"Sorry?" said Barbara, interrupting some sulky private babble with Jimmy.

"Requests?"

Barbara brightened.

"How about 'Diamonds Are a Girl's Best Friend'?" she said.

Doris let out a hoot.

"That's perfect."

"Lovely—thank you," said Menconi, with a bow. "It will be our next number."

Late the next morning, Doris and Barbara were again on deck, reclining in their deck chairs. The sea was remaining calm, and the day was much brighter than the previous one, with both the ocean and sky now luminous in shades of blue. From the promenade, stretching the twelve miles between them and the horizon, in a panorama of almost 180 degrees, was an infinite number of waves, each of which was throwing off a myriad of sparkles, yielding more sheer dazzlement to be beheld anywhere except on an ocean.

"You never told me about the gift shop yesterday," said Doris. "Did you find anything?"

"No, I didn't," said Barbara.

"So no ashtray with an eagle on it, grasping laurel leaves and arrows?"

"What? No."

"Not even a diamond?"

Barbara raised her head slightly in surprise, and then understood.

"*No*, not even a diamond," she sneered.

"You've never been a good liar, Babbo."

"So you knew?"

"Of course I knew. I was going to tell you last night, but I was too entertained by watching your face when they played 'Diamonds Are a Girl's Best Friend.'"

"Am I such a figure of sport?"

"That man showed me the same stone in Paris."

"He didn't say a word about you," said Barbara, sitting up in her deck chair.

"I didn't know he'd be aboard, but I recognized him immediately," said Doris.

"In fact, now that I think of it, he said I was the one and only person he was showing it to."

"Well, that might be true *now*—since I passed."

"Hmmh," said Barbara, gruffly. "May I ask why you passed? Isn't the thing real?"

"It looks real enough to me," said Doris. "But I don't believe any of that hokum about Astarte."

"You don't?"

"It sounds like something a college boy would make up."

"Is he a fraud, then?" said Barbara, settling back in her chair.

"Who knows?" said Doris. "It's a big stone. Maybe it's just a case of shady provenance. So many people are selling their things these days. I didn't look at the paperwork. May recommended that I simply pass. And I think you should, too."

"Hmmh."

"Anyway, Babbo—*two* forty-carat stones? What would you do with them? They're too big for earrings. And two of the same ring would look ridiculous . . ."

THE LAST AMERICAN HEIRESSES 265

"I could always commission Haseltine to do a full-size statue of a horse."

"Yes—in solid gold, with diamond eyes! What a good idea. Why don't you do that—you noodle?!"

They were silent for a minute; then Barbara spoke.

"Do you think that he could have gotten into the Bulgari archives, whoever he is, and had a diamond cut especially to look like mine looked when I bought it?"

"Interesting idea . . ." said Doris, though she was dubious.

"I know—let's make it a jape!" said Barbara, with sudden enthusiasm. "There's bound to be press at the dock in New York, right? We could leak a story about being pursued on the high seas by an international jewel thief, trying to outbid each other secretly for a rare stolen treasure. . . ."

Doris produced a pinched smile.

"Or is the game wearing thin?" she said.

"What do you mean?" said Barbara.

"We're in our forties, for God's sake. Are these hijinks for us anymore?"

"Aren't they?"

"I don't know. Is it childish?"

"Isn't that the fun of it? Dressing up for a costume ball is childish, too."

"Yes, but . . ."

"You think too much, Dodo. I just ask myself, 'What will make me happy?'"

"But what is 'happy,' Babbo? Real happiness, as my father used to remind me, comes from things like mucking out your own horse stall, if you see what I mean."

Barbara let out a groan that was almost a huff.

"You and your Tar Heel wisdom," she said.

CHAPTER 26

Ollie realized that in the old days, a trip like this to Monte Carlo might require several different kinds of clothes, and he would pack them all in his three-piece, matched set of T. Anthony luggage. Especially when traveling with Doris, this practice was standard for him. But traveling so opulently wasn't going to work for this trip; and actually, it hadn't been working for a decade or two. The last time he used all his luggage, on a junket to Paris in 2006, for the opening of the Quai Branly museum, he packed both hard cases *and* the trunk, as usual—with several suits, including black tie, several hats, and pairs of shoes. But since then, on jaunts to Europe, he'd been taking only the smaller case; though even that, when packed with his things, was proving too heavy to handle. Of course, every traveler he saw nowadays in airports and train stations were toting bags with wheels or spinners, the very sound of which, on any floor or pavement, made Ollie's skin crawl. To him, keeping one's luggage silent seemed a minimum standard of good travel manners. Also, the thousands he spent at the venerable Madison Avenue malletier in the 1970s, on luggage that was supposed to last forever, seemed to make it necessary to keep on using his classic black-canvas-and-leather goods until he couldn't lift them anymore. Well, that moment had now arrived.

"Here it is," said Mrs. Welland, entering Ollie's apartment, pulling an empty carry-on-size, spinner-wheeled suitcase in steel-gray polycarbonate.

"It's quite handsome," said Ollie.

"And you see, it's the kind with silent wheels."

In the living room, Mrs. Welland opened the case, showed Ollie its various straps and zippered compartments, explained the lock, and gave him the four-number code she'd set for it.

"It should absolutely do," said Ollie. "I'm not bringing a tuxedo or much of anything."

"Travel simply, that's what I always say, now that Horace is gone," said Mrs. Welland, who for years had lived between Oyster Bay and Palm Beach, before she lost her husband, Horace, a lawyer and investor, and settled in New York.

"The very idea of putting your clothes in someone else's bag . . ." said Ollie with a chuckle, playing with a strap designed to anchor the packed garments in place. "Tell me, Liz, have many other men had their clothes in here?"

Mrs. Welland chortled.

"Dozens, at least!" she said. "It's a fetish of mine."

"Mmm, Shalimar," said Ollie, catching the scent of the case's interior.

"Well, what did you expect?"

"That is exactly what I expected. And thank you very much for this, my dear. Gone are the days when I could not budge in my *Orient Express* cabin because it was stuffed with all my bags."

Ollie's steamer trunk was now serving as a bedside table in the bedroom, topped with a lamp, a tray with a water glass and carafe, and a pile of current, must-read books. The smaller cases were in the living room, comprising a decorative sculptural stack that was topped by an antique world globe representing national boundaries as they existed between the two world wars.

"I was just thinking that I haven't been to Monte Carlo since 1992."

"Ah, yes?"

"In my mind, it's 'my most recent trip to Monte.' Doris and I used to go all the time. Yet that was thirty years ago."

"Will you be making one of your stops in Zürich?"

"Yes, indeed, on the way home. Herr Einsner and I will have our lunch. I've told you about the restaurant we like near the bank."

"Lovely. There's something timeless about Zürich, isn't there? *Plus ça change . . .*"

"But that's just the thing. *C'est ne pas la même chose, pas de tout.* There are several new buildings there—office buildings, mind you—that are built of timber."

"Timber?"

"You wouldn't believe it. Ten stories tall! Apparently, the Swiss are making great advances in wood engineering. And it's Alpine, you see."

"I hope they're not cutting down old-growth forests."

"Now they've announced plans to build a new airport terminal out of timber . . ."

"Before I forget . . ." said Mrs. Welland, handing Ollie a manila envelope. "I printed out the relevant sections—project description, timeline, budget, etc."

"Thank you," said Ollie, with great sincerity.

"As always, just between us."

"Just between us."

"I know you can't tell me too much."

Mrs. Welland was a program officer at one of the city's top charitable foundations, where she had worked for ten years since the death of her husband. The foundation supported film and media projects, in addition to projects involving writing and the performing and visual arts. Her employment there was a way of staying active in the arts field, after the years she served on the board of Palm Beach's Kravis Center. The envelope contained the application that Emma had made to the foundation for a grant to support her film.

"Do you know why it was denied?" said Ollie.

"You know that I can't . . ."

"Of course, of course. You can't say why, and I shouldn't have asked."

"I wouldn't even know why, since I'm on the visual side. You know very well how many more really worthy applications we receive than we can accept."

"That's the thing, isn't it?" said Ollie, tapping the envelope with his forefinger. "Well, this is helpful and much appreciated, as always. Let's see if we can do yet another good deed."

PART 5

PALACES

CHAPTER 27

October 1948

When Doris Duke was named to the "Best Dressed" list, Nancy read all about it. When Doris wed Porfirio Rubirosa, Nancy read all about that, too. She learned that the wedding had taken place at the Dominican Embassy in Paris, and that Duke was wearing an ankle-length, green taffeta dress by Dior, with a green velvet hat. One of the papers featured a grainy black-and-white picture of Doris in the dress, which frustrated Nancy as much as it delighted her, since the draping of fabric and the play of flashbulb light upon it gave no clue, of course, about the dress's exact shade of green. Knowing something of Dior and current fashion, though, Nancy decided it must be something between a pine green and a forest green.

Though Nancy had been living in Prescottville for several months now, she still kept up with the doings of all her favorite boldface names and made it a point to pick up the New York papers every day at Eckstein's general store. She hadn't been back to the city for a visit yet, but New York was only a few hours away, and there was a pressing reason to get back there in December: the new musical *Kiss Me, Kate*, with songs by Cole Porter. It was a riff on Shakespeare's *The Taming of the Shrew*, and *everyone* was talking about it—anyway, the columns that Nancy read in the papers were talking about it, if not everyone in Prescottville.

Her father had bought a boxy, wood-frame house with a

steep pitched roof that was almost exactly the same size and configuration as their Brooklyn place, only instead of the paved alleyway between houses that they had in Bay Ridge, which led to a cramped garage, they had a real driveway in Prescottville and a fairly large field in back, with a barn where her father based his HVAC business. The dedicated gas pump that the property's former owner had installed near the barn door was a point of pride for her father, as was his new practice of buying gas in bulk. His business was doing well, so the move had been a success by his standards, and yet Nancy was still making more money than her father. Having been hired as a telephone operator just days after arriving in Prescottville—a job she was happy to take until she could investigate fashion retail opportunities in Kingston and Middletown, both of which were about an hour's drive away—she was quickly promoted to assistant supervisor and then to supervisor. It was a position of real responsibility, and she was already a respected member of the business community—a distinct accomplishment for any woman, let alone one so young. She sometimes chuckled to remember wondering back in Brooklyn whether or not any building in Prescottville would be tall enough to have a penthouse. Ironically, her office now was at the top of one of Prescottville's tallest buildings, on the fourth floor of the phone company's regional headquarters.

And though Nancy lived in the same house as her parents, her life was fairly independent. She had bought a secondhand Ford, and came and went as she liked, without her parents expecting to know where she was going and what she was doing. She made a few friends among her colleagues at the telephone office, and now and then went out with them for a drink, or bowling, or to a movie. Every so often, one of the nearby resort hotels would feature a musical act on tour from New York, and she and a few other gals would dress up and attend. It was not a bad life upstate, Nancy thought. She was trying her best to do what her esteemed former client, Miss Duke, had advised her to do, the day Nancy told her she had decided finally to go upstate with her family. "Make the most of what you have," said Miss Duke.

Nancy knew that this wisdom also meant trying to be fair to the young men she was meeting casually on social outings. Many were more sophisticated than she would have thought, some just out of college, some decorated veterans, some with business connections to the big city. She'd even met one, Donald Mancuso, the manager of the Starlight, a cocktail lounge that the gals liked to go to, whom she was attracted to purely on the basis of good looks and a warm, engaging manner. Yet Donald had made no more moves than the affable manager of a respectable business should make. He certainly dressed well for work—in a sport jacket and nice shirt, as any guy in the city might do. He was a decorated war vet, she learned. His father owned the Starlight and several other local businesses. Once when Donald showed Nancy and her friends to a booth for an after-work drink, he seemed to give Nancy a split-second more of his bright attention than he did the others; and then during one cocktail hour, Nancy noticed him looking over at her from behind the bar, as she and the gals were gabbing and sipping their gin rickeys; and she and Donald exchanged an innocent little wave with wiggling fingers.

But a minute after that wave, Nancy wasn't thinking seriously about Donald, or about anything her friends were saying. She was thinking about the daily New York paper she had picked up on her way to the Starlight, which she was eager to read. It was there in her tote bag, with her purse, next to her on the seat of the booth. She was wondering what her friend Miss Duke might be doing at that very moment, and what Miss Duke's so-called rival, if that's what Barbara Hutton really was, might herself might be doing. And Nancy would read all about it in the following day's paper. As it happened, at the very moment when Nancy was in the Starlight, Doris was in the sky, twelve thousand feet over the Atlantic Ocean, aboard TWA's luxury all-sleeper-service flight from Paris to New York. She was due the following day at the offices of *Harper's Bazaar*, where she would turn in her most recent story, an account of the sale of an ancient princely estate, and have lunch with editor Carmel Snow; and Barbara was on the ground in New York, hosting a dinner party at the Ritz for the likes of the Duke and Duchess of Windsor, Lady Diana and Duff Cooper, and Mr. Antenor Patiño and his wife Doña María Cristina de Borbón y Bosch-Labrús, third Duchess of Dúrcal and a cousin of the late Spanish king, Alfonso XIII. Nancy consumed all this news with great relish. The details were paramount! Barbara was serving her guests honeydew melon, caviar and blinis, cold salmon with tartar sauce, breast of chicken *pôelé nature*, asparagus with hollandaise sauce, fresh raspberries with vanilla ice cream, and liqueurs and champagne. Doris was traveling with a new, mid-length sealskin coat by Revillon; and interestingly, once back in New York, she was also scheduled to participate in a private demonstration of this newfangled, wireless telephone service that the newspapers and magazines were chirping about. "Truly one of the postwar miracles we've been waiting for," Doris was quoted as saying.

CHAPTER 28

It was an evening flight direct from New York to Nice, on Air France, in business class, so Emma and Ollie were able to sleep relatively comfortably and arrive relatively fresh. Ollie was delighted to find that his eighty-four-year-old bones and muscles were, by and large, still up to the challenges of travel.

When you land at Nice in the morning, you already know that you are in the domain of sea and sky, because from your window, you have seen plenty of both on the plane's final approach, and you've been caught, as the plane arcs into a descending turn, in the rays of low-angled sunlight piercing the cabin and sweeping across rows of seat backs and passenger heads. But then after walking through the terminal and emerging into the first moments of your stay on the fabled French Riviera, you are filled with the sheer pleasure of *azure*, if azure were not just the name of a color for sky and sea but of a full-body reaction to sea-freshened morning breezes, fragrant with botanicals, and daylight that is both shimmering and soft, making buildings and greenery and other human beings visually pop in a quietly sumptuous way. If you have been here before and know perfectly well how splendid an earthly spot this is, you may wonder why your memory, even if it is usually very good, does not measure up to the actual experience. And if it's your first time here, you may find yourself feeling frustrated that you can't quite take in all the splendor.

The plan was for a three-day shoot, to start on the following day in a small conference suite that Emma had booked at Monte

Carlo's Fairmont Hotel, a modern five-star establishment that Artemis recommended as best for a project like this, convenient and comfortable. In addition to covering Emma and Ollie's airfare, Artemis was generously putting them up at the Fairmont for four nights. The four-person, Nice-based crew that Emma had hired on the recommendation of a producer friend would make the half-hour drive to and from Monte Carlo each day. The shoot was planned to proceed at an easy pace. Each segment, with photography and any commentary from the owner of each piece of jewelry, would take only an hour or so. On the first day, they would do Artemis and her Duchess of Windsor pin; on the second, Artemis's Russian friend Lyudmila and her *Lusitania* tiara, and on the third day, Artemis's Emirati friend, Amaya, and her enormous Burmese ruby.

"We're all good," said Emma, tucking away her phone, as she and Ollie were being driven to the hotel. She had called Artemis to say they'd arrived safely and were looking forward to seeing her that evening for dinner. "Lyudmila and Amaya are all set for their sessions, so that's good. Oh, and she says she has something of Duke's that she wants to add to her shoot, tomorrow."

"Something of Doris Duke's?" said Ollie. "Some other bauble?"

"Mm-hmm."

"What is it?"

"She wants to surprise us."

"My goodness, this *is* exciting."

"Something from the 2004 auction, she said—that she just acquired."

"If it's something of Doris's, then I will probably know it. Yummy, yummy."

"You and she were such good friends, weren't you?"

Ollie was gazing out the car's window. They were on the Grand Corniche, and to the right were dazzling views of the Mediterranean.

"I was one of the gals, you see," he said, "which is probably why she didn't fire me. Or kill me."

Somewhere over the Atlantic, Ollie had told Emma the story of the kiss in the garden.

"So . . . do you think she really wanted sex? I mean, real sex?"

"Probably—in some corner of her mind, some *version* of sex. . . ."

"And how would that have gone?"

"Who knows."

"It's not like she had a plan."

"That's right. For her, it was a lovely moment in a garden at dusk. She was following the moment."

"Less lovely for you."

"That's right."

"You weren't up for it."

Ollie thought for a minute.

"I was and I wasn't," said Ollie. "I suppose I wanted to know more about it, but didn't know *how* to want it, or what I might particularly want. Don't ask me what I was masturbating to back then. I didn't masturbate all that much."

"I . . . wasn't going to ask you that."

"I know I was interested in *her* interest, because she was older and she was, you know, *her*."

"So, no rage?"

"From Doris? No. Maybe disappointment."

"Disappointment."

"More than sex, I think she was signaling me to sweep her off her feet. If I couldn't do that, you see, she didn't want anything else in the romance department. Joey and Eddie were both sweep-you-off-your-feet types, even if Eddie was a homosexual. Some men have it and some simply don't, irrespective of sexual identity. I don't happen to have it."

"You have it now."

Ollie turned to her, looking modestly gratified.

"Kind of you to say," he said. "Maybe something like that has been accruing to my account. Though a lot of good it can do me now, in my eighties."

The Fairmont had a kind of glitzy, Vegas-like glamour when it opened back in the 1970s as Loews Monte Carlo, explained Ollie, when they were arriving at the hotel, and there had been a glitzy casino! Half a century later, though, the hotel's bold

'70s-era design, like that of the Pompidou Center in Paris, looked positively quaint and a little sad, he said. After several changes of ownership and a couple of top-to-bottom refurbishments, the Fairmont had toned itself down into a quieter, more European kind of place. Ollie, himself, had always stayed at one of Monte Carlo's *grandes dames*, the Hermitage.

"Though of course, there was always room for *louche* on the Riviera. . . ."

Ollie stopped mid-sentence.

"I'm lecturing," he said, almost sheepishly. "You don't need me to explain the Riviera to you, do you?"

"You're fine," said Emma.

"I'm sorry."

"Why not save it for the camera? We'll want some background, some context . . ."

"Of course."

Both had suites with balconies overlooking the sea and part of the marina. Visible at the far end of the marina's main jetty were several large yachts, one of which, a sleek, gunmetal blade of a thing built along trimaran lines, looked at least three hundred feet long.

Artemis had said that her place was only a ten-minute walk from the hotel, just a few steps beyond the city's central square, the Place du Casino, so after a few hours that Emma spent on her laptop and Ollie spent at the rooftop pool with his audiobook edition of Amor Towles's *A Gentleman in Moscow*, they set out on a leisurely stroll.

"You may remember we had one of these at Rockefeller Center, a few years back," said Ollie, as they stopped in the square to admire Anish Kapoor's seductively reflective sculpture *Sky Mirror*, set into a terraced fountain with quietly burbling waters surrounded by beds of red and white cyclamen.

"Wow," said Emma.

"There's one in Russia, at the Hermitage. There are a few others. But I think this one works best."

"Why so?"

"It has the best light to reflect."

"Mm-hmm."

"I mean, they all deliver that science-fiction punch from another dimension. But beyond that *punctum*, as Roland Barthes might have termed it, there are more qualities to behold in this work, all about color and form, but mostly light—no?"

"Yes."

Commanding one side of the square with Belle Époque poise was Ollie's second-favorite Monte Carlo hotel, the Hôtel de Paris, and at the end of the square, facing the sea, was the Casino, a masterpiece of Beaux Arts stateliness leavened with just a touch of whimsy, by architect Charles Garnier of Paris Opéra fame. The luxury brand shops at the edge of the square, just beyond the palm and olive trees, were still open. Though plenty of people were out shopping or otherwise enjoying the early spring evening, the square was relatively calm and quiet.

"Not a blade of grass out of place," said Emma.

"Certainly not. The whole principality is like that," said Ollie. "No square foot of space that isn't beautifully built or landscaped and maintained. Before you and I get up tomorrow morning, an army of gardeners will have removed every petal and leaf that died or was dying today within the entire two square kilometers of Monaco."

Only some of the bits of conversation they overheard as they strolled were in French. There was also Russian, English, Italian, German. . . . Everyone was dressed, as Ollie said they would be, casually but expensively. Even the plain T-shirts and tank tops looked like the kind that cost hundreds of dollars in smart boutiques. Ollie was in a terra-cotta-colored blazer and white, open-collar shirt; and Emma was wearing a white, long-sleeve tunic-shirt with a pair of "good" jeans.

"You've been to her home before?" said Emma, puzzled as they were approaching the contemporary, commercial-looking building whose Avenue d'Ostende address Artemis had given her, marked with a map pin on her phone's screen.

"Oh, yes," said Ollie, with a hint of a smirk. "I may be blabby, but I didn't want to tell you anything about it and spoil the surprise."

"What surprise? That she lives in a bank?"

Featuring enormous ground-floor windows of plate glass, the building's pink granite façade looked nothing like that of a private residence. Ollie said nothing but walked Emma past what seemed to be the quietly grand public entrance of a now-closed place of business—perhaps a private bank? a brokerage firm?—to a smaller-scaled entrance at the far end of the building's façade, that featured a fan-shaped glass canopy and potted fig trees flanking a door made of glass and polished bronze. The door was opened for them from within, by an attendant in a black suit, and they were greeted by another man in exactly the same kind of suit, standing behind a sleek reception desk of highly polished burled wood.

"Good evening, Ms. Radetsky, Mr. Shaw," said the man, in British-accented English. "You're expected."

It might have been the lobby of a small museum—all in pink marble, with a vaulted ceiling. At the back of the lobby, where the elevator was located, a tall urn on an antique bombé chest was bursting with a spotlit arrangement of red roses, pink peonies, and reddish-orange gloriosa lilies. The door to the elevator was open, attended by a third man in black, who saw them into the car. The man remained discreetly facing the operating panel as he wordlessly pressed the button that was third from the top.

Like the men at the door and desk, the elevator man was wearing a small lapel badge with what looked like a corporate logo.

"It's his construction company, this is the headquarters," said Ollie.

"Ohhhh, right—the husband," said Emma.

"He built the building, mid-eighties."

"I see."

Ollie was speaking quietly, but making no effort to be inaudible.

"They have the penthouse," said Ollie. "The fifth and sixth floors. He built it especially for her. Well, you'll see."

What Artemis called home, Emma soon discovered, was a five-bedroom, twenty-one-thousand-square-foot duplex penthouse that included a double-height library, and an array of roof terraces with mature trees, bushes, flowerbeds, and an infinity pool.

"Darlings, you made it," said Artemis, floating into the palatial entry hall barefoot, in a flowing, powder blue caftan-like garment, with her hair down in a more youthful style than Emma had seen on her previously. Draped around Artemis's shoulders was a voluptuous silk scarf in lilac that covered her neck and chest.

Hugs and kisses were exchanged, while a maid stood by to take any wraps or personal items, but Emma and Ollie had brought none.

"I thought we'd be on the terrace, since it's such a lovely evening," said Artemis, leading the way through a vast formal dining room to a broad outdoor area overlooking the edge of the city and the sea beyond. As they went, Emma noticed two more men in black suits inside the residence—one stationed at the door to a room off the entry hall, and one at the far end of the lushly landscaped terrace they stepped onto. Next to a dining table set for four, with elegant stemware and a florid, crystal-and-ormolu girandole lamp, was a seating area. A young woman in jeans and a blue sleeveless blouse stood as they joined her.

"Ollie, I don't think you know my secretary, Honorine?" said Artemis. "I've asked her to join us."

Emma already knew Honorine, a dark-haired, young Swiss woman who'd been coordinating with her on shoot logistics.

"And Qasim—will he be joining us?" said Ollie.

"Afraid not," said Artemis. "He's in São Paulo—a new project for the president."

A butler served drinks, while a maid was giving final touches to the dining table. The corner of the terrace where they were was lined with lushly planted, raised garden beds replete with white hyacinths, the fragrance of which was mixing with the genial breeze.

"You're settled in?" said Artemis.

"Perfectly," said Emma. "The rooms are beautiful."

"I want you to see something of our little town, while you're here. You were very smart to give yourself such a manageable schedule."

"If you like cars, the Prince Rainier automobile collection is a treasure," said Honorine.

"Now that's something I've always meant to see," said Ollie. "In the palace garage?"

Honorine shook her head, with a modest giggle.

"It's in the marina," she said, pointing out from the terrace. It wasn't quite dusk yet, but some of the city's nighttime architectural and landscape illuminations were already switched on, as was the strand of lights strung over the funnel of a cruise ship parked in the marina.

In some sense, Monte Carlo was "a little town," as Artemis said. Tiny, densely populated, and efficiently packed into tight roadways and tidy properties, the municipality itself had a permanent population of only around fifteen thousand, whose wealth-derived sense of decorum and privacy was no doubt a big reason why the place didn't feel congested. The foursome exchanged thoughts about what to do and see in and around the larger principality; then Ollie said that the most beautiful things they were likely to see would be the *bijoux* that Artemis had lined up.

"We're excited that you're including a new piece," said Emma.

"Oh, yes! And now I can show it to you," said Artemis, gracefully letting her lilac scarf slip down from her shoulders, to reveal a turquoise, sapphire, and diamond fringe necklace whose design was distinctly Middle Eastern or Far Eastern in feeling.

Ollie gasped when he saw it.

"Oh, yes—magnificent," he said.

"Will it work—I mean, for the shoot?" said Artemis, doing an amusing bit of seated choreography, to show off the piece.

"Of course it will, absolutely," said Emma.

"David Webb, 1965?" said Ollie.

"Very good," said Artemis, a little surprised. "Then you know the piece."

"I do, indeed," said Ollie. "And you look beautiful in it. It suits you. Not everyone can pull off something that bold."

"Thank you. I think it's great fun."

Emma couldn't resist asking a question of Ollie that she hoped would not detract from the obvious gratification of their beautifully adorned hostess.

"Do you remember the first time you saw it?" said Emma.

"I . . . do indeed," said Ollie diffidently.

"Do tell, please," said Artemis.

Ollie shook his head slowly as if amused by the impossibly large number of years that had passed since then.

"Well, if you really don't mind. It was in London, 1969, April. We attended a Janis Joplin concert at Royal Albert Hall. . . ."

Artemis interrupted with a hoot of delight.

"Wonderful!" she said, clapping her hands at such an enticing story beginning.

"This was the 1960s, after all, and Doris was a very hip chick, you know, in her way," continued Ollie. "And she wanted to dress in that youthful, eclectic style that the kids were doing then, influenced by India and Bali and whatnot. But you know, with Doris, if she wanted a caftan, she went to Galitzine. If she wanted some hippie beads, she went to David Webb—in this case, she went with some of her own sketches."

Artemis clapped again, rocking a bit in her seat, completely amused by Ollie's recollection. The butler announced dinner, and a lively conversation about hippies and Janis Joplin and Swingin' London in the '60s was brought to the table when the party sat down.

Dinner was bouillabaisse and lamb, started off with *barbajuans*—a kind of fritter stuffed with a chard-ricotta-and-leek filling—which Artemis said was a local specialty.

"My cook makes them better than anywhere else in the city," she said. "I think she adds a touch of nutmeg."

Later, after dessert, talk returned to Artemis's necklace.

"So they're her mother's sapphires, you say?" said Artemis.

"That's right," said Ollie. "I believe they were from a piece that Doris inherited when her mother died," continued Ollie. "She hated her mother's taste."

"I wonder if they could be Ceylon," said Artemis.

"They well might be," said Ollie, "because nothing was too good for Nanaline Duke. But I know that we can't know for sure, because I included the necklace in a catalog piece I did for Rough Point a few years back, when they did a show about Doris's David Webb jewelry in the context of her involvement with design and architecture. I asked the David Webb people what they could tell me about the stones, and all they could say was that they were *probably* Ceylon, but since they didn't procure them, they couldn't know for sure."

"I'd love to see what you wrote," said Artemis.

"I'll email it to you when I get back to the hotel." Ollie chuckled. "Doris also had boxes and boxes of unset gems, you know."

"Did she? Just lying around the house?" said Artemis.

"Some, yes. But she learned from her father not to keep all her eggs in one basket. So other gems she kept in a Swiss bank where Buck Duke had established a private vault, thank you very much. There were hundreds of bars of gold bullion in there— I think to protect some of Duke's wealth from governmental scrutiny. This would have been around the time that income tax was invented."

"You saw this private vault?" asked Honorine.

"Oh, yes—many times. Doris often took me along to Zürich when she went to see her banker, Herr Aeppli. She insisted on staying in close touch with those who managed her assets. This, too, was something her father drilled into her. It was always lunch with Herr Aeppli at this charming Italian restaurant near the bank."

"Did she actually inspect her property on these visits?" said Honorine.

"Sometimes," said Ollie. "Sometimes she would inspect objects that she'd bought at auction in Europe and had sent to the bank, where they stayed until she figured out what to do with them—artwork, antiques, and such."

Afterward, following an after-dinner look into Artemis's library at some first-edition books, they said their warm goodnights and repeated how excited they were for the next morning's shoot.

It was only a weeknight, but the city seemed to be in a festive mood as Emma and Ollie walked back to the Fairmont.

"Is it always like this?" asked Emma.

"There used to be a season," said Ollie, "but now every season is the right season in Monte."

"Mmm."

"Apparently there is evidence of a Stone Age settlement in this exact spot."

"When I was in my twenties, and my friends and I would fly over to Europe for cultural adventures, somehow we always missed Monte Carlo. We did poke around other places nearby, smaller towns and villages on the coast, or in the hills, but somehow Monte Carlo always felt old-fashioned, stuffy to us—though I have no idea why we thought there would be nothing for us. My family used to bring me to Europe quite a lot, as you know, but somehow we never set foot here."

"Well, here's hoping that this will be a memorable first visit for you."

Emma made a little hum of assent. Their steps were slow, relaxed.

"That apartment, Ollie. . . !" she declared.

"I know! That's the way a billionaire lives."

"Old-master art."

"His father and grandfather were both collectors—Dutch and Flemish Renaissance. I spotted a Van Hemessen, a Van Cleve . . ."

"That still life in the dining room!"

"Gheeraerts, I think."

"The lamp on the dinner table . . ."

"Nineteenth-century, Louis XV-style. Original gilt, the crystal probably Baccarat."

"Just a little lighting for a picnic on the porch."

"You can have the same one for probably fifty thousand. Actually, no—you'd get the pair for that."

"Too much! Too much of everything, and everything so very exquisite."

"It's definitely too much. But if you ask me, it's the right kind of too much. A lot of rich people have the wrong kind of too much, and that's never nice."

"There were three people serving us."

"She's probably got a staff of five or six, not counting security."

"Security! Is that what those men in black are?"

"Darling, we just left the third-safest residence in the world. Putin's villa is the first, the White House is the second. I'm sure that building is impregnable."

"He has enemies?"

"*So* many enemies."

"That's why they had to leave the UK?"

"Among other reasons. The men in black suits. . . ?"

"Yes?"

"Former MI6, all of them."

"No."

"Armed, of course."

"No."

"Around the clock. Just in case."

"Really."

"I'm sure she'll have one of them with her tomorrow morning."

"Really?"

"You watch."

CHAPTER 29

April 1969

Dr. Boehme's main office was in London's prestigious Harley Street, though he was regularly summoned to see important clients in Paris, New York, and Hollywood. Doris had met the charismatic doctor one night at a party that she and Joey Castro gave at Falcon's Lair, the four-acre Bel Air estate that Doris bought in the 1950s. The house—built in 1929 by Rudolph Valentino in the Spanish Colonial Revival style and redecorated for Doris by Tony Duquette with his trademark flair for the fantastically stagey—was not very large, compared with Duke Farms and Rough Point, but it was a great spot for intimate parties that mixed movie people with members of the West Coast's visual arts, dance, music, and spiritual communities. A psychic and an "aura-hypnotherapy practitioner" with a background in reiki, the Japanese tradition of energy healing, Dr. Boehme had treated Doris several times in Los Angeles, cleansing her aura, "de-ruffling her biofield," and apparently causing her to lose a pound or two.

Since she was in London for the Joplin concert, and since Barbara, living in Tangier at the time, was at the Dorchester for a few days to see her British crowd, Doris decided to take her friend along to Harley Street for a special treatment that Dr. Boehme had agreed to perform on both of them.

Despite the loss of her mother and several friends and colleagues in recent years, Doris was in great shape. Her body was

still slender; her face was tan, even if her expression was looking a bit more drawn than in the past; her manner was eagerly,
if not strenuously, in tune with the youthquake-ishness of the
times. She was swimming regularly, noodling away often at her
jazz piano, and practicing as much hula and Afro-Cuban dance
as she could, and sometimes tap and even clogging. Whereas
dear Barbara, whom Doris was not seeing as often as she used
to, had been growing slower and wider, "more queenly than
regal," as Cecil described it. She had divorced her seventh and
avowedly last husband, Doan, and was suffering, certainly not
thriving, as a result of all the "treatments"—the pills, injections,
and alcohol—that she was subjecting herself to.

A nice de-ruffling would do her good, Doris thought. Ollie
would be arriving in London on Saturday, to meet Doris for the
Monday evening concert, so it was on Friday that Doris and
Barbara went along to No. 61 Harley Street to see the good
doctor.

"Really, Dodo? Auras that we can't see?"

They were sitting in the doctor's posh waiting room, which
was decorated in a clubby, Georgian-era manner.

"Artists have sensed they were there for centuries," said
Doris. "What do you think halos are?"

"It doesn't sound much like medicine to me," said Barbara.

"It's simply a different modality. There's no poking or cutting, or potions. It's all about the body's energy. It's in *here*,"
said Doris, tapping her sternum, then making a gesture that encompassed the whole room, "and through us and all around us."

Across the room, seated at an antique desk and doing some
kind of paperwork, was the pleasant, soft-spoken nurse-
receptionist who had admitted them. Soothingly, from hidden
speakers, came the sound of a sitar raga.

Barbara huffed and opened her purse, and was reaching for
her cigarette case when Doris stopped her.

"As I mentioned, we don't smoke in here," said Doris.

Barbara sighed and closed the purse.

They were almost sixty, and it had been clear for years that they were aging in widely different ways. This was a discovery that two teenage best friends had never foreseen making as adults. Through the years, no memos had arrived for either of them, charting the progress of variables like their happiness, patience, and calm, let alone diagramming their respective ranges of interest and levels of curiosity. Now that both the women and the times were a-changin', there was a question between them, for the most part unstated, about what should keep them together, if anything. Did they still share the same interests and values, or enough of them to matter? Did the mere fact of shared history still qualify them as good friends? And if so, what form should friendship take now? Lunch together now and then? Dinner once a year? Invitations to each other's most important parties, without really needing to have the other one show up? Referring to each other kindly in company, or, in the spirit of their adolescent game, wickedly?

In particular, America's political unrest had shaken Doris emotionally. Her sense of equality with others and fair play for all Americans had been challenged by the proliferation of demonstrations and riots. In the automatically *noblesse oblige* way of her father, her heart was largely with the underclass. The 1968 strike by African-American sanitation workers in Memphis—and the strike's underlying causes of unequal wages and bad working conditions—shocked Doris almost as much as the decade's terrible assassinations of King and the two Kennedys. The previous decade's social unrest, in fact, had caused her to move away from the old-fashioned patterns of philanthropy of her mother's generation toward a more socially active kind of philanthropy that reflected more up-to-date ideas about race and class. For years, Doris had been active in at least two Black churches, one in Harlem, one in Nutley, New Jersey, giving them money but also attending services and singing openheartedly with the choir. She had also established a program that gave money to a wide swath of southern Black churches for the express purpose of buying organs. And her restoration project in Newport, with the help of Jackie Onassis, was producing real results and reviving a significant portion of the town's nonrich neighborhoods. Whereas Barbara, thought Doris when in an uncharitable mood, had "only" opened a soup kitchen in Tangier and was still tossing away unwanted diamond necklaces on a whim, to friends who hardly deserved them.

Dr. Boehme was a neat, beaky little man with a Slavic accent and dark wavy hair streaked with silver. His consulting room, too, was traditionally Georgian—with tufted leather armchairs, gilt-framed engravings by Hogarth, and the like. With continental charm, he welcomed both ladies in and, for Barbara's benefit, gave an overview of his work.

"All living beings create their own aura, as they channel energy from the divine source," he intoned. "This aura exists both visually, in color and brightness, and psychically, in spiritual vibrations. So we observe and probe the aura for irregularities and imbalances, which express themselves in different colors and spiritual frequencies, and then we manipulate the patient's biofield and bring back harmony and balance."

"Huh?" said Barbara.

"This kind of medicine goes back five thousand years," said Doris.

"Farther than that," said Dr. Boehme. "Beyond the Egyptians, even, to the mother civilization."

"Atlantis," said Doris.

"We call it Atlantis because Plato did," said Dr. Boehme, "but one day, we may know what they called themselves."

The doctor stepped over to the bookcase and unfurled three wall charts, each depicting a human figure surrounded by penumbras of variegated colors.

"This is the proof," he said quietly.

Barbara studied the charts for a moment.

"Aren't those just pictures though, Doctor—illustrations?" she said.

"These are images—actual scientific evidence!—gathered by my colleagues in the Soviet Union, Semyon and Valentina Kirlian. Surely you've heard of them. These pioneering scientists are now capturing, with absolute clarity, these auras by a special photographic method of their own invention. Behold the human biofield!"

Doris and Barbara both remained focused on the three figures. One was surrounded predominantly by reds and purples; another, a combination of blues, reds, and greens; the third was similar to the second, but with patches of yellow.

"And then what, Doctor?" said Barbara. "You spoke of manipulating something."

"As I say, I observe and probe the biofield. . . ."

"Probe how. . . ?"

He raised his hands dramatically, wiggling splayed fingers.

"With these," he said, "and with my inner vision." With a finger, he touched a spot in the center of his forehead. "I adjust the shapes and the flows that I find there, which are produced by pain and worry and stress. . . ."

"Adjust them how? Into what?"

The doctor was responding to Barbara's questions with almost theatrical patience.

"Into better shapes and flows," he said. "With less pain and worry and stress."

For a moment, there was silence.

"And then your vital energy is so much better," said Doris.

"Exactly so," said Dr. Boehme. "Let me show you."

The doctor showed Doris and Barbara into his treatment room, which was the antithesis of a traditional Georgian interior. The room was modern, even futuristic, with featureless all-white walls, floor, and ceiling. A large window was shaded with a scrim that diffused the daylight into a generic glow. Along the walls was a built-in upholstered banquette in white, that turned its corners sexily in curves. The room was as silent as a padded cell.

In the center of the room were three armchairs of space-age design—one of which, facing the other two, was positioned next to a floor-mounted console that incorporated several elements: a control panel with several buttons, switches, and dials;

a sill bearing several small objects, including crystals, polished stones, metal tubes, and brush-like objects; another sill with a notebook and fountain pen; and, on top, a miniature version of what looked like a planetarium's star projector.

"If you'll have a seat, ladies," said the doctor, at the console, indicating the other chairs. Then he seated himself. With one hand on the control panel and the other one poised as if to conduct an orchestra, the doctor began the session.

"Today, at Miss Duke's request, we will be doing a brief aura check-in for both of you. And then, with your permission, Miss Hutton, a little tune-up for you. Does that sound alright?"

Both women said yes.

The doctor pressed a button, and a second window scrim descended mechanically to block out all outside light. At the same time, the room's initial lighting dimmed and gave way to a soft bluish glow that seemed to come from everywhere and nowhere. After a moment in this environment, with the floor, walls, and ceiling all glowing blue, it was easy to imagine floating weightlessly in the sky.

"This is our baseline, and now we optimize the ionization."

The doctor gave a dial a slow quarter turn. A low, pulsing sound, almost imperceptible, began to fill the room.

"May we speak?" said Barbara.

"Of course," said the doctor, turning another dial slightly, which added another subtle sound.

"Are we supposed to see something? I mean, besides the blue?"

"It's what *I* can see, Miss Hutton," said the doctor, focused on his controls.

"So then you take our photographs. . . ?"

"No, no, not in this session . . ." he said, turning a third dial, which produced a third layer of sound, after which the doctor seemed satisfied. "There!"

The doctor rose from his seat.

"What I take, dear lady, is my impression," he said, beginning to walk slowly around them, regarding them from all angles: now crouching a bit and looking up at them, now coming in from the side for a close-up on a hand or a head, but never touching them.

"I look, I sense . . . so I can *know*," said Dr. Boehme.

Occasionally, as he continued, the doctor emitted a small moan or gasp or "uh-huh," upon some discovery or observation that he didn't bother to fully verbalize.

Both women sat fairly still, graciously allowing themselves to be thus observed, not quite knowing if it was alright for them to turn their heads or even move their eyes while the doctor was aside or in back of them.

"Do you need us to remove our hats, Doctor?" said Doris.

"No, no—it's very good. Very good indeed."

Several times, Dr. Boehme returned to the console to make a few notes in his notebook. After a few minutes of this, the doctor reseated himself and brought the room's lighting and sound back to their original state.

"Thank you, ladies," he said.

"Thank you very much, I'm sure, Doctor," said Barbara. "Though I must admit I have no idea what just happened."

"I am delighted to report that I am finding a great deal of harmony here," said the doctor, bringing his hands briefly into something like the prayer position.

"Are you, Doctor?" said Doris.

"A great deal of green, for both of you—that is the heart chakra, passion. A great deal of blue—the throat chakra. . . ."

"Which is all about communication, vitality . . ." said Doris, for Barbara's sake.

"Yes, that's right," said the doctor. "And purple—the crown chakra. . . ."

"Spirit, vision," said Doris.

"For both of us?" asked Barbara.

"Yes, for both of you," said the doctor.

"So we have the same aura?" said Barbara.

"No, no. It's different from person to person, and from moment to moment. But this is the way you look to my mind's eye right now, here, together—sharing this experience."

"We're not different at all?" said Barbara.

"Forgive me if I am being unclear. My English! You each have these colors, but in unique and personal balances. Maybe Miss Duke has a touch more yellow."

"Really, Dr. Boehme—yellow?" said Doris.

"Solar plexus," said the doctor, nodding.

"Enthusiasm, optimism . . ." said Doris, again for Barbara's sake, and also with a touch of quiet pride.

"Oh, well . . ." said Barbara. "I suppose that makes sense."

"And now, Miss Hutton, may we go a little deeper with you?"

"I . . . certainly."

"There will be some very light touching involved—nothing to be concerned about."

"Alright."

"Will you consent to have Miss Duke present for the treatment?"

"It's to be a treatment, then? For what? Dodo, don't you dare let him cure me of my smoking."

Doris smirked.

"It's a general treatment, uplifting . . ." said the doctor. "Think of it as the equivalent of a vitamin shot, but for the spirit *in* the body."

"Alright. I'm for that."

"And Miss Duke may remain?"

"If she doesn't bother you, she doesn't bother me."

"Then let us begin."

Again, with his console, the doctor adjusted the room's environment. If the effect of the room in blue light produced a sensation of floating in the sky, now the light came as variegated, subtly morphing waves of blue and green shot with soft gray, producing the effect of being underwater in a still pond, while still being able to breathe. The sound that seemed to fill the room was the saturated, placental silence that one hears when suspended for a moment at the bottom of a swimming pool: is it the water pressure itself that's making a sound?

"The color environment will support the rebalancing," said the doctor quietly. In the dim light, the sound of his voice was more hypnotic than in the previous portion of the session. "I have selected these colors for you as an initial palette, based on what I have just learned during the check-in. Feel free to let your eyes wander at will. You may look at what I am doing or not. What I do ask you to do is listen—to me, to what I will be doing. In this portion of our visit, please refrain from speaking until we are finished. Just listen. The procedure will take about twenty minutes. Please nod if you understand."

Barbara nodded.

"Very good, Miss Hutton. Now please nod if you are ready."

Barbara nodded again.

Dr. Boehme pulled his chair an inch or two closer to Barbara. From his console, he took two small, polished black stones and began rolling them in his palm in such a way that they made light clicks as they struck each other. Several times he made a series of clicks, then swept the fist containing the stones in the air around Barbara's head, shoulders, and chest: clicking, sweeping; clicking, sweeping.

"This is the tourmaline," said the doctor. "We activate it and use it to disperse disruptive energies . . ."

Clicking, sweeping; clicking, sweeping. Barbara remained poised, breathing calmly, her eyes focused mostly straight ahead.

Dr. Boehme then did a series of clicking the stones, then applying them in a light touch to parts of Barbara's upper body, chiefly her shoulders, neck, and throat. Then he did a series of clicks and touches to the forehead and temples. Occasionally he emitted a whimper or went "Ahh."

"You've had quite a lot of coffee today, haven't you, Miss Hutton?" said the doctor.

Barbara started to respond by speaking, but the doctor raised a finger to silence her. She nodded yes.

"*Per*fectly alright," said the doctor in an almost musical way. "We are rebalancing the astral . . ."

With a surgeon's grace, Dr. Boehme returned the stones to their spot and took up one of the metal tubes, which was sealed at both ends and apparently contained small beads, because the tube produced a mild rattling sound when given a shake. Again the doctor performed a series of movements in the air close to Barbara, this time rattling and sweeping, and then came the light touches to her upper body and head.

Rattling, sweeping; rattling, sweeping, touching.

Purely sonically, the effect of the treatment was practically symphonic. In the dead silence of the room, in the midst of the flowing, hypnotic waves of underwater lighting effects, the clicks and rattles seemed to take on universal importance—as if some divine shreds of the very music of the spheres were being harnessed there in Harley Street.

"And now—the etheric . . ." sang Dr. Boehme.

He returned the metal tube to its spot and quietly rose from his chair. The final part of the treatment, he said, was for the "celestial aspect." Standing in front of Barbara, and then moving nimbly beside her, and then in back of her, almost in a dance, the doctor made a series of sweeping and waving and pushing gestures with his hands and arms, as if clearing away some smoke in the air or smoothing down layers of chiffon as a couturier's assistant might do to a long skirt on a mannequin as the master worked away on the bodice. This continued for several minutes, sometimes to some possibly involuntary humming from the doctor.

Then, with a satisfied exhalation, Dr. Boehme reseated himself. He took a moment or two of silence, then switched the room's environment back to normal. He placed his hands on his thighs and cocked his head. One side of his mouth twisted upward into half a smile.

"How do you feel, Miss Hutton? You may speak now."

Barbara took a second, then cocked her head, too.

"I feel fine, Doctor—thank you very much," she said.

It was clear that she was still processing the experience and didn't yet quite know what to say about it. Doris, for her part, was delighted to have witnessed the treatment, since she had had the highest hopes for it—and in general, for her old friend's well-being—but she hesitated to speak, because the doctor was still engaging with Barbara alone.

"Good, very good," said the doctor. "It sometimes takes a while to perceive what has shifted."

"Alright, then," said Barbara.

She smoothed her skirt and was about to rise from her seat, but it was clear that the doctor had something more to say.

"May I suggest, dear lady, that you consider a course of therapy that could go deeper?"

"What do you mean, 'deeper'?"

"We might address the matter of the psychic weight that you carry upon yourself."

"*Weight?!*"

It was a word that Barbara was not expecting to hear on a visit to a psychic aura-therapist.

"We all have it," said the doctor, reassuringly. "We rarely treat it. But it affects our lives, detracts from our well-being. . . ."

"*Weight*, Doctor?"

"The wounds we contract in everyday life, starting at birth. These are quite easy to heal, once they are identified."

"What kind of wounds?" said Barbara. "If you're talking about ex-husbands . . ."

She was speaking facetiously, out of sudden nervousness about her actual, physical weight, but the doctor had grown almost grave.

"I am detecting something very deep, about . . . your mother," he said.

Barbara looked surprised, even hurt.

"What about my mother?"

"Have you lost her?"

"Long ago."

"I believe this must be very painful. I believe . . ."

Barbara raised a palm against the doctor's words.

"Doctor, please," she said.

On Dr. Boehme's face was infinite concern and compassion.

"Very, very lonely . . ." he said, almost in a whisper.

Barbara began shaking her head and held her palm even more decisively. She was clearly shaken, but relying on her well-practiced sense of privilege and poise to get through the moment.

"*Please*, Doctor."

Dr. Boehme stopped speaking and nodded his head sympathetically.

"I just . . . can't," said Barbara simply.

Doris stirred.

"I think, Doctor, maybe we've had enough therapy for today," she said.

"Yes, of course, as you wish," said the doctor.

They all rose, and Dr. Boehme walked the women back through his consulting room to the front door of his office suite, where they said their thank-yous and goodbyes.

"I remain at your disposal, ladies," said the doctor, with a bow.

"Please send me your bill," said Doris.

Doris and Barbara walked out of the building in silence.

"Are you alright?" said Doris, outside on the sidewalk, before they stepped into the car that was waiting for them.

"Of course, Dodo," said Barbara. "He's actually a rather nice man, isn't he?"

"I think he has a good soul."

"And he's obviously talented at *something*."

"Yes."

"*Quel* performance. Did you tell him about my mother?"

"Of course not."

"Then how did he. . . ? Oh, well, I suppose he could have read all about the poor little four-year-old who discovered her dead mommy."

"Maybe, sure. And just maybe he *saw* something inside you and can help with it."

"Maybe. I just . . ."

Barbara shook her head.

"I know, I know," said Doris. "But, Babs, it *has* been over half a century. And I do think we carry around . . ."

"I know. I just didn't want to talk about it."

"Fair enough. But . . . have you *ever* talked about it—I mean, with a psychiatrist or something?"

"I don't believe in that. And I am not sure I believe in this. And I know we don't want to be late for tea."

Inside the car, Barbara reached again into her purse for her cigarette case.

"You're not going to stop me now, are you, after *that*?" she said.

"No, of course not," said Doris. "Go ahead, have it, by all means—though Daddy knew, even in 1910, that it killed people . . ."

CHAPTER 30

The breakfast buffet was already set up in the Fairmont's Salon Lacoste, a meeting room off the hotel's lobby, when Emma arrived at 8:30 a.m. to check on preparations. A member of the catering staff was arranging carafes of coffee, tea, and orange juice; and a manager from the hotel's events office was on hand to confirm that the room had been set up as Emma specified and to give her the requested number of key cards. The configuration was almost like the one she had at Christie's: catering laid out on a table near the entrance, and a set area put together at the other end, this time with ten comfortable chairs and a dining-level table, on top of which was a selection of neatly folded table coverings of various kinds, including the one Emma had asked for: basic, untextured white, rolled up rather than folded. Also on the table was the box of specialized items that Emma had FedExed from New York, for the display of the jewelry—small Plexiglas cubes, swatches of black velvet, a bust for necklace display, stands for brooch and earring display, and a mannequin hand for bracelet and ring display. The French crew would be bringing with them all the light, sound, and camera equipment they would need.

The day's schedule would be relatively relaxed, as shoots go, even with the addition of the turquoise-and-sapphire necklace. The crew would arrive at nine and set up; Ollie would show up sometime before eleven, which is when Artemis was due; the Duchess of Windsor shoot would run about an hour; Emma,

Artemis, and Ollie would be meeting Lyudmila for lunch at the hotel's Horizon Rooftop restaurant at twelve-thirty; and after lunch, it would take an hour to shoot the necklace. They would probably be done by four.

Emma had been emailing and videoconferencing regularly with Charles, the videographer, and finalized the day's shoot with him the night before, so when he arrived at the Salon Lacoste with the rest of the team—Sara, the lighting technician; Hakim, the sound technician,; and Sandhya, the makeup and hair artist—there was that automatic ease of cooperation and production-team camaraderie that Emma had seen on practically every shoot she'd ever taken part in. The team deployed their equipment and performed their tests so efficiently that there was plenty of time for all to enjoy the breakfast offerings, which included mini-croque madames. Ollie arrived after a morning stroll down to the marina and was conversing in French with Hakim about the glories of Rabat when Artemis arrived.

"Here we are! Good morning, everyone!" she said brightly, looking smart in jeans, a stylish white J. Lindeberg golf top, Ray-Ban aviators, and a thin, gold link necklace so light it was barely perceptible. Accompanying her, as Ollie had predicted, was a man she introduced as Nigel, who was carrying a Goyard suit bag and backpack. Though he may have been armed with a concealed Glock 19, Nigel was casually dressed in an outfit that any affluent Monte Carlo resident or tourist might be wearing: blue-and-white–striped Breton shirt, navy blazer, white jeans and tennis shoes, but with no corporate badge. As Emma was introducing the team to Artemis, Nigel took two jewelry cases from inside the backpack and was standing by with them.

"And here are the goodies," said Artemis, indicating the cases. "Now, where shall we put them, and how do you want me?"

"We're over here," said Emma, walking Artemis over to the set area, where two cameras had been set up on stands, facing a suspended sheet of seamless in front of which was a chair. To one side was the table, with its own lighting and camera setup.

"I brought some different looks," said Artemis. "You said 'casual,' but you know—collars and such."

Emma gave Artemis a thoughtful once-over.

"You look great. You nailed it."

"I thought white, *sportif.*"

"That's exactly right. We want the real person, not the lady at the gala. Then it's a lovely surprise when we flash some paparazzi shots of you really dressed for an evening."

"Oooh!"

"So you're there, in front of the seamless," continued Emma, "and Ollie and I are over here with Charles, who is operating both cameras. Camera number one here, camera number two there. We're using a boom mic, because I didn't want the messy, newscast look of a lavalier. I'm sure you've done this a million times."

"Not so much," said Artemis, "but I'm a quick study. Um, 'lavalier'. . . ?"

"Body mic. I knew you'd be carefully put together, and I didn't want to mess with that."

"Okay. So the mic is up there, but I speak normally."

"You speak normally, yes, and to the camera, please, not to us."

"Got it."

"And we just have a conversation, the three of us . . ." said Emma.

"More of exactly what we were doing last night," said Ollie. "Only maybe more complete sentences."

Artemis giggled.

"With the jewelry in front of us?" she said.

"No—that's the thing," said Emma. "Footage of that really wouldn't work. It's to be you talking, which we will edit, and then we do separate footage there at the table of the pieces themselves, properly displayed, close-up and all that."

"I see, good," said Artemis. "Yes, now that you mention it, I do see it might be horrid to watch someone clucking over this precious little thing she's got in her hand, or worse, wearing."

"Right."

"So it's me, then the pin, all before lunch."

"We'll go for thirty or forty minutes, talking. Then I'll set up the pin, and we'll grab some footage and some still shots of that. Easy-peasy."

In an almost military fashion, Nigel was remaining close to the jewelry. He had locked the door to the room after he and Artemis entered—"for security reasons," he explained quietly.

Emma and Ollie had sketched out some questions for the shoot, and it turned out that Artemis was able to respond to them in as practiced a way as any skilled media personality might.

"You met the Duchess of Windsor in the 1970s, I believe," said Emma. "Tell us about that. And if you could start your answers by restating the questions . . ."

"Sure," said Artemis, who launched into basically the same story she'd told Emma and Ollie in New York. "I met the Duchess in Paris, a few years after the death of the Duke. She was on the board of governors of the American Hospital, where my aunt was also on the board. She was probably around eighty at that point, but still so trim and chic. And I was invited with my aunt to lunch a few times at the Windsor home in the Bois de Boulogne. It was at one of those lunches, actually, when I first saw the pin and was fascinated by it."

"What did you find so fascinating about it?" asked Emma.

Artemis nodded to indicate that she understood the question and took a split second to formulate a response.

"I found the pin fascinating for so many reasons," said Artemis. "It was the perfect blend of whimsy and drop-dead glamour, if you know what I mean. None of the women in my family had jewelry that I liked. My mother had some very sober things that she inherited from *her* mother, which were old-ladyish a hundred years ago, yet still not exactly *chic à l'ancienne* today. On the other hand, my aunt Fanny liked anything that was eccentric or unusual—pins in the form of fruit bowls and flower arrangements—much too cute and girly. The flamingo, to me, exemplified how fun and serious could go together."

"Were you wearing much jewelry then?" said Emma. "You were, what, in your twenties at that point?"

Artemis smiled.

"I was in my twenties at that point, and wasn't wearing too terribly much jewelry at all. But as I got older and began entering a wider variety of social situations, I realized that jewelry could be a useful language. Well, one's whole appearance is a language, isn't it? And I realized one could speak either inadvertently or on purpose. I chose on purpose."

Emma nodded and mouthed the word "perfect."

"How did you come by the pin?" she said.

"The pin was a birthday present from my husband, who bought it in the 1987 auction of the Duchess's jewels, at Sotheby's. The sale was for the benefit of the Pasteur Institute—biomedical research, which is a field that's very important to my husband and me."

"And how did this very thoughtful husband know that the pin would be to your taste?"

Artemis giggled.

"He knew a lot about what I didn't like in jewelry because he is a very generous man," she said, "and once, shortly after we were married, he brought me back an extremely expensive, extremely hideous necklace from Singapore, where he had business. He knew instantly that I didn't like it, and because he is a very smart man who pays attention to important things, he asked me to explain what I did like and what I didn't, and why. Luckily, he had brought the necklace home only on approval . . ."

The questions that Emma asked were those whose responses would appeal to the film's more general audience. They evoked a story of the heart. Those that Ollie asked evoked responses that contained information Artemis had gathered over the years that might satisfy more connoisseur-like tastes while also prompting a general viewer to enhance both her knowledge and appreciation. This was more a story of history. Artemis explained that the Duke commissioned the brooch from Cartier in 1940, after the war interrupted the supply of gems and gold to France. Since clients had to provide their own materials, the Duke brought in a disused family necklace and several disused bracelets. With a selection of rubies, sapphires, emeralds, and diamonds to repurpose, the Cartier designers worked their magic.

At the end of fifty minutes, Emma paused a moment, then said thank-you.

"I think we have it."

"That was easy," said Artemis.

"Solid gold," said Ollie. "Well done."

"Was it good?" said Artemis.

"Better than good," said Emma. "We got exactly what we needed, exactly what I hoped for. You are so good at formulating responses!"

"Thank you. I feel that we could have gone on for hours."

Shooting the pin went smoothly. Nigel handed the jewelry case to Artemis, who opened it and showed everyone—to much *ooh*ing and *ahh*ing—then handed it to Emma.

"It's exquisite, isn't it?" said Emma, entranced by the design and workmanship of the pin: the delicate curve of the bird's neck, the sharp angle of its raised leg, the exuberant arcs of its tail feathers.

It took fifteen minutes to mount the pin on a display stand and twenty minutes to shoot it. Sara had worked in advertising and had experience lighting small objects like lipstick tubes and makeup compacts, so her pre-set lighting needed only a small refinement to maximize the pin's sparkle. Emma happily said yes when, at the end of the shoot, Artemis asked if she wanted to try on the pin for a photograph. On the gray sleeveless top Emma was wearing with a long, white cotton skirt, the pin looked perfectly at home.

"Emma, dear, what did you do to your elbow?" asked Artemis, noticing the small bandage that Emma was wearing over her biopsy incision.

"Nothing," said Emma. "Just a little fall." She had decided before the trip that it would be silly for her to wear long sleeves all the time, as if she were ashamed of something. The goal, she realized, was simply to minimize conversation about the bandage, and keep everyone's focus on the shoot.

Nigel stayed with the jewels in the Salon Lacoste and joined the film crew for the buffet lunch that was served there, while Emma, Artemis, and Ollie went up to the hotel's Horizon terrace.

The day was bright and temperate. It was early for lunch, and the Horizon was only half full with a pleasant, affluent-looking crowd.

"There she is!" said Artemis, waving to a pair of women seated at a table at the edge of the terrace, overlooking the sea and part of the marina. The older of the two women, who was wearing a raffia hat with a broad brim and black band, waved back.

As the threesome were heading for the table, Ollie discreetly drew Emma's attention to a man who was dressed like Nigel was, in a blazer and slacks, being seated alone at a table near theirs.

"Another one?" said Emma.

"*The* other one, I'm sure," said Ollie. "More than two would be showing off. He was probably posted outside the door."

"Lyudmila, darling," said Artemis, leaning over to kiss her friend on the cheek. "You look marvelous! And here is Emma and Ollie."

The other woman, Nadia, much younger than Lyudmila, was introduced as her friend, but after Emma noticed that Lyudmila was in a wheelchair and observed how attentive Nadia was to her, Emma concluded that Nadia was a nurse. Did Lyudmila, too, have a security man somewhere nearby? Artemis had explained that Lyudmila's husband owned a Russian oil and gas company; she and Lyudmila had met socially in London when Artemis still lived there. Now they saw each other chiefly in Monte Carlo, where Lyudmila spent part of the year, and in Montenegro, where Lyudmila and her husband had a villa on the Adriatic.

"I am very happy to be included in your film, Emma," said Lyudmila, a former Olympic skier for the Soviet Union who appeared to be around sixty-five or seventy. Her accent was French-inflected Russian.

"I'm honored that you're part of it," said Emma.

"And you've come so far to see us!"

"It's a pleasure, especially when you live in such a beautiful part of the world."

Lyudmila nodded with a tired smile.

"Roman and I are here only when it is too cold in Moscow and too rainy in London."

"They have a stunning place in Eaton Square," said Artemis.

"Next week we will go back."

"I see," said Emma. "So you have a place here, then?"

Lyudmila turned slightly and pointed in the direction of the marina. It wasn't clear what Lyudmila meant until she continued.

"We sail back and forth between Kotor and here," she said. "'The two Montes,' as we say."

Emma didn't quite know how to respond, realizing that Lyudmila had pointed to the massive, ultramodern trimaran yacht in the marina. This was new information for Ollie, too, as Emma noticed that he seemed the tiniest bit impressed to connect the lady with the largest boat in view.

"Life on a yacht is not . . . too inconvenient for you?" he said. It was clear what he meant—the wheelchair—and Emma saw in his question exactly the balance between directness and curiosity, coupled with the graciousness of a true gentleman, which Ollie commanded with such ease.

"No, no," said Lyudmila. "Just the opposite, Ollie. Design solves everything, as you know."

Ollie instantly understood.

"The yacht was built for you!"

"Yes."

"Bravo."

"In all the world, it's the easiest place for me to be now."

"Secure . . ." said Artemis.

"Well, yes," said Lyudmila, "but also the best place to entertain. It's the only place I can give big dinner parties anymore. It's very comfortable for me, because all the spaces have been thought out so well. I can get around and mingle with my guests."

"What is the yacht called?" said Ollie.

"*Stella Azzurra*," said Lyudmila.

"The Blue Star."

"It's practically the only place nowadays where I wear my designer gowns—the only place where I wear my jewels; the only place, in fact, where I wear my tiara, which you will see tomorrow."

Since Emma and Ollie had prepared for Lyudmila's shoot by discussing the lore behind the tiara—that it was rescued from the *Lusitania* as the ship was going down—Emma was sure that Ollie was on the verge of making some remark about the karma of sailing the seas while in possession of the ornament. But he said nothing.

CHAPTER 31

April 1969

Ollie arrived in London two days before the concert. By 1969, he had been working with Doris on various aspects of the Newport Restoration project, as well as advising her informally on a number of architectural renovations, including parts of Rough Point, and auction-house purchases—and this was in addition to his continuing work with David Hicks, who was now designing interiors for more clients in Manhattan. Ollie believed that Doris was now making it a point, since the incident in the garden, to tell people they were friends, just friends, so it would be clear that she was not thinking of him as a boyfriend or designated boyfriend-like companion—though Ollie did feel, and didn't mind, that being the friend Doris wanted meant he was pretty much hers and no one else's. After Eddie died, she would take him to performances or social events just as a friend, yet she would have been surprised and maybe even alarmed if he'd started doing the same thing with another great lady.

Joey Castro had pretty much been demoted from his position in Doris's life by then, having become possessive of his relationship with Doris and his social use of Falcon's Lair, which sometimes he acted as if he owned. There were spats, angry calls, and letters. Finally, Joey tried to "file for divorce," seeking some sort of remuneration after what he termed in the legal papers their "common law marriage." It was a ridiculous ploy, but as a way of soothing the situation, Doris did help fund a new record company for Joey, a corporate gig that would at least direct his energy toward good and profitable use. Ollie had always gotten along well with Joey, as he had with Eddie, though his loyalty to, and perhaps fear of, Doris kept him from remaining particularly close to Joey after the "divorce." In fact, a classless remark that Joey made to Ollie diminished him in Ollie's eyes. After Eddie's mysterious death, Joey warned Ollie bitterly that "You're next, buddy."

So there was nothing unusual about Ollie's staying in Doris's three-bedroom penthouse suite at the Dorchester, on this visit to London. By himself, he might be able to squeeze in a quick drink with a Hicks colleague or duck into one of his favorite small museums, like the John Soane House, but he was there in the city to accompany his dear friend to the Joplin concert. Indeed, Ollie had begun to entertain the idea that having a younger male friend like him—that is, not a boyfriend, nor a suitor, nor a husband, nor an ex-husband, let alone a walker—was something new for Doris and something that she liked. For her, the '60s was all about embracing new things, trying new ways—which Ollie found amusing, since for him. many of the decade's new ways, especially those involving love, were confusing and stupefying.

"He's cuter than I remember him," said Barbara.

"He *has* grown up, hasn't he?" said Doris.

"You gals, I'm right here," said Ollie.

They all laughed, but it wasn't exactly humor that was fueling the exchange. The three of them were taking afternoon tea at the Dorchester's salon-like Promenade, Doris and Barbara installed on a dainty, semicircular, sage-green banquette, Ollie across the table in a pink-upholstered chair; and between them pots of jam, butter, and clotted cream, and two three-tiered silver stands, one with finger sandwiches, the other with scones and cakes. Ollie ordered tea, but the ladies stuck to champagne.

"Boys *will* grow up," said Barbara.

"Not the boys *I* married," said Doris.

They paused for a contribution from Ollie.

"Don't look at me," he said. "I think I was born grown up. Anyway, I was never young."

Again, they laughed, though it wasn't clear precisely what was funny.

Barbara was smartly dressed in a gray suit and hat, a small fur piece that had been around her shoulders now across her lap, under her napkin. But she was heavily made-up, especially the eyes, which were defined with thick, black liner. Even now, at four in the afternoon, she seemed under the influence of some substance, with a glassy, vacant look; slow and deliberate of speech, sometimes uncertain, when she reached for her glass or a finger sandwich, exactly where the thing was positioned.

"So you're in town for a concert?" she said, managing an automatic smile.

"Janis Joplin," said Doris.

"Is that rock 'n' roll?"

"Something like that."

"Personally, I don't go for it."

"Why not?" said Ollie.

"The music, for one thing," said Barbara. "Simplistic, animalistic noise."

"That's the point," said Doris.

"The audience, for another," said Barbara.

"How so?" said Ollie.

"Simplistic, animalistic people. Armies of them."

"How would you know, anyway?" said Doris.

"And the way they dance to it, even at a concert, in the aisles. There are no steps! No steps at all! Didn't we have to learn all the steps, Dodo? That's just life. Well, now they just wiggle and flail, wiggle and flail. . . ."

"I think it's more than that," said Ollie. "The human body has been . . ."

But Barbara rattled on.

"I was in San Francisco last year—no, no, two years ago—for that Fillmore Auditorium thing—what was it. . . ?"

"They called it 'the summer of love,' if it's what I think you're talking about," said Ollie.

"Lance and the Mouseketeer took me. They said it was 'groovy.'"

"The Mouseketeer?"

"His wife, Cheryl. She used to be on that Mickey Mouse show."

"Anyway . . ." said Doris, impatiently.

"Well, it was a madhouse, the whole city was," said Barbara. "Bands with *airplane* and *dead* and *camel* in the title. Not at all what is done."

"Really, Babbo . . ." said Doris.

"Anarchy, pure anarchy," said Barbara. "That's the music of our times."

"You don't find it exciting," said Ollie, "some of it, sometimes. . . ?"

"I find none of it appealing," said Barbara.

Doris sighed.

"*Chacun à son goût,*" she said impassively.

"In Morocco, we have *chaabi* music," said Barbara. "I find that quite lovely—joyous, celebratory. . . ."

"Well I, for one, celebrate the hippies and the flower children," said Doris, "questioning authority, using anarchy, if that's what you want to call it, to shake up some of the conventions, sweep away the cobwebs—right, Ollie?"

"Uh, I guess so."

"I was at Shangri La when all that was happening, and I still regret not going to San Francisco for that festival, as people were doing; and I certainly don't want to miss out on anything else. I'm not going to make that mistake again. This summer, Ollie and I are going to the Woodstock festival. I already have the tickets."

"The what?" said Barbara.

"It's an outdoor music festival in upstate New York," said Doris. "It's going to be *very* groovy. All the bright young people I know are talking about it."

"Outdoors? Like Tanglewood?"

"It will probably be a little more like . . ." began Ollie, who already had doubts about the rosy Woodstock dreams that Doris and he had been hearing from the rich, international vagabonds she encountered on four continents.

"Yes, outdoors," said Doris. "In nature. Mother Nature—who has the power to heal us."

"Sounds messy," said Barbara, taking a sip of her champagne.

Just then, a man and a woman who were passing through the Promenade stopped abruptly at the table, both sporting long, dark hair, both dressed in identical white suits and wearing wire-rim spectacles with round, blue lenses. The woman was also wearing a white pork pie hat. It was John Lennon and Yoko Ono.

"My goodness, Ollie! How nice. . . !" said Ono, whom Ollie had met a few years before, at a London gallery that was showing some of her interactive sculpture. She and Lennon were accompanied by an assistant who seemed patiently impatient with the chance encounter, as if he were charged with keeping his stars on schedule.

"Yoko . . . hello," said Ollie, pleasantly surprised, rising for a kiss with Yoko. Then he introduced Doris and Barbara, and Ono tried to introduce Lennon, who was temporarily waylaid by an autograph seeker whose intention the assistant could not avert. Doris seemed keenly interested in the couple, but Barbara practically ignored them, choosing that moment to reach into her purse for her compact and lipstick.

"We're in town for the Joplin concert," explained Ollie, "Miss Duke and I."

"So are we," said Ono. "But we also had a press conference."

"I love Pearl's energy," said Lennon. "No bullshit there, no games."

"She sent John a tape for his birthday, singing 'Happy Birthday,'" said Ono.

"Pure soul," said Lennon.

There was a brief exchange about a so-called "bagism" event that Lennon and Ono had just presented in one of the Dorchester's ballrooms—a "pop-up protest" against racial prejudice.

"We were hidden inside a big white bag and spoke through a vocoder," said Ono.

"Well done," said Ollie. And then the couple abruptly said goodbye and were gone.

"Exciting," said Doris. "And I am not one to become giddy over famous people."

"That man is uncouth," mumbled Barbara.

"John Lennon?" said Doris.

"A few years ago, Lance insisted I come with him to the London Palladium, to see the Beatles. . . ."

"That son of yours is really trying to give you a good education," said Doris.

"Hah! So we go. And they play a song, and then another, and then another. At least some of them had melodies. It was fine, and then he stops the show, John Lennon does, to introduce a song, and he points to our box. Of course, he knows who's in the audience every night and where they're sitting. He points to the box and says, 'I'd like to dedicate this next song to Miss Barbara Hutton'. . . ."

"That's nice."

Barbara wagged her forefinger *no* and continued.

"He bows, and initially I'm flattered, and some people applaud, but not too many, because most of them are probably too young to know who I am—and then they start the song, and the words are 'Money can't buy me love'. . . ."

Doris giggled.

"Over and over again. 'Money can't buy me love, money can't buy me love,'" said Barbara. "It was *awful*. Uncouth and completely uncalled for. I'd never even met the man. I wanted to walk out right then."

"But you didn't?" said Doris brightly.

"How could I? I was with Lance and some of his friends, and they all thought it was terribly amusing. A little sport at Mother's expense—with two thousand people watching."

"It sounds like you've probably been to more rock concerts than I have," said Ollie, in an attempt to smooth the situation. But Barbara was focused elsewhere.

"Where's the waiter?" she said, looking around. "I want a vodka, and then I must run."

After tea, Doris and Ollie took a stroll in Hyde Park, along the Serpentine. The sun had come out, and though the temperature couldn't have been more than fifty degrees, one hardy soul was even swimming.

"I can understand why Barbara didn't exactly greet Lennon warmly," said Ollie, "but why didn't *he* greet *her*? Has Yoko Ono's influence over him made him more peaceful—and if so, why didn't he apologize?"

"Ollie, look at her," said Doris. "He probably didn't recognize her."

"You mean. . . ?"

"Her looks. They're deteriorating fast. Even a few years ago, she wasn't nearly as bloated and tired-looking."

"Ah—yeah."

"All those barbiturates and tranquillizers add up, let alone the alcohol. And then she slaps on all that makeup! She looks like a raccoon. You see the direction she's going in."

"*Tsk.*"

"She's an addict. And of course, she knows it, and is seeking all the wrong treatments, and never sticks with anything. She tried hypnotism, at Cary's request. Which might have worked, but she didn't stick with it. I love her, but she's an addict—and there is only so much you can do to help an addict."

From behind, three children ran past Doris and Ollie exuberantly, followed by a mother or nanny walking quickly to catch up.

"And she's as addicted to marriage as she is to drugs and alcohol," continued Doris.

"*Was* addicted to marriage," said Ollie. "Didn't she say she's swearing off husbands?"

Doris snuffled in sad amusement.

"That's the thing about addicts," she said. "You can never believe a thing they say."

Coming toward them was a man in an overcoat and fedora, with a pair of excited-looking Jack Russell terriers on leashes.

"We were once so similar, almost twins, a unique pair," said Doris, "united against these notions of wealth and publicity— talk about prejudice! Yet deep down, our flesh was different, our very cells. I'm no angel, Ollie, as you well know. I love men,

I love pleasure. I love vodka as much as the next girl. But my cells can take it. Poor Babbo, though—not hers."

With over five thousand seats arranged amphitheater-style, London's Royal Albert Hall was built to be impressive, in the imperial sense of the word. The place was colossal. Seated there for a classical music concert, with an Olympian-scale arcade far above your head, the lofty drum of the building's great dome, you felt both small and noble at the same time. But for a rock concert, incorporating multicolored lighting effects pierced with spotlights hitting the stage from all angles, it's the performers who seemed noble or even godlike.

On Monday, April 21, 1969, the god onstage was Janis Joplin, known to her friends as Pearl, incongruously tiny and dressed in an electric blue jumpsuit, in her first solo show in England. She appeared not with Big Brother and the Holding Company, the group she had parted from, but with the Kozmic Blues Band; and far more than five thousand Joplin fans showed up for the gig, which required some typically decorous British crowd control at the doors. Joplin had said that appearing in England as a newly solo blues artist was intimidating for her, because she felt that British audiences were more discriminating about authentic blues than American audiences were. In America, she said, reputations come cheap, and "it's easy to make people think you are a blues singer."

The concert's dress code was casual chic, and was spectacularly observed especially in the best seats, the center boxes, where Doris and Ollie were. On display there, in people's costumes and hair, was nothing less than a golden wish for a mythological Eden that was also a sumptuous presage of Valhalla to come; and in the air, emanating from folds and tresses, the sweet earthiness of patchouli laced with the acrid reek of hash and weed. Amidst a sea of psychedelically colored spring velvets and Indian brocade, groovy paisley and geometric patterns, faces painted with flowers and swirls, and accessories like beads, bangles, floppy hats, and dangly earrings, Doris stood out in a blue-and-purple caftan and her sapphire-and-turquoise necklace, her hair blown up into a gloriously shaggy, Goldie Hawn-like "big bob" hairdo with sprays of white silk lily of the valley, fashioned by a hairdresser from the Sassoon salon who had been summoned to the hotel.

Doris looked happy to be at the concert, which touched Ollie greatly. Music was one of the few areas where she could really let go. And Joplin on stage was electrifying, sharing with the audience every bit of her love and pain, yearning and ecstasy, and making everyone see that she was indeed a great blues singer, in a dozen songs that included "Raise a Hand," "Ball and Chain," and "Piece of My Heart," and in a far-out, switched-on-Bach-like intro, Gershwin's "Summertime," a song that Doris knew well and partially hummed along with.

Afterwards, some Hollywood people that Doris ran into invited her and Ollie to a VIP after-party at the Royal Garden Hotel, nearby.

"What I wouldn't give to be able to sing like that," said Doris, on the short walk over to the hotel.

"She's marvelous," said Ollie.

"She's more than that. She's truly alive—being her unique self with this vital energy. Especially now that she's going solo. You heard that, right? Her singing is the sound of truth. It reminds me very much of something Martha Graham once told me. It's your business to find that unique truth inside yourself and give it to the world. It's not your business to judge it, only to open your channel and keep it open."

The party was in someone's suite—forty or fifty people, the men in everything from black tie to blue jean bell-bottoms, the women in every kind of garment from mini to maxi. The fare was the usual drinks and nibbles; a DJ was keeping things lively with a mix of the year's hit sounds—Beatles, Stones, Marvin Gaye. . . . With Doris off talking to a movie producer, Ollie was at the bar ordering his second gin-and-tonic when he was greeted quietly by name by a young, long-haired gentleman he didn't recognize at first, who then came into focus as Ollie saw through the florid mustache and sideburns, the tinted glasses, and the green Carnaby Street suit with pinched-waist jacket and flowing, scarf-like necktie in purple-and-green paisley.

"Lawton, good Lord, how nice . . ." said Ollie.

It was a former colleague from David Hicks, the one with whom, a few years back, at the posh country house party, he'd shared a moment of fumbled affection that they both recoiled from in the best form possible. Back then, Lawton's wardrobe was quietly Savile Row. Now, it was . . . well, Ollie thought, the man's channel was clearly wide open.

"You're looking well," said Lawton.

"So are you, I must say—splendid," said Ollie.

"See the concert?"

"Yes, indeed. Wasn't she marvelous?"

"Absolutely marvelous!"

"Such fire."

"That's it—fire, absolutely! You're still with Hicks, I gather?"

"Yes, based in New York now," said Ollie. "We have a couple of projects there. I'm also involved independently with some architectural restoration. Now, when you left the firm, it was to travel, wasn't it. . . ?"

"It was, yes—to Bangkok, for eight months," said Lawton. "Then I returned to London and opened a little shop—selling this and that, on Portobello Road. You must come by, if you have the time."

Lawton gave Ollie his card.

"I will, I will," said Ollie, knowing that whether or not he'd be able to get to the shop on this visit would depend entirely on Doris.

"Is there . . . anyone?" said Lawton.

"No, no. Afraid not. I'm in town with a friend, actually—a lady I'm . . . advising on some purchases." Ollie found himself neglecting to name Doris for no good reason he could think of.

"I see."

"You?"

Lawton indicated another man talking with some people

nearby—handsome, lively, dressed stylishly but not flamboy-antly.

"Jonathan DeCourcy," he said. "A novelist—pretty well-known. Nice, funny, smart. . . . We met out there."

"Good for you, really," said Ollie.

"Who'd have imagined how fast things are changing, eh?"

"Like a freight train."

After a few more words and a promise to stay in touch, Ollie was alone—except for the people, the music, the din of lively conversations. . . . Across the room, Doris was laughing heart-ily, along with the four men she was standing with. She looked spectacular that night, Ollie thought. He'd never seen her wear her hair that way, yet she'd taken a chance, and it paid off. The caftan, which she'd commissioned with her own design, was ab-solutely right for her age and rank, and for a Janis Joplin concert on the verge of a new decade. The necklace, which she said was new and had also commissioned with her own design, from her great friend David Webb, was right, too. . . . Doris certainly had *her* channel, but does everyone have one?

Do I have a channel? wondered Ollie.

Something Doris had said earlier was sticking in his brain: that Barbara was an addict, and that this was partly because her body was programmed that way. So was addiction essential to Barbara's channel? Ollie wondered how *he* was programmed. Could he be gay, whatever that meant, if he wasn't programmed for matters of the flesh at all? What are you, if your flesh had no programming? In a sense, he envied Barbara her addictions. At least they were deeply hers, and she knew, everybody knew, that that was her nature.

Maybe I'm the opposite of an addict, thought Ollie—not "sober," not "in control," but lacking the kind of neediness Bar-bara had and the ability to feel the temporarily pleasurable con-sequences of that neediness.

Ollie chuckled to think himself so neuter, given the time he had spent with two of the least-neuter human beings of the twentieth century. Had he learned nothing from them? For in addition to matters of the flesh, Barbara's kind of neediness often led to gratification in other areas. Dear Babbo, addicted not simply to drugs and alcohol but to capricious, indulgent excess! He remembered sultry days and voluptuous nights in the palace of Sidi Hosni, where the capriciousness and indulgence were at their least inhibited, where the queen would spend hours in that vast marble tub filled with saltwater that locals brought up from the sea in buckets every day, because Barbara insisted that "that was the way it should be done"; sitting and chatting with her wealthy widow friends, brittle and weary women, but affecting lightness of wit, to the sound of a Berber flute player, whom Barbara paid to sit on silk pillows in the courtyard and spin haunting melodies that would drift through the tiled rooms like perfumed zephyrs. . . . Once, from one of these bath audiences, near midnight, Barbara called to him, "Ollie, dear, may I ask you to go to my dressing table and get me that golden pearl necklace, the one from the Empress of Japan? I want to give it to Mrs. Douglas here, since she's been so nice to me. And Ollie, dear, we'd *die* for two more Cokes. . . ."

CHAPTER 32

The second day's shooting in the Salon Lacoste went without a hitch. Emma and everyone else marveled over Lyudmila's tiara, which featured a Greek key, or meander, motif that was so fashionable in 1909 when it was commissioned by Canadian businessman Sir Hugh Montagu Allan for his wife, Marguerite.

"Since my accident, I wear more of my things, more of the time," said Lyudmila, with larger-than-life vivacity. "Why not? They're not just for special occasions. Rather, for me, now, every day is a special occasion."

When she was in her fifties, Lyudmila had injured her spine permanently in a skiing accident that might have killed her. Where Ollie's questions for Lyudmila had to do with the design and meaning of tiaras, Emma asked a lot of questions—probably more than the finished film would require—about the lady's indomitable spirit.

"I found myself relating to her almost as a daughter, seeking consolation for the boo-boo in my elbow," said Emma with a laugh that evening, in a corner of the lounge bar of the Monte Carlo Casino's palatial Salle Europe, where she and Ollie had gone for drinks. "I must've heard that idea a million times, that every day is a special occasion, but somehow Lyudmila made me get it."

"It's a Russian thing," said Ollie, "the flip side of their grim, pessimistic soul."

Nearby, a throaty singer in a slinky, shimmering black gown

was pouring her heart into what sounded like a Portuguese folk song, to the accompaniment of a bittersweet guitar. Across the room were several gaming tables, quietly in action. Around and above it all, lit by dazzling crystal chandeliers, were every Belle Epoque architectural form in the book: columns and cornices, scrolls and wreaths, cartouches and oculi, shells and shields, much of it gilded. And echoing every gilded detail, frighteningly but magnificently, were the maximalist patterns of the room's multicolored carpet.

They'd had dinner at Nobu, in the hotel, and were now, in the casino, on their second round of martinis. Ollie had suggested a festive evening, since he'd gone to the trouble of bringing a dinner jacket after all; and Emma had been tickled to hear his suggestion, since she had packed a sparkly top she bought the year before for a friend's wedding.

"May I ask you something, since we're talking about survival with grace?" said Emma.

"Anything, good Emma," said Ollie.

"It's about AIDS."

Ollie emitted a tiny, involuntary snort.

"What a relief," he said serenely. "I was afraid you were going to ask about something like wearing diamonds before dark."

"Really okay?"

"Of course. Shoot."

"I've been thinking. Is there any guilt involved in surviving a major threat to your health?"

"Oooh . . . okay."

Ollie thought about the question for a moment.

"I wasn't all that surprised to survive, for reasons that I won't bore you with now," he said. "But yes, I suppose there is some guilt. Why am I here when so many others aren't?"

Emma nodded.

"Did living through that era change your life?" she said. "Wait—as an interviewer, I know I should phrase that in a better way: *how* did living through that era affect your life?"

"Emma, I will tell you anything about my life that I can. And just to be clear, at the age of a hundred and two, I have no more wisdom about my life or anyone else's than I did when I was twenty. But may I ask first, if this is about . . ."

He pointed coyly to the elbow.

"Sure," she said. "It's just that I never wondered before my diagnosis if my next film would be my last—if my next anything would be my last."

"Ah. But isn't the prognosis fairly positive?"

"It is. But once the question has been raised, and the fantasy of invulnerability has been pierced. . . ."

Ollie took a deep breath and exhaled.

"Yeah," he said.

"Before Daddy went off to São Paulo and got himself killed, he was talking about a skiing trip he wanted us to take, as a family, to Aspen. So the previous time we were all in Aspen together, like the year before, was the last time he would ever ski, but he didn't know that. I'm trying to figure out how my knowing that there's, say, a ten percent chance of my dying in a year might be useful or valuable to me."

"I see."

"All I can come up with is, if it helps make my work the best it can be. But I am already trying to make it the best it can be—you see?"

"Yes."

"Or am I supposed to savor life, being here in Monte Carlo, any more than I already do? I mean, the sky at dusk today was already overwhelming—and I'm feeling totally unable to take in more than fifty percent of the beauty."

Those in the room playing table games were generally reserved, but a wave of low hooting rose for a second from one of the tables. Though listening carefully to Emma, Ollie also wondered if a fortune had been won or lost at that very moment.

"Taking your next breath is always a risk, and staying aware of that is a responsibility," said Ollie. "I guess that's what people mean when they talk about 'being present'—besides all the, you know, sunsets and such."

Emma took a sip of her martini.

"I don't know if I am managing to do that, Ollie," she said, "and it feels like a giant frustration."

"You *can* find the peace in it. There *is* peace in it."

"Is there?"

"I can only say that at this point, I feel free of that exhausting kind of active gratitude that people seem so thrilled about. I know that I've had my last run down Piz Nair long ago. Thank you very much. I am simply glad now for things like being ambulatory, being able to name every last decorative detail in a confounded room like this, and being able to help someone nice like you with her film."

Conversation during the third martini was about how Ollie heard of friends smuggling supplies of the experimental medicine AL-721 into hospitals for their dying comrades, during the AIDS crisis—he heard about it but didn't take part; how twenty-five years before that, he heard of friends trying to figure out how to end the war in Vietnam or at least avoid dying in it—he heard about it but didn't take part. And after he and Emma had returned to the hotel and said goodnight and retired to their rooms, Ollie rang room service for a carafe of martinis and a glass, then went out onto the balcony, where there was a little breeze. The sea was tranquil and black, except for pinpricks of light here and there. There were lights down in the marina, too—lamps along the walkways and docks, glowing decks and windows of several boats where maybe dinners or parties were in progress. On the walk back from the casino, he had been too absorbed in his conversation with Emma to notice the Kapoor. *How almost secretly it must reflect the nighttime sky*, he thought.

Not guilt so much as shame—that's what he might have told Emma, but he was only thinking of this now. Existential shame, to be sure, but still shame. That during the '60s, his interests were more or less hijacked by what Barbara and Doris were interested in, so he missed out on sit-ins and sip-ins and riots, let alone dates and parties and orgies, in which he could have grown his identity and practice as a gay man. This shame now felt like a cancerous organ that couldn't be surgically removed or shrunk by radiation—something that he had been living with for a long time and would still have a few more years with, assuming the metastasis had slowed to a crawl.

He'd come to Monte Carlo with Doris in the '60s practically as a boy—not for the first time, but for the first *best* time. It made all the difference then to know everyone, to sample everything, to discover that it was only a well-meant version of Monte Carlo that made its imposing self available to the common hordes, while its true self simultaneously effervesced for the kind of people it was built for. And there was still so much more to know about the place—what those ancient Ligurian settlements were like; which fauna and flora were native and which imported; who else, through the centuries, had come here to win and lose and love and dine and tan.

He knew exactly what had happened at the casino that night. Emma, who had once disliked him for his mandarin majesty, his closeted ways, and his supposedly bad influence on her father, finally saw the inner regret and sadness, which humanized him for her. Bravo. Discussion of her upcoming radiation treatment had led her to this insight, and little shifts like that are what the fear of cancer and cancer itself can do. Bravo. The idea of death can change you, if you let it. Doris changed after Eddie's death. Chiefly, her desire to help Barbara intensified at this time, along with her frustration that there were limits to helping, limits even to how connected two old friends can be, or ever were.

Ollie laughed out loud. For a moment, he considered saying or singing something to the sea, from his balcony. But what? Life was such a broad comedy.

I must be drunk, or close to it, he thought. *Bravo.*

Doris once told him that for a while during the '50s, after Barbara's divorce from Rubi, she was trying to persuade Barbara to consult Dr. Wilhelm Reich, whom Doris met at a conference in New York. They should both go, said Doris. Reich, who would later be jailed as a quack, was the infamous proponent of orgone energy, the putative life force that was also described by Freud as *libido*, which Reich said could be harnessed and amplified in orgone accumulators that he built—one of which was large enough for a human being to enter. This was right up Doris's alley! Orgone energy could cure cancer and, by the way, everything else bad for a person, including bitterness stemming from divorce. Barbara was initially interested in journeying with Doris up to the doctor's laboratory in Rangeley, Maine, to be treated—until she was shown a grainy black-and-white snapshot of the human-size accumulator and refused to travel for hours merely to be "shut in a broom closet lined with tin foil."

Ollie rose from his chair and stood at the balcony's railing.

"Hi-yo, Wilhelm, away!" he bellowed, in a voice as close to that of TV's Lone Ranger as he could muster.

What was his life adding up to? A footnote in the history of American wealth and incidentally a transitional figure between the semi-closeted companion-walkers that were born a decade before him, and the more self-actualized gay men who were born a decade after?

Ollie reseated himself. He noted that the balcony's deck furniture was of the same quality as the rest of the suite's décor: deluxe, but not "superior deluxe," as at the Hermitage.

"I can say 'transitional,' because I know my eras and categories," he mumbled to himself.

Living through the AIDS crisis with so many gay friends might have made him gay—that is, forced him to choose sides, learn more of the manners and modes of gay culture—if he hadn't already carved out a unique social identity for himself and been so indifferent to actual physical desire; *and* if his swath of smart society hadn't been so very gracious about, or indifferent to, an obviously gay man surviving with only half a soul. By the '80s, he was a recognized byline, which conveniently functioned as a force field shielding him from challenge; though who, moreover, was there to challenge him about something like *that,* soulless living? Certainly not Doris or Barbara, certainly not his editors, certainly not the out-and-proud gay men he encountered socially, who were perfectly happy to let the colorful dinosaur be, especially if it might have a smart thing or two to say about Anish Kapoor.

The sea—could he hear it? Waves must be beating against the rocks and concrete pilings below, but was he imagining hearing that sound, or was it just time passing?

Those nights at Sidi Hosni, the flute player in the courtyard, the songs that the player said were a thousand years old—that was sixty years ago! Yet those songs now, perhaps being played in Tangier or Paris or New York by the man's grandson, were still roughly a thousand years old. And those nights at Shangri La, also sixty years ago, when Doris's *kahuna* friend would speak hauntingly, by the light of a bonfire on the beach, about the next Hawaiian island, presently under the waves as the Kama'ehuakanaloa Seamount, but on its way to emerging from the ocean in a hundred-thousand years! History swallows little things like a lifetime. A lifetime ago, Doris used to say, with ladylike bawdiness, "I haven't had any greens lately," which was code for sex. *Venetian* was sometimes her code word for *homosexual*.

Ollie shook his head.

Some of that coding was so elegant! he thought. *Should I be ashamed of thinking that—and would good Emma, so keen on knowing the meaning of tiaras, understand. . . ?*

CHAPTER 33

April 1969

The day after the Joplin concert, Doris and Ollie had lunch at The Mangrove, a modest Caribbean restaurant in Notting Hill that was founded and run by Black civil rights activist Frank Crichlow. Doris knew that the place attracted the likes of Jimi Hendrix, Marvin Gaye, and Nina Simone, so a visit here was no less important to her than one to the British Museum's Islamic Gallery. Over plates of home-cooked Trinidadian curry beef and rice, which they spiced up with one of the hot pepper sauces sitting on the table, she and Ollie discussed various approaches that could be taken to refine the Tony Duquette interior she'd had installed a few years previously in her penthouse on Park Avenue. The ceiling and walls of the living room were lacquered black, and the room was accented with two dramatic *étagères* displaying specimens of quartz crystal. Doris admired the scheme but had come to find it "a little too drop-dead" to live with.

"Why not just consult with Tony and tell him your concerns?" suggested Ollie.

"Well, I can do that, but help me think through what I should say," said Doris. "I don't want to just order him to do such-and-such. The man is an artist."

"Right. So just talk about what you feel."

"That's just it. I don't know what I feel."

"That doesn't sound like you," said Ollie brightly.

"This is why I rely on you and other brilliant experts," said Doris, with a wink.

"Dodo, I have an idea. I have a friend, also on Park—Walton Alsop, do you know him . . . ?"

Doris shook her head.

"It's his parents' apartment, a very fancy duplex," continued Ollie. "They've been there since the place went up in 1930. Walt commissioned Tony to do a 'secret' room there that is like a fabulous tabernacle, 'fabulous' as in a fable . . ."

"Ooh, I like this . . ."

". . . And it's all colors of the rainbow, in reflective and iridescent finishes, with semiprecious jewels set right into the décor, absolutely bonkers *barocco*. Oh, and a suite of actual jewels that people can wear when they're in the room, like bracelets and pectorals and diadems. . . ."

"My goodness! I don't think he was doing that when he did Falcon's Lair."

"Actually, technically, it's his mother, a very *grande dame*, who commissioned it—she knows Tony from Hollywood—but Walt and Tony got along like a house on fire over all the design and construction details."

"I'd love to see the room, if I could, and then call Tony," said Doris. "It would be a perfect way for me to broach the subject."

"Let me arrange it," said Ollie.

"A tabernacle!"

"That's what I call it. I don't know if Walt thinks of it that way."

Around them was the pleasant hum of lunchtime conversation. The Mangrove attracted a nicely mixed clientele of individuals of different colors, different cultures, and different socio-economic levels, which was a refreshing anomaly in socially stratified London of the time. Doris often said that she felt more relaxed in restaurants that were friendly and inviting, and for months afterward, she made it a point to drop references to The Mangrove into conversations, though she rarely gave a second thought to the celebrated gastronomic temples she visited in Paris.

"Excuse me, I couldn't help overhearing," said a young man from the next table—white, sensitive-looking, well-dressed, clearly American. "Miss Duke, may I introduce myself? I'm Selwyn Stanfield, from New York."

He was younger than Ollie, maybe barely twenty, but was confident and poised.

"Mr. Stanfield," said Doris genially. "This is Mr. Shaw, my associate."

"You see, architecture and design are interests of mine, too," said Selwyn. "I'm in the media business—well, my father's business, media investments—but my real hope is to restore a traditional *haveli* in India or Nepal."

"I am involved in restoration myself," said Doris. "Mr. Shaw and I both are."

Doris invited Selwyn to join her and Ollie at their table for an after-lunch coffee, and they all talked for an hour, about the Le Corbusier villa near Monaco that Selwyn had just visited, about the time Doris's great friend Barbara played a prank on her by redecorating her Hawaiian retreat after a stay there in Doris's absence. Amazingly, Selwyn knew about the Hudson Valley mountaintop estate where Doris and Ollie had met. He had accompanied his father to the very same house, probably around the same time, to inspect it for possible purchase, but the father declined. Doris, Ollie, and Selwyn laughed when Doris mentioned the difficulties of helicopter access to the place. Then Selwyn had to run off to an appointment, and the usual promises about staying in touch were made.

"Nice guy," said Ollie, after Selwyn left.

"Indeed," said Doris, summoning the waiter with a gesture. "Now, Ollie, before returning to New York, I need to stop in Zürich, and I want you to come with me."

"Really? What's in Zürich—an auction?" said Ollie.

"I need to speak with my banker, Herr Aeppli, and I want him to meet you."

"Me? Why me?"

"I'll explain when we get there."

"I thought you banked in New York."

"I do. But there's been a family account in Zürich since my father's time, which I use now for certain . . . private things."

"Yes, miss?" said the waiter when he arrived.

"May we have the check please?" said Doris.

"The gentleman has taken care of it," said the waiter, "the one who was sitting with you."

The headquarters of the bank then known as the United Bank of Switzerland, on Zürich's Bahnhofstrasse, was imposing but sober, like the city itself. Six triple-story columns framed five stately arches whose keystones were carved with heads of vigilant-looking Mercury, Demeter, and other guardians of wealth. At eleven in the morning sharp, white-haired Herr Aeppli met Doris and Ollie in the bank's echoing marble entry hall, accompanied by his young assistant, Herr Einsner.

"A pleasure, as always," said Aeppli, in German-inflected English.

"The pleasure is mine," said Doris.

After introductions, Aeppli led Doris, Ollie, and Einsner to his office, where Doris confirmed the idea she had already written to the banker about: she was making Ollie a trustee of one of the funds she had established several years back for private philanthropy—donations made to artists, health practitioners, and other worthies that for various reasons, mainly speed and secrecy, she didn't want to funnel through her foundation, which was public. She was empowering Ollie thusly, she explained, because she trusted his judgment and taste, and was one of the few people she could imagine carrying on this more personal side of her philanthropy after she was gone.

Aeppli balked chivalrously at the reference to Doris's eventual death, and put a few questions to Ollie that were perforce quite general—"Do you understand the responsibility Miss Duke is placing in your hands?"—because the bank would do whatever Miss Duke wished. Ollie agreed, and tried to look as responsible as he could, in his newly bought Savile Row suit, but already his mind was generating a thousand questions he'd have to ask Doris later—about her intentions, her reasons, her purpose. Were these philanthropic activities on a case-by-case basis? How did Doris use this fund, and would Ollie be expected to use it the same way? Did Ollie even know enough about who and what projects, what kind of projects, would be suitable for their—his!—beneficence? He tried to look as though he and Doris had already discussed the plan thoroughly. Einsner, who was there more as a witness than anything else, merely beamed and appeared to approve.

"I'm not going to drive this one. *You* are," whispered Doris, in an aside to Ollie. "When we get back to New York, I'll show you the basics—budget, previous recipients, all that. But I want you to follow your own ideas, because this is going to be in your hands now, not mine. That's the point."

But how. . . ? thought Ollie.

The rest was procedural. Papers were produced and signed. Doris said she would leave the review of the rest of the accounts to her business manager, who was due in Zürich in a few weeks.

The rest of the accounts. . . ? thought Ollie.

Then Aeppli rose.

"It's almost noon," he said. "Will you go to the vault now?"

"Yes, please," said Doris.

"Herr Einsner will accompany you. May I ask how much time you will need?"

"Only a few minutes."

"Then I can tell the restaurant to expect us at one o'clock?"

"Perfect," said Doris.

"I will meet you in the lobby at ten minutes to one," said Aeppli.

Wordlessly, Doris and Ollie followed Einsner through a marble corridor, back into the bank's entry hall, and then into a grand, ballroom-like space that was the vault area's anteroom. Two armed and uniformed guards flanked the great circular door of stainless steel and brass, almost seven feet in diameter and three feet thick, with a turning wheel latch and formidable-looking cylinders. Beyond a steel-and-glass "day gate" was the safe-deposit vault, a large room with a table and chairs in the center, lined with what Einsner said were three thousand steel-doored drawers and cabinets of various sizes, from document-size to jewelry-size, to artwork-size; and beyond that, the gate to a general-use cash vault. But Einsner led Doris and Ollie through a short passageway, past another day gate and metal vault doors marked ROTHSCHILD, ESTE, and THURN UND TAXIS, to one marked DUKE. This opened onto a private vault as large as someone's living room, and decorated in a similar manner—meaning that in addition to baroque-style wood paneling and shelves bearing books that Ollie supposed were quite rare, were paintings hanging on the walls, several pieces of antique furniture arranged on a Persian carpet as they might be in someone's home, and wood-paneled doors to various cabinets.

"I'll be right outside," said Einsner. "Take all the time you need."

"This will only take a moment," said Doris, approaching one of the cabinets.

Doris's father, Buck Duke, had been banking with this establishment since the turn of the century, and this private vault was built to his specifications when the bank constructed this new headquarters building in 1917. Presumably the paintings, mostly landscapes and still lifes, were by Old Masters. Ollie spotted a few crates that looked like they contained goods bought at auction and were yet unopened. The vault's basic office-type lighting was supplemented by a small crystal chandelier. Since the walls were presumably among the thickest in Europe, there were no sounds inside the vault except the ones they were making.

"Feel free to look around," said Doris.

But Ollie was riveted by the sight, on one side of the vault, of a long steel rack of shelves upon shelves of gleaming, yellow bricks neatly stacked four high—gold bullion. There were hundreds of bricks.

He was speechless—filled with questions about the origins and value of this horde—but if there were ever a thing to be discreet about, he thought, this is it: a pile of gold as large as a truck.

"Come, look," said Doris, seating herself on a little settee in front of an antique card table with a green baize-lined top. Ollie drew up a chair. She opened a velvet-covered box, not much larger than a pack of cigarettes, that was full of unset diamonds of various size and cut. Carefully, she shook a spoonful amount or so of them onto the table. "Fun, right?"

"*Fun?!*" said Ollie. There were no words. Several of the diamonds were quite large—five or six carats, Ollie guessed.

"These are what I came for," said Doris. "They were mostly my mother's. I'm having them made into a belt—something I can wear with blue jeans."

"A belt?"

"At the party the other night, they were talking about the riots in Newark last year—that's only thirty miles from Duke Farms, you know—and how we have to be prepared for anything. Don't you agree?"

"I suppose so."

"The producer I was talking to said that his wife had had a belt made with secret pockets for cash and jewels—something she could flee the house with, if necessary."

"Lord. Is it coming to that?"

"Who knows. If these riots keep happening. I thought, good idea, but why be so refugee about it? Why not a fashionable belt with visible diamonds that everyone will assume are rhinestones? Wouldn't that be fun?"

That word again.

"Only you, Doris," said Ollie, "would think of such a thing *and* be able to pull it off."

"I'm going to see if I can get Irene and David"—the designer Galitzine and the jeweler Webb—"to collaborate on something."

"That would be wonderful."

"Okay, then," she said, scooping the diamonds back into the box and tucking the box into a tote bag she was carrying with her purse. "Ready for lunch? Herr Aeppli and I like to go to this Italian restaurant around the corner, where they have a great shrimp cannelloni with red pepper cream sauce. You'll love it."

* * *

On the third morning in Monte Carlo, Emma interviewed
Artemis's friend Amaya, who brought with her not a security
detail but her sister Sarai. Both women had beautiful dark eyes
and were wearing elegant hijabs that they did not lower for the
shoot. Amaya was actually wearing her twenty-six-carat, pigeon-
blood-red Burmese ruby as a ring, the only piece of jewelry, in
fact, that she had on. Set between two large, shield-shaped diamonds, the cushion-cut stone was the perfect accessory for her
stylishly tailored, sand-colored pants suit. After the shoot, Ollie
whispered to Emma that he had never spoken to anyone who
was sporting a thirty-million-dollar *anything*, and he got a kick
out of it.

After a leisurely lunch with Amaya and Sarai, which Artemis
joined, Emma and Ollie were walking back to the hotel when
Emma brought up their flight home, scheduled for the following
day. Ollie surprised her by saying that his plans had changed.

"I'm afraid I won't be able to fly back with you," he said.

"What do you mean?" said Emma. "We have round-trip
tickets."

"I changed mine. I was going to tell you at dinner."

"Why the change?"

"A colleague called with a painting he wants me to look at—
something he's considering buying."

"Oh—damn. Well, fine. But I'm sorry I won't have the pleasure of your company for the flight."

"You'll have plenty of it when I return to New York. This is
only a day's detour. It can't be helped."

"Alright. Where to, by the way?"

"Oh, uh, Bonn."

"Bonn," repeated Emma, nodding her head but not commenting.

Ollie almost said "Zürich" automatically, because that was
where he was going, then realized that Bonn was a safe name
that would arouse no interest or expectations.

PART 6

MIRACLES

CHAPTER 34

May 1979

Doris did have her mother's diamonds made into a belt. It was designed by Galitzine and Webb, and crafted by the artisans at Mark Cross, all of whom signed a nondisclosure agreement about their work on the project. Inspired by a nineteenth-century Ottoman bridal accessory, made of tooled leather with a wine-red velvet lining, the belt incorporated a chunky three-panel gold buckle—finished to look like brass and not gold—that was studded with diamond "rhinestones" in an elaborate floral pattern. For added efficacy, the buckle was reversible, so that its plain, un-bejeweled back side could face outward; and the velvet lining featured pockets around the entire waist that could conceal a passel of loose stones. Doris referred to the thing as "the revolution belt," and was tickled to think that it was worth several times more than what Barbara's golden horse heads were worth, yet so much more practical as portable wealth, come the revolution.

But the worst of the nation's social unrest had subsided, and the idea of having to flee your home as torch-bearing peasants stormed the front door had faded, so during the '70s, Doris wore the belt as a fashion accessory, delighted that it could really work the way she and the designers intended, as well with jeans and a T-shirt as with a minimalist sheath by Halston. In fact, Doris was wearing the belt with a three-piece, burgundy pants suit by Halston aboard her private DC-8, when she and

Ollie flew to Los Angeles in May of 1979, to see a weakening Barbara, who had just been released from a long stay at the Cedars-Sinai Medical Center.

Two months earlier, Barbara had entered Cedars-Sinai after collapsing with what she thought was pneumonia but turned out to be congestive cardiomyopathy, a condition in which the heart cannot pump blood efficiently to the rest of the body, resulting in fatigue, shortness of breath, and heart palpitations. Her body was ravaged by all the drugs she had been taking for years. She was underweight and malnourished, spending her days largely in bed, with the drapes drawn, smoking endlessly and alternating between Coca-Cola and vodka. Under the care of several, high-priced doctors who were "helping" in a decidedly uncoordinated effort that sometimes led to squabbles among them, she rarely went out, and when she did, she had to be carried in and out of the car by her chauffeur, since her foot and leg muscles had become so atrophied after a broken hip she'd suffered the year before, in Rome. She was in bad shape spiritually, too, since the death of her son, Lance. Seven years before, Lance's Cessna slammed into a mountainside near Aspen, as he was scouting for a resort property to buy. His own life by then had become fairly aimless, too. His enthusiasm for auto racing dimmed, he was flitting from skiing to polo to sailing, trying not to fall into the aimless playboy routine by doing all the things that aimless playboys do.

After Lance's death, Barbara grieved at Sidi Hosni for a few years, then sold the place and dropped back into drifting from watering hole to watering hole on the jet-set circuit, with her cortège of rich and/or titled idlers, which did little to help bring her life back into focus. Several times, under the influence, she attempted suicide—once on her private plane *en route* to Mexico, when she drunkenly tried to open the emergency door and throw herself out, and once when an attending nurse found her in a nightgown at the edge of the terrace of her penthouse suite at the Beverly Wilshire Hotel. Often, when drunk, she vowed to swallow a mass of pills "and be done with it," but then she would rally and arrange to be dressed and made up and carried around by her chauffeur for an evening date with a young man she'd met—which by this time meant any of the handsome, twenty-something actor-slash-models whom one of her remaining lady friends would bring up to her hotel suite for "tea." Under these conditions, Barbara would still venture out with her escorts to L.A.'s most fashionable restaurants and lounges, even hot clubs—a strangely magnificent, aging mad queen from some Grand Guignol spectacle, her face painted theatrically in layers of powder and rouge, her eyes smudged thickly with mascara, her mouth—and, occasionally, other parts of her face—smeared with lipstick. She'd give her dates gold watches, gold cigarette cases, and the like. When the couple was caught by the paparazzi coming out of a lounge or restaurant on one of these "dates," the attending chauffeur would stand Barbara up, shift her weight onto her young man, and step out of the shot, impassive, while the young man would do his headshot best to look like an up-and-coming Hollywood personality, and Barbara, on his arm debutante-style, would just stare into the lens, looking haunted but too frail to be very ghoulish.

The Beverly Wilshire was now Barbara's home base, since her financial manager, who had supervised the sale of Sidi Hosni, terminated the lease on her suite at the Pierre in New York, too. He was also selling off many of her other assets, including fine art. It wasn't clear what kind of plan this manager had for Barbara's fortune, or how much he was profiting from his efforts, or how welcome he found Barbara's indifference to the financial options he presented her with. Friends who heard that she had sold her Paris apartment questioned the man's wisdom and suggested that Barbara fire him. But she remained apathetic. "What difference does it make?" she groused. "They're all corrupt anyway."

She told Doris that she felt she was being pulled into some kind of terminal spiral, and Doris feared that she was right— which is why Doris was rethinking the most recent and most-elaborately planned of their rivalries, which they referred to as the "MoMA Gambit": Who could give the best gift to the Museum of Modern Art?

For a while after Lance's death, their fond yet bitter games continued automatically. It was an established thing, this love-hate connection they were familiar with, that was actually among the most meaningful relationships in both their lives. Doris's break in 1976 with Moroccan decorator Leon Amar, the last romantic interest she would ever have, left her as needy as Barbara was for connection to someone as dependable as a family member, even if the family was dysfunctional. As in the past, this gambit they dreamed up paradoxically kept them together, even if each of them was angling to make the splashier donation to the museum, that would result in the more prestigious attribution in catalogs, essays, and the institution's annual report. The contest this time concerned legacies, which both of them had been thinking about seriously, after a lunch they shared in which Barbara bragged about having been one of the founding sponsors of Lincoln Center, which Doris had not been.

"John D. hollered, and of course I answered the call," said Barbara blithely.

"Don't be smug, Babbo," said Doris. "I happen to know that Elsa Maxwell convinced you to do it, because Maria Callas told her that Lincoln Center was such an important project to support. Besides, as you know, I've been busy for years with my own philanthropic endeavors."

"Anyway, we are now at the age where we must be thinking about strategic bequests. That's why I am thinking about giving my Picasso to a museum."

"Are you, indeed?"

When this art-centered contest began, Barbara was planning to donate a Picasso of the Blue Period, *La Cruche Blanche*—"*The White Jug*"—that she'd bought years before from a French collector. It had been hanging in her living room at the Pierre, before she had it shipped to her suite at the Beverly Wilshire. Doris, for her part, was to contribute a Rodin sculpture that she would purchase for the museum, a full-size male nude entitled *Le Vaincu*—"*The Conquered One*"—from a Belgian family collection whose founder bought the piece in 1875 from the sculptor's studio. That was the plan. They were sure to get

some gossip column inches out of the supposedly rival donations. Then, without telling Barbara, Doris initiated arrangements to substitute an even splashier donation to the museum
than the Rodin, something fashionably contemporary; and she
took some glee in planning to trump her friend this way, until a
growing awareness of Barbara's decline caused Doris to worry
that any contest between them now was too predatory. Trying
to earn a big publicity splash at Barbara's expense would be
wrong.

When Doris concurrently heard that Barbara's offer to the
museum had actually been withdrawn, she suspected she knew
why. Barbara was not just ill but out of money, said the rumors.
This was the main reason why Doris had invited herself to visit
her old friend in Los Angeles, on her way to Shangri La. She
wanted to see for herself what was going on and decide after
that what to do about her updated donation plan, which was
already in motion.

Fitted out for commercial use, Doris's DC-8 would have been
able to seat a hundred and eighty passengers. For Doris, the
plane was configured with a living room, two bedroom suites,
a media lounge and dining room, a large galley, and an aft seating area for those occasions when the owner might be traveling
with a small party. The interior appointments were coordinated
in colors of green ranging from celadon to spruce, and featured
walnut paneling and patterned carpets that were more in line
with the library at Rough Point than a twentieth-century air-
craft.

"I saw this coming," said Doris, looking distressed. She and
Ollie were flying over a gleaming band of sinuous river in a hilly
stretch of Missouri. The three gold bangles at her wrist clanked
as she raised her Bloody Mary for a sip.

"Saw what?" said Ollie.

"She's spent all her money on boyfriends. She's surrounded
by people who have no respect for her or her interests, let alone
her soul."

They were speaking comfortably in their normal voices. The
plane's interior was noticeably quieter than that of a commercial

jet, as extra soundproofing had been applied to the cabin during customization.

"You've been a good friend," said Ollie. "She'll be so happy to see you."

"I could have been a better friend," said Doris.

"But *could* you, Doris. . . ?"

She shook her head.

"Do you remember Marbella?" she said.

Ollie searched his memory.

"Mmm—something about a girls-only meet-up. . . ?" he said.

"That's right—a spa retreat. I arranged it for her just after Lance died. She was down in the dumps, so I called her . . .

"'Can you be there on Thursday?' I said.

"'I guess so,' she said.

"'I'll book adjoining suites. My treat. The Hotel los Monteros—the Beach Club, La Cabane. . . . It's new.'

"'Alright.'

"'There is a massage therapist there that they say is a genius.'

"'Okay.'

"I wanted to do something for her spirit, her health. And she shows up with that bullfighter, Angel. . . . Ollie, he was only twenty-four and already a so-called 'ladies' man.' Adorable, of course, and quite aware of it. Wearing a gold ring she gave him. I thought she was grieving. Lance was no more than a month dead, and she brings this creature to our girls-only retreat."

"Bad form," said Ollie.

"But bad for *her*," spat Doris. "She's never been on very solid ground when taking care of herself. Anyway, that's how this whole MoMA thing got started. I knew she wanted to donate the Picasso, and I frankly wanted to one-up her. I knew I jumped into it for the wrong reasons. Now, of course, I regret it."

"You're not going to withdraw your own offer to the museum—the new work?"

Doris made a sour face.

"Can't very well do that, can I?" she said. "Talk about bad form."

CHAPTER 35

The first thing Ollie did after arriving home from Zürich was return the suitcase he borrowed from Mrs. Welland. She invited him to sit down for a cozy tea.

"Was it a good trip?" she said.

"Very successful," said Ollie.

"Monte Carlo is fun, isn't it? Though I haven't been there for years."

"It was great fun to be there *on assignment.*"

"You make it sound like a job."

"It was, Liz, and I adored every minute of it."

"Horace and I used to have a villa in Juan-les-Pins that we rented now and then, for a week. Just a simple place. Sometimes we'd drive to the casino for an evening, but only to eat and drink, never to gamble. Horace was no gambler."

"And you? Why do I see you at the roulette table in a slinky red dress with a plunging neckline. . . ?"

Mrs. Welland made a scoffing sound.

"I had no money—not of my own," she said.

"No?"

"Grandpa did a good job of losing it all in the Crash—well, most of it, anyway. Luckily, Dad married well. Though Lord knows, it was always iffy about the house."

"How do you mean? All I know about your past is that you used to live between Palm Beach and Oyster Bay, and that you attended Vassar."

"Ollie, the house I grew up in was a big old thing, a century-and-a-half old."

"Old money. I knew it."

"Well, old-ish. The place was falling to pieces when my sister and I were children."

"Those places are so hard to keep up."

"My sister wound up there after she was married and kept the place going as best she could. Then her husband wrapped his car around a tree."

"Lord. Suicide?"

"That's not what we called it. But probably."

"And she's still there?"

"No, no. She died some years back. My niece lives there now."

"With a woodstove in the one room where vines haven't pushed in through the windows?"

"Ha—no. My nephew—my dear late nephew—restored the place rather nicely. He was in real estate. He had planned to live there with his husband, but then—*pfft*. Drugs."

Ollie shook his head.

"Terrible, sad. Where is this magical castle, anyway?"

"Upstate."

"Upstate New York?"

"Uh-huh—Hudson Valley. On top of a little mountain in Ulster County."

This rang a bell for Ollie.

"May I ask what town?" he said.

"Prescottville," said Mrs. Welland. "My maiden name is Prescott. The family's been there ever since—"

"Church Lake Road?" interrupted Ollie.

"Why, yes!" exclaimed Mrs. Welland. "How did you know that?"

Ollie looked dumbfounded.

"There's a church there on the property. . . ."

"A chapel."

"Yes. Doris said it would be nice to have a sacred place on the property."

"Doris Duke?"

Ollie was doing his best to contain his delight.

"I was *there*, Liz!" he said. "And you were, too."

"Huh?"

"I visited that house in the sixties—probably '64 or '65—and I believe I saw you there. There were two young girls?"

"My sister and me, I guess. But when?"

"You don't remember, I'm sure, but Barbara Hutton was one of the people interested in buying that property. She drove up from New York to see it with a young design consultant in tow, and that was me."

"Ah—this might be ringing a bell. . . ."

Mrs. Welland looked surprised and pleased.

"And then," continued Ollie, "Doris arrived and stole me away from Barbara, because *she* wanted a design consultant, too. They had this little game going on between them. Don't you remember a nerdy young guy with them?"

"I don't think so. But now that I think of it, I do remember a lady coming to visit one day, and then a helicopter landing, with another lady. But I didn't quite register who . . ."

"Yes! That's how Doris arrived, in a helicopter. And then twenty minutes later, she got in it again and flew away, taking me with her."

"You? I'm afraid I don't remember the part with you, Ollie, but I do remember the helicopter. It was exciting but scary, as I recall. I was probably ten at the time."

"Isn't this the funniest thing?"

"But I do remember a young man that the helicopter lady had in tow—a very stylish guy in a sport jacket who reminded me of Paul Drake on *Perry Mason*. Remember *Perry Mason*?"

"I do."

"Dad explained that he was trying to sell the place, and my sister, Maggie, and I were upset about it."

"Aw . . ."

"Then a lot of other people came through."

"And you never knew it was Doris Duke and Barbara Hutton. Isn't that interesting?"

"I guess I hadn't quite registered that, no. Dad would not

have made a big deal about it. I doubt I would have known who they were then, anyway. It was a fairly remote life up on that mountain, at least until I went away to school. . . ."

"Were you and your sister close?"

"Terribly close," said Mrs. Welland, visibly moved by nostalgia. "Best friends, really—partly because we were so isolated from our classmates, up there on that mountain. We wound up playing together a lot, pretending, just her and me. That old house was our castle, our royal palace, our ocean liner. . . ."

"I can imagine."

Ollie chuckled.

"How about that?" he mused. "You walk up to a lovely person at a benefit for the Central Park Conservancy and say hello. You become friends, you wind up in the same apartment building, and you never realize that you visited her house fifty years before. I love New York!"

"Well, is that New York?" said Mrs. Welland. "Or is it just life?"

CHAPTER 36

May 1979

Still two hours away from landing in Los Angeles, Doris and Ollie decided to have lunch where they were seated, in two plush leather seats with a small built-in table between them, rather than move to the plane's formal dining area, which could comfortably accommodate twelve. A steward brought them steak sandwiches and mineral water. Among the things they discussed were more logistical details of the contemporary artwork that Doris was now donating to MoMA, that before Barbara's decline she'd been hoping would make splashier news than the Rodin would.

"The Zanobi project is going to be so much better than a hundred-year-old bronze nude," said Ollie, gleefully. "Everyone I'm talking to at the museum is excited about it—even the austere folks in Painting and Sculpture."

Several weeks before, in late March, before Doris knew how badly Barbara was doing, negotiations had broken down on the purchase of the Rodin, which belonged to a noble family in Belgium whose younger generation was squabbling over ownership. After Doris walked away, Ollie suggested a different approach to the donation entirely, "more in line with the interests of some of the museum's younger curators." He proposed that Doris commission a work from the Italian artist Luca Zanobi, a socially conscious conceptualist influenced by the postwar Arte Povera movement that had drawn so much attention in avant-garde circles a few years back. Zanobi's star was on the rise. A work by him at the previous year's Venice Biennale, *Bottles and Cans*—a gallery full of vessels he had acquired among Rome's homeless population—had drawn much praise. The commission and donation of a work by him would be more excitingly contemporary, said Ollie, and might garner Doris more of the good publicity she was aiming for at the time.

The donation would also have the benefit of reflecting Doris's progressive vision as a cultural mover and shaker better than the canonical Rodin would. And while Zanobi showed often in prestigious venues in Europe, he had yet to have an exhibition in a major American art venue—though an installation of his happened to be on view at the very time he brought the idea to Doris's attention, at Bergdorf Goodman. The installation comprised seven display windows featuring barren, post-apocalyptic landscapes created by the artist with a palette of "poor" materials like soil, rocks, twigs, dead leaves, and assorted bits of trash. And in line with the artist's critical use of such materials, which was meant to challenge the consumerist values that support the commercialized contemporary gallery system, the high-priced fashion garments also featured in Zanobi's Bergdorf windows were shown crumpled and strewn over the ground as if blown there by a nuclear blast.

"He's quite a crusader, isn't he?" said Ollie, on the day when he and Doris took a stroll over to Bergdorf's to inspect the windows.

"Yes, and I'm sure it's also very nice for him to receive a hefty paycheck from the store," said Doris.

On the sidewalk that day, though the displays had been on view for weeks, were several individuals and couples moving respectfully from window to window, observing, contemplating, discussing.

"It's a public rostrum," said Ollie, "and I think the store should be congratulated for doing it. I'm told that every curator, gallerist, and collector in town has been over here. Not to mention the press."

"I love it," said Doris. "How do we get in touch with the artist?"

The commission centered on an idea that occurred to Doris

in a flash one Sunday at the First Baptist Church of Nutley, New Jersey, where she sometimes attended Sunday services—a practice not at all unusual for her, since participation in Black churches was part of her father's family tradition. The affinity she acquired as a child for Black communities and cultures was a large part of what prompted her later to create the program for buying new organs for Black churches; it also led her into deeper immersions in the arts—to the study of dance with Black dance pioneer Katherine Dunham, for instance, and to vocal training from Reverend C. L. Franklin, the father of Aretha Franklin and pastor of the New Bethel Baptist Church of Detroit, to which she flew regularly for lessons. Doris supported the Nutley church with funds for operations, property maintenance, and food for the church's pantry and soup kitchen programs; and at Sunday services, she was often welcomed there into the choir, where she heartily joined the voices raised in praise.

On the Sunday following their visit to Bergdorf's, she brought Ollie along to Nutley, not only to experience the service but to verify that her idea might be right to present to Zanobi: an immersive, site-specific installation inspired by the ongoing outdoor rummage sale hosted by the church on its sidewalk, on Saturdays and Sundays throughout the warmer months.

Doris made sure that she and Ollie arrived at the church around ten o'clock, so they would have plenty of time before the eleven o'clock service to look over sale offerings and say hello to some of the church ladies who staffed the sale. It was a warm day in mid-April. Under pear trees just beginning to leaf out and dapple the sunlight was a profusion of items displayed on tables upon tables, in plastic bins and crates, and on racks upon racks lining both sides of the sidewalk—items for sale that had been collected in successive waves of donation drives among congregation households, such as furniture, kitchenware, and small appliances; toys, games, dolls, and action figures; all manner of bric-a-brac, including vases, bowls, clocks, wall sconces, spice racks, and planters; even cleaning supplies and other household goods. Some items were new, most were gently used; all were for sale to benefit the church. Some independent vendors were also part of the sale, offering brand-new items like sneakers, sweatshirts, track pants, T-shirts, caps, and jewelry, the proceeds from which were split with the church.

Sitting on folding beach chairs among the tables and racks were several well-dressed ladies whom Doris knew.

"Good morning, sister," said a lady in a smart yellow suit and matching straw boater. "Nice to see you back again."

"Good morning, sister," said Doris warmly. "You're looking well."

Doris made it a point to dress nicely but not conspicuously on these occasions.

"Good morning, Miss Duke," said a lady in a dressy blue shift and matching hat of straw and organza ruffle.

"Good morning, Mrs. Owens."

"Sometimes I wear a wig to church," Doris confided to Ollie. "I'm obviously not fooling anybody, but it helps me inhabit the spirit I want to be in—just Doris, not Miss Duke."

"No wig today, though?" said Ollie.

"Nope," said Doris. "Just me."

Sunlight glinted from the facets of a fake cut-glass candy bowl, glowed dully from a brass lamp that needed polishing, glared from a stack of white plastic dinner plates, and a drawer organizer full of mismatched stainless-steel flatware. Now and then, Doris stopped to pick up an item and share an observation with Ollie. She made it a point to buy a china ashtray in the shape of a clamshell, which she tucked away in her handbag. It was her idea that this whole thing—the community ritual of a rummage sale, humankind's eternal exchange of goods—should be the inspiration of her Zanobi gift to MoMA.

"This little market represents so much devotion, sometimes even sacrifice, for the common good," Doris told Ollie. "I am always touched by that. My writing a check for a million dollars doesn't compare to this, which is real charity at work."

Ollie was agog at the sheer mass of items in the sale, and the fact that they were arranged neither by category, nor price, nor any other classification he could discern. It was just masses of stuff. Though all the items were of modest value, the effect of them cumulatively was of great wealth.

"There must be ten thousand items out here," he said, as they inspected the tables. "The sheer labor of putting them out every time, then carting them back into the church, to some massive storeroom—that alone is an act of devotion. Just to witness it is somehow . . . heartwarming."

"You've got it," said Doris. "And the fact that every single item was owned by someone probably living within ten or twenty blocks of here . . . or that there are items like a vase, sitting right now on someone's windowsill, that will wind up here before long. . . !"

"I think Zanobi will find it interesting."

And then, a week after that church visit, following a series of transatlantic phone calls to the artist and two meetings with museum officials—one with a team of curators, one with a committee of museum board members—Doris flew Zanobi to New York, put him up at the Waldorf Astoria, and brought him out to Nutley.

"It's fantastic!" exclaimed the artist, snapping away madly, outside the church, with his Canon F-1. "It will make a fantastic piece."

Zanobi was as amenable to working with ideas from Doris as her chosen architects, fashion designers, and jewelry makers were. On the spot, the artist began chatting with the church ladies, asking about specific items—who had contributed it, who might be buying it. . . . And when Doris told him about her history of singing in the church choir, he suggested that a recording of the choir could run as a loop for the museum installation, as "environmental sound."

Mrs. Owens, who ran the sale, was flabbergasted when Doris asked how much it would cost to purchase the entire inventory.

"All at once? The whole thing—everything here?"

"The whole thing."

"I'd have to talk to the pastor. But Miss Duke, then we

wouldn't have anything to sell, and people like our sale. They come here especially."

"That's easily solved."

Doris asked how many days of the year the sale ran and how much, on average, was brought in each day. Mrs. Owens was in the middle of that calculation when Doris offered to pay the estimate plus ten thousand dollars for the entire lot, *and* provide an equal amount for the purchase of new merchandise for the church to sell, so the sidewalk market could continue. And after that day's service, Doris and Zanobi met with Mrs. Owens and the church's pastor and agreed on a date when the goods would be collected by movers and taken to a temporary studio in Long Island City. They also agreed on dates when the artist could come and chat further with the church ladies and oversee the recording of the choir. To the church, Doris wrote a check on the spot, from a private account. To Zanobi, she had already given a check for a hundred and fifty thousand.

"These people are wonderful," said Zanobi, in the car, on the way back to New York from Nutley. "I like to be working with joy, in this piece. Instead of bitterness, always bitterness."

Doris was pleased to hear this.

"I doubt I could ever get my friends to come to Nutley and see how nice these services are," she said. "But if I can get them into the Museum of Modern Art and think a little bit about the objects they see and where they came from, that will be a big deal."

Zanobi was impressed by his day in Nutley and came up with a title for the piece, *Count Your Blessings*, while watching Doris from his pew as she sang with the choir:

When you look at others with their lands and gold,
Think that Christ has promised you His wealth untold;
Count your many blessings—wealth can never buy
Your reward in Heaven, nor your home on high.

Count your blessings, name them one by one,
Count your blessings, see what God has done. . . !

CHAPTER 37

Memorial Sloan Kettering's department of radiation oncology had ten treatment suites with linear accelerators, and Emma was usually treated in the newest of these, whose walls, said the technician, were only one foot thick, because they were constructed with a new type of aggregate material, instead of the usual three-foot-thick concrete. The room's chief fixture was the machine itself, its hulking, eight-foot-high gantry dwarfing the patient, who is positioned on a table underneath the bulbous treatment head, but unlike the other treatment rooms that Emma had seen, which were fairly featureless, this one had a wall paneled with slats of blond wood in a decorative herringbone pattern, and a simulated window-wall at one end, with simulated daylight and a waist-high row of wooden planter boxes containing some kind of greenery. As cancer treatment spaces went, this was chic. Without the LINAC machine, as the technician called it, but furnished with two queen-size beds, an armchair, a desk, and a TV, it might have been a room in a mid-scale boutique hotel. Emma's treatments were usually only ten or fifteen minutes long, and the staff got her in and out of the room with laudable efficiency, so she never had much time to contemplate her surroundings, unlike in a doctor's examination room, where every piece of artwork, every diploma, every manufacture's label on a piece of equipment—"Midmark 604 Manual Exam Table, Dayton, Ohio"—can start a program running in the brain. Yet Emma did have enough time in the radiation room to wonder why there was no art at all, not even a generically cheery print depicting a rural stream, and whether or not the greenery in the planter boxes was real. Could real plants grow in a room officially termed a bunker, which was entered from a corridor referred to as a maze, designed to baffle stray photons?

Dr. Lee had consulted with a radiation oncologist and a dosimetrist to determine exactly how much radiation Emma would receive, how often, and for how long. Four weeks had been decided on, and the course of treatments had gone smoothly, with barely any of the nausea, fatigue, or skin irritation that Dr. Lee said could happen. During that time, some of the dread Emma had felt about cancer abated, not so much dissolved by hope but dispersed by the realistically positive, day-at-a-time attitude that she discovered at the hospital among staff and patients alike. "Live the best way you can, with hope but no guarantees," was the way Emma came to think that anyone's life should be running, cancer or no cancer. She had set aside those weeks to finalize the script with Ollie, and it was looking good, though Ollie had declined the producer credit she offered him, for reasons he didn't explain. Then, together with Emma's colleague Kelly, they reviewed a few dozen audio clips of professional narrators and selected for the film a British woman who spoke English in what her agent described as a "posh, contemporary RP" accent—so-called "received pronunciation," a way of speaking that has long been associated with the privileged class who assumed it should be widely and easily received and understood.

The fifty-thousand-dollar gift that Emma had received from her mother was almost used up, and still there was editing and sound to pay for, which were going to be expensive. Kelly was looking into distribution options and the festival circuit, and lining up a few final shoots that would take place in the studio at Christie's. One shoot that happened just before the radiation sabbatical, of a ruby-and-diamond necklace, particularly pleased Emma, since there was a historical photograph of it being worn by its former owner, Miss Barbara Hutton. Designed with palmette and lotus flowers in a style meant to recall ancient

Egypt, the necklace had been given by Barbara to the mother of its present owner, a sharp Upper East Sider named Letty, during the last year of Barbara's life. Letty didn't want to be shot herself for Emma's film—"Who wants *me*?" she said—but she did agree to chat with Ollie for background.

"Chaumet?" said Ollie.

"Van Cleef and Arpels," said Letty.

"Ah. Burmese rubies?"

"That's what I'm told."

"You've had it looked at?"

"Of course."

"And I understand it was once the property of Queen Amélie of Portugal?"

"Well, that's the thing. Mom didn't remember exactly what Barbara told her, except that Barbara seemed a little confused at the time. Actually, very confused. This wasn't too long before her death, poor thing."

"Hutton's death?"

"Yes. Mom died in '91."

"I see."

"Barbara apparently had another ruby-and-diamond necklace that *was* by Chaumet. What we think is that *these* rubies were from a different necklace, owned either by Amélie of Portugal or Amalia of Solms, Princess Consort of Frederick Henry, Prince of Orange."

"My goodness! You've really looked into this."

"I had help. So few of these things are reliably identified, don't you find?"

"I do."

"Even some quite reputable houses sometimes have their facts wrong. Or they peddle hearsay as facts. I'm no scholar, but I do take note when I hear two contradictory statements."

"So your mother received this marvelous gift shortly before Barbara died?"

"It was Christmas '78, and I believe that Barbara died the following May."

"It was a Christmas present. . . !"

"Well, nominally, I suppose. But Barbara would often just take off something that she was wearing and give it to you, as you probably know."

"She was a very generous soul."

"Mmm. Maybe a little capricious, too."

"Maybe."

"But she and Mom had been friends since school, and Mom said she had the impression that Barbara knew she was dying."

"Ah."

"She was a little out of it, you see, toward the end."

"Quite sad."

"Her property was being sold off, for the benefit of those doing the selling, I'm told. And she was hanging on physically to the things she valued most, literally in the room with her, like her jewelry, like a Picasso that she loved."

"*The White Jug.*"

"Mom said she absolutely cherished that painting."

"I'll bet."

"It can be worn as a tiara, you know—the necklace. She was wearing it as a tiara when she gave it to Mom."

"Was she really? Wearing it in bed?"

"In bed, and in a bedjacket that had food stains on it. That's what Mom said. Red stains, which she said was either spaghetti sauce or blood. We preferred to think it was spaghetti sauce."

"Lord."

"She took off the tiara and gave it to Mom quickly, as if someone were watching. 'Put it in your bag,' she said. 'Don't let him see it.' But they were alone in the room."

"Who was she talking about?"

"Mom thought her lawyer, or whoever was selling off her things."

"Do you wear it as a tiara?" asked Ollie.

Letty laughed.

"I can barely pull off a hat," she said. "No, I wear it as a necklace with jeans and tell people it's costume."

*   *   *

Ollie hadn't expected that he and Emma would become friends by way of their work together, but it didn't surprise him that that was what seemed to be happening. Their meetings often touched on life issues, especially the uncertainty Emma was dealing with regarding what she now matter-of-factly referred to as mortality. Was the constant awareness of mortality a gift too often wasted on the old?

"So you're seeing Dr. Lee tomorrow," said Ollie.

"We'll be talking about a treatment plan," said Emma.

"Surgery?"

"Unless I am too far gone for that."

They both uttered a little chuckle.

"I think I am going to hear revised numbers about being alive after five years—that sort of thing," said Emma.

"Want some company at the doctor's office?"

"Ollie, do you mean it? I'd really love that. Kelly's out of town."

"Of course. Just tell me when and where. I'll take you to lunch or coffee, before or after, if you have the time."

"I realize," said Emma deliberately, "as I listen to you speak about Doris and Barbara and some of the other amazing people you've known, that you're a great friend. There's an art in that."

"Thank you. I try."

"I suspect you were a great friend to my dad, too. I must admit I never quite saw it that way. I think the generation gap must have gotten in the way."

"Maybe. It's good that you and I have finally reached the same age."

"Ha."

"Also, I think I've finally started, just a little bit, doing what Doris always said, about keeping your channel open. It doesn't simply pop open the minute you hear about the concept."

"You have to think about it."

"You have to kind of get used to it, more than think about it. It's more emotional than cognitive, and God knows how long some of *those* things take."

"Is that why you never . . ."

"Had a boyfriend?"

"Forgive me if . . ."

"No, no—it's alright. Friends can ask each other these questions."

"I've often wondered if your family was very conservative or religious. I think Dad, for instance, regarding sexual identity, had some family-related religious issues he was dealing with."

"Oh, no. My mother did a much worse job on me than that, by instilling the dread of social opprobrium."

"Oh, that."

"Yes, that. Which I could have burst through. Which, Lord knows, the times encouraged me to burst through. Which once or twice I *almost* burst through." He paused. "But no critical mass, I guess. And then there was Doris, and some people do rather fill up your entire life. They're that big."

"She was big. I see."

"And it hasn't been such a bad life."

"And it's not nearly over. Is it?"

"Well, I'll give you 'not over,' anyway."

"Okay."

"And if we die tomorrow, the film will be a handsome part of our respective legacies, if I may say so."

"Doris would be proud of you."

Ollie flashed on all of Doris's spiritual searching, her encounters with the great people and the fraudsters of the world, her own search for love and how that finally was sublimated into . . . something higher. He thought how her charity work did help open an unexpected channel—for him.

"Yes," said Ollie. "I think she might be."

CHAPTER 38

May 1979

It was a short drive from Falcon's Lair to the Beverly Wilshire Hotel. Doris and Ollie were silent for most of the trip, dreading what they might find. They were met by a nurse in the elevator foyer of Barbara's penthouse, where Colin, a strapping Australian six-footer who functioned as Barbara's chauffeur, secretary, and security man, had a desk.

"How is she doing today?" asked Doris.

"About the same," said the nurse.

They followed her past a palatial living room and dining room, whose windows offered dramatic views of the Hollywood Hills, to Barbara's bedroom, where a wasted little body was installed in a bed as expansive as some suburban backyards. A maid was taking away a lunch tray that looked like it hadn't been touched. Then the nurse left them, reminding Barbara that she would remain just outside the door.

"Babbo, darling, don't get up . . ." said Doris in a pointedly jocular manner, approaching the bed where her friend, with a lit cigarette between her fingers, was sitting up, propped against several pillows. Looking emaciated, Barbara closed her eyes and mustered a wan smile to accept the little kiss that Doris bent in to bestow. The scent of Barbara's Joy was mixed with something medicinal and minty. Her long gray hair was up, but in more of a pile than the usual well-tended upsweep.

"How are you?" said Barbara, appearing to make an effort

to be gracious and gesturing toward two armchairs that were positioned close to the head of the bed.

"Very well, dear," said Doris. "But may I just . . ." Before sitting, Doris took a tissue from a bedside dispenser and wiped a bit of stray lipstick from Barbara's otherwise white cheek. "Little smudge. All better."

"Thank you," said Barbara, taking a puff of the cigarette. The nails on her gnarled gray hands were impeccably manicured in coral. On her finger was the enormous Pasha diamond.

The bedroom, like the rest of the suite, was decorated in a restrained Rococo *moderne* style, in a fashionably neutral color palette, with generously proportioned furnishings. The room's heavy, beige satin drapes were pulled shut. Barbara seemed not to recognize Ollie, but merely acknowledged his presence with a gracious smile inflected with the tiniest residue of coquettishness. Next to her, on a bed tray, were an ashtray, a pack of cigarettes, a lighter, and a crystal glass containing an inch of colorless liquid. Her bed linens, which were white and otherwise tidy, were pockmarked with several fresh-looking, black-edged burn holes. Her face was heavily made up, though it all stopped abruptly at the neck, where the pinkish-beige of foundation and powder gave way abruptly to the pallor of semi-desiccated flesh.

"I have to do it myself now," she muttered, almost to herself.

"Do what?" said Doris.

Barbara shook her head with a sour look and gestured toward the door.

"Makeup. This one doesn't do it the way I like."

The eyeliner was far from symmetrical and more thickly applied than ever—so thickly that it was textured with lumps.

"Let me send someone over," said Doris. "I know a very good beautician who works on all the stars. I could ask her to come and see you."

"You didn't come all this way to see me," said Barbara, with sudden sharpness.

"Yes, dear, we certainly did," said Doris, understanding that something was wrong with Barbara beyond weakness and fatigue. Her mood seemed unstable—the pace of her words and even her breathing seemed to change from moment to moment. "We're at Falcon's Lair for a few days, and we stopped specially to see you. Then we're on to Shangri La. You know, if you're feeling up to it, you could join us there, for some sun."

"I should never be in the sun. Doctor's orders. It's one of those pills."

"Well, then we can always enjoy the evenings. . . ."

"Will *you* be there, Cary. . . ?"

It took Doris and Ollie a second to realize that Barbara meant Ollie—although it wasn't clear whether she was attempting to be funny, or, if she wasn't, whether she was asking seductively, or sarcastically, or in some other way that an ex-husband might be addressed. Or, indeed, whether she didn't remember ever being married to Cary Grant and thought she was beholding the handsome star of *My Favorite Wife* and *His Girl Friday* for the first time and indicating she might *possibly* be interested in him.

Doris and Ollie exchanged a brief look, before Doris spoke.

"It's Ollie, dear—you remember Ollie."

But Barbara appeared not to register the information.

"Oh. Okay," she said blankly, with a shallow breath.

"I hope we didn't interrupt your lunch."

"No."

"We brought you a tin of caviar. I gave it to the nurse."

"Okay."

Doris and Ollie were both wondering how profound this mental haziness might be, and whether its cause might be among the profusion of medicine bottles on the night table, underneath the four-foot-tall lamp in the form of a golden sheaf of wheat: Nembutal, a sedative; Doriden, a sleeping pill; Dilaudid, a painkiller; Valium and Librium, for anxiety; which Barbara took in addition to the injections of Thorazine that the nurse said had been ordered for symptoms of schizophrenia, and L-Dopa, for tremors that were probably caused by all the other drugs in combination with the champagne and vodka that Barbara constantly consumed.

Doris had visited the suite often before, and immediately noticed the absence of the Picasso, which had been hanging in a place of honor in the bedroom above a gold-lacquered, Imperial Japanese chest—the painting that had started their race to donate to the Museum of Modern Art.

"Babbo, what happened to the Picasso?" asked Doris, trying not to show any of the emotion she was feeling—chiefly alarm that Barbara had either sold the painting for needed cash or given it away absently to some maid.

"The what?"

"Your Picasso. The painting—that pretty Blue Period jug."

"Oh. Lance wanted that, so I gave it to him."

This made no sense, but Doris remained composed. Barbara's son had died long before, and Doris had seen the painting in the suite many times since then.

"You gave it to Lance?" said Doris.

"I was actually going to give it to you when I saw you next," said Barbara, "because I think we were talking about it, right? And you like it? But then they said Lance wanted it, and I said, 'Okay, take it.' You can't hold on to everything." She fondled her ring. "Then they said Lance wanted my Pasha, too, but I told them no, I'm going to keep that, because . . . well, I can't very well imagine *him* wearing it."

"Who is 'they,' if I may ask?" said Doris.

"Oh, people from the office. I let them handle everything. Until I get better."

Barbara returned her gaze to Ollie.

"Ollie . . ." she said. "It's so good to see you. I hope you've been well."

"Oh, uh . . . yes, very well, thank you, Barbara," he said.

They spoke a bit about Barbara's recent stay at Cedars-Sinai, and the findings about her heart, and the medical options being recommended, but Barbara seemed confused about many of the details and was also having difficulty forming sentences. Doris, all the while, was fitting the observations she was making into a bigger picture and resolving to take action.

"Babbo, look, I've had a wonderful idea, and I want you to consider it, really consider it," she said, speaking decisively, with the patience of a nurse and the protectiveness of a mother. "I'm going to send over a friend, a gentleman who helps me with my business, one of the top people in the country, and I want you to speak with him privately about helping you with *your* business. Will you do that?"

"Business. . . ?"

"Yes, darling, business. I'll phone you with the details, and we'll decide on the right time for him to come to you. I think we should do it very soon."

"But . . . I have someone."

"That's alright, Babs. I know you do. But this is someone who I think will be good for everyone. Don't you want that?"

But Barbara already seemed to be fading into a different, less energetic mood.

"If you say so," she said, sleepily.

"You'll like him. He's very nice."

"Mmm."

"I'll call you about it tomorrow, okay?"

Barbara nodded.

"I'm just going to rest my eyes," she whispered.

"Okay, Babs?" said Doris, taking her friend's hand gently and removing the lit cigarette, whose overgrown ash had already fallen onto the sheet. But Barbara was asleep.

Doris and Ollie stayed with Barbara for another ten minutes, half expecting her to wake up and continue the conversation. They were both too sad to say what they were feeling, and didn't want to be saying it in case Barbara should suddenly awaken and hear. In fact, it was as unclear now as when Barbara was awake whether or not they were actually in the presence of their old friend. In quiet tones, Doris spoke fondly to Ollie about horseback riding with Barbara when they were girls, of hijinks like evading family authorities to sneak out to see bawdy Broadway shows. Together, Doris and Ollie had a laugh over the way Doris had stolen Ollie away, years ago, on that mountaintop.

Then the nurse knocked gently and entered. "Dina and Cliff" were there to see Barbara—her cousin, actress and socialite Dina Merrill, and Dina's husband, actor Cliff Robertson. So after some quiet, genial greetings, Doris and Ollie left.

368 Stephen Greco

In the back seat of the car, practically as soon as the driver had shut the door, Doris was struggling to resist a bout of weeping.

"That poor baby," she said, with unsteady breath. "That poor, sweet baby."

Ollie, too, was fighting back tears, both in sadness over Barbara and in response to Doris's tender concern for her friend.

"She's lost so much weight . . ." he said.

"She can't walk," sputtered Doris. "That thing in Rome, when she broke her hip—it's never healed properly, and I'm sure she is in great pain. Or would be, without the pills. And now this heart thing. Oh, Ollie. . . !"

"Would it . . . do any good to. . . ? I mean . . . can anything be done?"

"I'll tell you one thing. I'm going to have someone look into what's going on there. It sounds very shady to me, and I won't stand for it. I didn't know how bad it was, but I won't allow it to continue."

"But Doris, what can you do? Her people must have power of attorney—all that. . . ."

"Damn power of attorney," said Doris fiercely, wiping away some tears with a handkerchief. "I can have that broken in a minute if there is the slightest bit of funny business going on."

Ollie sighed.

"You're a good friend, Doris Duke."

A wave of outright weeping seized Doris.

"She's hanging onto that ring because it's everything to her— the last bit of her beauty. They'd probably pry it off her finger if they could."

Ollie shook his head sadly.

"A friend told me she gave him one of her precious jade pieces, just so her lawyer wouldn't get his hands on it," he said.

"Really? He said that? But what if she is really out of money?" said Doris, bitterly. "What if selling things is the only way to keep her in vodka and pills? Then what?"

"I don't know."

"Ollie, I've got this terrible feeling that we should have been saying goodbye, that we won't have her for much longer. But that's such a terrible thing to do to someone, isn't it? I mean, she and I are both the same age, for goodness' sake."

As the car made its way up Benedict Canyon, toward the house, the mood lightened.

"Did you see she was wearing a whistle?" said Ollie.

"Charming," said Doris. "To summon the maid, I suppose."

"*Toot-toot!* Front and center!"

Doris laughed, then Ollie did, then they were quiet again, until Doris spoke.

"I don't want to lose her, Ollie."

"I know."

"Yet it has to happen sometime. It was always in the future, and now it's suddenly here."

"Mm-hmm."

"I feel . . . guilty. I could have done more for her, I could have done something sooner."

"You were there for her. You *are* there for her."

"We've been needlessly silly with each other, needlessly cruel. It was all such a waste."

"It was a way of surviving. Forgive yourself. Hopefully she'll get through this, and you'll have her around for a good long while."

"Maybe."

"Maybe."

Doris took on a faraway look.

"We were twins, Ollie. We were supposed to take care of each other. We promised we would."

"Twin spirits. Some people don't get that, ever. What do you say we do a ceremony for her, a blessing or something, when we get to Hawaii?"

Doris brightened.

"What a good idea."

Planned for their stay at Shangri La was a ceremony that Doris organized annually to bless the memory of the daughter she lost, Arden. An old friend of Doris's, a *kahuna po'o*, or high priest, was the usual officiant.

"Two ceremonies," said Doris. "One for Barbara's spirit and

life, one for Arden's spirit and afterlife journey. Thank you, Ollie."

"Thank me? For what?"

"You're a lifesaver."

"Thanks, Dodo, but you're the lifesaver. You have the power, and you use it wisely, and will do so for years. The calendar stretches before us."

"The calendar may stretch before *you*, dear, but some of us may be down to hours."

Doris contacted her financial man later that day, and arrangements were made via Barbara's secretary/chauffeur Colin for a meeting with Barbara a week after that. But that meeting never happened. It was just a few days after Doris and Ollie arrived at Shangri La that they received word that Barbara had had a heart attack and died.

A small, private funeral took place in the Woolworth Chapel at New York's Woodlawn Cemetery, in the Bronx. Then there was interment in the Woolworth family mausoleum nearby, an imposing limestone edifice in the Egyptian Revival style, whose great bronze door was flanked by papyriform columns and guarded by drastically buxom sphynxes. Only ten mourners were present for the funeral, including Merrill and Robertson, but no press or ex-husbands or any of the international glamour crowd whom Barbara had spent so much time with. The poor little rich girl had only thirty-five-hundred dollars left when she died, which prompted more than one columnist to quote that sad American expression about "shirtsleeves to shirtsleeves in three generations": one generation acquires the fortune, the next one inherits it, the third one destroys it.

As it happened, the funeral in the Bronx, which began at ten-thirty in the morning of May 25, took place simultaneously with the traditional Hawaiian ceremony that Doris organized at Shangri La for dawn of the same day, which was 5:30 a.m. local time. Thus, inside both the fieldstone chapel in the Bronx, dressed in black and seated in wooden pews designed like garden benches, and halfway around the world, dressed in white and seated in lotus positions on a tree-shaded lawn with a view of the ocean, those who loved Barbara Hutton most came together with each other to bless her memory.

For Doris and Ollie, the *kahuna po'o*, an old man with a white beard, wrapped in a traditional *kihei* robe, began:

> *E ala e, ka lā i ka hikina,*
>> Awaken, the sun in the east
>
> *I ka moana, ka moana hohonu,*
>> From the ocean, the deep ocean,
>
> *Pi'i ka lewa, ka lewa nu'u,*
>> Climbing to heaven, the highest heaven,
>
> *I ka hikina, aia ka lā, e ala e!*
>> In the east, there is the sun, arise. . . !

For the mourners in the chapel, it was Cliff Robertson who spoke, since Barbara's will stipulated that no clergyman should officiate. Robertson began with the King James version of the eighty-fourth psalm:

> *How amiable are thy tabernacles, O Lord of hosts!*
> *My soul longeth, yea, even fainteth for the courts of the*
>> *Lord.*
> *My heart and my flesh crieth out for the living God.*
> *Yea, the sparrow hath found a house,*
> *And the swallow a nest for herself,*
> *Where she may lay her young, even thine altars,*
> *O Lord of hosts, my King, and my God.*
> *Blessed are they that dwell in thy house.*
> *They will ever be praising thee.*

CHAPTER 39

The news from Dr. Lee was good. The radiation had shrunk Emma's tumor significantly, and an operation would now be easier. A full recovery could be expected.

"But what does 'full recovery' mean, Doctor?" said Emma.

"It means that you will recover completely from the treatment and the surgery," said Dr. Lee.

"But not that I will be cured of cancer?"

"As I've explained, some cancer cells can remain in your body, and soft tissue sarcoma can return, sometimes after years."

"The elbow again."

"Well, the elbow or somewhere else. It's a tricky thing."

"Ucch."

"The upside is that you will be monitoring yourself for lumps and such, and if anything happens, you will come back to me ASAP. We'll stay on top of it, and that gives us a strong advantage. If anything does happen, I can get you into a clinical trial, or one of the very interesting immunotherapy programs we have going on here."

"Experimental drugs."

"Look at it this way. Nobody loves cancer. But we're living in a time and place where more is known about it, more can be done about it, than ever before. The expertise in this building represents millions of hours of study and research and treatment. That's not nothing, and our goal here is to make all of it available to you."

Half an hour later, Emma and Ollie were at Felice, a wine bar not far from Dr. Lee's office. It was 11:45, and lunch service would not begin until noon, but the kindly maître d' let them take a table and order Garibaldis to sip—Campari and orange juice—until the kitchen was ready.

"Here's the thing about cancer . . ." began Emma.

"Oh—the thing about cancer," mocked Ollie. "Let me get out my pencil."

She smirked, then continued.

"The thing about cancer—and I know that lots of people have more deadly cancers than I do, God bless them—the thing about it is that before, I was just a filmmaker and an Upper West Side girl. Now, I'm a *vigilant.*"

She said it semi-comically, and Ollie laughed.

"A star in your very own after-school special," he said.

"Yes—except that I don't know my lines and can't remember what happens in the next scene."

"We never know that, dear," said Ollie. "That's always been the point. That's why we all need a little something to hang on to. In fact . . ."

He reached into the pocket of his jacket, took out a small brown box, and placed it in front of her, on top of the menu that the maître d' had laid beside the charger.

"What's this?" said Emma.

"It's a little something I got you as a wrap gift, that I thought you should have now, for being such a brave survivor."

"Ollie!"

"Open it."

"This is so sweet of you."

Inside the box was a silken envelope, and inside that was a brilliantly faceted, colorless, octagonal-cut gemstone as large as a silver dollar.

"Is it what I think it is?" said Emma.

"It's a copy of what you may think it is," said Ollie.

"The Pasha?"

"In your very own hands. I thought you should have a big rock."

It was a precise replica of the original, forty-carat octagonal version of Barbara's Pasha diamond, made of cubic zirconia. It had been created by a man in New Mexico who specialized in replicas of famous diamonds.

"It's fabulous," said Emma, holding the stone up to catch the light coming from the wine bar's window, then placing it on the back of her hand to see how it might look as a ring. "I love it. It's perfect! Thank you."

The stone clearly caught the eye of the waiter, who arrived at their table to take their order but was too discreet to say anything. Emma tucked the thing away.

"Thirty-nine dollars for a piece of salmon flown in from the Faroe Islands," commented Ollie, after the waiter went away with their orders. "And to think that some of the people who once lived in this building slept in bedrooms that never saw natural light."

"It's a tenement building, originally? How do you know that?"

"My eyeballs. I just looked up as we were approaching the building."

"I'll bet those apartments are ridiculously expensive now."

"Of course they are. But they have no more natural light than they did in 1910, do they?"

"Ha."

"Which is around the time, as you will recall, when Miss Hutton was born in blinding luxury, just a few blocks that-a-way."

Ollie pointed west, beyond the wine bar's front window.

"So, Ollie, you remember how happy I was when we shot Barbara's ruby necklace, because there was a photograph of it. . . ."

"The Hoyningen-Huene."

"Yes. Well, then there's the Cecil Beaton photograph of her in the emerald tiara. It would be so great if we were able to track down the Pasha diamond and talk to the person who owns it now, and actually shoot it. Kelly's been investigating but hasn't been able to turn up any clues."

"Oh, I know where that is. Paris."

"What?!"

"The property of a lady, as they say in auction catalogs. A socialite. She's the daughter of one of Barbara's best friends."

"Really?"

"Yes."

"Do you think we could. . . ?"

"Not a chance," said Ollie. "She's beyond private."

"But aren't you our wrangler for such creatures?"

"You give me too much credit. I only talk to them once they're wrangled."

"So the diamond didn't get snatched away and sold without Barbara's knowledge."

"Apparently it was still on her finger when she died. I gather it passed through the will, which stipulated that Boubou—I mean, this daughter of Barbara's friend—should have it."

"I only think that the film needs just one more piece, maybe even a little one, that tells a personal story through the years, linking everything together—the lore and meaning of it. That would be powerful, don't you think?" A look of dreaminess came over Emma's face. "I wonder when Boubou wears her Pasha, how she wears it, where she keeps it. Whether she has a daughter whom she will pass it on to and how *she* would wear it. . . ."

"I gather there is a daughter, in her twenties, but I'd wager that she is too *au courant* to be wearing giant diamonds around. I'm not sure young people do too much of that nowadays."

"Oh, they should."

"Alright. Then I will expect you to take your own Pasha over to Cartier and have them set it in a big, juicy ring."

May 1979

"What did you mean that day when you called Barbara's Pasha ring 'her beauty'?" asked Ollie.

"Don't get me wrong," said Doris. "She was a beautiful girl, herself—her face, that perfect oval face, those adorable eyes.

But that ring . . . I think it represented the beauty of the hopes she had for herself."

"The beauty of her hopes."

"It became her attribute—you know, the way each Muse has her attribute: Thalia, her mask; Erato, her lyre. . . ."

"I see, yes. The diamond wasn't simply a piece of her wealth, or a device to display wealth. It was a symbol of the good things that wealth can bring. A talisman."

"Something like that. I think it served that purpose for her even after the rest of the actual wealth was gone."

They were sitting by the pool at Shangri La, a few days after their Hawaiian ceremony to bless the memory of their friend.

"Sidi Hosni was like that for her, too—essential, defining," said Doris. "Like this place is for me. I think she was most happy there in Tangier. I know she was. In fact, I was there when the ring was photographed, on the occasion of a great ball she gave there. This was before I met you, probably before you met her—'61, I believe. It was a great moment in her life—it meant so much to her."

"I know the photograph. Queen of the East."

"Hah, yes," said Doris, nodding fondly. "She commissioned Cecil because she knew he could tell the story, not just capture her looks and possessions. Because he photographed the Royal Family, and somehow even those very formal images tell a deeper story of majesty and service to the people."

"Tell me about the ball."

"Well, I went alone. Joey was somewhere or other on a gig. It was August, which is actually not too hot in Tangier, especially in the evening. . . ."

August 1961

The photograph that Cecil Beaton took of Barbara wearing the Pasha diamond was taken the day before an elaborate ball that Barbara gave at her Moroccan palace for a hundred or so of her very best friends and three or four well-dressed gatecrashers. Cecil and his companion, Kin, the young champion fencer, were houseguests at the time, having arrived two days earlier so Cecil would have ample time to do the portrait. She wanted it to be shot in or around a double-story courtyard of carved columns and arches, patterned *zellige* tile, and wooden *mashrabiya* latticework; and she wanted to be done up splendidly herself, in a caftan-like robe and draped in a golden silk brocade shawl, adorned not only with the great diamond ring but the Romanoff emerald tiara and earrings, the Marie Antoinette pearls, and a bracelet of Golconda diamonds. In the course of a long morning, they went through several poses. In one shot, Cecil suggested that Barbara pick up the antique *oud*—a Moroccan lute—that she had on display nearby, and hold it as if playing it. That turned out to be her favorite shot, though the one that all the magazines and newspapers picked up was the one that most prominently featured the ring.

Though Barbara liked giving dinner parties for ten or twelve at Sidi Hosni, this was a sprawling house party that she called a "ball," to which she invited notable Tangier residents, local dignitaries, and numerous old friends who happened to be in town or willing to fly or sail in for the occasion. Repeatedly Barbara sent her car to meet people at the airport or the dock at the Royal Yacht Club—a custom-made Rolls-Royce that she'd ordered shorter and narrower than normal, to better navigate Tangier's smaller streets. In addition to Cecil and Kin, and Doris, who was also a houseguest, invitees included Charlie and Oona Chaplin, Ari Onassis and Maria Callas, an ailing Elsa Maxwell and her partner, Dorothy Fellowes-Gordon, and Tennessee Williams, who was more famous than ever, after the Broadway success of his play *Sweet Bird of Youth*, the year before. Williams was there with his boyfriend, Frank Merlo, a handsome, young working-class guy from New Jersey. For the occasion, Barbara's Asian, African, and European antiques were supplemented with divans piled with cushions of velvet and pillows of embroidered silk, and scores of polished brass tray tables. The house and terraces were filled with floral arrangements created for the occasion by a character whom Cecil sometimes called "the other queen of Tangier," his and Barbara's great friend David Herbert, a British socialite, writer, and aesthete whose grand house on the outskirts of the city was another center of high-stratum social life. Exotic lighting effects had been designed for all of Sidi Hosni's main interior spaces, as well as the courtyards and rooftop terraces, the latter of which were set up with airy tents in scarlet and orange, surrounded by planters bursting with marigolds, zinnias, and sunflowers. From the terraces of this palace—which actually comprised several contiguous three-hundred-year-old mansions—were dramatic views of the city below and the Bay of Tangier.

May 1979

"She was forty-nine at that point," Doris told Ollie, "and fifty was looming darkly. I think she was angry about having to say goodbye to her youth, though in that passive way of hers. She certainly hadn't come up with a suitable approach to the adventure of aging, as I think we all must, unless we want to become very bitter. I'm sure that most of the guests thought this ball was just another of her extravagances, but I knew it was meant to mark this important moment of her life. She was a poet, remember. That's the way she thought about these things."

August 1961

Lined up in front of the house was an honor guard of twenty camels and drivers that had been brought in specially from their homes in the desert. Not far away, on the edge of the grounds under an orange tent, servants were distributing meals to any of the kasbah's residents who might be hungry—the same food that was being served inside, to the guests. The ball was called for ten-thirty, and by eleven, the house was full of people in both European attire—black tie, gowns, and uniforms—and various forms of North African and Eastern dress, including caftans, djellabas, and saris. Throughout the house were lavish buffets and elaborate entertainments, like belly dancers, snake charmers, and musicians playing classical Arab-Andalusian music. And then, around eleven-thirty, the hostess made her entrance to a special lighting cue in shades of green, dressed in a white-and-silver silk robe and the same suite of jewels she had worn for her portrait, the tiara authenticating the ball as a ceremony as grand as England's State Opening of Parliament. As she descended a stairway, there was a wave of applause; then the party rolled on.

May 1979

"She spent most of the evening in the most regal of the roof tents," recounted Doris, "greeting friends, dignitaries, special guests, drinking and laughing, enjoying herself. I don't think I've ever seen her happier."

"Tennessee Williams was there?" said Ollie.

"Oh, yes. He found us in one of the other tents, where we were having a gay ol' time—Cecil, Kin, and me, and Cecil's friend David Herbert, a very fancy expat gentleman with a raspberry-colored house in a fashionable neighborhood called the New Mountain. . . ."

August 1961

The maze of Sidi Hosni's rooftop terraces and flowerbeds, all finished in spotless white stucco, were threaded together by a network of stairways and walkways that guests were giddily navigating constantly that night in search of friends or a bar or a bathroom. The happy sound of *chaabi* music, offered by a Moroccan singer in a red knit skullcap, accompanied by a trio of musicians on the central terrace, carried to all parts of the roof, in varying degrees of volume.

"So this is where you all have been hidin'," said Williams, in his rich Southern drawl, coming upon Doris, Cecil, and party, who were reclining on divans among colorful silk pillows and on rugs laid down on the terrace floor. "I should have known this is where you'd be. Rooftops and fire escapes are where all the cool kids congregate at parties."

"Join us, Tom," said Doris.

"Pull up a cushion or two," said Cecil. "Recline like the Tangerines do."

Williams seemed pleasantly buzzed.

"Thank God we found you," said the playwright, as Merlo helped him settle into a large orange pillow on the ground. "I was trapped downstairs by a string of consuls' and ambassadors' wives, which I suppose is what I'm here for, but it was *no* fun."

Everyone knew everyone—except Kin, who didn't know Frank Merlo and asked what Merlo did. Merlo, a sometime actor who had been with Williams for more than ten years, was long used to this question and replied brightly, "I sleep with Mr. Williams."

Everyone laughed, as this was the kind of role that many among the guests that evening might well admit to playing, including Kin.

"That line's gettin' old, Frankie, but you deliver it *so* well," said Williams, saucily.

From nearby planters drifted the fragrance of night-blooming jasmine.

"Isn't it a splendid evening?" said Doris. "Wonderful weather for it."

"It never rains here in August," said David Herbert, holding a cigarette with cursory elegance. He was wearing three rings on each hand, and was dressed in an indigo blue djellaba with matching headscarf. "We get it in the spring."

"Do you know what our hostess told me?" said Williams. "She said, 'I *adore* the spring when it rains here.'" He was speaking theatrically in a voice that an actress playing Barbara might use. "'Sitting in a loggia skimmed by the rain-scented breeze, listening to the sound of showers echoing through tiled archways. . . . Sometimes I have a musician come and play Berber songs on a reed flute, as a descant to the music from the sky . . .'"

Williams chuckled at his own impromptu performance.

"Well, the rain here *is* quite beautiful," said David Herbert, with a slight touchiness in his voice.

After some conversation about Williams's next play, *Night of the Iguana*, and what Cecil hoped was going to be his next project, the movie of *My Fair Lady*—and a big groan of disapproval when Kin tried to change the subject to the rise of the Berlin Wall, which was all over the news—Barbara appeared at their tent.

"My lovelies. . . ! Make room," she said, insinuating herself into a semi-recumbent posture between Doris and Cecil, who happily made space for her on the divan. On her feet, she was wearing delicate sheepskin *babouche* slippers in silver, embossed in gold. "What am I interrupting?"

"Party talk," said Williams. "You'd be very proud of us. Nothing remotely serious."

"Good," said Barbara. "Have some champagne."

Attending Barbara that evening was a personal champagne steward, an attractive young Moroccan man with dark eyes and hair, dressed in a djellaba made of the same silver-embroidered white silk that Barbara's robe was made of. And attending the steward, in turn, was a barefoot boy bearing a bucket containing two champagne bottles and ice.

"Tom was telling us about his next play," said Doris. "It's set in Mexico."

"Oh?" said Barbara.

"Something about a lizard," said Cecil.

"*Iguana*, sir, if you please. *Iguana*," said Williams languidly.

"Is there a difference?" asked Kin.

"Women are fine, and sheep are divine, but iguanas are *numero uno*," said Williams, who was more than slightly tipsy.

"Does the creature have any good lines?" asked Barbara. Then she caught herself. "But what am I saying? All your characters have good lines."

"Thank you, Barbara, but no," said Williams. "It's a non-speaking part. It spends part of the play leashed up on the veranda, *observin'*. . . ."

"Will you actually have a live animal there onstage?" said Doris.

"Now that's a very good question," said Williams. "We're working that out. It's a symbol, of course, but we're going to see what Broadway allows."

"A symbol of what, if I may ask?" said Kin.

"*Oooh*—all tied up by the bonds of society," intoned Williams, with cheerful grandeur.

"Tom, dear," said Barbara, sitting up, "which of us are you going to depict in your next play after that, Miss Duke or me?"

Everyone felt the charge of a potentially deadly question being asked in a playful way, and Williams took a second to consider it.

"Now that, dear lady, is a very difficult question, because you both have such delicious . . . *qualities*, as we say in the theater."

"Come on, Tommy, you can do better than that," groaned Cecil.

"Give me a moment, baby. I wasn't finished," said Williams. "If I may, and since you were kind enough to ask: Doris, you belong in a delightful, airy, eighteenth-century comedy, full of amorous servants and randy nobles: 'The Duke's garden, after midnight. Enter the Duchess, in disguise'—that sort of thing."

Giggles from everyone in the tent.

"And you, Barbara, belong in something more gothic, nineteenth-century—an offstage suicide, an old man with hearing loss, and a sister whose heart is like a fine piano that no one can play because the key is lost. . . ."

"Not bad . . ." said Cecil.

"So I think the answer is . . . I will simply have to write an airy comedy dripping with sadness, with starring roles for both of you!"

Doris applauded, while Barbara just tilted her head, regarding the playwright thoughtfully.

"You really are a great poet—you know that?" she said. "That's part of what makes your plays so great—the poetry."

"Why, thank you, Miss Hutton. 'Permit me voyage, love, into your hands . . .'"

May 1979

"He quoted Hart Crane," explained Doris to Ollie.

"The poet?" said Ollie.

"Yes. I saw her connect with artists often this way—genuinely, as a fellow artist, not simply as a fan. I always admired that about her."

"She gave me a volume of her poetry, but I never really read it."

"You should."

August 1961

The mayor of Tangier and his party appeared at the tent, to say they were leaving and to thank Barbara for inviting them to such a brilliant gathering.

"*Ce fut un plaisir, votre excellence. Vous honorez ma maison*," said Barbara grandly, extending her hand, which the mayor bent over crisply to kiss.

"Oh, brother," whispered Cecil, once the mayor's party stepped away.

"No, no, that's quite right, quite right," said Williams. "If you ask me, a scene like that *needs* to be overplayed. Right, Barbara? Nothing less for persons extraordinary and plenipotentiary. . . ."

Since the champagne steward's assistant was closer to Williams than the steward was, Williams motioned for the boy to fill up his champagne glass. The boy, probably no older than ten or eleven, looked like he didn't know what to do; then the steward noticed, horrified, and took over the refilling.

May 1979

"Tom was drinking heavily," said Doris, "and possibly under the influence of something else. He wound up arguing with Frankie terribly that evening and stormed off alone."

"Why Hart Crane?" said Ollie.

"Barbara asked the same thing. Tom said he'd fallen in love with Crane's poetry as a boy. Something about the power of mystery. He said that there were references to Crane in all his work, and he wanted to write a play based on Crane's relationship with his mother. Apparently, she was monstrous."

"Right up his alley."

"And Ollie, he said he wanted to give himself back to 'the great mother of the sea,' the way Crane did. Do you know Crane's story?"

"I know nothing about Hart Crane. Though of course now I will go and read everything."

"Tom told us the story as if he were onstage. Crane was a tortured homosexual, and was sailing back to New York from Mexico, when he made advances on a Mexican crew member one night on deck, and got beaten up for it. Apparently both of them had been drinking. Then Crane staggered to the railing and jumped overboard, into the Gulf of Mexico."

"Golly. Just like that?"

"Several people on deck saw it happen. He said 'Goodbye, goodbye!' and jumped. The body was never recovered."

"What an exit."

"So, Ollie, there we were at this lovely party, at a palace in Tangier, and the music was playing, and the jasmine was blooming all around us, and everybody was drunk, and Barbara leans over to tell me, 'I'd want to go that way, too, if I could.' I said, 'Babbo, what do you mean?' And she said, 'That's the way a poet should die, Dodo. But I'm no poet, not really. I let the poet in me be drowned by . . . *this*.' You know—she gestured to indicate the party around us."

Ollie shuddered.

"Chilling," he said.

"I thought so, too," said Doris, becoming emotional. "And then she raised the hand with the diamond and looked into it intently. 'This is my memorial to the dead poet within. It's her temple. . . .'"

Ollie was stunned, both by the meaning of Barbara's pronouncement and the touching way that Doris recounted the moment.

"I . . . don't know what to say," said Ollie.

"I didn't either," said Doris, wiping away a small tear. "The others weren't paying attention. They were trying to contain our increasingly voluble friend, the playwright."

"What did you do?"

"I hugged her. What else was there to do? Then she got up and said she'd better check on the Ambassador, whoever that was, and floated off with her servants."

"How long did the party go on?"

"Probably 'til dawn. But I went to bed. She'd put me in a suite that was in a private wing, very Moorish, all in blue, and I could faintly hear the music drifting in through the window as I fell asleep. . . ."

PART 7

MEMORIES

CHAPTER 40

June 1979

Ollie was drawn closer to Doris after Barbara's death, but not necessarily as someone to offer daily witness. Doris and Barbara had never offered each other that. Rather, Ollie was one of the few people left who was able to comprehend the quality and dimensions of Doris's life. It was simple human nature, she told Ollie, that people whose names and faces were so well-known to the public should feel a strong desire to be truly *seen* by someone close.

During that first year after Barbara's death, Doris repeatedly told Ollie how grateful she was to have his continuing presence in her life.

"Otherwise," she said sadly, "it would be too lonely."

"Your butler sees much more of you than I do," joked Ollie.

"He may see more, but you see better."

It also helped that Ollie had known Barbara so well, and could share recollections about her with Doris. He was now the only other person who knew about the unique friendship that the two women had constructed for themselves.

In her grief over losing Barbara, Doris consigned the memory of her friend tenderly to the same kind of mental reliquary where she kept the memory of Arden, the infant daughter she never knew. In meditation, she entered each reliquary often, to pray and mystically unify past, present, and future so she could once more be together momentarily with her lost loved ones. But

Doris's reaction to the public discourse around Barbara's death was anything but tender. Bitterly, she complained that Barbara's name was, as ever, a plaything of the media and now the center of a gothic myth that was entrenching itself in the public mind.

The obituary that appeared in the *New York Times* said that Barbara "spent much of her life searching for a happiness that apparently eluded her." Doris found this ludicrous.

"Everybody is searching for something," she spat. "This is much too obvious to state."

The obituary also reported, with dollar amounts, the financial arrangements that attended several of Barbara's seven marriages.

"Does it get any more vulgar than that? Is this really the best the *Times* can do?"

People repeated with gleeful horror that one of America's great fortunes had been depleted chiefly through a woman's extravagance and seeming indifference to the bad judgment—or, as some claimed, the bad intentions—of her lawyers and business managers. The generosity that Barbara often showed to friends while alive, and the bequests to them specified in her will—precious objects of jade, rare antique rugs, costly pieces of jewelry—were overlooked, as were her bequests of art and antiques to museums like the Norton Simon in Pasadena and the de Young in San Francisco. What stuck in people's imagination was the report that the rest of Barbara's personal property had to be auctioned off to pay for what were described as "substantial debts."

"Is that all that's left, common gossip?"

The first things you search for in life are the things you were trained as a child to want, said Doris: a husband, a position in society, maybe a constructive role in the community. The things you wind up searching for as an adult, if you're lucky, or well-guided, or favored by the gods, are things you learn you *need*: chiefly, meaningful connections with other human beings in which you are truly seen, known, accepted. Doris's greatest blessing, she claimed, was her instinct to begin addressing the most important needs early in life, through music and art and dance, even as she gamely went about marriage and the social whirl. Now, as a new decade was beginning, the 1980s, Doris resolved to respond to the death of her friend by addressing her own important needs ever more diligently. She said she wanted to redouble her search for "whatever else might be out there," not only in the spiritual arena, under the guidance of her gurus and psychics, but in the physical one. Intent on avoiding the health pitfalls that Barbara had encountered, Doris continued to exercise and swim every day. She strictly regulated her diet and avoided refined sugar and flour; she consumed masses of ginseng, which she believed boosted the immune system, protected against cancer, and improved sexual function. Indeed, over the next decade, these healthy pursuits could sometimes become parodies of themselves: a weeklong diet consisting only of sardines and mineral water; a jaunt to Bimini in search of the lithium-laced waters of the Fountain of Youth; a string of hour-long, in-and-out "dates" at the Park Avenue penthouse with raffish young jazz musicians she met in Harlem; regular visits to a clinic in Switzerland for expensive shots of sheep's placenta; periodic sessions on an Buick-sized machine in a basement at Duke Farms that she claimed "dynamized bodily energies."

She had no plans to die, she once told Ollie. It was thrilling to command the resources that might help her discover a path around death. Mention of this eccentric goal raised a flag for Ollie, yet he felt that it was more admirable than the eccentricities Barbara had manifested during her final years, when she seemed practically resigned to death. Anyway, what alternative was there for Ollie but to go along with Doris, if he wanted to remain her good friend?

There were fewer dinners in the garden room at Rough Point; more quirky indulgences like moving a massive, custom-made bathtub from Park Avenue to Shangri La, which involved a crane outside the building and a plumber to travel with the tub; more lavish attention to the pets at Rough Point, the German shepherds Foxie and Rexie, which were allowed access to all parts of the house including the bedrooms and swimming pool, and the Bactrian camels Princess and Baby, which Doris had acquired in the deal with Saudi arms dealer Adnan Khashoggi when he sold her a 737 jet. There was a more relaxed attitude about the dogs soiling the antique Oriental carpets and the camels soiling the lawns and flowerbeds, but a distinctly sharper one toward household staff when they failed to clean up these pet accidents as quickly as Doris expected.

"She said she'd fire me if I didn't get it immediately the next time," grumbled Hank, a senior gardener.

"Is it true she gave the camels a coming-out party when they arrived?" said John, a junior gardener.

"Just remember," said Mary, a cook, "the animals live here, and you don't."

Ollie overheard this exchange one day in the kitchen at Rough Point, when he was staying with Doris for some Newport restoration meetings. And he understood immediately that the tense atmosphere characterizing Doris's households during those years was partly a result of her fear of slipping into the same kind of carelessness and squalor that Barbara had slipped into. There was nothing for Ollie to say to Doris about all this, of course. He relied on her cues as to whether or not to reminisce about Barbara, let alone discuss the effects of her loss. Which is why he was glad to be able to help Doris focus on her arts projects. In a way, they were all she had now, besides Ollie and the other new best friends she took on during the decade after Barbara's death, like Imelda Marcos, the former Philippine First Lady to whom Doris lent five million dollars and the frequent use of her plane, before Doris tired of Imelda's repeated pleas of poverty and dropped her; like Chandi Heffner, the thirty-two-year-old, free-spirited Hare Krishna devotee whom Doris adopted as a daughter, before Doris tired of Chandi's increasingly troublesome material demands and dropped and disinherited *her*; and like Bernard Lafferty, the ponytailed butler Doris hired, who was canny and solicitous and became comfortable wielding quantities of Doris's wealth for his own benefit, but would be allowed to stay with her until her death.

Moreover, Barbara's death felt like a symptom of a world that was once again remaking itself radically. This was the '80s!

Money was less embarrassed about itself than ever before; and for those who had it, the discontinuity between them and those who didn't have it mattered less than ever before. At least during the Gilded Age, the rich, who carried on their circumvolutions largely out of view of the poor, still remembered to drop some crumbs from the table, like public libraries, concert halls, and botanical gardens. Now the rich, especially the new young rich, were not only unembarrassedly selfish, but happy to be glaringly visible to everyone, as if to show that their wealth proved some axiom that the entire world needed to know. Doris had been born into a gracious world of dance cards and chaperones, and adapted to the arrival of Café Society and then the Jet Set, and was now hanging on while society headed . . . where? Poor Babbo had never been able to accommodate herself fully to the evolving crassness of modern society, so for dear life she enveloped herself in a backward-looking bubble, with other relics like herself. And occasionally, out of habit, she slapped on a face and bribed a young man to join her in the bubble for a few drinks. Whereas Doris, entering her seventies, was doing her best to keep up with the parade, at the risk of appearing ridiculous—even if, as she mused one day to Ollie when dressing for an evening in a voguish gown that revealed her still-slim figure, "trying to stay young might be just as desperate as hiring the young."

CHAPTER 41

Ollie met Emma at the hospital on the morning of her operation and waited, while she was in surgery, in the broad, commodious sitting area that he was directed to. Featuring a concierge desk, library nook, café bar, decorative planters, and seating areas configured with plush sofas and chairs, and tall-table workstations with stools, the brightly lit space was designed as something between a business hotel lobby and a first-class airport lounge. Neutral wood tones and light, fashionable colors were accented with pops of high style in sculptural table lamps and wall treatment accents. Except for a few visits with dying friends in cramped, semi-private rooms during the AIDS crisis, Ollie had very little experience with hospitals. He was surprised here not only by the expensive-looking furnishings and finishes, but by the very concept of the space itself, obviously meant to offer respite and support with what the hospitality industry called "amenities." How different this was from the room Ollie remembered waiting in when he was three, in 1942, after his father entered the hospital with liver failure and died of cirrhosis—a room so dreary that it seemed to produce its own stress and anxiety. Institutional furniture made of tubular steel, with cracked leather upholstery; pedestal ashtrays full of cigarette butts; stained green-and-yellow carpeting in a jittery, stylized floral pattern; framed mirrors on walls painted white but yellowed by cigarette smoke; a solitary, sickly palm tree in a moldy terra-cotta pot.

So horrid, that day was, when his father died: everyone on edge because of the war, his mother beset with panic over the loss of her husband and the imminent loss of their fine, large house. So horrid, the days and months following: his mother having to go to work and find a small, decent apartment where she could bring up Ollie and his younger brother, Ambrose, only a baby, under what sanctimonious voices termed "underprivileged" circumstances. Ollie's mother made do as best she could, always managing to put supper on the table, but not always able to buy the boys the new pants and shirts and shoes they wanted. She was never complaining, but always embarrassed and constantly insisting that the family should maintain its respectability by behaving properly and making sure they were seen doing things properly, by neighbors and schoolmates and shopkeepers, if not by old friends in their former neighborhood, whom they rarely saw anymore.

And it was that same dreary hospital waiting room where, fifteen years later, Ollie and his mother waited during surgery after Ambrose's motorcycle accident, and were given the news of his death—the framed mirrors replaced by framed sculptural reliefs; the hideous green-and-yellow carpeting replaced by hideous beige carpeting; the cracked leather replaced by simulated leather. The sanctimonious voices called Ambrose a "juvenile delinquent."

Odd, Ollie thought, how different he and his brother were, but right up until Ambrose's death, there was little friction between them. They often laughed at the same jokes, and were even curious about each other's respective interests. Ambrose listened to Ollie's stories of the historic house museum where Ollie sometimes worked, and Ollie was genuinely fascinated by the tales Ambrose told of adventures like shooting rats at a local landfill with boys "from the other side of the tracks"—boys who were too young for drivers' licenses but nonetheless drove cars and rode motorcycles. Ambrose had a tender side that few people other than Ollie and their mother saw.

One day, when Ollie was on duty at Robertson's flower shop, Ambrose came in and said he needed a bouquet.

"Of course," said Ollie, surprised but willing to help.

"Nothing expensive," said Ambrose.

"On the house. Who's it for?"

"It's a friend's birthday."

"Anybody I know?"

"You really don't know any of my friends."

"I guess you're right. What's her name?"

"It's just a friend, a guy. It's sort of a goof."

Because of that small incident, Ollie had always wondered if, had Ambrose lived, he and his brother might have discovered they had more in common than parents—though they would certainly have remained very different kinds of men.

As he waited for news of Emma, Ollie thought how nice the present was as a place to escape to, when you feel mired in too much memory, even if you happen to be in your eighties and your gait isn't quite as steady as it used to be. The present is what you have created for yourself, not what was once plopped in your lap, and that can be so comforting, despite your wobbly legs.

It was almost two hours before a nurse arrived to tell Ollie that Emma was out of surgery and to show him the way to the recovery room. The operation was a complete success, said the nurse, and Emma was doing beautifully.

CHAPTER 42

June 1979

A few weeks after learning the terms of Barbara's will, Doris tried to discover who now owned the Blue Period Picasso. Her intention was to buy it quietly and donate it to MoMA in Barbara's name, in addition to her own gift of the Luca Zanobi work. But she couldn't find out anything about the painting. She did decide, though, to downplay her MoMA gift, asking the museum to keep the use of her name to a minimum. Since the gift had originated in her contest with Barbara, she remained convinced that making too much of it would constitute bad form.

Count Your Blessings opened a year after Barbara's death. MoMA gave a big opening-night party for patrons and other VIPs. The work was installed in the largest of the museum's first-floor d'Harnoncourt Galleries, and took the form of almost exactly the same piles and cascades of rummage-sale goods as were once displayed on the sidewalk of the First Baptist Church of Nutley, New Jersey. As planned, the installation was accompanied by a soundtrack of gospel music performed by the church's choir. Masses of guests milled through it all eagerly, marveling at the sheer profusion of objects, making remarks that ranged from the obtuse and the obvious to the overintellectual and the pseudo-sociological; some guests even grasped the relationship between the "poor" materials and the point about wealth and community that Zanobi was trying to make. Among the guests were several of Doris's friends from the church, including Mrs. Owens and her husband, Pastor Walker and his wife, and members of the choir, who after some brief remarks by Richard Oldenburg, the museum's director, performed a fifteen-minute live set of spirited church music. Mayor Ed Koch, who attended with Bess Myerson, the actress and former Miss America he poignantly called his "First Lady," was given the honor of conducting the choir's first song.

Doris attended with Ollie, who by now was a fairly well-known man-about-town in both New York and London. He was writing more and more, for respected arts and cultural publications, and advising collectors in many areas of both the fine and decorative arts. His column "Poking Around" was often quoted. He went out with many of the "great gals" who were mentioned in the society columns, in a merry round of so many dinners, parties, concerts, art openings, and book launches that he maintained two tuxedos and visited the barbershop at least once a week.

At the museum opening, Doris and Ollie had just finished chatting with Lee Radziwill and the architect John Warnecke when another couple joined them.

"Excuse me, Miss Duke? I wonder if you might remember me."

The gentleman, dressed in black tie, accompanied by a young woman in a chic black suit and two-inch slingback heels, was now ten years older, but Ollie recognized him.

"London, '68 or '69," he offered.

"Selwyn Stanfield," said the gentleman, with a little bow.

"That Caribbean restaurant . . ."

"Mr. Stanfield, of course," said Doris, extending her hand. "You remember Oliver Shaw."

"I do," said Selwyn. "This is my girlfriend, MaryAnn Dessault."

"A pleasure, Miss Duke," said MaryAnn. "We're both fans of your work, Mr. Shaw."

"MaryAnn is with the Mary Boone Gallery," said Selwyn.

"SoHo," said Ollie.

"I know it well—the gallery building," said Doris.

After an exchange among the four of them about the Zanobi installation, Ollie slipped into a conversation about an upcoming gallery show that MaryAnn was working on, while Doris and Selwyn chatted about artistic patronage and cultural philanthropy.

"I hear such wonderful things about Newport," said Selwyn.

"Please come and see for yourself, anytime," said Doris.

"They're the old houses. . . ?"

"Yes, the original housing stock—eighteenth- and early nineteenth-century. We restore them and rent them as private residences."

"One by one?"

"A few at a time. Then we maintain them with a full-time crew of carpenters and painters."

"Marvelous. So they're of wood, I imagine?"

"Mostly wood-frame, with wood shingles and clapboards. But some are brick."

"Not-for-profit?"

"Of course. We're a five-oh-one-C-three. We call our tenants 'stewards.' Really, you should come and see for yourself."

"We should."

"As I recall, Mr. Stanfield . . ."

"Please—Selwyn."

"And please call me Doris. As I recall, you were interested in Indian *havelis*."

"That's right—you remember!—Indian and Nepalese," said Selwyn. "My business takes me frequently to Asia, and I always try to make time to look at old houses and talk to historians and preservationists. It's so inspiring, isn't it? Architecture just . . . speaks to me."

"I know exactly what you mean," said Doris. "My eyes were opened when I first went to India in 1935, on my honeymoon. I started collecting things on the spot—artworks, architectural elements."

"I've heard about your place in Honolulu."

"Shangri La. It really is a world apart."

"A retreat for you?"

"Well, yes, now. But I hope it can be more than that, after I'm gone."

"Ah. I've been thinking a lot about this—what remains after we're gone. I don't know if I mentioned it to you, but my father built the business that I'm now running."

"Television, isn't it. . . ?"

"Telecommunications. I wanted to go into the arts, but I felt it my duty to honor what my father created. And really, the business is about connecting people, elevating them, so there's that. I want to serve humanity, and I think good business does that. But Doris, I must tell you, India changed me. When we met in London, I was on my way back from there. I had negotiated a deal for my father, but I became immersed in a culture where people connected with each other and valued each other in a more . . . in a *truer* way than we do here."

"Yes."

"I am always thinking about going back there and finding a house and restoring it, and living there, simply."

"Then you must, you must," said Doris, finding Selwyn's story more interesting than the usual party chat.

". . . While also leaving the company in good hands, so it continues to prosper."

"I understand. My father was exactly like that."

"We serve on boards, of course, and that's a privilege. But I think to be effective, we need to get out of the boardroom . . ."

". . . To something simpler."

"To something realer, right? For sheer personal survival. And then, maybe after some spiritual strengthening, we can return to business life, renewed, replenished. . . ."

"Yes!"

"Or am I dreaming?"

Doris and Selwyn shared a laugh, while around them, bathed in the sounds of choral praise and opening-night conversations, scores of art lovers were inspecting new and used ashtrays, vases, salt-and-pepper shakers, baby dolls, board games, album cassettes, basketballs, T-shirts, hooded sweatshirts, and the like. In one corner, Luca Zanobi, outfitted in a decidedly plain sport jacket, T-shirt, and baggy jeans, was speaking with a curator and several museum patrons.

"You're not dreaming, Selwyn," said Doris. "In fact, who knows? You might find a way of performing your service to humanity invisibly, anonymously—and don't the wise men always say that that's a higher order of business?"

"Interesting."

"Though that kind of thing would be a challenge for some of us to achieve."

Selwyn groaned in assent.

"To be honest, I've always been attracted to the idea of going *sannyasin*," he said. "Owning nothing but a homespun robe and a begging bowl, going from kitchen door to kitchen door, for scraps of food."

"It's an appealing idea."

"Or would stepping away from my life be more like jumping out of a speeding car?"

Next to them, Ollie and MaryAnn were chatting away.

"Tell me, is your girlfriend aligned with you on this?" said Doris, leaning in closely to Selwyn. "She appears to be wearing Chanel."

Selwyn was surprised at such a sharp, personal question, but he liked Doris's directness.

"Honestly, I don't know," he said, with a chuckle. "I've never asked. Would she want to drop everything and run away to Kathmandu with me? Somehow, I think not."

Doris's eyes sparkled.

"Well, she wouldn't necessarily have to switch from Chanel to homespun. In today's India, it could be *that*," she said, gesturing toward a rack of pink and blue cotton fleece tracksuits.

They agreed to stay in touch, and Selwyn and MaryAnn moved off to greet Mayor Koch.

Since Doris and Ollie had a dinner reservation at a small Italian restaurant that she liked near her place, she suggested that they head over there. On the way out of the museum, they ran into a dancer whom Doris knew.

"Look, Ollie, it's Susan," she said, and exchanged a little kiss with the woman.

Susan Varda was a contemporary dancer and choreographer trained in both classical and folk dance forms. She led a small company of six dancers that existed on a tiny budget and appeared periodically at small venues like Dance Theater Workshop in Chelsea, above a garage on West 19th Street, and The Kitchen in SoHo, on the second floor of a hundred-year-old building at the corner of Wooster and Broome. Doris sometimes attended the daily class that Susan gave for her company at a rehearsal studio near City Hall, and made a relatively small annual donation to the company, though she had always declined a board position. Doris not only liked Susan personally, but prized her work as emotional and story-based, unlike many of the more formalist and abstract dance artists of Susan's generation.

"Here for the Zanobi?" said Doris. Sounds from the party were echoing into the reception lobby, where they were standing. People were coming and going.

"Yes, indeed! My dancer Mariuccia is friends with Luca from Milan, so he invited all of us. So exciting!"

"We loved it—it's extraordinary," said Doris, modestly omitting the fact that she had commissioned the artist. "And how are things with you? Preparing for an upcoming performance?"

Varda made a sad face.

"Not exactly," she said. "We have a residency at Jacob's Pillow starting on Monday, to create a new piece, and I was going to drive everyone up there in my trusty VW van. But of course, this is the moment when the thing decides to fall apart."

"Oh, no!"

"Engine mounts shot. Clutch cable shot."

"What about repairs?"

"Long story. Usually I take it home to Pennsylvania, where I get a good deal from my father's friend's garage. But I don't think I can even drive it there."

"So how will you get to the Pillow?"

Varda sighed.

"I'll figure it out," she said. "There's no budget for it, but I am going to think about all of that tomorrow, and tonight I am just going to enjoy the art and the party."

"Tell you what," said Doris, with barely a hesitation. "Ollie, you have calling cards with you, don't you? Be an angel and let me have one."

From a small silver case, Ollie took one of his blue Pineider calling cards, with his name engraved in classic Copperplate Light Extended capitals, and gave it to Doris. With a silver pen from her purse, Doris wrote an East 55th Street address on the card and gave it to Varda.

"Come to this address tomorrow morning," said Doris. "It's an apartment building. Give the gentleman at the front desk your name and say that Miss Duke told you to come and pick up an envelope."

"What. . . ?"

"I will leave an envelope there for you. You have to get up to your residency, make the most of it—that's all there is to it. There's no time for paperwork."

Reflexively, Varda examined both sides of the card two or three times, as if she could find there a more explicit explanation of Doris's words.

"You mean . . ."

"I mean I'd love for you to accept a small gift, so you can get yourself a better car and get your dancers up to Becket."

Varda seemed overcome.

"Miss Duke, this is . . . so incredibly nice of you," she said. "I don't . . . know what to say."

'You don't have to say a thing, Susan." Doris took Varda's hands in hers. "Just have fun making your new piece. And be sure to let me know when it comes time for you to perform it."

"I will. Thank you, thank you. I can't thank you enough."

After another kiss and promises to stay in touch, Varda went off into the party, and Doris and Ollie stepped out into the night air.

"That was nice of you," said Ollie.

"She works hard, that girl," said Doris. "Her dancers are beautiful. Dance is persistently the least remunerated art form there is, and sometimes I think it gives the most to us."

"You're right."

"So before dinner, Ollie, I want to make a stop."

"Alrighty."

They started walking east on 53rd Street. The roar of some building's massive HVAC system, somewhere above them, was bullying the otherwise quiet street.

"There's a small office where I go . . ." said Doris, taking Ollie's arm.

"Ah, yes . . ." said Ollie. He had already put together in his mind oblique references that Doris made in the past about a place on East 55th Street.

"You may have heard me mention it."

"Where you go to be alone."

"It's more of a business office, where during the day I have an accountant and a bookkeeper to handle my personal affairs, separate from the Duke business offices and foundation offices."

"I see."

"But I do go there at night sometimes, when no one else is around, to look over the books and keep current. It's where I do my personal gifts—the private ones that don't need to pass through the foundation. I've been meaning to show you around since our visit to Zürich."

"Okay."

"It will just take a moment, and then we can go to dinner. The restaurant is not far from there."

CHAPTER 43

Emma's operation went as smoothly as anyone could have hoped. Since the tumor had not invaded any bones, no reconstruction would be necessary. Ollie was delighted to notice her brighten when she saw him enter the recovery room.

"There you are," he said. "How are you doing?"

"Okay," said Emma, as a nurse rechecked her vital signs and made sure she was comfortable. Her hair was matted but neat.

"I hear it went beautifully."

"Yeah. How are you?" she said, still a little groggy, but upbeat.

"I'm perfectly splendid, thank you very much," said Ollie, "now that I see your smiling face."

Emma, who hadn't been smiling, managed a sort of grin.

The surgeon came in directly, to look at Emma and confirm that everything had gone well and that, as planned, Emma would be able to go home that day, as soon as she felt able to make the trip. Ollie mentioned that he was the one who would be seeing her home safely, and another nurse came in to review Emma's discharge instructions and answer any questions she might have. But Emma had none at the moment.

Ollie had a question, though.

"For pain, Nurse?"

"We've phoned in a prescription for ibuprofen to your pharmacy—basically, it's super Advil—and here are two more for later today and tonight." She placed an envelope on the tray table next to Emma's gurney. "One around three, if you need it, and one before bed."

"Can I work?" said Emma.

The question did not surprise the nurse.

"Well, today you'll probably want to take it easy," she said. "But tomorrow, if you mean working at your computer, you should be able to do that, if you want to. Just see what feels comfortable for the elbow."

An hour later, when Emma had regrouped and felt ready to leave the recovery room, she found that she needed help dressing. Ollie, flustered for a moment, called for a nurse and stepped out of the room when she arrived.

Outside the hospital, in the pick-up zone of the building's entry drive, Ollie helped Emma gently into the back of an Uber Black. He was suddenly amused by his familiarity with this kind of moment.

This again . . . he thought.

The motions of this part of escorting—identifying the car from the curb, signaling the driver, offering his companion an arm, opening the door, steadying her as she entered, saying that he would go around the other side so she didn't have to scooch over, closing the door, scanning for moving vehicles in the outer lane, checking to see if the act of touching the car's door handle and roof had soiled his hands; walking through all this with a smooth and confident cadence—all of it triggered a sense memory that was well-entrenched in his mind, the awareness of which that day was heightened by the extreme concern for Emma that he was trying his best to hide.

Here I am at eighty-four, he thought, *helping yet another great gal into a car—this one not even born in '79, when my first great gal, Barbara, died.*

And Emma was probably nine or ten years old when Ollie first met her. He was old even then—sixty. It was at one of Martin and Janet's dinner parties, and Ollie was surprised that after the cute act of assisting her mother by passing a tray of hors d'oeuvres, Emma took a seat at the dinner table with the adults. The next older person at the table was a bookish *Nota*

Bene editor in his twenties. Yet Emma held her own in a discussion of the possible Y2K crisis that was looming at the end of that year, and even brought an insight into the discussion that none of the adults happened to offer: that banks, governments, and corporations had been busy deploying software patches across their networks, a fact that Emma learned from one of her friends in the technology lab at St. Ann's. She reported that all her schoolmates, in fact, were hugely entertained by the unnecessary millennium bug alarm being clucked over in the media.

Extraordinary child, thought Ollie at the time—as smart and self-assured as he might expect a child of his precocious editor and the editor's gifted artist wife to be; dressed for dinner in simple jeans, sweater, and T-shirt, her mid-length hair barely styled, like a properly bohemian St. Ann's girl, instead of some adorably accessorized Chanel-via-*Clueless* outfit that a Chapin girl might be in.

"Isn't school awfully far from here?" Ollie asked Emma, after dessert.

"Forty-five minutes," said Emma.

"By subway?"

Emma nodded.

"The Number One is right here," she said. "A switch to the Two-Three at Seventy-second or wherever, then it's express to Clark Street."

"Is it safe—I mean, do you feel safe?"

"I read the *Times*, when there's room enough to open it. Nobody bothers me."

She told Ollie that she was in the fifth grade and most fond of puppetry and philosophy classes, the latter of which was currently focused on logic. *How many ten-year-olds would have much to say about Bertrand Russell?* wondered Ollie as they spoke. Yet Emma delighted in recounting a story of Russell during the Cuban missile crisis, sending telegrams to both Kennedy and Khrushchev, appealing for "an end to the madness."

"Shouldn't world leaders be philosophers?" asked Emma intently.

"Why can't they be more philosophical, do you mean?" said Ollie.

"No, I mean why does every American president and senator have to be a lawyer?"

"Fair point. And may I ask what you are working toward yourself?"

"What do you mean, 'working toward'?"

"I'm trying to ask, 'What do you want to be when you grow up?'—without using the terribly condescending phrase 'when you grow up,' since you're so . . .'"

"She's amazing, isn't she?" said Martin, joining them and resting his hand lovingly on Emma's shoulder.

"That she is," said Ollie.

"Thanks, Dad. Maybe an artist, Mr. Shaw," said Emma. "But okay if I go help Mom clean up?"

"Sure," said Martin.

"Excuse me," said Emma. "I'm supposed to be part-servant tonight."

"I'm glad you came," said Martin, after Emma went off.

"How could I not?" said Ollie. "We're friends as well as colleagues, no?"

"And you owe me a piece."

"Right—about my tailor!"

"How's it going?"

"He's copying a Katharine Hamnett jacket for me—showed me exactly how he examines the original and builds the copy. It's going to be gripping."

Fifteen years before, a year or so after Martin and Janet were married, Ollie and Martin were attending an awards dinner together in Lower Manhattan. Martin, then a bright, young star in the publishing world, was a junior editor at *Nota Bene*; and Ollie was a well-known columnist, feature writer, and man-about-town, with an international circle of friends like pianist Radu Lupu, architect I. M. Pei, columnist Liz Smith, chef Paul Bocuse, Senator Daniel Patrick Moynihan, socialite Doris Duke, and such. In a cab after the dinner, a bit of warm and wine-soaked conversation led to some back-seat snogging that lasted only for a few blocks of uptown-bound travel on Church Street, but to nothing after that. The twenty-three-year-old man found the intellectual authority and social smoothness of the older one momentarily alluring; the forty-six-year-old found the energy and ambition of the younger man curiously appealing; neither had specific thoughts they were aware of about the physical appeal of the other—the noble shape of a nose, the lush configuration of lips, the intelligent brightness of eyes, the sturdiness and solidity of fingers—none of that played a role consciously in either man's wanting to put his mouth on the mouth of the other. There was no enchantment, no falling for or into anything. There were no ulterior motives.

If anything deeper were at play—a scent that subconsciously recalled a favorite uncle, a vocal resonance that vibrated with fatherly magnetism—neither was particularly aware of it. And for Martin, the younger party, the incident would be dismissed more than remembered; whereas for Ollie, of an older generation, programmed longer ago in history, the incident would not register solidly enough in the brain either to dismiss or to remember. For each, in different ways, it was a non-event. If Eros were involved at all, neither of these men would have identified it as such. It was just a moment that happened between a newly married man who thought of himself as primarily straight but did acknowledge the little bit of bisexual experience he'd had in college and still had, occasionally, in a public park or an airport men's room; and a confirmed bachelor who'd never had sex with a woman or ever wanted to, but once or twice, when younger, did have a pallid version of pre-sex with a man and accepted that he'd probably never want to try it again.

For a decade or so after that, Ollie and Martin found themselves avoiding close contact with each other, though they continued working together out of necessity, because a great magazine needs its great writers. And maybe some mental murmur of Martin did remain with Ollie—he couldn't call it more than that—even with the snogging incident long past; some recurring notice of Martin's lambent modes of expression, which were still . . . catching. Yet Ollie had always wiggled out of being caught by these catching things, and that was that. So mostly he avoided thinking about things in Martin that might still catch him, and things about him that he thought might catch Martin. And then Martin invited Ollie to one of his dinner parties—that first time that Ollie was welcomed into Martin and Janet's charmed social circle—and he remained there, purely as colleague and friend, until the circle dissolved with Martin's death and Janet's decampment to London. It was only Emma, initially as a searching ten-year-old, who wondered if there might be something hidden between her dad and this older man.

"What's it like to have a kid?" Ollie asked Martin after dinner, after Emma and a Broadway performer had installed themselves at the piano, where they were amusing some of the other guests with a rendition of the song "Steam Heat."

"You know—great," said Martin. "Marvelous. Mysterious. You never wanted one?"

Ollie frowned in a friendly way.

"I don't think so," he said. "It would be like . . . like having an orchard. I wouldn't know what to do with an orchard—what it needs, how to take care of it, what to do with the fruit."

CHAPTER 44

June 1979

Doris's secret hideaway office was in a good but nondescript postwar apartment building on East 55th Street just off Park Avenue, markedly less glamorous than her penthouse on Park, three blocks uptown.

"Good evening, Miss Duke," said the doorman.

"Hello, Charles," said Doris. "How's the wisdom tooth?"

"Had it out, ma'am."

"Much better—good for you."

She and Ollie went to the elevator, Doris pressed 7, and within a minute, they were inside Apartment #7C. Doris showed Ollie around, turning on lights as they went. It was an undistinguished, two-bedroom apartment whose dining room and master bedroom were given over to business, furnished with several standard, green metal office desks, two banks of four-drawer, green metal filing cabinets, and several bookcases of ledgers and file binders. The living room was furnished as it might be if someone lived there, with a sofa, chairs, and a coffee table, tasteful but unremarkable, and the smaller bedroom was furnished like a mid-level hotel room, designed with function, not fanciness in mind. There was a full kitchen that looked unused except for a coffee maker and bottled water dispenser. The apartment featured none of the artworks, objects, or décor elements to be found in Doris's residences. It was as far from Tony Duquette as possible, Doris joked. She laughed when she compared her visits there to the *sannyasin* lifestyle that she mentioned discussing with Selwyn Stanfield at the party.

"I am usually wearing something very plain when I come here," said Doris, dropping her wrap and bag on the living room sofa. "A big hat, usually sunglasses, even at night; sometimes even a wig. The doormen know my disguises, and of course, I take care of them. I usually come at night for a few hours. Every now and then I stay 'til the morning."

She ushered Ollie into the dining room, to one of the larger desks, the top of which was clear except for a clock, a pen-and-pencil cup, a notepad, and two short piles of ledger books.

"You have people running your business here?" said Ollie.

"Two people, for my private business—the households, mostly. I have the foundation for the churches, the dance companies, an animal protection program, a land-use project. . . ."

"Wow."

"Then this, for private giving. Funded by a Swiss account."

"I see," said Ollie, noticing Doris transform subtly, despite the aquamarine-colored silk tunic and harem pants she'd chosen to wear for the opening, from socialite into businesswoman.

"Make yourself comfortable," she said.

Doris seated herself at the desk and switched on the lamp, while Ollie took a seat on the chair beside the desk.

"Once a week," she said, "they send over updated reports from all the Duke enterprise books and the foundation books, so I can always get a snapshot of everything here."

"You look at the books that often?"

"When I am in New York, yes. I like to stay in the picture."

Ollie was intrigued to see that Doris was a different creature here than the one he had just seen at the museum party. There was little of the glamorous, larger-than-life quality she normally radiated. Here, she was just a smart lady intent on staying in control of her affairs. And in this way, Ollie understood that Doris's East 55th Street hideaway shared a characteristic with the rivalry that she had designed for herself and Barbara: it was a construct in which she could be who she wanted to be only for herself, not for the public.

From the desk drawer, Doris took out a large binder of three-on-a-page checks.

"Ten thousand should do it, no?" she said, smoothing the page and picking up a pen.

"For Susan? I should think so," said Ollie.

She began filling out the check.

"She could buy a new car," said Doris, "but it would probably be smarter of her to rent one and get her people up there that way, and use the rest for gen op."

"Mmm," said Ollie.

"Anyway, it's her call. But I bet that's what she'll do—general operations. These dancers are very smart about surviving. They always use their money well."

Doris unzipped the check neatly from the page and popped it into an envelope with a little note: *Enjoy the big stone! —DD.* Then she shut the binder and put it away.

"There," she said. "All done. Branzino!"

"Doris, may I ask a serious question?" said Ollie, as they headed back into the living room. "How do you decide what to give away—to whom and how much?"

Her expression took on a glow of interest.

"I've been wondering if and when you'd ever ask me that question," she said.

She gestured toward the sofa and chairs, and they both sat. Tidy and well-kept but without artwork or accent, the room was conspicuously plain, its décor in unassertive greens and browns—dull, really, as if someone had specified this as a conscious design choice.

"I've been wanting to ask it since that day in Zürich," said Ollie, "but I didn't want . . . to question your intentions."

"I only wanted you to feel totally free to use your own judgment and be autonomous."

Ollie nodded.

"You made it very clear that I wasn't required to report to anyone," he said, "that you wanted it to be *my* fund, *my* work. And I've tried to do my best."

"I wanted to give you something meaningful, Ollie, because

I realized back then that I had come to trust you. That was my way of expressing it."

"I'm grateful, Doris. I think you know that. But I'm so eager to do it right! Every grant I make is me trying to find my way."

"Sure."

"As I understand it, from a friend of mine who works at a large foundation, there's no school for philanthropy, and barely a universally accepted set of best practices."

"Well, there are legal boundaries and ethical ones, but I think we can do better than simply observing the rules."

"Better how?"

"We follow our hearts, of course, but I think we have to have a bigger thought about what we're doing—an instinct, if you will, about how it all brings civilization forward, in the long run."

"Hmm."

"Do you know what I mean? I hope this doesn't sound pretentious. Simple generosity is all very well. You're in the schoolyard, and Mummy has packed your lunch bag with two pieces of fruit, and you give one to a friend. Or a stranger. Lovely. But making generosity work on a larger scale does require some planning."

"Can you tell me how you have gone about it?"

Philanthropy was a habit she learned from her father, Doris told Ollie. And his habit was probably an extension of an old Southern tradition of responsibility to the community. People rely on each other, she said; this was something to be honored and respected. Wealth could be like a sacrament, if you handled it as such. Lucre was filthy only if you conceived of it that way.

"At the foundation, we have some very smart people who are at the forefront of thinking about these issues," said Doris. "They've created quite a sophisticated program. They handle it all, but I like to think that we have a dialogue. I listen to them, and they listen to me—and not just about what dance companies I happen to like. It has to be bigger than that—for me, anyway. Not just giving a million dollars to the ballet so you can go swanning about on opening night."

These were the thoughts, Ollie realized, of someone who had taken an inheritance of a hundred million and overseen its growth into a fortune of over a billion. And as he sat there amidst file cabinets and ledger books, he knew that Doris knew where every last nickel of this fortune was located. This was also a woman he'd seen repair a broken porcelain vase herself, at Rough Point, because "It's got to be fixed, and I can do it better than most people."

Ollie had been giving away one or two grants per year, since Doris conferred control of that "secret" fund upon him. Though he was under no obligation to do so, he had been sending Doris a memo and dossier on each project, in case she was interested, but she had never made a comment on any of them.

"I share your thoughts about the greater good these grants can do," he said, "and I always stay anonymous, of course."

"There's no 'of course' in these matters, though I do recommend anonymity, at least at the beginning, until you find your philanthropic persona," said Doris.

"But sometimes I wrestle with an idea for a grant. I think the recipient is worthy, the work is terrific, but I wonder about it being as useful to the world as I hope it will be."

Ollie's most recent grant was to an American furniture maker who restored fine French furniture for museums and important private collections. The man was one of the top restorers in the world. He had studied at the Louvre and inherited, from an ancient French master craftsman, an historic collection of rare *boiseries*, that was now stored in a studio in Brooklyn. The restorer lived modestly and used much of his earnings to pay apprentices, yet he worked with priceless, museum-level treasures and could probably devise a business model that would yield him much greater profits. How correct was it to award a grant to this man?

"Correct?" said Doris. "There are courts of law, but no court of charitable correctness. It can be useful, Ollie, to have someone to talk to about this. Maybe you need some kind of partner in this work."

"I suppose so."

"Every writer needs an editor. Every philanthropist needs one, too. Perhaps the friend you spoke of, who works at a foundation . . ."

"Yes . . ." said Ollie, thinking of Liz Welland. Maybe he *should* confide in her.

Doris asked Ollie how he would describe his "sweet spot"— the interest most dear to him, the one he most enjoyed supporting.

"I haven't thought about it, to be honest," he said. "I'm interested in so many things."

"Well, I recommend you think about it and talk about that with someone, too," said Doris. "Knowing this can turn generous impulses from caprice into something noble. For me, it's dance, and I don't mean simply that thing that we may see on a stage, a show, a spectacle. It's a phenomenon of body and spirit, of sex and identity, of gender, and class, and race. . . . See? Is it any wonder that we're in the middle of what they're calling a 'dance boom'—with all that's been going on in the world in the last few decades, all the change, all the growth. . . ?

"I try to talk about dance with as many people as I can— and not just dancers, but writers, scientists, politicians. . . . I try to understand where the important transformations can come. Otherwise, I am just giving away cars to nice people."

Doris paused.

"Or diamond necklaces to random gals who already have a diamond necklace," she added dolefully.

Ollie understood the reference to their dear, deceased friend, Babbo.

"Doris, you've given me a lot to think about," he said.

"Have I? Good," said Doris, rising from her seat. "So, *now* branzino!"

On their way out of the building, she left the envelope with the doorman and said goodnight to him. Then she and Ollie walked to the restaurant, a few blocks away, and enjoyed a late supper.

CHAPTER 45

Ollie was reminiscing with Emma one day at her place, where she was editing the film. She had asked about Doris's final years.

"Her attempts during the eighties to find a suitable playmate were doomed," he said. "Babbo was gone, and she was now the last of the species. No one else had gone horseback riding with her as a girl in the fields of Miss Porter's, and talked about peeing in the shower, and had a picnic lunch in the back of a limousine driven by a chauffeur-collaborator named Henrik. No one. Not a beauty-queen dictatress like Imelda or a belly-dancing Krisha cultress like Chandi. Those two just didn't cut it. She took them up and then dropped them—in the latter case, took up and legally adopted, then dropped and legally disinherited."

"Oh," said Emma, "and the butler?"

"He wasn't terrible. Just . . . kind of classless, despite the airs he took on."

"How did they meet?"

"The butler? Doris needed somebody to run the house at Duke Farms, and Chandi suggested Bernard, whom she had met in that Honolulu rich-and-supposedly-cool crowd she was hanging out with. He knew stars—Elizabeth Taylor, Sophia Loren; he had spent some time as the maître d' of the Bellevue Stratford's dining room, in Philadelphia. And he wound up running all of Doris's houses and becoming very devoted to her, and she to him. By the end, he was managing her life and business and even her body—you know, through doctors and meds and things."

"I see. But not evil?"

"Bernard? I never thought so. He filled a void, and did seem to have her welfare in mind, even if he never grasped the loftiest part of her vision for the foundation. Even if he drank *terribly*, on and off the job."

"What did the foundation have to do with it?"

"Doris made him a director."

"Did she!"

"At the same time, she made him a co-executor of her will."

"Wasn't that shady?"

"Not particularly, in my view. And she didn't think so, either. People do things like that. She liked his spirit. She never did really lose any marbles at the end, you know. What was shady was his taste in the luxury goods he bought for himself with her money."

"Really?"

"Emma—a full array of rather cheesy gold rings and watches and diamond earrings. A gold clip that he wore on his pony-tail. . . ."

"A ponytail?"

"Oh, my, yes. Bernard was a flower child, you see. He learned how to tend orchids like her. He even dyed his hair to her shade, once. I understood him, because we were both the sons of Irish washerwomen—figuratively speaking, of course. And both of us had a gift, I think, for friendship with her."

"No jealousy between you and him?"

Ollie feigned horror.

"Hardly," he said. "We both knew I was out of his class, intellectually."

"Knew? He's gone?"

"Died three years after she did. Had his ashes scattered over the ocean at Shangri La, in the same place where we scattered *her* ashes."

"Poetic."

"Isn't it just?"

"Spiritual."

"That's nearer the mark—spiritual. And speaking of filling a void, she was attracted to Chandi ultimately because she thought the girl was the reincarnation of Arden."

"The daughter she lost."

"Her child with Duke Kahanamoku. Which could not be allowed to exist, after all, given the racial prejudice of the 1940s; which I think led her to some kind of induced miscarriage resulting from continued swimming and surfing; and which I think she felt terribly guilty about, always. In a way, with Chandi, I think she felt that she'd been given a second chance at motherhood, the one role she hadn't played yet—this rich lady in her seventies. . . ."

July 1990

It was the middle of a warm Hawaiian night, and everyone in the house had gone to bed hours before. In the most private of the house's sanctums, a darkened bedroom suite designed as if for a Moghul empress, a single flickering votive candle housed in a minaret-shaped brass lantern was illuminating a patch of white marble wall inlaid with red and green jasper in classical, scrolling iris and narcissus motifs. To one side, on a long, low divan, a naked woman lay on her side, half draped in sheer silk. She woke suddenly, though peacefully, from dreamless sleep; and now, as her eyes adjusted to the room's dim light, the sound of a tranquil ocean nudging in through delicate, lattice-screened arches, she wondered if this were a waking dream. Because standing there across the room, draped all in white, her silver hair loose and flowing, was a woman—an apparition?— her flesh pearlescent and her kind, gray eyes radiant, somehow enveloped in her own soft illumination.

"Do-do, Do-do . . ." sang the apparition breathily, in a warm whisper.

Hmm?

"Do-do . . ."

What?

"Yes—it's me. . . !" The whispered words were almost lilting, as if expressing delight.

"Barbara?"

"You've helped show me the way, dear friend . . ."

"What?"

How could this be?

Remaining in place, across from the divan, the apparition made a slow, almost maternal gesture that indicated *From my heart to you.*

"Across the river . . ." it said.

How could this be Barbara?

Doris propped herself up on one elbow and brushed a lock of hair out of her eyes. Diaphanous silk curtains ruffled silently in the open archways to the bedroom's ocean terrace.

"Am I asleep?" she said, to herself. Besides the calm swash of waves lapping on the breakwater below, the only sound in the room was the words Doris was speaking. The words of the apparition seemed to register not through the ears but, somehow, through some physical sensation of the body.

"Sooo much sleep, darling," murmured the apparition. "We're born that way. And then we awaken . . ."

Several spiritual disciplines could explain a phenomenon like this, thought Doris hazily. Some condition of physics or metaphysics or astral physics might well explain this apparent visit from a long-departed friend. She would have to consult Dr. Boehme about this. But couldn't it also be simply a dream? Or was it the result of ingesting some substance that had been mixed into that last cup of herbal tea, before bed? The empty cup and saucer were right there next to the lantern.

Could someone be . . . dosing me with something?

"What can I do?" said Doris, daring to address the glowing figure. "Can I . . . help in some way?"

Gentle waves, rhythmically surging.

"I will always remain with you, Dodo. Always."

Goodness.

Was this some paranormal faculty that Doris had in fact been developing up during the course of her spiritual explorations? Some talent or knack that had been quietly opening up within her etheric body?

"Do you . . . want anything?" said Doris.

Then there was a palpable pulse of silent contentment through the candlelit gloom.

"You are so beautiful," uttered the apparition. "You have always been so beautiful. . . ."

Doris's mind was clearing, even as she wished to stay in the moment. She had been warned by a longtime family attorney of the shoddy methods that "some well-placed persons" had been known to use within rich families, to consolidate their access to money and power; and she knew exactly whom the lawyer might be talking about. But *drugs*? How would that even work? Would drugs be meant to diminish her capacity, and somehow make her more dependent or suggestible? Still, if this vision, or apparition, or dream, or whatever it was, were the result of a drug, then that was certainly worth pondering . . .

And then the moment faded.

"I will always remain, dear Dodo—I will always remain . . ."

The echo of the voice sank away, and then the apparition—Barbara—was gone.

Doris sat up. What had happened? She was left only with the sound of the ocean. Something inside her suggested that she turn on a light, or even wake the house, or maybe even call a private detective—right then, in the middle of the night—to launch an investigation, beginning with the teacup. Yet something else suggested, *Just sit with it. Think about it. See how it feels . . .*

Doris decided that she would act, in her own way, but not immediately. It would be in her own time, soon.

But first, I must try to summon her back, from my end, she thought—*for I will always remain, too. Always.*

Two months later, Chandi decided to throw a party celebrating the relationship between her friend Paul Reubens, aka Pee-wee Herman, and Paul's boyfriend, Mark, who were renting a beachfront house owned by Doris's friend, actor and singer Jim Nabors, a few doors down from Shangri La. Chandi and Paul were "like brother and sister," people said—a bubbly pair of twins who shopped together in L.A. and New York and Honolulu, and gabbed together endlessly, and drank and danced and sang. Chandi wanted to do something nice for Paul, and the best place to do it, she thought, would be Shangri La, since she was living there with Doris at the time.

Party plans evolved excitedly into wedding plans, but as Chandi went about ordering masses of flowers and leis for the ceremony, the local press got wind that something big was going to take place at the Duke estate, and they began asking around. When they heard there was to be a wedding involving the famous TV star Pee-wee Herman, Paul panicked, at which point Chandi let it "slip" strategically that it was actually she and Paul who were getting married. Then Doris got involved and decided that a wedding with vows and gifts was not as modern and spiritually advanced as it should be to reflect the love that everybody in her rarefied circle should feel for everybody else—including not only Chandi and Paul, but Nabors and his partner, Stan; Joey Castro, who was still tangentially in the picture; Ollie Shaw, who was then visiting Shangri La to help Doris decide where to install an antique, carved marble *jali* screen she had bought; and, of course, Imelda Marcos, who'd been recently widowed and was spending lots of time with Doris. So Doris morphed the ceremony into a celebration of enduring, universal love that would culminate in a communal blessing of the bonds between the living and the departed, because she wanted the spirits of Arden and Barbara and President Ferdinand Marcos also to be included.

The ceremony would be for the *ohana*, family and dear friends—eight altogether, counting the *kahuna* and his assistant. Imelda and Jim would sing. Chandi would dance. Joey would formulate a special libation with premium, single-batch *rhum agricole* from an historic island distillery. And it would take place in Shangri La's most sanctified space, the *mihrab* room—a wide hall between the living room and dining room that featured a rare, thirteenth-century ceramic *mihrab*, or prayer niche, from an ancient Iranian tomb, that Doris had purchased and installed some years before. The *kahuna* who was to have performed the original wedding ceremony was perfectly happy to officiate at a universal love fest instead. He said that there were hundreds of traditional Hawaiian rituals and blessings to choose from, and assured Doris that he could put together something "healing" for whatever kind of gathering she was planning.

Even then, tensions were mounting between Doris and both Chandi and Imelda, whom Doris saw as hanging on to their respective relationships with her as an appurtenance to a lavish lifestyle. They'd all had some giddy fun among Honolulu's flower children and the Hollywood milieu of spiritualists and movie stars; in New York clubs like Studio 54 and on shopping sprees in Paris, London, Rome. . . . But Doris had long thought that these capers were a distraction from the serious matters of life that she wanted to stay focused on. Increasingly, she understood that she was far from being seen for herself by either Chandi or Imelda. She was growing tired of Chandi's increasing demands and her bossiness with household staff; she was growing resentful of Imelda's clinginess and constant expectation of extravagant favors. The situation with Chandi was particularly sticky, though—apart from the adoption, which Doris was certain she could have reversed or invalidated legally. The background was that shortly after meeting Chandi, Doris was told by one of her favorite psychics that the girl was the reincarnation of Arden. And a year or two after that, the same psychic affirmed, by way of her self-described prodigious powers of spiritual insight, that two people can be reincarnated in the *same* living person, and that Chandi "probably" embodied not only Arden but Barbara Hutton, too. Hence, despite the tensions, Doris's high hopes for the universal love fest.

It started calmly enough. The evening was warm and balmy. All the sliding doors and window panels of the house's main rooms were thrown open to the evening breezes. The ocean was serene, and the sound of the waves lapping the breakwater below the house was soothing. The house was darkened except for the light from scores of candle lanterns that had been placed in the living and dining rooms, in the *mihrab* room, and on the oceanfront lanai, off the dining room, where the ceremony was planned to conclude. From hidden speakers inside the walls of the house—via an extraordinary sound system that Doris had had installed, run from a small control room hidden off the main hall—came the strains of an ancient Hawaiian nose flute, which gave way to chanting accompanied by soft drums. Rum cocktails were served in the living room, and then everyone gathered in the *mihrab* room and took their places on silk pillows in a semicircle around the *kahuna,* who was seated directly in front of the sacred niche.

Consisting of numerous panels of molded cobalt- and turquoise-glazed lusterware set into the room's wall, the twelve-foot-high *mirhab* abounded magnificently with floral motifs, arabesques, and inscriptions from the Quran. Imelda was the only one who brought her gold-trimmed cocktail glass in with her from the living room. Everyone was splendidly dressed in flowing robes of saffron and lavender that Doris had hired a dressmaker to create especially for the occasion. A squad of six servants, also clad in specially made robes, theirs of saffron only, distributed plumeria leis to all the guests, and Doris herself, as host, presented one each to the *kahuna* and his assistant.

The recorded music was silenced, and after a moment, the *kahuna* began chanting in Hawaiian, while the assistant softly repeated the same words in English:

O ke au i kahuli wela ka honua
    At the time that turned the heat of the earth
O ke au i kahuli lole ka lani
    At the time when the heavens turned and changed
O ke au i kukaʻiaka ka la
    At the time when the light of the sun was subdued
E hoʻomalamalama i ka malama
    To cause light to break forth,
O ke au o Makaliʻi ka po
    At the time of the night of Makaliʻi
O ka walewale hoʻokumu honua ia
    Then began the slime which established the earth . . .

It was the first part of a traditional Hawaiian creation chant called the *Kumulipo,* translated, said the assistant, by Queen Liliʻuokalani herself. Doris and the *kahuna* had agreed that only the first part of the chant would be needed for the ceremony, since the *Kumulipo* is over two thousand lines long. And after that portion of the ceremony, the *kahuna* invoked the ancestors—everybody's ancestors—and then launched into a series of blessings of the individual bonds that Doris had requested: Paul and Mark, Doris and Chandi, Doris and Imelda, Chandi and Paul; Jim and Stan, Doris and Ollie, Imelda and Ferdinand, Doris and Arden, Doris and Barbara. Each blessing entailed chanting and the pouring of holy water over hands from a small ceremonial bowl. Joey was pointedly not included among the requested blessings, nor were the four servants remaining at the edge of the room, nor those in the dining room, who were preparing the buffet to be served after the ceremony.

It was all going beautifully, but when the guests moved to the lanai, with its sweeping views of the Pacific at dusk—for the part of the ceremony when the *kahuna* blessed the earth, and the sun, and the moon, and the stars, and everyone was served more cocktails and invited to offer their own personal blessings in the presence of the great Mother Ocean—Doris became upset. Almost everyone's blessing was short and humble, consisting of only a few words. Nabors blessed the doctors of the American Liver Foundation; Chandi blessed the tenderness and love of Lord Krishna; Paul blessed his pet goldfish with a quiet rendition of the made-up incantation from his television show, "Mecca-lecka-hi, mecca-hiney-ho." But Imelda, by contrast, now quite affected by the delicious rum cocktails, launched heartily into an extravagant panegyric to her recently deceased husband and the great Filipino people "out there on the other side of the broad Pacific." And as if addressing a stadium full of people, she charged into a chorus of "Lupang Hinirang," the Philippine national anthem. To judge from the strength of her full-throated soprano, her blessing was intended to reach across the ocean, all the way to Manila. But coming as it did directly before the quietly prayerful blessing that Doris was planning to offer for her dearest friend, Barbara, it was too much.

"I'm going for a walk," said Doris, suddenly, with a sharpness everyone felt. "Ollie, come with me?"

"Uh, certainly," said Ollie, surprised.

"I'll see you all in the dining room shortly," said Doris. "Ollie and I need some air."

As Doris and Ollie walked silently along the lanai to the lawn, past the stately row of slender Achaemenid-style columns that Doris had had shipped from Iran, Ollie noticed she was weeping. They made their way down to one of the two massive lava rock breakwaters created when Doris and Jimmy Cromwell built Shangri La's harbor basin in 1937, and then to the hewn-rock steps that descended into the ocean. The steps were dark and slippery.

"Careful," said Ollie, not sure if Doris was planning to immerse herself. It was not the most conducive place or time of day for ocean swimming.

"Don't worry," said Doris, steadying herself on Ollie's arm while she removed her silk slippers one at a time and stepped down onto the first submerged step. "I just needed to feel the ocean with my toes." She sniffed a few times and wiped away a tear with a manicured finger.

"I think Mrs. Marcos may have had one too many," offered Ollie.

"Is it me, or is that woman insane?" said Doris bitingly. It was an uncharacteristically nasty remark. "Or am I being uncharitable?"

"We did not need a national anthem at that point, no."

Doris exhaled stoutly.

"I know she just lost her husband—she's lost everything, probably," she said. "There's a huge legal mess, a political mess. But there are limits." She paused. "That ridiculous song! Like a nightclub singer, in the limelight. Just when I was feeling closest to Barbara, which really was the whole point of this ceremony for me."

"I know it was," said Ollie.

They stood there for a moment, facing the darkening ocean.

"Chandi's becoming untenable, too," said Doris.

"I know."

"I feel so . . . alone."

"Oh, Doris . . ."

"None of these people are 'til death do us part."

"Nope."

"Barbara was."

"She was."

Wafting faintly from speakers on the lanai and in the dining room was the sound of vintage bossa nova music, from Doris's extensive collection of records and tapes and, now, CDs. She'd been among the first to take up bossa nova when it appeared on American and European shores from Brazil. Easily she'd learned its subtle rhythm and could render it expertly both on the piano and in song. Every now and then, Ollie caught her humming a bit of "The Girl from Ipanema," which, of course, Doris would render as "The Boy from Ipanema"—"tall and tan and young and handsome. . . ." She'd even been persuaded, one night when they were at a club in Paris, to go onstage and sing the song with the band.

"You know, they had a nightclub in the palace—an actual nightclub, that they built," said Doris.

"The Marcoses?"

"Uh-huh. Malacañang Palace. Eighteenth-century, Spanish Colonial. She remodeled it extensively and put in a nightclub. They liked to invite people in for parties. They sang, both of them. The whole family does. The Filipinos are tremendous party people. Did you know there's a tea-dance in every big hotel in Manila, practically every day at cocktail hour? It's quite civilized, really."

"I've never been to Manila."

"We'll go sometime. It's a wonderful place. Sometimes she put me up in this extravagant guesthouse she built on the bay. The Coconut Palace—made of . . . well, can you guess?"

"Umm, coconut shells?"

Doris drew another deep breath and released it.

"Exactly," she said contemplatively. "But the Pope wouldn't stay there when he visited the Philippines, because it was too opulent, and she was miffed."

They were quiet for a while and stood listening to the sound of the waves.

"Barbara was a real friend," said Ollie. "You're not going to get another one like that."

"No, I won't," said Doris. "But you're my friend, too, darling. I think you see me, and I think I've earned the right to call you that."

"I do, and I am, Doris."

Doris shot him a soft look of tenderness.

"You can call me Dodo," she said.

Ollie laughed silently.

"Alright, Dodo."

The sky had gone almost black.

"Take your shoes off and get your feet in the water," she said playfully.

"Mmm—not now, thanks," said Ollie. "Maybe tomorrow."

PART 8

LEGACIES

CHAPTER 46

October 1991

As the '80s gave way to the '90s, Doris became frailer. A broken hip and two knee replacements reduced her mobility and ended, to her great dismay, her ability to dance and swim. She saw friends less frequently, yet she was still traveling often to Europe and Asia, as well as to and from Hawaii, and she was managing to stay in the picture socially, for events that she thought important enough and that she was assured would be easy to get in and out of, since she now often used a cane. Old friends would greet her enthusiastically, and strangers would thrill when they caught a glimpse of her, especially younger people, who welcomed the stylish lady of advanced years who showed up for the party.

"I think I'm finally getting used to this feeding frenzy," she whispered to Ollie, one evening in 1991, in New York, on the sidewalk outside the then-trendy supper club Tatou, as they arrived for a small, private dinner party to a gaggle of paparazzi and a coruscade of camera flashes. "It's only taken me, what, a hundred years?"

For a moment, she stopped to allow the head-to-toe shots the photographers wanted, with a bit of *grande dame* posturing in her gold lamé top and matching scarf, black-and-white leopard-print pants, emerald-and-diamond Moghul-style David Webb ear pendants, and golden slippers. Then, with a hand gesture that meant both "thank you" and "enough," she turned toward the door that was being held open for her.

Inside, she and Ollie greeted the guest of honor, Sophia Loren, whom Doris knew well from encounters in Hollywood, London, and Rome. The star was attired goddess-like in a gown of baroque fuchsia-pink-and-green swags and tucks, with quite a low neckline.

"You look marvelous," said Loren, as the two women bent in to exchange air kisses.

"Look who's talking," said Doris, warmly.

"Bernard must have helped you dress."

"Ha! How did you know?"

Loren gently fingered the edge of Doris's lamé scarf.

"He loves gold, that boy," she said, and they both laughed.

Hosted by an old friend of Doris's, film producer Franco Rossellini, the party was in honor of the Museum of Modern Art's thirtieth-anniversary showing of Vittorio De Sica's classic film *Two Women*, which Loren starred in. Doris and Ollie were seated at Loren and Rossellini's table, as were a distinguished-looking couple in their fifties, David, a white-haired oil company executive in black tie, and his wife, Beverly, a member of the Museum of Modern Art's board of directors, in a red Galanos evening suit. Dinner conversation was lively, centering on the best places around the world to swim, dive, and snorkel, then on the dangers facing the planet's coral reefs and oceans, then on the best hotels in Bali. And then plates with the remains of grilled quail were cleared, and Rossellini and Loren chatted with socialite Pat Buckley, who stopped by the table, while David offered Doris and Ollie his unrequested thoughts on current events.

"Russia is over," he stated gruffly.

"Russia is eternal, dear," said Beverly patiently. "It's the Soviet Union that's over."

Across the room, on a tiny stage, a piano-drum-and-bass trio was playing "My Unknown Someone" from *The Will Rogers Follies*.

"I guarantee you, total dissolution in Moscow by Christmas," said David. "Seventy-five years wasted. A social experiment failed. They can't do government. Never could. Never learned how."

"But surely it will be good for business, no?" said Ollie. "Privatization? Investors moving in?"

"We'll see. Maybe," said David. "Lots of risk, though. Lots of risk."

"Ollie, you were in Russia this year, weren't you?" said Beverly, attempting gently to steer her husband away from business talk.

"Yes, indeed."

"Ollie was a guest of the Hermitage," said Doris proudly.

"I saw your piece on the Malachite Room in *Nota Bene*," said Beverly.

"I was a guest of Mr. Gubenko, the Minister of Culture," said Ollie. "He was kind enough to show me around. I was also able to see—"

"They'll dissolve that ministry, you watch," interrupted David, with a raised finger.

"Yes, well, what I learned," said Ollie, "is that they are dissolving the Ministry of Culture of the USSR and reconstituting it the same day as the Ministry of Culture of the Russian Federation. So that's rather neat, don't you think?"

"Neat?!" squawked David.

"We want to go there in the spring," said Doris.

"They're planning to restore several sections of the Hermitage," said Ollie, "including the Imperial Theater. We want to learn more about it."

"Ahhh," said Beverly.

"It's exquisite," said Ollie. "Eighteenth-century. A chamber theater, really—only two-hundred-fifty seats. Hasn't been open to the public for decades."

"Quarenghi?"

"That's absolutely right—good for you!" said Ollie. "You know your St. Petersburg."

"We've been to Russia several times, over the years."

"Damned Russians!" mumbled David. "They missed the Renaissance, they missed the Reformation, they missed the Enlightenment. . . ."

"Some of the great visionaries and psychics have been Russian," said Doris.

"My point exactly," said David. "You can't have a nation of mystics."

"And the collection. . . !" said Beverly, still talking about the Hermitage.

"I know," said Ollie, groaning with pleasure. "I had never been face-to-face with *The Prodigal Son* before."

"Ah, the Rembrandt. . . !" said Beverly.

"We were walking through, alone, the museum was closed, and suddenly . . . there it was. I was stunned; I couldn't move," said Ollie.

Beverly gasped in delight.

"Nikolai was . . . that is, Minister Gubenko was more than understanding," continued Ollie. "He said he had seen this happen often before."

"Thrilling."

"And then you do move, and get closer to the picture, because you want to make sure you're seeing everything that's in it."

"Are you going to write about that?"

"I'll be writing about the theater restoration."

"They're forming an international committee, to help," said Doris. "Like with Venice."

"I want to know more about that," said Beverly.

Talk of Broadway shows bubbled up after waiters placed plates of double-chocolate terrine in front of them. Later, when there was drinking and dancing, Doris went to the ladies' lounge and found Loren there in front of one of the gold-framed mirrors, touching up her lipstick.

"I don't know how you do it, Sophia," said Doris. "You just don't age."

The star laughed modestly.

"I age all right, Doris," she said, "but I've learned how to cover up the telltale signs. For now."

Doris checked her makeup, too.

"Bernard reminded me that you won an Oscar for *Two Women*. What was it like to go up on that stage and accept?"

Loren shrugged comically.

"I wasn't there."

This surprised Doris.

"No? Why not? Were you ill?"

"Not at all. Honestly, I didn't think I had a chance. It was not an English-language film, remember, and I was up against four wonderful actresses, including Geraldine Page, for *Summer and Smoke*. That's who I thought would win. So I stayed in Rome."

"Well, when did you hear?"

"Carlo and I were awake all night, in case someone would call. Then, just as we were about to go to bed, Cary Grant called. It was six in the morning—when the ceremony in Los Angeles just ended. Wasn't that nice of him?"

"Did he really? That's marvelous."

"The marvelous thing was that we opened a bottle of champagne and drank it with breakfast."

Loren's charmingly Italian-accented English seemed to admit tiny inflections of British pronunciation.

"Here's to having made so many good films, including tonight's masterpiece," said Doris.

"Thank you very much," said Loren. "But you, Doris—you have so many masterpieces in your own life. Which one means the most to you?"

"That's a very good question. I've been thinking about that," said Doris, while trying to tame a few stray strands of wispy, dyed-blond hair. "I would say my house in Hawaii, which will one day be a public museum."

"I admire that. Such dedication," said Loren. "That's something I could never do."

"No, no. Your movies make people's lives so much richer, don't they? And they reach millions worldwide! I can only aim toward that kind of reach, with the resources I have—to help improve people's lives. Do you know what I mean?"

"I do. And I think you're very noble, like almost all of the people at this party."

"*Almost* all? You mean there's someone here who isn't noble?"

Loren giggled at the genially sarcastic remark.

"Green dress," she said unassumingly, eyes darting heavenward.

Doris flashed a knowing expression.

"Well, sure," she said. *"Her . . ."*

Within a year, Doris had pretty much closed the door to all but Ollie, two or three psychics, and a quorum of doctors. She curtailed her traveling and socializing, and allowed herself to be relocated more or less permanently to Los Angeles, under the increasingly devoted care of Bernard, who pointed out that Falcon's Lair was conveniently midway between her homes on the East Coast and her retreat in Hawaii. The arrangement also happened to suit the butler, who was completely at home among the dyed and facelifted denizens of Beverly Hills.

Ollie saw Doris twice during the week she died, at Falcon's Lair, in October of 1993. In the previous two decades, when visiting Doris in Los Angeles to consult on some renovation for the house, or shop for accessories or attend a dance performance with her, Ollie would be Doris's houseguest and be put in his favorite bedroom, with a tiny balcony facing a grove of cypress trees. This time, Doris said, Bernard thought it best that Ollie stay at a hotel, so she got him a suite at the Beverly Hills Hotel.

The eleven-bedroom main house was a Spanish-style villa of white stucco, with a red-tiled roof. Overlooking Benedict Canyon with views toward the city, it was built in 1923 by a developer and purchased in 1925 by Rudolf Valentino, who called it "Falcon Lair," after a lavish but never-finished costume epic that he had starred in the year before, *The Hooded Falcon*.

Situated on four hilltop acres, the estate comprised a guesthouse, a swimming pool and grotto-like pool pavilion, a classical Italian garden, exotically planted terraces, and a horse stable, in addition to the main house and garage. After Valentino, the estate went through several owners, including a group of women who wanted to turn it into a Valentino shrine. When Doris bought the place in 1953, after a visit there to Gloria Swanson, who was renting the place, she changed the name to "Falcon's Lair," which she thought sounded better. For Valentino, the estate had functioned as a refuge from his hordes of fans, because in the '20s, before that part of Los Angeles was very built up, the estate was relatively remote, and getting there meant a drive up a semi-rural road. During the '50s and '60s, though, when Doris was spending lots of time there among Hollywood folks, in the company of Joey Castro, Eddie Tirella, and other handsome young men, gated villas and mansions sprang up beneath and around Falcon's Lair, as did retaining walls for landscaped terraces; and by the time Doris spent her final years there, parts of the once semi-rural neighborhood had become practically as dense as a Brazilian *favela*. For her, during those years, the estate was a place to spend the early part of December, after jetting in from the East Coast on her private 737 and before jetting off to Shangri La for the holidays.

The first of Ollie's last two visits took place on a cloudless day, with a temperature in the comfortable low 80s. For the jaunt up Benedict Canyon Drive, Ollie had the top down on his rented, metallic blue Mitsubishi Eclipse. At the gate of the estate, he drove up to the intercom post and leaned over to press the keypad's CALL button.

"Good morning," came the tinny response.

The greeting was impersonal, though it sounded like Bernard, who was obviously expecting Ollie at that hour.

"It's Ollie Shaw, for Miss Duke."

There was no verbal response, only two quick beeps from the intercom and the sound of the gate unlocking and sliding open. Ollie entered the circular drive court and pulled around the fountain to park in a spot that he knew was reserved for guests. Bernard greeted him at the massive wooden front door.

"Good morning, Mr. Shaw."

"Good morning, Bernard. How are you today?"

"Well, thank you. And you?"

"Very well, thank you. Always nice for a New Yorker to get behind the wheel of a convertible."

Bernard was dressed in a white butler's jacket and gray flannel slacks. As he led the way across the hall and up the stairs, Ollie noticed that on Bernard's feet were what appeared to be a gentleman's evening pumps in black velvet—awfully fancy foot-wear for a butler, he thought with a chuckle. Bernard was also wearing a diamond stud in his right earlobe.

"How's our girl?" said Ollie.

"Better today, I think," said Bernard. "Breathing comfortably."

"That's good."

The original plan for Ollie's visit to Doris in Los Angeles this time had been for him to accompany her to visit some friends and attend an auction at Sotheby's Beverly Hills, but she had had an attack involving weakness and shortness of breath, and had been confined to her home by a doctor and put on new medications for her heart.

The house was quiet and much as Ollie had seen it last, a dramatic stage set in the classically opulent Old Hollywood style: Spanish-Italian Baroque Revival spruced up by the whimsical updates that Tony Duquette added shortly after Doris moved in—like a wall of polka-dot wallpaper that had since been re-covered with an expensive, custom-made paper of the same design—and some of the overscale Moderne pieces that Eddie Tirella had brought in.

Doris was installed in a chair in the sitting room of her bedroom suite, when Ollie entered.

"Dodorshka, darling," he said, approaching and kissing her lightly on the cheek. "Looking very glamorous, I see."

Doris angled her cheek to receive the kiss, smiling, and gestured toward the other chair. Over parrot-green silk pajamas, she was wearing a bed jacket of embroidered blue and gold silk, in a resplendent floral pattern.

"My Fragrant Oleander . . ." she said, using a nickname she sometimes used for Ollie.

"I'll bring lunch immediately, Miss Duke," said Bernard. "Mr. Shaw, is there anything I can get you right now?"

"Nothing, thank you."

The butler withdrew with a little bow.

"Awfully formal," said Ollie.

"Oh, yes," said Doris. "Terribly *comme il faut.* Even more so these days."

"Is it just him now?"

"Heavens, no. We've still got a cook, two maids, and a gardener down there. Same as always."

"But the house seems so quiet."

"He insists on that. I'm supposed to have peace."

She sniggered as she smoothed the hem of the bed jacket.

"So here we are again, kiddo," she said. "Only no trip to Sotheby's this time. I'm not getting around too well just now."

"He told me. How are you doing?"

"I'll be fine. But it's such an ordeal to move me, so he thought it would be better if I were discovered here like this, sitting in place, like a character in a play when the curtain goes up."

She made a florid gesture with one arm.

"Ha!" said Ollie. "Well, you make being discovered in place as dramatic as a grand entrance."

He was trying to stay bright for Doris, but privately, he was shocked to find her so clearly immobile. Her hair, though now quite thin, was neatly arranged in the plain way that she liked, though; her makeup was neat, if a tad too dramatic for a lunch date. He wanted to ask more pointedly how she was doing—how she felt, what the doctors were telling her, how Bernard was treating her—but outwardly, there was no cause for alarm, and he didn't want her to think that he was alarmed, in case *that* would alarm her. So his plan for the visit was to be as agreeable as possible, and as interested as she was in anything she might bring up. And he had a few anodyne subjects ready, should he need temporarily to take the lead in conversation: the pleasure of driving a convertible, the beauty of the mass of viburnum in the house's forecourt, the progress being made on the newest Newport restoration project.

They chatted about a young jazz pianist whom Doris helped support, whose Sunset Boulevard club gig Doris was missing, owing to her bad health; about Toni Morrison's historical novel *Jazz,* which Doris adored, and the author's recent Nobel Prize win; and the photographs of James Van Der Zee, which Doris also adored. . . . The French doors to the balcony were open, and beyond them, Ollie could see all the way to the towers of hazy downtown Los Angeles. He could remember so many of the parties that had taken place in that house, full of Hollywood stars and other creative people that Doris liked to mix with; so many times when he helped her select something to wear in that very room—a long dress, an oriental robe, a sari, a piece of jewelry, even one of the Tony Duquette trinkets she'd acquired, which she made a point of wearing when the designer and his wife were among the guests. He would have liked to reminisce about any of this, but would do so only if she seemed to want to. Maybe others would find it odd, his hesitation, he thought. Surely a good friend should have the instinct to know what to say and how to gauge a response. Yet at this stage of their friendship, even though he'd known Doris for decades, he still had a sense of the boundaries involved—his as well as hers—that he didn't want to risk trespassing beyond.

Or was the instinct here simply good manners? Doris was weak; lunch had to be an effort for her.

Bernard brought in a tray of tiny sandwiches—tea sandwiches, really, served on a tiered serving stand, as at afternoon tea. Following him was a maid with a tray of tea, water, and Diet Coke. Lunch was set up and served, and then Doris and Ollie were alone again.

"My diet is so restricted," she said. "I can't have much salt. He sees to that."

That was Ollie's cue.

"So Bernard is taking good care of you?"

"He's capable, and I find him very dear."

"That's good to hear."

"What, did you think he was holding me hostage or something?"

"No, no . . ."

"He's got his foibles, of course. I mean, the man's illiterate. Can't make heads or tails out of Islamic art, or any art, really.

He wears makeup. He drinks—I suppose you know that—but somehow the drinking always makes him nicer. I know that sounds odd. Lord knows, Ollie, we've both known some nasty drunks, haven't we?"

"He-he."

"With Bernard—he becomes like a sweet little schoolboy, and at the same time almost motherly."

"Oh, my."

"He doesn't know me as you do. We can't really talk about the things that interest me. And Ollie, this lack of conversation is almost as painful to me as not being able to dance." She took a slow breath. "But that's the way things are now."

The sitting room was decorated in an antique Persian style, with a tucked fabric wall treatment in an elaborate blue-green-and-white floral pattern and a tented ceiling in blue-and-white stripes. On the walls were a series of early twentieth-century sepia photographs of Persian cities, mounted in delicate silver frames.

"Are you able to exercise at all?" said Ollie.

Doris snorted.

"I *am* exercised," she said. "On a table. By a very nice man in a white tank top—Mike. That's about as good as it gets. The thing that Bernard is really good at is keeping away the people I don't want to see. And there are lots of 'em, these days. They all want my money. I told you I made a new will, didn't I?"

"You told me you were thinking about it."

"I made Bernard co-executor."

"Oh."

"And don't look at me that way. I know exactly what I'm doing."

"So Chandi . . ."

"She's out. Gone. I'm sure there will be some squabbling after I'm dead. She'll probably sue the estate." Doris cackled. "Now she'll have to deal with *him*, to get any kind of settlement."

Each tea sandwich was small enough to be consumed in exactly two bites. Doris had eaten one-and-a-half of them. Ollie did notice that the sandwiches, though good in every other way—pretty to look at, composed of lovely fresh ingredients—were decidedly unsalty.

"She's in India, running a public health charity," continued Doris. "I suppose I am at least proud of that. She was probably no more trouble than any daughter would have been." She glanced toward the open window. "I sometimes wonder what her office is like, what she wears to work—whether it's those hippie peasant things she likes or a proper suit, like an executive should wear. . . ."

For much of their conversation, Doris seemed both sharp and hazy at the same time. She was certainly able to remember things, and never seemed less than focused in the present moment. She was decisive, even, yet there were times when some other focus—the past? the possible future?—seemed to be beckoning her.

Taking off from her musing about Chandi's work attire, she told a story of visiting a Fifth Avenue department store after World War II, with her friend Pansy, who was also director of the first formal organization that Doris set up and funded to do charitable work, Independent Aid. Doris was looking for a suit to wear to a meeting at the organization's office—"the kind of suit that any American working woman of the era might wear," not something from the salons of Paris couturiers where Doris usually shopped. The saleswoman who sold Doris a suit that day impressed her. "Nancy was her name," recounted Doris—and Ollie was surprised that she could remember the name of a saleswoman who had helped her forty-five years before. For Doris, Nancy embodied the new generation of American women who were benefitting from postwar society's more liberal attitudes—women who could work and earn their own money and think for themselves, who were expecting, as they looked forward to the 1950s and '60s, to change society and business and even family life for the better. Nancy also sold Doris a simple gold circle pin that day, to accessorize the suit "appropriately," somehow knowing that Doris, for *that* suit and *that* meeting, would not be inclined to reach into her safe and pull out a flashy Cartier treasure to pin on her sober lapel. Doris was impressed by Nancy's selection of that pin for her and had thought, If this woman has such insight into me and into how modern American women are dressing today, then she is someone whom Pansy and I should be hiring for Independent Aid.

Doris offered Nancy a job on the spot, and Nancy was grateful but had to decline. She said that her father, in whose Brooklyn house she lived, was moving the whole family upstate, in pursuit of better business prospects for *him*—though Nancy said with some pride that at the department store, she was already earning more than what her father was making as a plumbing contractor. It was sad, Doris said, and often since then, she had regretted not proposing to find an apartment for Nancy, to sweeten the job offer. Yet she had respect for the young woman's decision, and did see how a dutiful child, no matter how modern, might feel compelled to comply with a father's wishes.

"Once though, during the seventies," said Doris, "I was thinking about Nancy again and actually hired a private detective to go poking around in Brooklyn and upstate, to see if we could find her. I was curious about what happened to her—maybe I could help with whatever she was doing."

"And?" said Ollie.

"We couldn't find her. She must not have stayed in fashion. I never got her last name."

"Oh, too bad. It wasn't on the, uh, bill?"

Doris made a smiley frown.

"I have to say that I wouldn't have checked the bill for that particular purchase, since the amount was so small."

"Too bad."

"So nothing came of the whole thing."

After lunch with Doris, on the breezy drive back to Beverly Hills, past lushly landscaped mansion after lushly landscape mansion, Ollie couldn't help comparing Doris's situation with that in which they found Barbara during her last days. Then it dawned on him that any comparison of medical crises and mental states and financial situations was beside the point. By far the dominant issue here was the sadness that both women—all women, all men—have a limited time on earth and never enough opportunity to make the most of it. There is always the pressure to find and take advantage of more opportunity.

Well, I am sad about my dear friend, thought Ollie as he drove, *and perhaps, by extension, myself, since one day I, too, will be eighty, but today the weather is glorious, the damn top is down, and I'm glad I took the Eclipse instead of the duddy BMW sedan they first suggested to me.*

Ollie also decided, after the visit, to extend his stay in Los Angeles, at his own expense, since when he was leaving the house, Bernard confided quietly that "despite appearances, things could really be serious this time."

In bed that night, at the Beverly Hills Hotel, after consuming a room-service cheeseburger with a carafe of martinis, Ollie had strange dreams in which he was visiting Doris in a new residence she'd moved into, on a vast, sprawling, undivided floor of an old warehouse building that had been fashionably repurposed, which others occupied, too, in their own little areas separated by empty space. The floor was a vista of these scattered, little indoor encampments. Doris, like the others, had some of her possessions around her, including an antique Moorish divan and a marquetry chest whose inlays contained bits of mirror, and, on top of the chest, a framed Roman micromosaic on a small easel and an antique burl wood box containing jewelry. But with no walls or doors except on the floor's perimeter, these precious possessions were alarmingly exposed and unprotected—yet in the dream, it was Ollie, not Doris, who was worried about security. Doris, for her part, was happy with her modern, new living arrangement and unconcerned that strangers were walking around freely, throughout the space. It was an unnerving dream that Ollie fell back into after rising from the bed for a moment, blearily, to go to the hotel room door and make sure the safety latch was engaged.

CHAPTER 47

November 1948

Prescottville's Starlight Lounge wasn't the Rainbow Room, but someone had made an effort. Physically, it was just an ordinary storefront space on Center Street, on a block shared with a hardware store, a shoe store, and a furniture store; in a two-story building whose second-floor apartment, entered by a rickety wooden staircase from a parking lot in back, was rented by a schoolteacher. But inside the Lounge, a moody darkness was bedizened with swags of Christmas lights above the bar and, along the walls, an aurora of blues and purples glowing from behind a black plywood soffit pierced with the shapes of comets and stars. Early on a weekday evening, when Nancy entered alone, looking sensational in a tailored black-and cream houndstooth suit from her alma mater, Best & Co., the place was practically empty and as quiet as a church.

She installed herself in a booth and was checking her makeup in her compact's mirror when the Andrews Sisters' "Toolie Oolie Doolie" started up the jukebox. Donald Mancuso appeared just as she was tucking away the compact.

"Hi there. Where are your friends?"

"Oh, hi. It's just me and Delores tonight. And she's late!"

"I see."

"No waitress?"

"Her shift starts at seven. What can I get for you?"

"How about a gin rickey?"

"Shall I bring two? Wouldn't Delores like it if she found one waiting for her when she arrives?"

"I suppose so, yeah. Thank you."

Nancy was still alone when Donald arrived with the drinks on a small cork-lined serving tray.

"I'll make a fresh one if she's late," he said, setting the drinks on the table. "On the house."

"That girl!" said Nancy.

"Listen, uh, I see they're holding *Sorry, Wrong Number* over at the Shadowland. Have you seen it?"

"No, not yet. You know how it is—one thing or another."

"I know. So would you . . . wanna catch it some night—I mean, with me? I hear Barbara Stanwyck's pretty good."

"I hear that, too."

"So what do you think?"

This wasn't exactly what Nancy would have thought was in the cards for her, but she did flash on the thought, *What would women like Doris Duke or Barbara Hutton do in this situation?* And she knew that they would do exactly what they wanted to do.

"Okay, sure," said Nancy. "Later this week?"

Donald flashed a smile.

"How about Friday? The early show?"

"Sounds good."

When Delores arrived and slid into the booth moments later, she was glad to find her gin rickey all ready for her.

"Why are you so smiley?" she asked Nancy.

Nancy cocked her head.

"Because I am doing something that a wise woman once told me to do. Make the most of what you've got."

October 1993

After his lunch with Doris at Falcon's Lair, Ollie was content to remain in Los Angeles more or less on call for her, uncertain as to whether she would want, or be able, to pick up on some of their plans. Then Ollie got a call from a distressed-sounding Bernard.

"I think you should come and see Doris."

"Oh, no."

"It's not for me to say, but you might consider saying good-bye."

Doris was in terrible shape when Ollie found her, in bed—weaker, vaguer. A doctor and nurse were with her, and they and Bernard left the room when Ollie arrived, so he and Doris could be alone.

Ollie had decided not to say goodbye, under any circumstances. It felt too final, expressing a kind of hopelessness that Doris would never approve of. Yet this time, she was fatalistic.

"This might be it, Ollie."

Her voice was barely supported by any breath.

"You always surprise us, Doris."

"Do I?"

"Always."

"I'm afraid I must *look* surprising."

She had been neatly arranged in bed, and her nightgown and bedclothes were impeccable, but she wasn't wearing any makeup and did look old and emaciated. Her hair, though tidy, was lifeless.

"The glow is still there, baby."

She mustered a breath that would have been a chuckle, if she had had more strength.

"I know I was never particularly beautiful, so losing my looks isn't the tragedy that it was for Babbo. For so long, she was as pretty as a doll. Wasn't she?"

"She sure was."

"For me, the tragedy was losing the ability to dance. I think it's killing me. I didn't think it could ever happen. I always knew older dancers who were in better shape than the rest of us. Even when they walked, there was energy."

Ollie was holding her hand, sitting in a bedside chair that he had pulled close. Her eyes were half-closed.

"Once, at a garden party—we were very young—" said Doris softly, "I saw Babbo walking across the terrace—such an elegant stride, in white satin pumps, mind you; a long skirt flowing behind her, her face glowing in that late-afternoon sunlight. . . . It was the energy of a performance. Energy and lyricism. This was before all the maladies. She could have been a dancer. I tried to get her to come to dance classes with me. Several times. But she would just make that face—you know . . ."

Weakly, Doris mimicked Barbara's faint grin of disapproval. Ollie nodded, quietly containing the sad joy of seeing Doris marshal a tiny flash of wit.

"That was Babbo," whispered Doris.

She rested for a moment, then took as deep a breath as she could.

"Ollie, I'm sorry about that time in the garden . . ."

Surprised, Ollie shook his head slowly.

"Ohhh, now . . ." he moaned.

"No, no," said Doris. "I'm really sorry. It was just my . . . energy. And—well, sometimes it's not the time and place for that, is it?"

"You've always meant the world to me—always, Doris. Remember, I know the real you. I know that part of you is dancing right now, under the covers."

"Ha."

She could barely move her head or arms.

They spoke a bit more about dance, about some new plantings she was thinking about for Shangri La; then she went silent. She looked sleepy. Ollie knew well that a visit with someone under circumstances like this is not usually about extended conversation, so he said he thought he would run along and let her rest. She nodded okay.

"Can I come back tomorrow?"

At first, she didn't answer. Then she said, "You never named your grant, did you?"

It took Ollie a second to realize she must be speaking about the Zürich fund.

"As a matter of fact, no," he said, mildly stunned that she was thinking about this.

"Why not?"

"I don't know."

"May I make a suggestion? Only a suggestion."

"Of course."

She pointed to the dresser near the bed, on top of which were standing some framed photographs, among which was a framed, handwritten poem. The paper, which looked like a page torn neatly from a notebook, was yellow with age, its handwriting spidery, careful and graceful, in dark blue ink.

"Sometimes, a line from a poem can suggest a good name," said Doris.

Ollie picked up the poem and read it.

Appeal

Show your face to me
And guide the way across
The river great and wide,
Dear friend;
Your words are always
Clear and strong,
And tamp the doubt
That rattles in my soul.

Flows fast the river
And deep, which drowns weak souls.
My fear is great,
And skills alone,
I know, can fail me.

Won't you smile and speak
Then, from that far shore,
And show the way—
And more, the faith
That any way there exists. . . ?

"Is that . . . one of hers?" said Ollie, as he gently placed the poem back in its spot on the dresser.

Doris nodded yes.

"It's just a thought," she whispered. "I'm worried that there's nothing left with her imprint. And you loved her, too."

Ollie understood and looked pleased.

"It's a wonderful idea," he said.

Doris raised an arm and gestured toward the dresser.

"Take it," she said. "If Bernard says anything, tell him I gave it to you."

Did I love Barbara? Do I love dear Doris? Was it really love with either of them? Did they love me—or was it something else?

He and Doris had said "see you soon!" and shared the same casual kind of goodbye kiss that they always did, but when Ollie left Falcon's Lair, he was fairly certain that he'd seen Doris for the last time. And he became aware as he drove back to the hotel that the sadness he was feeling was laced not only with regret but with disappointment, too, in surmising that he wouldn't be with Doris at the very end. Bernard would be. Presumably, if Doris had wanted things any different, she would have said something.

I mean, I would have been happy to be there, but . . . does companionship have a different end, or leave a different residue, from love?

Yet, sure—it was a kind of love, with both of them, wasn't it . . . ?

Doris had given Ollie many gifts over the years, but control of the Zürich account was more than a gift. It was a sacred responsibility, and he cherished her thinking him worthy of such a thing much more than he did any artwork she ever gave him. It was one of the many secret bank accounts that Buck Duke set up around the time his daughter was born, she said—"secret" meaning that even the men in the Duke business and legal offices didn't know details about them. These were assets that for different reasons would not even pass through Doris's will—including Ollie's account, which was now under his ownership exclusively. When she passed control to him, on that day in Zürich, she told him only to do good things with it. "Sometimes we can make our money behave more like nice people than we ourselves can do personally," she said. For Ollie, this was a gift just as fine as love. And Ollie had taken this guidance to heart, in his own way; and in the years since 1969, with a series of as yet unnamed grants, he had given away hundreds of thousands of dollars anonymously to progressive social and cultural causes, including many focused on LGBTQ issues. To be able to do all that, and still to be doing it now, with Mrs. Welland's quiet assistance, helped him feel—much more than did his stellar reputation as a writer and intellectual—that he was not a complete washout as a human being.

On the twenty-eighth, a few hours before Ollie was due to drive up to Falcon's Lair for another visit, Bernard reached him by phone and gravely announced that Doris had died.

"It was a stroke."

"The dear girl," said Ollie.

"There was no one like her," said the butler, who was sounding quite emotional.

"I'm sorry for your loss, Bernard. I know you were devoted."

"Thank you for saying that, Mr. Shaw. I'm so sorry for yours. I know you were great friends. We've lost a great lady."

"Is there anything I can do?"

"She left very clear instructions," said Bernard, recomposing himself. "Cremation, as soon as possible. The ashes to be scattered over the ocean at Shangri La. We'll have a small memorial service sometime in New York, probably after the holidays. Very private, though she did make it a point to include you."

"That's . . . so nice."

Now Ollie was feeling overcome, finding it a little difficult to speak.

"Well, just let me know," he said feebly.

"Will you be staying in Los Angeles very long?" asked Bernard.

It took Ollie a moment to process a response.

"No, I suppose not," he said. "Unless, again, I can help with anything."

"Thank you, but I've got it all under control, carrying out her wishes. If I may, I'll be in touch soon with further details."

"Very well, Bernard. Thank you for calling. Stay strong."

"You too, Mr. Shaw."

CHAPTER 48

In the months that followed Doris's death, it pained Ollie to hear reports of squabbling over the estate. There were family members who felt short-shrifted. There was Chandi, who did indeed sue the estate. There were questions about Bernard's both co-executing the will and being named in it. Eventually Bernard was removed as co-executor. A few years after that, he died in his sleep of a heart attack, in a three-point-five-million-dollar Bel Air mansion that he bought with the five million that Doris left him. To Ollie, Doris had left a seventeenth-century Safavid ceramic floor panel that he had helped her purchase. Consisting of forty-eight separate tiles and designed like a carpet, with a border and a central field decorated in tree and flower motifs, the thing was meant for the floor of a courtyard or great hall of a palace. Ollie had seen it assembled only once, at the auction house, and Doris had never installed it anywhere. Obviously, it could not be installed as designed in Ollie's tiny East 77th Street apartment. When it arrived there, disassembled, in two great crates, Ollie rearranged his foyer to make room for it, the unopened crates now an imposing sculptural element as haunting as a wrapped monument by Christo and Jeanne-Claude.

Maybe someday I'll have a grand house where I can show it, he thought, with the gently sarcastic humor of a confirmed apartment-dweller.

Ollie was still going out a fair bit at this time, and didn't mind going out alone, though there were always bright young editors of several genders ready to tag along with him to some event—people whose enthusiasm and curiosity he identified with. Without Doris, though, his social position didn't feel the same with some of the grandees they used to see together. When he was out alone or with a young editor, the less enthusiastic and curious of the grandees—who for this reason were certainly not among Doris's favorite people—seemed to hold Ollie somehow less essential now to that wedding they were planning for their daughter in Provence, or that group skiing trip to Patagonia they were organizing for July. Whereas previously he'd have been included in the invitation, quite apart from all the erudition that he normally expected to be valued for. These were the same people, he sometimes observed to a young editor, who were happy to tell you something about an artwork of theirs, but didn't necessarily want you to tell them anything more about it unless they asked—"and they ask far less often than you'd think."

An exception was Selwyn Stanfield, a man whom Ollie knew had two or three billion dollars but was always eager to hear more about his possessions—like the cheerfully evil Philip Guston, or the lyrical Cy Twombly drawings, or the noble bronze head by Maillol—all of which Ollie sometimes saw at parties at the West 9th Street townhouse where Selwyn lived with Mary-Ann Dessault, who was now his wife. Selwyn had sent Ollie a nice note of condolence after Doris died, and the two stayed in touch. When Selwyn and MaryAnn hosted their "Thanksgiving in town" get-togethers, Ollie was often invited. It was at one of these festive get-togethers that MaryAnn, who now owned a big gallery of her own in Chelsea, was lining up donors for a new arts center devoted to multimedia and performance work that she was involved in. She asked Ollie to consider joining the center's board.

"It sounds like a terrific project . . ." he began tentatively.

"We're looking for lead donors," she said.

"A million or more, I understand."

"Yes, that's right."

They were standing in one corner of the very crowded dining

room, which also featured the buffet. Ollie had heard all about the arts center and knew that MaryAnn was raising money for it, but he was surprised to be asked, himself, to participate at the level she was suggesting, even if he knew that people sometimes assumed he was rich. Selwyn, who was standing with them, knew better, and in fact rather suspected that writers like Ollie who may appear to live well do so on a limited budget.

"MaryAnn," said Selwyn, "Ollie's got so much to bring to your project in other ways."

"Well, of course," said MaryAnn, "but I had to put it out there. And Ollie knows so many fabulous friends of the arts. . . ."

With a coy smile, she brushed a bit of hair behind her ear, conveniently making a display of the enormous diamond ring she was wearing on her finger.

"Quite so," said Ollie graciously. "And I'd love to know more. Sorry I'm not in a position myself to join your board."

"Well, the publicist will keep you in the loop," she said, suddenly excusing herself after spotting a newly arrived guest who probably did have a million or two to spare.

"Sorry about that," said Selwyn.

"It's the suit," said Ollie, self-mockingly slipping a finger under the lapel of his custom-made Sandro Trapani jacket. "But it does sound like a great project."

"She's the cutting-edge art lover in the family. I'm more twentieth-century and older."

"The classics," said Ollie. "But I will take a closer look at the project. If I can help with some ink, or in some other way, I'll consider it seriously."

Several weeks later, Ollie and Selwyn were having a glass of prosecco at Bottino after an afternoon art walk around Chelsea. They discussed the artist MaryAnn was showing at the time, a young painter named Langley who depicted mounds of whipped cream in immense, white-on-white canvases, and then Selwyn mentioned that plans for his wife's arts center project were progressing well.

"Are they? That's great," said Ollie.

"People are beginning to hear about it."

"Yes, I imagine so. A place for performance art, installation art . . . it's a great idea—something the city needs."

"Out of nowhere, they received a donation from one foundation that no one had ever heard of. A hundred thousand dollars."

"I guess fundraising isn't as difficult as everybody says."

"It was a foundation with a strange name."

"Is that so?"

"Something like 'Show Me the Money.'"

"Oh, my—that can't be right."

"Something like that."

"That *is* odd . . ."

When Ollie arrived at Emma's place for a meeting they'd scheduled about language for the film's credits and acknowledgments, he could see from the moment they sat down that she was upset. Instead of the usual intrepid calm, there was a jittery quality he hadn't seen before in her.

"You seem . . . well, how are you?" he said.

"Ollie, how do you think I am?"

"I'm not sure I ever . . ."

"I'm spending money that I don't have!" she said emphatically, then made an effort to calm herself. "I sit here with an editor, racking up bills I don't know how to pay. Sometimes I lose track of the story I'm trying to tell. I keep going, because I have to finish this thing, but I don't even know why, anymore."

"Kelly's got some festival dates lined up, doesn't she?"

"She does, and that's great. I just . . . can't see myself *there* yet."

"So it's the money?"

"That's a big part of it. I don't want to go back to my mother. I don't want to take money from Robert. I don't want to take *anything* from Robert. Your dear Dodo and Babbo sure didn't take any crap from men."

"No, they didn't."

"Maxing out a credit card makes me feel like a drug addict. I don't want to take one of these pictures off the wall and sell it. Well, I couldn't do that anyway, since they're not mine. But do you see? I am thinking demented things like that, and I feel like some kind of . . . loser."

Ollie listened as Emma vented, about her frustration with money and production and distribution issues, and he resisted the urge to jump in with any advice or guidance, until she explicitly asked for it. And then she did ask.

"So let me share a thought," he responded.

"Please do," said Emma, exhaustedly.

"I believe the issues you're describing are solvable."

"But where do I . . ."

Ollie made a kindly gesture that was meant to be calming.

"Except, for the moment, the money—I understand," he said. "So I want to suggest that since there are a few channels lining up for exhibition or distribution, your job is to stay focused. *Be a little bit in denial about the damned costs. Denial can be so helpful here*—for a month or two, then see where you are. Find some faith that in the conversations you're having with people who are interested in the film, financial opportunities will present themselves—because your work is good, and *that* inspires people."

"You're telling me to hang in there?"

"I am, yeah, basically."

Emma sighed.

"Okay," she said.

"Also," continued Ollie, "I don't necessarily want to medicalize your crisis, but darling, you've just been through a cancer episode, and your body is undoubtedly still speaking to you about that experience, on several levels. Cancer is not something that you simply go through and get over. This is part of you now—the experience, not the cancer—and it's vast. You keep processing it as you move forward, and it becomes part of your life and work. In fact, your life and work are your triumph over the *fears* around the disease, if you will. You may already get all this, and if so, I'm sorry. I don't mean to bore you. But that is what I think I am hearing right now, as we're talking: a little film, a little cancer."

Emma was shaking her head and trying to keep from weeping. She was relieved to have her feelings out in the open, and grateful for Ollie's being there to listen to her.

"Sometimes, it's all too much," she said, with a sniffle. "You know?"

"I know," said Ollie. "But if I may say so, life itself is always too much, for everyone, and we are always in a state of wrestling with it. It's when we are oblivious to mortality and fragility and contingency that we really go numb and start sliding toward the grave."

"I guess so."

"I just think that the key is always to be telling the people close to you exactly what you're going through, and accepting the witness of it that they offer, along with any other thoughts they may have."

"Witness."

"It's key, I think."

Emma snickered.

"You know, I think, in a funny way, that's what's keeping Robert and me together longer than we should have been," she said, "the witness part of our relationship. Coming in and having someone to complain to about a subway delay."

"Some people, that's all they have. It's not shabby."

"Also, I was thinking, Ollie. When I was younger, I never really defined myself by my looks, the way other girls did. Mommy and Daddy both found that extremely superficial, and it rubbed off on me. But recently, sometimes I find myself looking in the mirror, or I catch a reflection of myself in some store window, and I think two thoughts, which are linked: one, *I've never looked better*, and two, *I'm never going to look this good again*. You know? I've never particularly wanted kids, so I really haven't been thinking in terms of reproductive shelf-life. But here I am, suddenly thinking about my attractiveness shelf-life."

"Mmm."

"So let's say I cut and run with Robert. What kind of shape am I in for my next go, if I want one?"

"Aging never stopped Doris and Barbara from having another go."

"No, but they had a million dollars in each fist, didn't they?" said Emma.

Laughter, and then Ollie grew pensive.

"It takes the time it takes for a person to know that she is sufficient," he said. "It often happens at a certain age, *n'est-ce pas?*"

It occurred to both of them that there might be a lot more to say about all this, but they were happy to step away from it at the moment and return to talking about the film.

"I still wish we had a piece, even a small piece," said Emma, "some *bauble* that explicitly told the kind of story that I realize now I've been looking for—a story that embodies all the issues we're talking about. Not just design, value, context, but sentiment, emotional meaning—something we see on the screen . . ."

"But aren't you almost finished with the editing?"

"I am, but for the right piece, I would shoot a few more minutes and cut it in, to express the right frame for the whole project."

"Let's see what happens. I think it's great right now, actually."

Emma looked fondly at her friend.

"You've been such a support, Ollie," she said. "I hope you know how much I appreciate it."

"*You* appreciate it? I've gotten much more out of this project than I ever expected. I mean, I have always known that jewelry was interesting, but in working with you, I have come to see much deeper into my own interest in those issues you're always talking about—power and personal expression and all that. In a way, what was once just an interest is now an actual sweet spot. That's quite a gift."

"You're welcome," Emma said, brightening.

"You know, Doris always used to say that when you're a teenager and become sexually active, there are, say, four things that you like to do in bed, and you keep pursuing those four things as you get out there in the world. And that's great, because most people only have one or two things they're interested in sexually, and they pursue those, God bless them. But even when you have four things, someone may suddenly try a fifth thing on you one day, and your first reaction may be 'Hey, wait a minute,' until you realize, 'Wow, I really like this,' and you're clobbered! Then you include that fifth thing among the things you're always looking for, and eventually it dawns on you, 'Hey, if this great fifth thing was out there and I didn't know about it, then what else is out there that I might also like—a sixth thing? A seventh thing? A tenth thing?' And that's when you start kind of going beyond your awareness and become hungry for *more* awareness, as much as possible."

"Yeah."

"Your film has kind of done that for me. And now, at the age of a hundred and two, I find that exciting."

"We should be looking for new things to clobber us, at any age."

"The eternal pursuit of clobberation."

CHAPTER 49

"Doris gave her a pin?"

"A circle pin. Very plain, considering."

"Just took it off her chest and pinned it on your sister?"

"Just like that."

Ollie and Mrs. Welland were chatting again, in his apartment, about that day long ago on an upstate mountaintop when two great ladies appeared at the family home of Mrs. Welland and her sister, Maggie, then young girls—one lady whom Mrs. Welland now knew was Barbara Hutton, who had arrived by limousine with a young Oliver Wendell Shaw; the other lady, Doris Duke, who dropped in by helicopter and dramatically stole Ollie away in it. Until now, Mrs. Welland hadn't mentioned this important detail—that upon hearing Maggie's distress about being dressed identically with her older sister, Doris swapped the three-strand gold circle pin she happened to be wearing for the plainer one that the girl was wearing.

"Maggie could be very persuasive," said Mrs. Welland. "And needless to say, we were both perfectly adorable little girls."

"I'm sure of that," said Ollie. "Does your sister still have the pin?"

"She died a few years ago and left it to me. Dear Maggie—I miss her so. And wouldn't you know it? She left our grandmother's Tiffany diamond ring to my niece Claire, who was . . ."

"Wait a minute. You mean you have the pin, the one that

Doris Duke gave your sister on the day I was there, on the day when we were all there. . . ?"

"Yes, I do."

Ollie widened his eyes, opened his mouth, and pointed dramatically toward his foyer and front door.

"Eh bien, ma chère, montrez-le-moi instantanément, s'il vous plait!"

Without a word, Mrs. Welland rose, left the apartment, and returned a few minutes later with a small jewelry box and a photo album. From the box, she took the pin and gave it to Ollie—three intertwined strands of eighteen-karat gold, stamped on the back with TRABERT & HOEFFER and REFLEC-TION. It was a sweet little thing, modest but elegant.

"Wow," he said.

"I don't know anything about it, except that Trabert and Hoeffer is a Chicago firm, still in business, and Reflection, I suppose, was their line of jewelry, or one of their lines."

"Fascinating," said Ollie, carefully inspecting all aspects of the piece. "And so different from the kind of thing Doris usually collected."

"She liked exotic things, didn't she?"

"Oh, wildly exotic. And she commissioned great jewelers—Cartier, Webb—to make fabulous things for her. This one is so absolutely restrained and sober. I wonder what drew her to it?"

"Maggie loved it. And you know, our mother never noticed that it was different from the ones she'd bought for both of us. She was dressing us alike, at that point. Then Maggie and I started doing more individual looks. Doris told her it was our little secret—like the 'secret' bracelet that the other lady gave to me, in consolation."

Ollie did a double-take.

"What?!"

From the jewelry box, Mrs. Welland took out the Cartier gold bangle with tiger heads and black enamel stripes.

"No!" warbled Ollie, his eyes bright with recognition. "I remember that thing! I often saw it on her wrist! I didn't realize she was wearing it that day."

"Of course, a ten-year-old had no place to wear such a thing," said Mrs. Welland, handing the bracelet to Ollie.

"I'm . . . speechless," he said. "Emeralds for the eyes!"

"And frankly, at the time, I found it a little scary."

"Again, Barbara just slips it off. . . ?"

"She slipped it off her wrist and tucked it into the pocket of my jumper, and told me the same thing that Doris told Maggie, to keep it a secret."

"Did you?"

"I did. I mean, even now I find it a bit too racy to wear. You've never seen me wear it, have you?"

"No, but Liz, you must! On New Year's Eve, with a slinky, floor-length dress of oyster satin."

"I did wear it once, as a kind of joke, to a school dance with a Roman theme. As I was going out of the house, my mother asked where I got the bracelet, and I told her I found it at Woolworth's for ninety-nine cents. There was a very nice Woolworth's in Prescottville."

"Ha. Well, in a way, it did come from Woolworth's, didn't it?"

"Oh, my goodness . . . I never thought of that!"

"Wow."

"And this is me at the party."

Mrs. Welland opened the photo album and turned to a faded color snapshot of four teenage girls in bedsheet togas, with their hair done up in fancy upsweeps and laced with ribbons. On the white edge of the photo, in ballpoint pen, was written, "Binky, Betty, Liddy, Jo. 1969." And there was the bracelet, on Liddy's wrist.

"You're Liddy?" said Ollie.

"That's what my friends called me. My family did, too. But nobody calls me that anymore."

Ollie called Emma the next day to tell her about Mrs. Welland's pin and bracelet, and that there was a cute, fifty-year-old photograph of the bracelet being worn by Mrs. Welland, and that she had agreed to let both be shot for the film and to tell the story of both of these pieces of jewelry.

"I think it's just the kind of personal story you're looking for," he said. "And it makes a nice contrast with enormous Burmese rubies and such."

"You're right, and that's great," said Emma. "I can get the crew back to Christie's whenever it suits her—the sooner the better."

"I'm glad you like the idea."

"But Ollie, Ollie, I have even better news!"

He paused a moment, and then, with a kind of Cheshire Cat silkiness that was not meant for Emma to pick up, he said, "Do you?"

Emma told him that a letter had arrived from a Swiss bank with a document awarding her one hundred fifty thousand dollars for "Ms. Emma Radetzky's full-length documentary film project focused on historic jewelry and the women who own it." It was going to be enough for Emma to finish the film.

"Was this something you applied for?" said Ollie.

"No, not at all. But the letter uses some of the exact same language that was in my proposal and applications. So some kind of invisible philanthropic physics must be at work here."

"That good ol' invisible philanthropic physics!"

"I have the letter in my hand right now—from a bank in Zürich, with a branch in New York, where I am to go and arrange to access the funds."

"Fancy that! So is it the bank itself that's giving you this money?"

"No," said Emma. "The document refers to an organization called Show Your Face to Me. Isn't that a weird name for a foundation or whatever it is?"

"I don't know," said Ollie. "Show Your Face to Me. Hmm. No weirder than Be a Dear and Donate a Brassiere."

"Seriously? That's a thing?"

"That *is* a thing."

"And Ollie, the letter says that should I be seeking funding for my next project, they would be delighted to have a first look at it."

"That's good."

"I'm excited."

"Any ideas?"

"For the next one? I've been thinking a lot about architectural restoration."

"Newport? I'm delighted."

"No, no—not American. I've been looking into those Nepalese houses you were telling me about."

"*Havelis.*"

"Yes, *havelis.* Didn't you say you knew someone who was involved in Nepalese domestic architecture?"

"I did several years ago—a nice gentleman, Selwyn Stanfield, married to MaryAnn Dessault, the art dealer. Your mother probably knows her. But I haven't seen or heard about him in a long time."

"Maybe he's dead?"

"I suppose maybe. But more likely, he just gave up his business and went to live in Nepal. He always seemed a bit of a dreamer to me—you know, for a businessman. I'll make some inquiries."

The film's final shoot, of the circle pin and the tiger-head bracelet, went smoothly. Mrs. Welland was willing to speak on camera and did so with surprising eloquence about both pieces. Her remarks about Barbara's tiger-head bracelet were humorous, but it was those about the pin that provided the golden moment that Emma was hoping for, for the film.

"It's such a darling piece," said Mrs. Welland, holding the pin in the palm of her hand and regarding it with tender affection. In this case, unlike with the other pieces of jewelry that had been shot, Emma decided it would be best if the owner did actually hold it; and sure enough, that choice did provoke strong feelings in Mrs. Welland, which opened up that bit of footage emotionally and added intensity to the spot in the film where Emma placed it, at the climax.

"I never wear it," said Mrs. Welland softly. "But it's a lovely souvenir of that day, of my dear sister. This brings her back, it really does. Maggie was also my best friend, you see. . . ."

She smiled wistfully and brushed away a tear.

"It was a wonderful time in our lives. I wish I could remember those days more clearly—it was so long ago. I'm afraid I just don't recall the details of the encounter with those two women, which is sad, because I'll bet they were damned impressive. If only we could just rewind the tape and play it all again! Wouldn't it be nice if the universe worked that way? Think how much more we would see, the second time around. . . !"

Mrs. Welland sighed when Emma asked if the little gold pin might keep that moment with the two great ladies alive forever.

"Well, what it reminds me, and perhaps the viewers of your film," mused the older woman, "is that what should live forever isn't just a moment, but everything that was there *filling up* that moment—that wonderful old house, those two marvelous ladies, the freshness of the air that day, the hijinks my sister and I were up to . . . I want to hope that the contents of any moment remains alive in some form, somehow, long after we're gone and all the gold in the world has melted away and diamonds have turned into dust."

A month later, *Radiant: Great Women of the 20th Century and Their Historic Jewelry* was submitted to several festivals on the circuit, and within six months, it had been scheduled for four of them. For the unofficial premiere at Christie's—for VIP clients and guests, and several socialites whose jewelry appeared in the film—the auction house graciously made space and time available for a cocktail reception and screening. The event nicely coincided with the preview Christie's mounted of its upcoming sale, Magnificent Jewels of the World.

The night before the premiere, Robert called Emma.

"I wanted to wish you luck."

"That's nice of you. Thank you."

"I can't wait to see it."

"I think it turned out pretty well. It'll be at the Film Forum eventually. I'll keep you posted."

"Thanks."

For a second, there was silence; then Robert continued.

"So we're set for Friday morning."

"We are," said Emma.

"You're okay with my guy's conference room?"

"It's fine."

"Good."

"I'll bring the ring with me. My guy says it's best to do it with witnesses."

"We don't have to . . . well, okay, sure. God—*witnesses, lawyers.* . . . It sounds so . . ."

"I know."

"Right?"

Another silence.

"Look, this may be a legal proceeding," said Emma, "but I'm trying not to think of it as a *divorce*-divorce—as in, you know, that fifties thing. We're both perfectly sufficient as human beings, and that's a good thing we have going for us, right? All we're doing is recognizing our incompatibility. That's how I'm trying to frame it, in the terms our therapist gave us: a recognition of incompatibility."

"That's such a mouthful."

"It is."

"I suppose we could call it an ROI, for short."

Emma snorted.

"If that's meant to be wit . . . I approve," she said.

"Thank you," said Robert.

"You're welcome. I never said you weren't witty."

CHAPTER 50

May 1964

Liddy and Maggie were upstairs in their bedroom when the limousine with the lady and her party arrived. They didn't understand exactly who "Miss Hutton" was or why she was so important, but as instructed, the girls had dressed alike to be presented to her, in neat white blouses and plaid jumpers whose right shoulders were adorned with identical little circle pins that their mother had bought for them at Schneider's jewelry store, in Kingston. Twins but not really twins, because everybody could see that Liddy, who was ten, was slightly taller than Maggie, who was eight. Their mother thought it was cute when they dressed like this, and the girls had enjoyed it for years, only now they admitted to each other that they wanted to be more individual, and somehow, they had to figure out a way of making their mother understand this without hurting her feelings.

They watched from their window as the big black Cadillac pulled up and the lady emerged, and was greeted warmly by their father and their father's lawyer. A young woman was with the lady, and a young man, too, both of whom were dressed neatly but casually and acted like assistants. The young man's shirt was in a bold paisley pattern in bright colors—something neither girl had ever seen on a man before. The lady was visiting, their father had told them, because she might be buying their house, but this was an idea that the girls were not in favor of. So they made a plan to ward off this fate. They would drape themselves with bedsheets and make ghostly noises from secret places in the house, in the hope of scaring the lady away. The girls knew very well there was no such thing as ghosts. They had been told this repeatedly by their parents, in response to ridiculous claims that some people made, who didn't know any better, that their big, hundred-year-old Gothic Revival house was haunted. The girls did know better—but wasn't it possible that this New York lady did believe in ghosts and might be scared away?

Their father had been talking about selling the house for weeks now. He and their mother kept talking about how they couldn't afford to "keep the place up," whatever that meant. The girls didn't understand why it should be so difficult simply to live in their house, since they were told that the family was already "saving money" by not buying new kitchen appliances and not making repairs on the front terrace steps. They loved living there, up on the mountain, in their practically castle-like house. With the nearest neighbor down on the highway, half a mile away, and the town down in the valley, two miles away, it was like living in their own kingdom. Their friends and schoolmates who lived in town had perfectly nice houses, but *their* neighbors were only a yard or alley away, and that felt uncomfortably close. People could see into each other's windows. The girls liked to visit their friends and see them at school, but it was so nice every day to slip out of the town and drive up the mountain, to go home. Their father explained that even John, who did cleaning and gardening for the family and often did errands for them, like driving the girls to and from school, was "too expensive" anymore. He said, "You don't want to be prisoners on the mountain and die up here with no food, do you?" They solemnly shook their heads no. But who else could live there in their house, on their mountain? It was a strange idea. They had always heard proud tales of their ancestors—four generations of Prescotts who lived in the house, because Dewitt Prescott bought the property from the Dutch, who'd bought it from the Indians, and his son Cornelius Dewitt Prescott built the house and also railroads and canals for a growing nation, which was so grateful to him. How could all that suddenly not be true?

Not only did the girls have wide-open spaces, indoors and outdoors, in which to play explorers and settlers and Greek gods, according to stories they were taught in school and histories they learned from the books in great-grand-uncle Hartley Prescott's library, they could play in the unfinished stone chapel down the road, that their grandfather had been building for their grandmother when what their father called the "Crash of '29" occurred. The crash was an event that the girls understood was very bad, but not actually a car or train crash. The chapel made such a good Roman forum, and Valhalla, and an Egyptian tomb, and the Chinese Forbidden City. Losing that was unthinkable. And besides, how could anyone who hadn't grown up in that spot ever understand the magic in those stones, the secrets behind the unfinished carvings of the big stone block still sitting there in the chapel yard, now with grass grown up around it and moss on its north-facing corner?

It was hardly reassuring that their father said he was going to try to find someone to buy the place who could afford to treat it beautifully and would honor its history. He said there were very few people who could do that, but that this Miss Hutton was one of them. When their father had explained that the lady was coming up from the city, they understood a little about what that meant. New Yorkers dressed well, spoke quickly, and seemed smart. The girls were sometimes brought down to the city to visit the big museums there. Once they'd even walked past the grand old mansion that their father said his own father and mother lived in long ago. The mansion was now an embassy, and their father explained what an embassy was. But why would a New Yorker like this lady want a house so far away, on a mountaintop, with a kitchen that needed a new refrigerator?

Determined to execute their plan, the girls concealed them-

selves in sheets, slipped stealthily out of their bedroom, and tip-
toed down to the place where they had planned to make their
first round of ghostly sounds, a semi-concealed spot on the landing where the staircase turned on its way down into the main
hall. They started making their sounds—*wooooh! wooooh!*—
but nobody could hear them. The adults were all standing outside on the terrace, chattering away—the lady and their father
and the lawyer, while the young woman and young man were
conferring with each other and occasionally scribbling in note-
books. Then Liddy and Maggie descended the rest of the way
to the hall and found a spot in back of the front door, which
was open, and started making more ghostly sounds. *Wooooh!*
Wooooh! But still no one heard. Finally, the girls decided to
abandon the ghost idea.

"We might as well just say hi to them," said Maggie.

"Okay," said Liddy.

They left the bedsheets draped over a four-foot-high Chinese
floor vase that stood near the door and stepped out onto the
terrace.

They were presented to the great lady, exchanged a few polite
words with her, and then trailed along as their father brought
the party inside the house and began showing them around:
front hall, drawing room, library, dining room, kitchen, back
hall, back stairs, bedrooms, front stairs, front hall. It was after
everyone wound up back on the terrace, and their father was
answering a question from the lady's secretary, when the other
lady arrived, in a spectacular manner, with a helicopter that
made the loudest noise the girls had ever heard—even louder
than their school's fire-drill alarms. This was Miss Duke, they
overheard, and she was accompanied by a young man of her
own, this one dressed and groomed quite a bit more sharply
than the other lady's young man, in a sport jacket, with shiny,
wavy hair, like a TV star.

The ladies asked questions of their father about the house, in
a way that made it seem as though each of the ladies was trying
to best the other. Was this a game? The girls were both terrified

and strangely delighted by these two grand creatures. The ladies were certainly nothing like Marge Stapleton, or Janeane Adler, or the rest of their mother's friends from the country club, or their school's principal, Mrs. Slater, whom their mother once described as "redoubtable," which they knew meant something good. Only one lady in town was nearly as glamorous as these visitors: Nancy Mancuso, the director of the telephone company. And Mrs. Mancuso's job was so important that she might well go flying around in a helicopter. One of three local leaders who had recently addressed a school-wide assembly that both Liddy and Maggie attended, Mrs. Mancuso was so impressive, speaking about the future of communications satellites and fiber-optic cable, that more hands shot up with questions for her at the end of the presentation than did for the two other leaders, both of whom were men—the director of the county's largest factory and the owner of the area's biggest resort hotel.

"That Nancy Mancuso is always so put-together," their mother said. "As stylish as a First Lady. So smart and poised. She could run for Congress, if she wanted to. She has real flare. I wonder where she gets it."

Then the ladies asked Liddy and Maggie's father for a moment alone and began chatting together, off to one side of the terrace, easily, intimately, with some quiet laughter between them. They seemed to be such good friends, and both Maggie and Liddy understood instantly that though this was so, the ladies, for some reason, were pretending for their father to be rivals. The girls sometimes used the same tactic themselves, with their parents and schoolteachers, and it always worked.

Maggie thought that the very tall lady was exotic-looking, because her eyes sort of slanted upwards and her cheekbones were so angular. But the lady did seem nice, with a bright, buoyant personality. The shorter lady was much more conventionally pretty, with a mouth as perfect as a baby doll's, though she was wearing an awful lot of makeup. She was pretending to be annoyed by her friend, but she obviously really wasn't.

If these ladies knew each other so well, why hadn't they arrived together? Did they want to live in the house together?

It was an exceptionally fine day, with fresh breezes and characteristically strong mountain sunlight that, except for the occasional shadow of a roving cloud pushing over the landscape, ignited a thousand shades of green that were on view from the porch: yellowish and brownish greens of the lawn and the meadow, bluish greens of the shrubs and trees beyond, cool gray-greens of the hills far beyond that, on the other side of the valley, which were partially visible because the property's terrain itself had been cannily altered a hundred years before, to afford good views from the house.

The ladies were gabbing away.

"They're probably talking about their boyfriends," groaned Liddy.

"Do you think that's who those guys with them are, their boyfriends?" said Maggie.

"I don't know. Maybe they're bodyguards?"

"I don't think bodyguards act like that."

Then the ladies spotted the girls watching them, and the tall one waved them closer. Maggie and Liddy approached. These ladies weren't so scary after all, they saw. They just had something different from what their mother and all the other women in their lives had, something *more*, something *bigger*—some special way of moving or even just standing there. And there was something different about the way you wanted to be with them, too . . .

Even their perfumes were more indescribably wonderful than anything either girl had ever breathed before. One lady smelled like pure happiness; the other was somehow wrapped in sparkle. Genially, the ladies halted their conversation—something about a prince that someone had paid for—as the girls came up to them and said a polite hello.

The tall lady smiled and bent slightly toward the younger girl, lowering her sunglasses, her proximity radiant with the freshness of forest rain and fizziness of ginger ale. The lady's eyes fixed on Maggie with a kind of calm intensity.

"And who do we have here?" said Doris.

While Barbara stood by, fixing her makeup—reapplying the burgundy-red "Mysterieuse" lipstick that Doris had earlier sniped was "vampier" than necessary for a spring day in the mountains—Doris chatted amiably with Maggie. And within a few moments, Doris was exchanging the gold circle pin she was wearing for the one that the girl was wearing. A unique piece of jewelry was such a nice way for Maggie to distinguish herself from her older, identically dressed sister, they agreed! Then Doris crouched low for a few additional words with Maggie, in whispers that she didn't want Barbara to overhear.

"But I want you to remember that you're lucky to have a sister," said Doris. "Barbara and I didn't have sisters when we were little. We had everything else, but we didn't have sisters, and we were very sad about that. So we decided to be sisters for each other. Do you understand?"

Maggie nodded.

"You should always love your sister, despite your differences, even when you have squabbles. Do you know what squabbles are?"

Maggie shook her head.

"They're little fights," continued Doris. "They happen all the time. Sometimes Barbara and I squabble with each other, but for fun. It's like a game. But we always hang on to each other, and so should you and your sister. Because there are a million crazy things in the world that try to come between you. So stick together, okay?"

"Okay," said Maggie.

"You won't forget?"

"Uh-uh."

"Good girl."

Doris stood and turned to Barbara.

"So . . . Madame Nosferatu," she said, "the kidnapping—are you in?"

Barbara, obviously relieved that the Auntie Duke moment was over, summoned an anemic smile and said "fine." She added that she thought Ollie would be happy with the prank they were pulling, since now he'd be able to make the new Carol Burnett musical that he had tickets for that evening.

"That boy likes a good show," she said.

"We all like a good show," said Doris. "So let's get this one on the road, shall we?"

AUTHOR'S NOTE

I am grateful to editor and publisher extraordinaire John Scognamiglio for his enduring support and invaluable creative suggestions, and for the efforts of his accomplished team at Kensington, especially Kristine Noble, Lorraine Freeney, and Vida Engstrand.

With massive thanks I bow to my agent Mitchell Waters, of Brandt & Hochman. I feel lucky to be a beneficiary of Mitchell's deep knowledge of story, character, and language; his savvy about the marketplace; and his insights about where an author might find the most rewarding literary challenges.

My sincere thanks also go to friends and colleagues who shared valuable advice during the writing process: Victor Bumbalo, Craig Hensala, Lesley Maia Horowitz, Matthue Keck, Eric Latzky, Tom O'Connor, David Anthony Perez, Adam Snyder, Sarah Van Arsdale, and Matt Wagner.

Gratefully, I acknowledge the excellent biographies and other books about Doris Duke and Barbara Hutton that I relied on for research, including *The Diaries of Cecil Beaton*, *The Silver Swan* by Sallie Bingham, *Too Rich* by Pony Duke and Jason Thomas, *Poor Little Rich Girl* by C. David Heymann, *The Richest Girl in the World* by Stephanie Mansfield, *I Married the World* by Elsa Maxwell, and *Daddy's Duchess* by Tom Valentine.

I am also grateful to the scores of media workers who have covered these figures in print and electronic media, over the years. Respectfully in this regard, I acknowledge Andrew Anthony,

Laird Borrelli-Persson, Bob Colacello, Peter Collier, Amy Fine Collins, David Patrick Columbia, Rebecca Cope, Jessica Diehl, Liz Elliot, Marion Fasel, Tyler Golsen, Vivian Gornick, Leslie Hogan, Cathy Horyn, Barbara Jones, Laurence Leamer, Andrew Morton, Mitchell Owens, Evgenia Peretz, Adrian Prisca, James Reginato, Elisa Rolle, Susan Ronald, Spencer Rumsey, Zeon Santos, Benjamin Schwarz, Mort Sheinman, Michael Shulman, Dinitia Smith, Danielle Stein, Sadie Stein, Daniela Sunde-Brown, Rupert Taylor, Stellene Volandes, Mike Wallace, Stephanie Waldek, and Sheila Weller.

Several well-organized websites also proved valuable for research, including those of the Doris Duke Foundation; Duke University Libraries; the Newport Restoration Foundation; the SS United States Conservancy; the Shangri La Museum of Islamic Art, Culture & Design; and the auction houses of Christie's and Sotheby's.

Finally, I am indebted to the legends and legacies of Doris Duke and Barbara Hutton, two extraordinary women who, quite apart from their fortunes, can be said to have lived life on their own terms. My story about them is a fictional one, and though they revealed little about their inner selves to the world directly, a thoughtful reader can discern, within the massive amounts of gossip, slander, and opinion written about them, two generous and creative individuals.

THE LAST AMERICAN HEIRESSES

ABOUT THIS GUIDE

The suggested questions are included to enhance your group's reading of Stephen Greco's *The Last American Heiresses*!

Discussion Questions

1. How much did you know about Doris Duke and Barbara Hutton before reading *The Last American Heiresses*? Did your impression of these women, and/or the women of their class or generation, change as you read the book?

2. What aspects of Doris and Barbara's heiress lifestyle appeals to you the most and the least? Are there any aspects of that lifestyle that seem particularly wonderful or egregious?

3. What do you think are the main reasons why the debutante system declined so dramatically during the twentieth century? Would you have wanted to be a debutante? Why or why not?

4. What does the way that each of these women wielded material wealth say about their personalities and their goals in life? How do you think the wealth affected their marriages and other personal relationships?

5. In what ways did Doris and Barbara take advantage of the new social possibilities opening up for women at specific points in the twentieth century—the 1930s, the 1950s, the 1970s. . . ?

6. How does the gossip published in the newspapers about Doris and Barbara during their lifetimes compare with gossip today in all media about the rich and famous? Would you count Doris and Barbara among the "influencers" of their time—and, if so, do you think they enjoyed this role?

7. Doris and Barbara were often said to be "frenemies"— mostly by the press and others who didn't know them personally. What do you think the chances are that we can

know what these women really thought about each other, and why?

8. Are there any ways in which you think Doris and Barbara would be called feminist pioneers? For those who read about Doris and Barbara during their lifetimes, in the gossip columns and society pages, what aspects of these celebrity lives do you think were the most and least admirable?

Visit our website at
KensingtonBooks.com
to sign up for our newsletters, read
more from your favorite authors, see
books by series, view reading group
guides, and more!

Become a Part of Our
Between the Chapters Book Club
Community and Join the Conversation